DECLAN'S CROSS

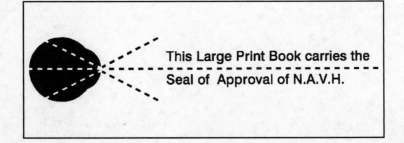

This Large Print Book carries the
Seal of Approval of N.A.V.H.

DECLAN'S CROSS

CARLA NEGGERS

THORNDIKE PRESS
A part of Gale, Cengage Learning

Detr

GALE
CENGAGE Learning®

LIBRARY OF CONGRESS CATALOGING-IN-PUBLICATION DATA

Neggers, Carla.
  Declan's Cross / By Carla Neggers.
    pages cm. (Thorndike press large print basic)
    ISBN 978-1-4104-6283-1 (hardcover) — ISBN 1-4104-6283-8 (hardcover)
  1. Ireland—Fiction. 2. Large type books. I. Title.
PS3564.E2628D43 2013
813'.54—dc23   2013026705

...hed in 2013 by arrangement with Harlequin Books S.A.

To Oona, daughter of my daughter.
Welcome, baby girl!

PROLOGUE

A cold, gusty wind swept up from the Celtic Sea, whistling and shrieking in the rocks and ruins as Lindsey Hargreaves jumped over a puddle in the muddy, rutted lane. She didn't care about the weather. She was happy to be out of her car. She would never get used to Irish roads, and this one was worse than most — if one could call it a road. It curved up from the tiny village of Declan's Cross, hugging sea cliffs, twisting through fields of grazing sheep and finally dead-ending at a stone wall tucked between two small hills at the tip of what locals called Shepherd Head.

Her rented Mini barely fit into the small hollow, but she was confident it wouldn't be spotted from the water or farther down the lane.

That was good. She didn't want anyone to see her.

She noticed a holly tree poking up from

the November-browned hedges, rushes and ferns that grew along the stone wall. Its waxen, evergreen leaves glistened with raindrops from an earlier shower.

Wasn't holly supposed to bring good luck?

"I hope so," she whispered.

A muddy trail led up through wind-stunted trees to a rock ledge with a precipitous drop to the cobble-and-boulder coastline. Lindsey had never been up there and couldn't see the ledge from the lane, but she had seen it from the water.

And the crosses.

She'd seen them, too. Three stone Celtic crosses rising from golden-copper grass on the small hill at the tip of the headland. She looked up at them now, standing tall against the gray clouds of the damp, gloomy November afternoon. They marked old graves next to the ruin of a small church on the other side of the stone wall. She'd read there'd been a church dedicated to Saint Declan on this spot for more than a thousand years.

Whose graves, Lindsey wondered, were up there on the hill? She tried to imagine the rough, simple life the last residents of this place must have endured. Had they died in the horrible mid-nineteenth century Irish famine? Had they joined the mass emigration to other parts of the world? America, Canada, Australia?

What would she have done in their position?

Survived, she thought.

Her natural enthusiasm and optimism, coupled with her instinct for survival, would see her through what she had to do out here.

She tightened her sweater around her. She hadn't brought a jacket or even a raincoat. She wore too-tight jeans, the same dark gray as her sweater, and black boots more suited to the Dublin streets where she'd spent the past two days than out here on the south Irish coast. An Hermès scarf with its cheerful mix of reds, blues and purples added a splash of color to her outfit. It was a birthday gift from her father, his first birthday gift to her in years. She'd deliberately worn it to breakfast with him in Dublin that morning.

Handsome, wealthy, lonely David Hargreaves. Smiling awkwardly as he'd complimented her on the scarf, forgetting he'd bought it for her himself just a few months ago.

Lindsey hadn't reminded him. She couldn't let the gift or his offer to have her move into the guesthouse of his home on Boston's North Shore fool her. He would always be the reluctant adoptive father who kept her at a safe, arm's-length distance.

She'd picked him up at the Dublin airport on Saturday and had spent yesterday with him, taking him to her favorite Dublin sights. The Book of Kells and the Long Room at Trinity College Library, Dublin Castle, Temple Bar, Grafton Street. They'd strolled through quiet St. Stephen's Green and Georgian Dublin with its famous painted doors, then had dinner at a five-star restaurant, talking about their mutual love for the world's oceans.

"I'm enjoying this father-daughter time together," he'd told her.

Lindsey believed him, but she had no illusions. He preferred solitude. He always had, even during his eight-year marriage to her mother.

Her sweet, artistic, vulnerable mother who had died drunk and broke, still desperate for his attention and approval.

They'd married when Lindsey was five and divorced when she was thirteen. Her mother had kept the Hargreaves name and died when Lindsey was eighteen. She was twenty-eight now. Time to put past hurts behind her.

She just had to do it her way.

Her father had caught her off-guard that

morning at breakfast when he'd told her he was extending his stay in Ireland. His business in London, his reason for this overseas trip, could wait.

He'd be in Ardmore tonight. Declan's Cross tomorrow.

"I've booked a couple of nights at a two-bedroom cottage on the grounds of a boutique hotel in Declan's Cross," he'd told her. *"I plan to arrive late tomorrow afternoon. You're more than welcome to stay with me."*

Lindsey had felt cornered.

She'd told him so many lies.

He knows, she'd thought, staring at her plain yogurt and berries — which she'd ordered because it was what he'd ordered.

Finally she'd mumbled, *"I know the hotel you mean. It's only been open a year. You'll love it. I'd join you, but I'm staying with a friend. We're sharing a cottage within walking distance of the village."*

"What friend is this?"

"She's a marine biologist from Maine."

Lindsey had welcomed the change in subject and, as she'd left breakfast, told her father she looked forward to seeing him in Declan's Cross.

"Enjoy Ardmore," she'd said, keeping any bitterness out of her tone.

His pale blue eyes had taken on a warmth

and a distance that together she found disconcerting. *"You understand why I'm going, don't you?"*

"I do, Dad, yes."

"Your mother loved Ardmore." He'd looked away, then added, *"Good memories."*

Lindsey had pretended she hadn't heard him. Good memories? When they'd gotten back from Ireland, he and her mother had separated.

But her mother had loved the south Irish coast. *"It's magical, Lindsey. Absolutely magical."*

Lindsey didn't want to see her father in Declan's Cross. She couldn't bear having him confront her about her lies.

So many lies.

She blinked back tears. She needed to concentrate. If she tripped and were incapacitated, she'd fast be in danger of hypothermia in the cold, wet conditions. No one would come looking for her. No one even knew she was in Declan's Cross, never mind out here. She'd made sure.

She was on her own.

"I can pull this off," she said aloud.

The wind shrieked again, whipping her scarf into her face.

She thought she heard someone above her on the trail, but it had to be the wind, the ocean, maybe a bird. No one else was out here — except maybe the ghosts of the Irish dead.

She suppressed a shudder and stepped over another puddle in the muddy lane.

Lies, lies and more lies.

It was her way.

1

Emma Sharpe paused atop a craggy knoll and looked out at the ripples of barren hills, not a house, a road, a car or another person in sight. She didn't know what had become of her hiking partner. Maybe he had stepped up to his midcalves in mud and muck, too, but she doubted it. It wasn't that Colin Donovan wasn't capable of taking a misstep. It was that she'd have heard him cursing if he had.

A fat, woolly sheep stared up at her from the boggy grass as if to say, *"You might be an FBI agent back in Boston, but out here in the Irish hills, you're just another hiker with wet feet."*

"This is true," Emma said, setting her backpack on the expanse of rough gray rock. "However, I'm prepared. I have dry socks."

She unzipped her pack and dug out a pair of fresh wool socks. The sheep bleated and meandered off, disappearing behind another knoll, one of a series on the windswept ridge on the Beara Peninsula, one of the fingers of land that jutted into the North Atlantic off the southwest coast of Ireland. It had been centuries since these hills were forested. She could see peeks of Kenmare Bay in the distance, its calm waters blue-gray in the midafternoon November light. Across the bay, shrouded in mist but still distinct, were the jagged ridges of the Macgillicuddy Reeks.

Emma kicked off her shoes, sat on the bare rock ledge and pulled off her wet socks. She glanced down at the narrow valley directly below her, a small lake shimmering in the fading sunlight. She and Colin were five hours into their six-hour hike. With the short November days, they would get back to their car just before dark.

As she put on her dry socks, he came around the knoll where her sheep had disappeared. A light breeze caught the ends of his dark hair, and he had his backpack hooked on one arm as he jumped over the wet spot that had fooled her.

He climbed up onto her knoll and dropped his pack next to hers. "I like having you walk point," he said with a grin.

"No fair. You saw my footprint in the mud."

"I'll never tell."

Emma leaned back against her outstretched arms. She had on a wool hat, her fair hair knotted at the nape of her neck. She had pulled her gloves on and off over the course of the day. She didn't know if Colin had even packed a hat and gloves. He was, she thought, the sexiest man she had ever met. Small scars on his right cheek and by his left eye from fights he said he had won. She had no doubt. He was strongly built, rugged and utterly relentless.

A good man to have on your side in a fight.

She was fit and lean and could handle herself in a fight, and although she wasn't tiny, he could easily carry her up a flight of stairs. In fact, he had, more than once.

They had set out early. For the past two weeks, they had explored the southwest Irish coast on foot and by car, by mutual agreement avoiding talk of arms traffickers, thieves, poison, attempted murder and alligators. Colin would wink at her and say he especially didn't want to talk about alligators, not that he had seen one on his narrow escape from killers in South Florida. Thinking about them had been enough.

By unspoken agreement, he and Emma

17

also avoided talk of their futures with the FBI — or even each other. His months of intense undercover work, in an environment where everyone was a potential enemy, had taken a toll, and he needed this time to be in the present, to be himself.

Emma's needs were simpler. She just wanted to be with him.

It was her life that was complicated.

She sat up straight, noticing that Colin's boots and cargo pants were splattered with mud but not wet like hers. She grinned at him. "You do know I've spent more time hiking the Irish hills than you have, don't you?"

"Beneath that placid exterior beats the heart of a competitive federal agent." He made no move to sit next to her. "Your mishap gives me an excuse to run a hot bath for you when we get back to the cottage."

"Life could be worse. You're not bored, are you?"

"I can go more than two weeks without anyone trying to kill me."

As he stood next to her on her boulder, his smile almost reached his stone-gray eyes.

Almost.

He offered her a sip from his water bottle, but she shook her head. He took a long drink as he gazed out at the hills. Except for the occasional *baa* of the grazing, half-wild sheep, the silence was complete.

"What are you thinking about, Colin?"

"Guinness."

"A cold pint and a warm pub. Sounds perfect."

He leaned down and touched the curve of his hand to her cheek. "It's been good being here with you." He winked at her as he stood straight. "Mud and sheep dung and all."

Emma sighed as she slipped back into her trail shoes and tied the laces. "No escaping sheep dung out here, is there? I wasn't distracted when I stepped in the wet spot. I just misjudged. There's a difference."

"But you do have a lot on your mind," Colin said.

She always did. Their jobs with the FBI attested to their different natures. He was an undercover agent. She specialized in art crimes. She was analytical, methodical, detail-oriented. He was direct, intuitive, quick and decisive — and independent to a fault. Six weeks ago, he had been assigned to her small team in Boston, if only because the senior agent in charge was determined to rein him in.

Good luck with that, Emma thought. She stood, lifted her backpack and slung it over her shoulders. "The rest of the way is all downhill."

"Have you ever done this hike before?"

She shook her head. "First time."

"It's a good spot," he said, tucking his water bottle in his pack.

"I'm glad we did this before I go home."

"Yeah. Me, too."

It was Monday. She had a flight back to Boston on Friday. She'd be at her desk a week from today. Colin had more time before he had to decide what was next for him. Not a lot more time, but he could stay in Ireland for a while longer, without her.

She angled a look at him. "Anything on your mind, Colin?"

"I had an email from Andy in my in-box this morning. He sent it last night. I didn't read it until just now, while I ate an energy bar and admired the view. Reading email is against our hiking rules, I know."

"A sign it's time to get back to work, maybe." Emma gave him a moment but he didn't take the bait and respond, and she let it go. "How are things in Rock Point?"

"Andy says Julianne Maroney is leaving for Ireland tonight."

"Tonight? Isn't that sudden?"

"She's just accepted a marine biology internship in Cork that starts in January.

20

She decided to come for a couple weeks now and get herself sorted out. It's sudden, but that's Julianne."

"So, she's staying in Cork?"

"A village east of Cork. Declan's Cross."

Declan's Cross.

Emma went still as a dozen images came at her at once. A pretty seaside Irish village of brightly colored shops and residences. A romantic mansion with sweeping views of cliffs and sea. Haunting Celtic crosses on a grassy hilltop.

A tight-lipped old Irish sheep farmer.

Her grandfather, Wendell Sharpe, a renowned art detective, pacing in his Dublin office as he admitted he and Sharpe Fine Art Recovery were after a thief they couldn't catch.

A thief, Emma thought, who had first struck in tiny Declan's Cross on a lonely, rainy, dark November night ten years ago.

She'd only become involved in the case four years ago, in the months between her life as Sister Brigid at the coastal Maine convent of the Sisters of the Joyful Heart and her life as a special agent with the Federal Bureau of Investigation. She'd worked side by side with her grandfather in Dublin, learning everything he knew.

Not everything.

Wendell Sharpe never told anyone everything.

She was aware of Colin's eyes narrowed on her. He wouldn't know about the thief. There was no reason for him to know.

She pushed back her thoughts. "Why Declan's Cross, Colin?"

"Emma . . ."

"Just tell me what you know. Please."

"All right." He was plainly suspicious now. "A woman who's launching a marine science research facility in Declan's Cross stopped in Rock Point last week. She and Julianne hit it off. Now Julianne's meeting her there."

"To help with this research facility?"

"Andy doesn't have any details. He hasn't talked to Julianne himself."

"Then who told him?"

"Her brother. Ryan. He's in the Coast Guard, but he's in Rock Point visiting for a few days. He found out from their grandmother. Julianne lives with her."

Rock Point was a small, tight-knit southern Maine fishing village. Everyone knew everyone else's business, but Julianne's short-lived romance with Andy Donovan, third-born of the four Donovan brothers, apparently had come as a surprise, especially since she'd vowed never to get involved with

22

a Donovan. Emma didn't know either Andy or Julianne well. She'd only met Colin in September and was still figuring out who was who in his hometown.

"What's this woman's name?" she asked. "Do we know her?"

"Her name's Lindsey Hargreaves. I don't know her."

Hargreaves. Emma searched her memory but shook her head. "I don't, either. Did she come to Rock Point looking for Julianne?"

"I don't have any details. I just know Julianne's on her way to Ireland."

"And you don't like it."

"Julianne's as smart as they come, but she's impulsive and she's had a rough time lately. She's never been that far from home. I doubt she's been farther than Nova Scotia. Now all of a sudden she's meeting some strange woman in a little Irish village."

"Are you concerned she's running away because of her breakup with Andy?"

"I know she is," Colin said half under his breath. "This trip could be exactly what she needs, but I'd feel better if she wasn't alone."

"We could drive over to Declan's Cross tomorrow," Emma said.

He tilted his head back, eyed her again.

"We could, but what's going on? I noticed your look when I mentioned Declan's Cross. Emma, is there a Sharpe connection to this village?"

She sighed. "We can talk on the hike back to the car."

2

They didn't talk on the hike back to their car or the drive back to their borrowed cottage in the Kerry hills across Kenmare Bay. Colin drove. He'd adjusted quickly to driving on the left, but the high, thick hedges and narrow roads — each with its own quirks — kept him on alert.

He'd known he and Emma wouldn't talk the moment he'd mentioned Declan's Cross and she'd given him that tight look. He liked to joke that he could do deep-cover work because he himself wasn't deep, but Emma was. She had layers of secrets. Sharpe secrets, Sister Brigid secrets, FBI secrets.

Emma secrets.

He didn't have secrets. He just had stuff he couldn't talk about.

And he had his demons. He'd come to Ireland because of them. His months of undercover work had taken a toll not just on him but on his family and friends — and on Emma, even in the short time they'd known each other. They'd met in September on his brief respite at home in Rock Point.

Then he went away again, and when he came back, he'd brought some of his bad guys with him.

The short version, he thought as he pulled into the gravel driveway of the little stone cottage he and Emma had shared for the past two weeks. He'd stayed here on his own for several days before she couldn't stand it any longer — as she'd put it — and got on a plane in Boston, flew to Shannon, rented a car and found him.

Colin hadn't asked her to turn around and go back to Boston without him.

Maybe he should have.

It was dark now, the wind shifting, turning blustery. He glanced at Emma, but she had already clicked off her seat belt and was slipping out of the car.

Definitely preoccupied.

He was in no rush. Let her take all the time she needed before she told him about the Sharpes and Declan's Cross. Wendell Sharpe had lived and worked in Dublin for the past fifteen years. Whatever was on her mind likely involved him. Colin had drunk whiskey with old Wendell. Interesting fellow. Maybe not quite the analytical thinker his granddaughter was but definitely a man with secrets.

Colin got out of the car, not minding the spray of cold rain. He grabbed their packs from the back and headed up a pebbled path to the cottage. The front door was painted a glossy blue, a contrast to the gray stone exterior. Finian Bracken, the owner, an Irish priest serving a parish in Rock Point, had told Colin to stay as long as he wanted. They'd become friends over the past few months, maybe as much because of their differences as in spite of them.

Fin couldn't bring himself to stay in the cottage. It was a reminder of his life before the priesthood, when he'd been a successful businessman, a husband and a father. He and his wife had renovated the tiny ruin of a place, adding a bathroom, kitchen, skylights, richly colored fabrics. It had been their refuge, he'd told Colin, a favorite spot to spend time with their two daughters.

Never in Fin's worst nightmares had he imagined he would lose all three of them. Sally, little Kathleen and Mary. They'd drowned seven years ago in a freak sailing accident.

Fin had removed any personal mementoes, but Colin thought he could feel the presence of his friend's lost wife and daughters and the happy times they'd had there.

He set the packs on the tile floor and pulled the door shut behind him. He liked being here. He liked having Emma here. The rest would sort itself out.

He watched her as she got on her knees and carefully, methodically, placed sods of turf in the stone fireplace. Colin liked the smell of burning peat, and a fire would warm up the single room and loft in minutes.

She rolled back onto her heels and stared at the fire as it took hold. Then she glanced up at him, the flames reflecting in her green eyes. "I hate to leave this place," she said.

"Ah, yes." He moved closer to her. "The cold, cruel world awaits."

She stood, and he slipped an arm around her waist, kissed the top of her head. Even her hair smelled like mud, but he didn't mind. She leaned into him. "I thought we'd have a few more nights together here. It's the most romantic cottage ever, isn't it? But we need to go to Declan's Cross, Colin. At least I do."

"There is a Sharpe connection to this village, then."

She eased an arm around his middle, the lingering tentativeness of even two weeks ago gone now. "I've reserved a room at the

O'Byrne House Hotel," she said. "It's on the water, right in the village of Declan's Cross."

"That was fast."

"The joys of smartphones."

And she'd had her plan fixed in her mind when they'd arrived back from their hike. "Have you ever been to Declan's Cross?" he asked.

"Once, when I worked with my grandfather in Dublin. I was only there for the day. The O'Byrne House wasn't a hotel then. It was a rambling, boarded-up private home. It opened as a hotel last fall. Apparently its spa is quite nice."

"A spa," Colin said, as if he were translating a foreign language.

"I bet it offers a couple's massage."

"Dream on, Emma."

She grinned. "I think you'd enjoy a hot stone massage."

"I'd rather have you heat up my stones, Special Agent Sharpe."

"You're hopeless." She tightened her hold on him, her grin gone now. "Massages are good for demon fighting."

He wasn't going to be distracted by talk of his demons. He drew her against him. "What's good for extracting Sharpe secrets?"

"There are secrets and there are confidences, and there are things I just can't tell you." She broke away from him and grabbed a black-iron poker, stirred the fire. "I wish I had a fireplace in my apartment in Boston."

"Emma."

She turned, and now the hot flames deepened the green of her eyes. "It was a great hike today, but I smell like dried mud, sweat and sheep dung."

"Just mud," he said.

"Such a gentleman. I've no regrets. I love hiking the Irish hills."

Still trying to change the subject, or at least delay telling him what was going on. He wasn't easily put off. "Roaming the Irish hills is different from figuring out what drives people to steal art. Is Declan's Cross the scene of an art heist the Sharpes investigated?"

Emma sank onto a bright blue-and-white rug in front of the fireplace, kicked off her shoes and tucked her knees under her chin as she stared at the flames. "It's the scene of an art heist we're still investigating."

Colin remained on his feet. He was restless, but he knew he had to be patient. An unsolved art theft was right up Emma's alley as both a Sharpe and an FBI agent. "What was stolen?" he asked.

"Three Irish landscape paintings and an unusual Celtic cross." She still didn't look up from the fire. "They were stolen from the O'Byrne House ten years ago, on a dark November night much like tonight."

"Your grandfather investigated?"

"Not at first. Not until after another theft in Amsterdam six months later."

"The work of the same thief?"

"We believe so, yes. He's struck at least eight more times since then. London, Paris, Oslo, Venice, San Francisco, Dallas, Brussels and Prague."

"A different city each time?"

"Yes."

"Patterns?"

She hesitated, then said, "Some."

She didn't go on. Colin sat next to her, feeling the warmth of the slow-burning fire, her intensity. "Declan's Cross was his first hit?"

"We believe so, yes. It's also the smallest location, and the only one in Ireland."

"Any viable leads?"

"Almost none."

"And of all the cute Irish villages, Julianne picks this one. Okay. I get it. You want to make sure her choice of Declan's Cross doesn't have anything to do with your thief."

"I have no reason to suspect it does. We

31

can scoot over there tomorrow, welcome Julianne to Ireland, spend the night in a romantic Irish hotel and then get out of the way and let her enjoy her stay."

"Without a Donovan breathing down her neck," Colin added.

"If she's making this trip in part to get over Andy . . . then, yes, she deserves to be Donovan-free."

Colin stretched out his legs. "All right. Let's check out Declan's Cross and see what Julianne's up to. If it's just whales and dolphins, you're on for that couple's massage."

"You jest now, but wait until you've had one."

"Jest." He smiled at her. "I don't know if I've ever used *jest* in a sentence."

"Making fun of me, are you?"

She didn't look at all worried. "Never." He edged closer to her. "What were you like four years ago when you were working with old Wendell in Dublin?"

"Not as good with a gun for one thing."

"Quantico changed you."

"I learned new things there, most certainly. Did it change you?"

He shrugged. "Not that much."

"You were in law enforcement before you entered the academy. I wasn't. My grandfather can't break the law, but he doesn't have to follow the same rules we do."

"In other words, he doesn't care about prosecuting this thief. He just cares about catching him."

"I wouldn't put it quite like that."

"You're a complex woman of many interests. I'm a simple man of limited interests. Whiskey, sex and —" Colin grinned at her. "I can get by on whiskey and sex for some time."

"That can be arranged."

"Good." He lowered his mouth to hers. "No more questions, Emma. No more thinking. Not tonight."

3

Julianne Maroney was half in love with Father Bracken and totally in love with Andy Donovan, and that, she thought, was reason enough to head to Ireland. She grabbed a coffeepot and headed across the dining room to Father Bracken's table. It was a dreary afternoon in southern Maine, and she was wrapping up her shift at Hurley's, a popular, rustic restaurant on Rock Point harbor.

This time tomorrow, she'd be in Declan's Cross on the south Irish coast.

She'd accepted a marine biology internship in Cork, but it didn't start until January. Impatient, going crazy, she'd jumped when opportunity had knocked last week in the shape of Lindsey Hargreaves, a diver, a marine science enthusiast and a member of the family that had founded the prestigious Hargreaves Oceanographic Institute in Massachusetts.

Impulsive, maybe, but Julianne didn't care. She was packed. Her flight to Shannon left tonight.

She arrived at Father Bracken's table overlooking the harbor. "Not much of a view today, Father," she said, refilling his mug. "Gray rain, gray sky, gray ocean."

He smiled up at her. "I'm Irish. Wet weather doesn't bother me."

He'd ordered fried eggs, ham, toast and jam, a late breakfast by Rock Point standards but not, he insisted, all that late by Irish standards. He'd taken his time, reading a book and jotting notes in a black Moleskine. The lunch crowd, such as it was on a Monday in November, was in now, mostly locals — fishermen, carpenters, retirees, a group of young mothers with babies in tow.

No Donovans, at least not yet.

There were four Donovan brothers — gray-eyed, dark-haired, rugged, sexier than any men had a right to be and not one of them even remotely easy.

They said Finian Bracken reminded them of Bono. Maybe with a little Colin Firth, Julianne thought as she checked to make sure he had enough cream in the little stainless-steel pitcher. He was in his late thirties, relatively new to the priesthood. In

35

his early twenties, he and his twin brother, Declan, had started a whiskey business in Ireland. Bracken Distillers was a success, but the tragic deaths of Finian's wife and daughters had changed everything.

Julianne didn't have many details and wasn't sure she wanted any. She couldn't fathom such a loss. He'd left Ireland in June to serve a one-year assignment at struggling St. Patrick's, the Maroney family's church a few blocks from Rock Point harbor.

He wore his usual priestly black garb. She had on knee-high boots, dark brown leggings and a Hurley's-required white shirt and dark blue apron. She had her hair tied back. It was golden brown, and Andy used to tell her its natural highlights matched the gold flecks in her hazel eyes.

"You must be about to leave for the airport," Father Bracken said. "How are you getting there?"

"My brother's dropping me off."

"Will you be seeing Colin and Emma while you're in Ireland?"

She almost reminded him that Colin was a Donovan but instead said, "They're in the southwest, and they're supposed to be relaxing."

Father Bracken's midnight-blue eyes leveled on her. He had to be aware of the complicated dynamics of Colin's relationship with Emma Sharpe and the reaction of his family and friends in Rock Point to her. An FBI agent, an ex-nun, a Sharpe. She and Colin were, to say the least, an eyebrow-raising match.

"Have you told them you're coming?" Father Bracken asked.

"No, but it's fine. They don't need to know. I wouldn't want to interrupt their time together." Julianne stopped herself, which wasn't her style. Usually she said too much, not too little. "You haven't told them about my trip, have you?"

"I wouldn't without your permission," he said simply.

She felt her cheeks flame. "Oh, right, of course not. I hope they're having a good time, and Emma isn't finding out the hard way what rock heads the Donovan men can be." She gave Father Bracken a quick smile. "Sorry, Father."

His mouth twitched with humor. "No worries."

"I can handle Colin. It's not that. I'm used to Donovans."

And she'd never slept with Colin. Never even considered it. She'd known better than to get mixed up with any of the Donovans. Mike, the eldest, was an ex-army wilderness guide on Maine's Bold Coast. Then came Colin, an FBI agent. Kevin, the youngest, was a Maine state marine patrol officer. But it was third-born Andy, a lobsterman who restored classic boats on the side, who had captured her heart.

She'd slept with him, all right. One of the stupidest things she'd ever done.

Father Bracken was frowning at her, but if he guessed what she was thinking, he kept it to himself. She smiled. "Sorry. Mind wandering."

"No apology necessary. Be sure to tell Sean Murphy I said hello."

Sean Murphy owned the cottage Julianne was renting in Declan's Cross. She'd expected to stay in a bed-and-breakfast, but Father Bracken had arranged for the cottage after she'd brought him his fried eggs yesterday morning and told him about her trip. He and his fellow Irishman were friends somehow. Julianne didn't have any details. She was curious but felt awkward prying into Father Bracken's private life.

"I will," she said. "He's not a priest, is he?"

"No, but he'll look after you if you need anything."

"This will be great. I'm really excited. I can get the lay of the land, figure things out ahead of my internship. I've never been anywhere. I've told my folks and my brother, and Granny, naturally, but I don't need everyone in town knowing my business."

"Meaning the Donovans," Father Bracken said with a smile.

"Trust me, it'll be easier if I just go on my way without the benefit of their opinion of my sanity."

"Well, then. Godspeed, Julianne. Give my love to Ireland."

"Thanks, Father, I will."

She withdrew with her coffeepot. She felt good about her impromptu trip. It wasn't just a chance to get things sorted out for January or even to put space between her and Andy. She would also be helping with her new friend's marine science field station.

She and Lindsey Hargreaves had hit it off when Lindsey had stopped at Hurley's last Wednesday. Not even a week ago. Lindsey had explained that she and some diving friends had been diving in Declan's Cross that fall, and she'd had the idea of launching a field station there. She'd flown home for a few days to work on some of the details.

A mutual friend in Declan's Cross had mentioned Finian Bracken, co-owner of

Bracken Distillers and now a priest in America, and Lindsey had thought it would be fun to say hello while she was in southern Maine for a day trip. She hadn't given Julianne the name of the mutual friend, but now she wondered if it was Sean Murphy.

Short, slim, dark-haired and dark-eyed, Lindsey had a contagious energy and enthusiasm about her, and Julianne had volunteered to show her around the area. They'd spent the afternoon together, then stayed in touch by email after Lindsey went home that night and returned to Ireland on an overnight flight on Thursday. When she indicated she'd love to get Julianne's take on the field station, Julianne had seized the moment and booked a round-trip ticket for a two-week stay.

Tomorrow, they would be sharing the cottage Father Bracken had arranged. Lindsey had been only too happy to take a break from the "primitive" conditions at the building she'd rented in Declan's Cross for her soon-to-be field station.

Julianne was convinced that as last-minute as this trip was, it was the right thing for her to do. Her grandfather would be pleased, too, she thought with a rush of affection. Jack Maroney had died last year, far too soon. He'd unexpectedly left her some money, with instructions that she was to go a little nuts with it, have some fun and not be in such a grind all the time. Julianne thought he'd love Declan's Cross. If the photographs she'd found on the internet were at all accurate, it was as adorable an Irish village as she could ever imagine.

She'd had a hard time after her grandfather's death. She still had her parents and older brother — who were all skeptical of her Ireland adventure. It was November, she was going alone, she was going at the last minute and she didn't really know the woman who'd invited her. *And* she had limited funds, even with her grandfather's mad money. She needed to finish her thesis and get a real job, which she hoped this trip and then her internship would help facilitate.

She had it all rationalized in her mind.

Barely able to contain her excitement, she ducked into a back room and changed into a sweater and jacket. She could smell lunch cooking in Hurley's spotless kitchen. The kitchen was hopelessly outdated, but some of the best clam chowder in New England came out of its dented pots.

By the time she went back through the dining room, Kevin and Andy Donovan were approaching Father Bracken's table.

There was no way to get out of there without passing them. Julianne tried zipping up her jacket to give herself an excuse not to make eye contact, but Kevin said, "Hey, Julianne. Hanging out with Father Bracken?"

She found the knowing note in his voice annoying. It wasn't as if she were *seriously* fixated on Father Bracken. Just mildly fixated. "Not really. You boys having lunch? The soup special is a nice butternut squash bisque. You'll like it."

"It sounds orange," Kevin said.

Andy grinned, then settled his dark gray eyes on her. "I didn't see your car outside. How are you getting home?"

"Walking."

"It's about to rain."

"Good. I like rain."

She didn't tell him she was walking because she knew she had a long drive to the airport and then a long flight ahead of her. She got out of there. She didn't want Andy finding out about her trip until she was safely aboard her Aer Lingus plane. Rock Point had always been home for her, but she'd lived on campus much of the year as an undergraduate and then a graduate student at the University of Maine. Then in August, immersed in her master's thesis, struggling with finances, she'd moved in with her recently widowed grandmother in Rock Point and had taken on as many hours as she could at Hurley's. It didn't matter what time she was working. A Donovan was *always* there.

Overexposed, she'd weakened, violating her personal Golden Rule never to get involved with a Donovan. When Andy, the rake, the heartbreaker of Rock Point, had stayed after closing one misty September night, she'd let him walk her home.

She'd been lost from the moment he'd brushed his arm against hers.

This, she thought as the cold November air hit her, was why she was going to Ireland. She had to let go of her anger and misery. She had to get Andy Donovan out of her system and find herself again.

Forty minutes later, Julianne set her purple soft-sided suitcase on the rug in the entry of her grandmother's small house on a quiet street between St. Patrick's Church and Colin Donovan's Craftsman-style house. Her grandmother stood in the living room doorway, her thin arms crossed on her chest in worried anticipation. At seventy-five, Franny Maroney didn't bother to pretend she wasn't a worrier. Her hair used to be as thick and golden brown as Julianne's, but now it was white, carefully curled once a week at the only beauty parlor in Rock Point.

Granny had dug the purple suitcase out of the attic and presented it to her only granddaughter for her trip, telling her in no uncertain terms that every young woman should have her own suitcase. Not that Granny had ever done much traveling herself. Hence, the pristine condition of the fifteen-year-old suitcase.

"Do you have your passport?" she asked for at least the sixth time.

"Yes, Granny." Julianne patted the tote bag — her own tote bag — that she planned to take on the plane. "It's right in here."

"You're sure? Sometimes I think I've put something in my bag and discover later it's still home on my dresser. I suppose that's because I'm old."

It wasn't because she was old. Her grandmother had been forgetful for as long as Julianne could remember. "It could also be because you always have a million things going on. You're not one to be idle."

Granny seemed to like that. "You'll send me a postcard from Ireland?"

Julianne smiled. "I'll send one every day."

"That's too expensive. One will do. I don't

mind if you email me photos but I'd love to have a real postcard from Ireland." She lowered her arms and frowned, her eyes a true blue, unlike Julianne's gold-flecked hazel. "Do you have a plan for emergencies?"

"I do, Granny."

It amounted to taking care not to max out her credit card and calling the Irish police if she had an accident or got into trouble, but Julianne didn't tell her grandmother that. Granny was all about planning for disaster to strike. She'd already warned Julianne about dark fairies. *"Not all fairies are good, you know."*

Her grandmother had been telling her as much since she was a tot, reading her bedtime stories about nasty pookas, scary banshees and mischievous leprechauns. Julianne wasn't inclined to believe in fairies, good or bad. The prospect of a pot of gold at the end of a rainbow or a shrieking banshee warning of imminent death didn't faze her. She was a marine biologist, not a folklorist.

"Have you told Father Bracken you believe in fairies?"

Granny waved a slender hand. "He'd understand."

Probably he would, if not just because he

was Irish. Church attendance was up at St. Patrick's since Father Bracken's arrival in Rock Point. Parishioners insisted they wanted Father Callaghan to return from his yearlong sabbatical, but they were falling in love with their Irish priest. He'd helped Granny get past her anger at God for her husband's death. Whatever spiritual guidance Finian Bracken had offered, Franny Maroney was back at church and not as depressed and irritable.

Julianne wondered if her crush on Father Bracken was a sin. She would have to find someone else to ask, that was for sure.

She gave her grandmother a quick hug. "You have fun while I'm off to Ireland, okay, Granny?"

"Don't you worry about me. You just live your life and be happy. I'm fine here on my own."

"I know you are."

As Julianne started to grab her suitcase, her grandmother tucked a twenty-dollar bill in her hand. "Buy yourself a Guinness or two while you're over there."

Julianne beamed her a smile. "Thanks, Granny. You're a love."

"Ireland's the best place to heal a broken heart."

Franny Maroney had never stepped foot

in her ancestral homeland, either, but Julianne appreciated the sentiment. Everyone in Rock Point knew she had a broken heart, because that's what Andy Donovan was. A heartbreaker.

She carried her tote bag and suitcase — no wheels — outside and down the front walk to the street. Her brother would be here any minute. Ryan was thirty, the same age as Andy, four years older than she was, and tight with all the Donovans. More proof she'd been dumb to get involved with one of them.

But it wasn't Ryan's black truck that pulled in next to her. It was Andy's rust-colored truck. He had the passenger window rolled down and patted the seat next to him. "Hop in, Jules. I'm driving you to the airport. Ryan can't make it and I volunteered."

It was a conspiracy. No doubt in Julianne's mind, but she had no choice — which Andy would know. She needed to leave now in order to get to Logan Airport the requested three hours ahead of her flight's departure time. She was following all the rules and guidelines. She'd provided the requested preflight boarding information, checked in online at the appropriate time and printed out her boarding pass. She had any liquids she wanted on board with her in a clear plastic bag. She'd read about what exercises to do on the plane and would fill her empty water bottle after she cleared security. Andy wouldn't have bothered with any of it. He'd have said, "Use common sense," and shown up at the airport in the nick of time.

Julianne shoved her suitcase behind the passenger seat and climbed in next to him. She wanted to think it was his rules-breaking nature that had nearly gotten him killed a few weeks ago, but it really wasn't. He'd been blindsided, attacked by thugs. She'd found him unconscious, drowning in the harbor. As mad as she'd been at him, she'd done all she could to save him. She couldn't let him just *die.*

The thugs had been related to one of Colin's FBI cases.

Obviously he didn't just work at a desk at FBI headquarters in Washington, as he'd tried to get everyone in Rock Point to believe.

Emma had been involved in the case, too.

Complicated, those two.

"All set?" Andy asked.

Julianne nodded. "Yes. Thanks."

He had on a thick deep red flannel shirt over jeans. No coat, despite the November cold. She'd debated and debated until finally deciding to wear a long, shawl-like sweater that would keep her warm enough on the way to the airport and once in Ireland but wouldn't be too bulky and awkward on the plane. She'd packed layers in her suitcase to accommodate whatever conditions she was likely to encounter once she arrived in Declan's Cross.

She adjusted her sweater. She still had her hair in a ponytail. Back when he'd noticed such things, Andy had told her he'd liked her hair that way. She put that thought right out of her mind and gave him a calm, neutral smile. As if he were a cabdriver. "Did you get out to check your traps this morning?"

"Nope. Not back on the water yet after my mishap. Couple more days."

His "mishap." Only a Donovan would regard attempted murder as a mishap. Julianne angled him a look. "You're following doctor's orders, aren't you?"

"More or less."

"What's the 'less'?"

He grinned over at her. "Beer."

She didn't know if he was kidding. "If you're not back on the water yet, is it too much for you to drive me to the airport?"

"Driving to Boston is different from hauling lobster traps, and I wouldn't be doing it if it was too much."

Julianne looked out her window without responding. They hadn't parted as friends when they'd broken up over Columbus Day weekend. She hadn't, anyway. She'd parted angry, hurt, wanting to smother him in his sleep. No high road for her. As much as anything, it was his obliviousness to her feelings that had gotten to her. He'd been so matter-of-fact in dumping her. *"Hey, Jules, we've had a good run, but you need to focus on your thesis and finish up your degree. I'm just distracting you."*

He didn't get it that she'd actually fallen in love with him, never mind that she'd told him so. Another dumb move on her part.

When he'd been attacked by those thugs, she'd wondered if on some level she'd helped make it happen. If all that negative energy she'd lasered at him in her mind had put him in the wrong place at the wrong time.

It wasn't healthy, that kind of thinking. It wasn't a sin, though, was it? She hadn't told Father Bracken because she knew, deep down, that she hadn't wanted Andy hurt. Not really.

No. She really *had* wanted him hurt. Or thought she had.

"What's on your mind, Jules?"

"My trip. I'm excited." It wasn't an out-right lie since for most of the past few days, since she'd first considered an early trip to Ireland, it was all she'd thought about. "Do you want to go to Ireland someday?"

"I guess. I don't know. Maybe I could pick up an Irish accent. That could be good. You should hear my mother go on about Finian's Irish accent."

"Granny, too. She loves it. You call Father Bracken by his first name? I can't. It feels . . . I don't know. Too familiar."

"I'm not that much of a churchgoer. Mostly he and I just have the occasional shot of whiskey together."

"But if something happened to you, you'd want —" Julianne gulped in a breath at what she'd been about to say. "Never mind."

Andy cast her an amused look. "I'd want him to bury me, you mean?"

"Visit you in the hospital is what I was thinking."

His grin broadened. "No, it wasn't. Finian did visit me when I was recuperating."

"Right. Of course."

She remembered the terror she'd felt when she'd spotted Andy unconscious in the water. She'd jumped off the dock, tried to save him as his brothers had come running in response to her screams for help.

They'd leaped into the water and dragged him out to safety.

Suddenly she was desperate to change the subject. "Aer Lingus is in Terminal E."

"You'll be in Ireland two weeks?"

"That's right."

"Renting a car?"

She shook her head.

He eased his truck into the right lane, traffic picking up as they got closer to the city. "Driving on the left makes you nervous?"

It did, but she wasn't admitting as much to him, in part because it wasn't the main reason she wasn't renting a car. "Renting a car is expensive, and I won't need one."

"Is someone picking you up at the airport, or are you taking a bus or something?"

"Lindsey Hargreaves is meeting me at the airport."

"She's American, right? Not Irish?"

Julianne nodded. "That's right."

"Another marine biologist?"

"She's a diver and a marine science enthusiast. She loves whales and dolphins."

He shrugged. "Everyone loves whales and dolphins." He held up a hand. "Don't get mad, Jules. I'm not making fun of you."

As a biologist, she specialized in marine mammal research. Andy wasn't a student. He could be defensive, or maybe she just thought he could be defensive — it didn't matter anymore, did it? She sighed, kept her tone neutral as she said, "That's good."

He drove with one hand on the wheel, as confident in Boston traffic as he was in his boat on the Atlantic. "How do you know this Lindsey woman is for real?"

Julianne felt herself bristle. "What do you mean, 'for real'? I met her. I drove her around the area when she was up here for the day. We've stayed in touch by email since then."

"I mean do we know she is who she says she is?"

"What, you think I should have taken fingerprints off her water glass and had one of your law enforcement brothers run them?"

He frowned at her. "Why are you so defensive?"

"Why are you grilling me? Am I not allowed to make new friends?"

"I'm not grilling you, and you can have all the friends you want. I'm just making conversation."

"You're grilling me, Andy," she said, waving a hand. "Never mind. I'm not letting you get to me. I appreciate the ride to the airport."

"You can afford to go to Ireland now and

53

again in January?"

"I guess I can since that's what I'm doing," she said, struggling now not to pop off at him. Half the problem was being so close to him again, next to him in his truck. She hadn't touched him since she'd helped save his damn life in late October. Before that . . .

She sighed again. Best not to think about their hot, mad weeks together.

She could see the muscles in his hand tighten as he gripped the wheel. "Don't you think it's weird that Emma and Colin happen to be away, in Ireland, and then this Lindsey woman shows up in Rock Point, saying a friend told her about Fin Bracken?"

"You think Lindsey invited me to Declan's Cross because of Emma and Colin? That makes no sense, Andy. They're not marine scientists. You've been around your law enforcement father and brothers too much. That's just so paranoid."

"Just be careful," he said.

"Thank you for your concern, but I'll be fine."

"That's you, isn't it, Jules? Self-sufficient to a fault."

She didn't answer and stared out her window as they entered the tunnel that would take them to Logan Airport. She couldn't remember which one it was. It was

Callahan going one way and Sumner the other way, and there was the Ted Williams tunnel, too. She couldn't keep them straight, but she'd never been big on Boston. Give her a stretch of rocky Maine coast any day.

She noticed a sign for the airport and pointed. "Right lane."

"Got it. Thanks."

She heard the irritation in Andy's voice, as if he'd been chewing on what bugged him about her. "Just trying to help," she said, unclenching her teeth.

He downshifted. "I know."

"You were annoyed —"

"No, I wasn't. Quit trying to read into things. When I'm annoyed, I'll say so."

"Like now?"

"Not annoyed, Jules."

He didn't sound that annoyed, she realized. More resigned than anything. Fatalistic. As if he knew he couldn't say anything right and should give up trying. But what difference did it make whether he was resigned, frustrated or just plain irritated with her? In another few minutes, they'd be going their separate ways. She'd be dragging Granny's purple suitcase to the Aer Lingus counter and on to Ireland. He'd be turning around and driving back to Rock Point.

He pulled in front of the terminal. Julianne pushed open her door, jumped out and reached in back for her bag. "Thanks for the ride. I hope you get back to work full-time without a hitch."

"Appreciate that. Have a good trip. Call me if you need anything."

"Right. I will. Thanks again."

She shut the door and carried her suitcase and tote bag into the airport, past travelers with sleek wheeled black bags. She really did need her own suitcase. Granny said she liked the idea of her suitcase going to Ireland even if she couldn't.

As far as Julianne knew, Andy hadn't taken up with another woman since their falling out. That was a long time for him. But, clearly, he was back on his feet after the attack on him. He had to be restless.

She felt herself tense. There was no question in her mind that Andy would have another woman on his arm before she was back in Rock Point in two weeks.

She saw the emerald-green of the Aer Lingus sign and forced a smile.

Never mind two weeks. She wouldn't be surprised if he had another woman before she landed in Shannon, Ireland.

Julianne figured she slept all of seven minutes on the plane, not because it was a bad flight or she was afraid of flying or nervous about Ireland, but because she was so excited. She refused to think about Andy — at least she more or less refused — and focused on the thrill of her first transatlantic flight.

She loved the green of Ireland, even in November, as the big plane landed in Shannon. She'd already changed her watch to Irish time, five hours ahead of Boston. Mentally, she told herself it was 6:00 a.m. and not 1:00 a.m.

Getting through customs was a breeze. She picked up her suitcase at baggage claim and carried it out to the main lobby, where Lindsey had indicated she'd be waiting.

No Lindsey.

Julianne checked the ladies' room, the coffee shop and the books-and-sundries shop, but didn't find her new friend. Shannon Airport wasn't Logan. There weren't many places Lindsey could be.

Maybe she couldn't find a parking space or was running late.

Her tote bag hoisted on one shoulder and her suitcase on the other, Julianne went through the sliding glass doors, welcoming the rush of the chilly early Irish morning. She set her suitcase on the sidewalk, plopped her tote bag on top of it and stretched her arms up over her head, her muscles stiff after six hours on a plane. She wasn't hungry, but she wanted coffee, badly.

The airport parking lot didn't look crowded. Lindsey couldn't have had trouble finding a parking space. Other travelers left the terminal, passing Julianne as they headed for the car rental lot or were picked up by family and friends. Airport workers went about their business.

Julianne dug out her phone. No new emails, texts or voice mails from Lindsey. What if Lindsey had gotten mixed up and was meeting her at the Dublin airport?

"What to do, what to do," Julianne muttered, then decided to send a short text message.

After a few minutes without a response, she dialed Lindsey's number and got her voice mail but disconnected without leaving a message. Somehow they had gotten their wires crossed.

Fuzzy-headed after the long flight, Julianne carried her suitcase and tote bag back into the terminal and bought herself a latte and scone at a small, uncrowded coffee shop. Most of the people from her flight had departed. The lobby was dead. She checked her email messages on her phone and found the one from Lindsey confirming the pickup: I'll meet you in the lobby. We'll stop for a full Irish breakfast and be in Declan's Cross for lunch. Can't wait to see you! xo Lindsey

Straightforward enough. Julianne double-checked to make sure she had given Lindsey the correct date, and she had.

She slathered her scone with butter and jam. The only thing to do at this point was to get herself to Declan's Cross.

She finished her coffee and scone and made her way to the rental car counter. A car was available. Irish roads being what they were, collision coverage was extra and highly recommended. She had enough room on her credit card, but she'd have to find a fancier place to wait tables than Hurley's in Rock Point, Maine, to pay it off if she didn't want to dip deeper into the money from her grandfather. She decided to worry about that later. Father Bracken had jotted down directions to the cottage, and she'd put them in her Ireland folder.

She bought a bottle of water, a latte and another scone and somehow got everything out to the rental car lot. Her red Nissan Micra was one of the smallest cars they offered, and it had a standard transmission — a car with automatic transmission was another fortune on top of the rental fee and collision coverage. Her suitcase fit in back, just barely, and she set her tote bag on the front seat and arranged her water, latte and scone next to her. No way could she eat and drive, so she downed most of the latte while she familiarized herself with the car and got used to the idea of shifting with her left hand.

Her first roundabout nearly gave her a heart attack, but she didn't stall out, didn't hit anything — or anyone — and was now wide-awake with the adrenaline rush.

When she cleared Limerick and entered a pretty village, she pulled over to the side of the road. She ate the rest of her scone and checked her messages but there was still nothing from Lindsey.

A half-dozen children passed her car, giggling on their way to school. Julianne rolled down her window and smiled, letting the cool air invigorate her, reminding herself that she was a serious marine biologist and accustomed to being on her own.

She had no intention of calling or emailing Andy to tell him he was right.

There was nothing a Donovan liked better than being right.

4

An elfin-faced, black-haired Kitty O'Byrne Doyle showed Emma and Colin to their room on the second floor of the graceful, ivy-covered O'Byrne House Hotel. Once a private residence owned by Kitty's uncle, the boutique hotel occupied a scenic stretch of south Irish coast in the small village of Declan's Cross. "Fin Bracken is a great friend of mine," Kitty said as she set the door key on a gleaming mahogany side table in the attractive room. "I saw you were from Maine and emailed him on the off chance he knew you. He said he did and told me I should take good care of you. That sounds like Fin, doesn't it?"

Emma started to assure Kitty there was no need to go to any trouble on their account, but Colin grinned and said, "It does sound like him. He's stayed here?"

"He's had a drink or two here. We haven't been open quite a year yet." Kitty adjusted a tie on a drape of a tall window overlooking the hotel's extensive gardens and, beyond, the Celtic Sea. "Fin's well?"

"He just survived his first authentic Maine bean-hole supper," Colin said.

Kitty turned from the window. "Heavens. That sounds ominous. Dare I ask?"

"You dig a hole, light a fire in it, add a cast-iron pot of beans and let them bake. After twenty-four hours or so, you dig them up and serve them. It's a Maine tradition."

"So is wild blueberry pie," Emma added with a smile.

"I'll be sure to try them both if I'm ever in Maine," Kitty said. "I'll let you two get settled. Let me know if you need anything."

Emma followed her to the door. "Did Finian mention that a friend of ours from Rock Point is arriving in Declan's Cross today?"

Kitty's hand faltered on the door latch. She was in her late thirties, in a chunky wool sweater and a slim skirt in a dark blue that matched her eyes. "Yes — yes, Fin told me about her. A marine biologist. He put her in touch with a local man. Sean Murphy." She recovered her emotions. "Your friend is staying at a cottage on the Murphy sheep farm. It's up on Shepherd Head."

"Walking distance?" Colin asked.

"It's a good walk, if you don't mind hills. Easiest is to go through the garden and out the back gate. Don't go right — go left, all the way down to the bookshop. You can't miss it. It's painted red. You can go straight or go right. Don't go straight. Turn right up the hill, continue on past the cliffs, then bear left. The cottage is just there." She smiled, her cheeks pink. "It's easier than I make it sound. You'll have no trouble at all."

Emma thanked her. Kitty glanced around the room as if for a final inspection and then withdrew. When the door closed, Colin said, "She knows who you are."

"You beam 'FBI' more than I do."

"I don't mean FBI. I mean that our Kitty recognized the Sharpe name. As in Wendell Sharpe and Sharpe Fine Art Recovery."

"I assumed she would, actually." Emma walked over to the window and looked out at the sea, quiet under a blue-gray sky. "It's a pretty hotel, isn't it? Contemporary Irish art and clean, cheerful colors. I like it. John O'Byrne, Kitty's uncle, left this place to Kitty and her younger sister, Aoife. Aoife's an accomplished artist. I think some of the art in the hotel is hers."

"They're from Declan's Cross?"

Emma shook her head. "They grew up in Dublin. Their uncle was the eldest of seven.

I think he was in his forties already when they were born. I never met him."

"Your grandfather did?"

"Yes."

Colin stood next to her at the window. "Good view."

He wasn't interested in the view. She could tell. "What else is on your mind?"

"What do you know about our Kitty and our sheep farmer?"

"Not as much as you think I do, and not as much as I'd like."

"An Emma Sharpe answer if I've ever heard one." He looked out the window as if the view of gardens and sea offered answers. He'd done the driving to Declan's Cross, stopping only once. "It's too early for lunch and way too early for whiskey."

"We can walk up to the Murphy farm and have a look at Julianne's cottage," Emma said. "She'll be here soon if she's not already. Or I could go up there on my own, in case she's in no mood to deal with a Donovan."

Colin moved back from the window. "She and Andy got in over their heads. Just one of those things."

"Maybe to Andy."

"We all warned him about breaking her heart. Mike, Kevin and I. He didn't listen.

A family trait. After that, we stayed out of it. I'm not worried about Julianne's state of mind. She's tough. She's more likely to shoot me than shoot herself."

"That's what you see on the exterior," Emma said, zipping her rain jacket. "She's not going to let you all see how hurt she is by what happened between her and Andy."

"The Maroneys are all proud and stubborn." Colin grabbed the room key off the table and opened the door. "After you."

Emma went past him into the hall. He shut the door behind them, slid the key into his jacket pocket and touched her cheek. "Being here brings back memories, doesn't it?"

"My work with Granddad in Dublin was an intense time for me. I was at a crossroads, sure I had made the right decision in leaving the sisters but not sure what came next." She raised her eyes to his. "Not unlike what you're going through now."

"Taking tourists on puffin tours was on your list of new career possibilities?"

She rolled her eyes and bit back a smile. He would always try to make her laugh, despite the seriousness of what was on her mind — or his. Since the arrests of his arms traffickers and the breakup of their network, he'd been half jokingly talking about quitting the FBI and setting himself up as a tour boat operator off the coast of Maine, maybe returning to lobstering to supplement his income.

She understood the temptations of a different life.

"No puffin tours," she said. "I knew it was Sharpe Fine Art Recovery or the FBI. I briefly considered teaching or working in a museum, but they weren't for me. You know you have options besides becoming Cap'n Colin and taking tourists on puffin tours."

"We'd see seals and bald eagles, too, and I could do whale watches."

She'd meant options within the FBI, but he knew that. Getting him to talk to her about his career crisis — his personal crisis — since his undercover mission had led murderous thugs to Rock Point in October wasn't easy. He was a deep, complex man, but that didn't mean he liked to talk.

"We'll continue this conversation another time," she said as they headed down the hall.

Emma paused at a reading room at the top of the curving stairs. Its double doors were open, inviting passersby in among the comfortable-looking sofas and chairs. A round table in the middle of a thick, colorful Persian carpet displayed books on Irish history, geography, art and food. The basic lines and layout of the room hadn't changed in the extensive renovations that had transformed the musty, run-down mansion into a quirky, upscale boutique hotel.

"Is this where the stolen art was located?" Colin asked.

"The paintings were here."

Four years ago, Paddy Murphy, the part-time caretaker, had let her peek into what had then been a library. Emma had observed musty furnishings, a threadbare rug and oppressive wallpaper. John O'Byrne had died the previous year. It had been late summer, a beautiful day on the south Irish coast. She'd already decided to have a go at Quantico. She hadn't known if she'd make it through the training and become an FBI agent, but she'd known she'd had to try. That trying was part of whatever was next for her.

"Thinking again, Emma?" he asked.

She smiled. "Always."

He winked, slipped an arm around her. "Not always."

They descended the stairs and headed into the bar lounge, a low fire in its marble fireplace, and outside through French doors to a tiled terrace. Colorful pots of ivy and scarlet and lavender cyclamen glistened in the morning sun. A half-dozen tables over-looked the gardens, pebbled paths meandering among rosebushes, hydrangeas, rhododendrons and raised flower and herb beds, inviting even now, in early November.

Emma sighed, admiring the gardens. "It's a perfect spot for a romantic getaway."

"Can't argue with that."

They took a walkway past beds of deep-colored pansies, rows of trimmed-back hedges and pale pink cyclamen that had taken over a corner by the ornate iron gate.

Colin opened the gate. "Did your thief go in and out this way?"

"It's a good guess, but that's all it is," Emma said. "We don't know. It was a dark, rainy night. He could have escaped several different ways without being seen."

"You're sure it's a he?"

"Another good guess but we don't know."

" 'We' meaning the Sharpes or the FBI?"

"Both."

They went out the gate, shutting it behind them, and turned left onto a narrow street, following Kitty's directions.

"My question bugged you," Colin said calmly.

"I expected it," Emma said. "I'd have asked it myself in your place."

"It still bugged you."

They passed a gray stone house with dark

green shutters and white lace curtains in tall, sparkling windows. Most of the buildings in the village were painted in a range of primary colors, with colorful awnings, flower boxes and flowerpots, the occasional bench out front. Simple, lovely — Emma wished she could dismiss her nagging doubts about Julianne's choice of Declan's Cross and just enjoy the day.

They came to the promised red-painted bookshop on the north end of the village and turned right, as Kitty had instructed, onto a narrow lane that took them uphill. Emma felt herself relax as she breathed in the cool, salt-tinged air. The lane leveled off, curving along dramatic cliffs that dropped straight down to the sea, then winding through a patchwork of rolling fields dotted with grazing sheep.

She remembered how much she'd loved the atmosphere of Declan's Cross on her one visit. So much had changed in the past four years. She wondered how she'd have responded to Colin if he'd turned up in Dublin back then, or if she'd run into him on her day trip down here. He was already an FBI agent, on his first undercover assignment.

Ten to one that Colin Donovan wasn't any

different from the one walking next to her now.

"Smiling at the view of the Celtic Sea?" he asked her.

"It's spectacular, but no. I was thinking about you and what it would have been like if we'd met sooner."

"How much sooner?"

"Well, not when I was with the sisters. I expect I needed that time so that I'd be ready when we did meet."

He laughed. "Learning to shoot probably helped, too."

"A wonder I didn't run into you even before the sisters, since we grew up within a few miles of each other. Maybe we did and just didn't know it." She slowed her pace and noticed a few yellow blossoms on a cluster of prickly gorse along the edge of the lane. *So pretty,* she thought, then squinted out at the horizon in the distance as she answered the question that hung between them. "I know my background as a Sharpe is complicated, but growing up around our family business, working for my grandfather, learning as much as I have from him — all of that's a plus, Colin. Being a Sharpe is an asset in my art crimes work."

"Mostly an asset," he said without hesitation.

She glanced sideways at him. "Are you trying to provoke me?"

"Just trying to get you to admit that I already have provoked you."

She sighed. "I'm not as hotheaded as you are."

"You have doubts, Emma. You're not sure you're where you're supposed to be."

"I'm here with you." She knew he meant the FBI and not him. "That's good enough for me."

"No argument from me. We'll save the deep talk for another time. I may not know all your secrets, but I know you. I know you're worried that being a Sharpe is getting in the way of your work." He took her hand and drew her close. "Your fingers are cold."

She was relieved he hadn't pushed her for answers. "I left my gloves at the hotel."

"We'll have to keep each other warm, then."

She smiled. "Sometimes we do think alike."

A few minutes later, they came to a tan cinder-block bungalow in a small lot bordered on three sides by fields and more sheep. Emma stopped at a barbed-wire fence where four woolly ewes had gathered. They didn't seem to mind the stiff breeze off the water, but it was colder than she expected, prompting her to pull up her jacket collar. "It's a beautiful spot for Julianne's stay," she said, glancing at Colin. "If you decide you never want to leave Ireland after all, you could always take up sheep farming."

He patted a ewe's head. She bleated and pushed against his palm. He grinned. "I do have a way with women, don't you think?"

"Very funny."

"I don't see myself taking up sheep farming in Ireland. Whale watches, maybe. Irish coastal waters are a sanctuary for whales, dolphins and porpoises."

"Colin, you're not serious, are you?"

His smoky gray eyes settled on her. "I'm kidding, Emma. I won't be staying in Ireland forever. Whatever's next for me is back home."

"You won't be going back with me on Friday. You need more time on your own here, without me."

"It wasn't a mistake for you to have come," he said.

"I'm glad of that."

He stood back from the sheep, the wind

catching the ends of his dark hair. He hadn't asked her to join him in Ireland. When he'd left without her, she'd understood that he'd believed some time on his own in Finian Bracken's Irish cottage was a way for him to decompress after his months undercover, and at least to start the process of figuring out what came next for him. She'd followed him there because she'd wanted, simply, to be with him. If he'd asked her to go back to Boston, she'd have gone.

But he hadn't asked her to leave. They'd taken long walks, laughed in pubs, made love on dark, rain-soaked nights. She'd relished every minute of being with him, but that didn't mean she'd made the right decision in coming here. Leaving without him didn't seem right, either, but she still was booked on a flight back to Boston on Friday.

The sheep about-faced and wandered back into the field. Emma turned from the fence and looked across the lane, past a stone wall and a strip of golden grass to a steep, rocky slope that angled down to the water, sparkling under a mix of clouds and sun. Not a boat was in sight.

"Do you know anything about this Sean Murphy?" Colin asked.

She shook her head. "Not really, no."

It wasn't a complete answer, and she suspected he knew it. The Murphy farmhouse was up through the fields behind the cottage, not as close to the water. She remembered it from her day trip four years ago. But she needed to pull her thoughts about Declan's Cross together before she explained everything to Colin, not explain scattershot — not let herself feel pressured to tell him things about the theft and the investigation that she couldn't tell him, shouldn't tell him.

His approach would be simple and direct. He'd tell her he wanted to know whatever she knew. All of it. Now. No waiting, no thinking. It wasn't a question of trust, he'd say, as much as a matter of being practical. He was a deep-cover federal agent. It wasn't as if he couldn't handle the facts of a serial art thief.

"It's a beautiful view," Emma said, taking in the gray-blue sea as it melted into the horizon. "Of course, you're a former lobsterman and marine patrol officer. You probably don't see what I see when you look out at the ocean."

Colin moved back from the fence and stood next to her. "Julianne's a marine biologist. She probably sees things neither of us would notice."

"Do you want to wait for her?"

"We can at least catch our breath."

Even as he spoke, a small red car appeared down the lane, inching toward the cottage. As it came closer, Emma recognized Julianne Maroney at the wheel and frowned at Colin. "I thought her friend was picking her up."

"So did I." He nodded toward the creeping car. "She's not setting any land-speed records, is she?"

"First time driving in Ireland? Fresh off a plane? I wouldn't be, either."

The tiny Micra came to a crooked stop in front of the cottage. Julianne leaped out as if the front seat had caught fire. "I made it alive. Damn. A miracle if there ever was one." She exhaled, placing a hand on her heart as if to steady her nerves, then focused on Emma and Colin. "What are you two doing here?"

"We thought we'd welcome you to Ireland," Emma said.

"How did you know —" Julianne stopped, sighed. "Andy." She glared at Colin. "He told you?"

Colin shrugged. "Emailed me after he talked to Ryan and then again last night."

"Figures. No secrets in Rock Point." She lowered her hand from her heart and gave an exaggerated shudder. "Jet lag, driving on the left, roundabouts, hedgerows — my heart was already in my throat. Then I get to this lane. Cliffs. No guardrails. No shoulder. It's insane. What if I'd met another car?"

Emma smiled. "Looks as if you did just fine."

"At least this place exists. I was starting to think I'd gotten all my wires crossed." Julianne hunched her shoulders, rubbed her neck with one hand. "Ugh. I'm so stiff. I must have tensed every muscle in my body driving. I didn't sleep much on the plane. It still feels like the middle of the night."

"Get some sunlight in your eyes," Colin said. "You'll be fine."

She bristled. "I know I'll be fine."

He glanced into her rented car. "What happened to your ride? Lindsey Hargreaves, right? She was picking you up in Shannon?"

"Yes, and I have no idea what happened to her." Julianne sounded slightly less combative. "I have a terrible feeling she's meeting me in Dublin instead of Shannon. I take it you haven't seen her? She's not here?"

Emma shook her head. "We only just got into Declan's Cross ourselves."

"I've called and texted her but nothing. I

must have screwed up. Right now I just feel stupid more than anything else."

"A little late to feel stupid," Colin said.

Julianne scowled at him. "Always count on a Donovan to make you feel better."

"You barely know this woman," he said, obviously not about to let Julianne off the hook. "You have no idea if she's reliable."

"I know that, Colin. I got here alive, didn't I?" She tightened her shawl-like sweater around her and sighed at the view. "What a great spot. It's going to be a fantastic two weeks." She turned to Emma. "Thanks for the welcome, but you and Colin can go on your way now."

Emma could see that Julianne was rattled and tired from her long, unexpected drive from Shannon, on little sleep, and she was defensive around Colin. Probably should have left him at the hotel, Emma thought, then said gently, "We're staying in the village. Just overnight. The O'Byrne House Hotel. It's really lovely. I hope you'll stop by before we leave."

"Wait, what? You're staying in Declan's Cross?" Julianne's dark hair blew in the wind, the last of her ponytail coming loose. "You're kidding, right?"

"No, ma'am," Colin said, blunt as ever. "Get yourself settled. We can talk later."

She stiffened visibly. "I'll do exactly as I please."

He turned to Emma. "That spa's looking better and better."

Julianne ignored him and headed up the walk to the bungalow. She tried the front door. It was unlocked, and she went in without so much as a backward glance.

Emma stood next to Colin by the little car. "You and Julianne go back a long way. I'll go talk to her and let her know how to reach us. Why don't you stay out here and count sheep?"

"I remember her bossing us around when she was six. She liked to carry around a bucket filled with seaweed and periwinkles."

"Not afraid of her, are you?"

He grinned. "Terrified. I have to remember she's almost finished with her master's in marine biology. She's always been smart. Andy is, too, but he never was a student. He dropped out of the only college that accepted him."

"Is that why he and Julianne aren't together anymore?"

"I haven't asked. Won't, either. He doesn't have a chip on his shoulder."

"Not that a Donovan ever would," Emma said. "He does well as a lobsterman, and his boat-restoration business seems to be getting off the ground. Do you think he's worried about keeping Julianne in Rock Point, somehow limiting her horizons?"

"I have no idea. They both do what they want. Always have." His tone softened. "Go on. I'll grab her suitcase. She won't thank me for it. You watch."

He seemed more amused and expectant than annoyed. Emma hoped Lindsey Hargreaves had left a note in the cottage to explain why she hadn't met Julianne at the airport. That would ease Julianne's mind. Colin's, too. He clearly didn't like that this woman hadn't shown up.

Julianne had left the front door open, and Emma stepped inside, entering a living room with a tile floor, throw rugs and IKEA-style furnishings in neutral colors. There was a fireplace, next to it a bin of kindling and peat.

A pine table served as a divider between the living room and a sunlit kitchen on the opposite end of the little one-story bungalow. Julianne stood by the table, looking out double windows at the front yard and across the lane to the sea.

"Sorry I snapped at Colin," she said, sounding more tired than apologetic. "Not that he can't take it."

Emma walked over to her. "We didn't

mean to upset you."

"You didn't. Really. I'm just frazzled. If I'd known Lindsey wasn't meeting me, I'd have been more prepared to drive." She glanced around the living room and adjoining kitchen. "It's a cute place, though, isn't it?"

"It is. It looks comfortable and well-equipped."

"Father Bracken knows the owner somehow. I didn't get the details. I'd planned to stay in a bed-and-breakfast, but I jumped at the chance to rent a cottage. Granny was reassured that Father Bracken recommended it."

"And you invited Lindsey to join you here?"

Julianne nodded. "It has two bedrooms, each with its own bathroom. Lindsey said conditions at the field station are a little primitive. She's been staying there."

"How long?"

"I don't know. A few weeks, maybe. I took a quick look around, but there's no sign she's arrived yet. I'm sure we just got our wires crossed." Julianne sighed at the view. "I wish Granny could see this. She's always wanted to go to Ireland."

Emma went into the kitchen. It had white cabinets and a white countertop, a sturdy stove and small refrigerator, and another window looking out at the sea. The back door was through an adjoining mudroom with a washer and dryer. On the counter was a welcome basket filled with bread, digestives, instant coffee, tea and a bottle of red wine. She peeked in the refrigerator and noticed milk, orange juice, eggs, butter, jam, cheese and a bottle of white wine.

"It's a bit more remote up here than I expected," Julianne said, coming into the kitchen. "I'm glad it's still within walking distance of the village. I love to walk, but I suppose I'll have to drive to get groceries. Helps to know I'm not likely to meet many cars."

"You'll get used to Irish roads."

"I just need a good night's sleep. I'm falling over on my feet."

As she spoke, Colin entered the cottage and set her suitcase and tote bag by the front door. He glanced around the living room, then joined her and Emma in the kitchen. "There's no cell service up here. No landline, either. Wi-Fi?"

"I don't know. I didn't ask because I don't care." Julianne pulled the bottle of wine out of the welcome basket. "I'll find a phone if I need one, and an internet connection, too. Don't worry, okay?"

"Looks like it's just you and this Sean Murphy up here." Colin took the digestives out of the basket. "These things are addictive. Light a fire, make some tea, kick back and relax." He grinned. "Not that I'm telling you what to do."

Julianne smiled, at least a little. "Sounds perfect. Maybe Lindsey ran into a delay and tried to get in touch with me but couldn't due to technical difficulties. I'm sure she'll turn up. I can't wait to check out the field station, but I need to get settled first."

"It's her brainchild?" Emma asked.

"That's what she told me. It's still in the early planning stages. I know I just met Lindsey and this trip is impulsive, but I'm not being reckless. I'm familiar with the Hargreaves Oceanographic Institute. It's solid. They do good work. I'll also be going into Cork to see about my internship." She grabbed the bread out of the basket and set it on the counter. "It's exciting. Being here."

Colin placed the digestives next to the bread. "What's the research focus of this field station?"

"Irish porpoises, whales and dolphins, as far as I know," Julianne said.

"As opposed to Welsh porpoises, whales and dolphins?"

She made a face. "That's something Andy

82

would say."

Colin winked at her. "Uh-oh."

Color rose in her cheeks. "Just don't tell him I got stood up at the airport. He won't ask, but don't tell him if he does. And don't volunteer anything. I know I'm being very seventh grade, but I've learned to head you Donovans off at the pass, so to speak. Learned the hard way, I might add."

"As if Maroneys aren't just as rock-headed," Colin said half under his breath.

"Maybe it's no wonder our hometown has 'rock' in its name." Julianne smiled, then stifled a yawn. "I'm so tired I could melt onto the floor. Now that I'm here . . ." She glanced around the compact, tidy kitchen. "I won't mind staying here on my own if Lindsey doesn't show up."

Colin stood back from the counter. "I'd like to know where she is."

"She's probably got a million things going on and just forgot. People forget things, you know. Not all of us are as perfect as the Donovans."

Their moment of near-camaraderie had passed, Emma saw, but she said nothing.

Colin sighed. "The Donovans aren't perfect, Julianne."

"I know that. I was being sarcastic. You're going all FBI on me and jumping from A to

Z without any good reason."

"I'm not jumping to anything. I'd just like to hear from this woman."

"I get that. That's why you're an FBI agent and I'm a marine biologist. You have a suspicious mind." Julianne had clearly lost what limited patience she had with him. "I'll let you know when I hear from Lindsey, okay? I have your number. I'll text you."

Emma started out of the kitchen into the living room. "We'd love to have you join us at the hotel for lunch, dinner, a Father Bracken–approved whiskey — whatever you're up for. It's nice to see someone from home."

"Thanks, Emma," Julianne said, her tone warmer. "Right now I'll be happy with a grilled cheese sandwich and a nap. Sorry if I'm being defensive. It's good to see you guys. Really. I'll stop at the field station later and find out if anyone there has heard from Lindsey."

"Colin and I can pop in on our way back to the hotel," Emma said. "We'll let you know if she's there or anyone there has heard from her. Enjoy your grilled cheese sandwich."

Colin said only, "You know where to find us."

"Yep. Thanks again."

Emma could see it was time to leave and all but elbowed Colin back outside. The air had turned cooler, and the sky was overcast, no sun now, although with the short November days, dusk would be coming early. "It's a cute place," she said. "Finian never would have recommended it if he thought it wasn't safe."

"I guess."

"Julianne's like a little sister to you."

"More like a thorn in my side." Colin glanced back at the lonely bungalow. "I guess there's no way I'm going to like leaving her up here by herself."

"As you said, she knows where to find us."

The ewes returned to the fence, baaing, crowding against each other. Colin grimaced. "The sheep can keep Julianne company." He tucked his hand into Emma's. "Let's go check out this field station."

5

Julianne lasted in the cottage for ten minutes before she had to get out into the Irish air. She couldn't believe she was finally here. She tightened her sweater around her and walked across the lane to a stone wall. She could hear waves whooshing on the rocks far below her, and the sigh of the wind in the grass and hollows.

So beautiful, so peaceful.

She breathed deeply, releasing some of the tension that had built up since she'd strapped herself into her little rented car and hit the Irish roads.

The lane continued past the cottage, narrowing even more as it turned to dirt and disappeared around a bend. She noticed a man come around the bend, ambling toward her. He wore muddy work clothes and muddy dark green Wellies, as if he'd just come in from the fields. As he approached her, she saw he had thick dark hair and piercing blue eyes, something of a devil-may-care look about him. She guessed he was in his late thirties — Father Bracken's age, maybe a little younger.

"You must be Julianne," he said in a pronounced Irish accent. "I'm Sean Murphy, Fin Bracken's friend. Welcome to Declan's Cross."

"Thank you. It's great to meet you, Mr. Murphy."

"Sean."

She smiled. "The cottage is fantastic. I'm glad it worked out on such short notice." The wind whipped her hair in her face as she stifled yet another yawn. "Father Bracken sends his best."

"He's been telling me tales of bean-hole suppers."

Better than tales of attempted murder, Julianne supposed. "I never got a chance to ask him how you two know each other. He's not from around here, is he?"

"He's from Kerry, but he's visited Declan's Cross many times." Sean glanced at her car, still parked crookedly on the side of the lane. "You drove yourself down from Shannon, did you?"

"I did. I'm a little wobbly, but I did okay. Necessity forced me out of my comfort zone. Lindsey Hargreaves was supposed to

87

meet me, but — well, she didn't, for whatever reason. Has she been in touch with you, by any chance?"

"No, she hasn't," the Irishman said. "She's not here, then?"

"I don't know if she's in Declan's Cross, but there's no sign of her at the cottage. You know her, though, right?"

"We've met. A friend of mine has done some diving with her." Sean glanced toward the sea a moment, then back at her. "Have you heard from Lindsey at all today?"

Julianne shook her head. "Not since Sunday afternoon. We emailed each other about plans to meet at the airport. She offered. I didn't ask. I didn't expect to hear from her again before I arrived this morning. My flight got in so early. I think my phone's working okay — I'll check my messages again when I go into the village. I gather there's no cell service up here."

"It's spotty at best."

"That's fine with me." She realized she sounded as if she didn't want to talk to anyone back home, but it was just Andy she didn't want to talk to. And her brother, since he'd ratted her out to Andy, who'd ratted her out to Colin. She pushed windblown hair out of her face and added, more cheerfully, "I'll let you know if I hear from

Lindsey. I'm sure I will."

Sean studied her a moment, as if she wasn't quite what he'd expected. "Fin says you're a marine biologist. I see dolphins and porpoises now and again." He nodded toward the water. "I saw a whale once."

"Recently?"

He smiled. "I was a boy."

Julianne didn't know what she expected an Irish farmer to be like, but Sean Murphy wasn't it. It was like having a mix of a young Liam Neeson and Colin Farrell up the lane. "I thought I'd get some fresh air while I can. They say sunlight can help jet lag. It's in short supply right now, but it was sunny on the drive down here. I'd rather crawl in bed and sleep, anyway."

"You'll find it gets dark early this time of year."

"Maine does, too, but Ireland's even farther north. The Gulf Stream helps keep the climate mild here, but it doesn't help with the short winter days." She suddenly felt self-conscious, as if she'd already said too much. "I'm thrilled to be here, though."

"You'll have to come back in June when it stays light until late into the evening."

She relaxed some. "That would be great. I start an internship in January in Cork that runs until May. I'd love to stay on a couple

89

more weeks just to go sightseeing. Maybe I'll get my grandmother to join me. She's always wanted to see Ireland."

"I noticed you had company earlier," Sean said, checking a wooden fence post that was leaning to one side. "Friends of yours?"

Julianne nodded. "Colin Donovan and Emma Sharpe. They're staying at a hotel in the village. The O'Byrne, I think they said."

"It's a good place." He straightened some of the wrapped-wire fencing strung between the posts. "Donovan — Fin's FBI friend?"

"That's right." She couldn't tell if he also recognized Emma's name. "He and Emma have been in Ireland a couple weeks. They borrowed Father Bracken's cottage — I think it's in County Kerry."

"She's with the FBI, too, as I recall."

Julianne wasn't that comfortable discussing Emma and Colin's FBI status. "They're not here on official business or anything like that. They just came to welcome me to Ireland." She decided to change the subject. "Have you always lived in Declan's Cross?"

He nodded to the bungalow. "I grew up right here. It's been redone since then."

"It must have been something, being a kid out here. The village lives up to the pictures I saw on the internet. Of course, my heart was in my throat when I drove through it

90

just now, but I'm looking forward to exploring. I love to walk."

"It's a good place for walking. If you need anything, just find me. My uncle is up here most days, too. Paddy Murphy. Give either of us a shout anytime."

Julianne found herself not wanting to be alone just yet. "Farming must be a ton of work," she said.

Sean smiled, fine lines at the corners of his eyes. "Most things worth anything are a lot of work, don't you think?"

"That's a good attitude. I've always loved whales and dolphins, but it's not as if organic chemistry came naturally to me." She turned her back to the water — and the wind — as she looked across the rolling fields. Several sheep stared back at her. "The sheep look all set for winter. Father Bracken says Irish winters are cold, dark and damp."

"He's right, but I wouldn't know any different."

"I hope he doesn't think a Maine winter will be any better. It's at least as long as an Irish winter, and it can get very cold and snowy. Helps to like to do things outside. I like cross-country skiing in perfect conditions, and snowshoeing's a lot of fun. I've never gone ice fishing." Julianne remembered that Andy was into ice fishing. She'd thought they'd be together over the winter, and he'd take her out to his fishing hut on a lake up north. She shook off that image before it could take shape. "I hope Father Bracken's enjoying Maine."

"From what he tells me he seems to be. He said you showed Lindsey the sights while she was in Maine last week."

"I did. We had a great time."

Sean stepped back onto the lane. "I've never been to Maine. I think of lighthouses and lobsters."

"We saw one lighthouse and a lot of lobsters, especially in Rock Point. I also showed her summer houses, art galleries, a nature trail, a couple of sandy beaches. We did a whirlwind grand tour."

"Was she interested in seeing anything in particular?"

"She was interested in everything." Sean Murphy might be an Irish sheep farmer, but he was starting to remind Julianne of Colin with the questions, the suspicion — but she was tired and on the defensive. She'd trust her reactions better after lunch and a nap. "I've kept you from your farm work long enough."

"Not at all." He zipped up his jacket

against the stiffening wind. "Have a good walk."

She thanked him again. As he headed back down the lane, he didn't really strike her as an Irish farmer — but what did she know about Irish farmers?

She decided to skip her walk and instead returned to the cottage, the wind whistling in the rocks now. A grilled cheese sandwich definitely sounded good, and maybe a nice fire to take the damp chill out of the air. She'd give it a while longer before she really started to worry about Lindsey Hargreaves.

6

That the unreliable, cheerful Lindsey Hargreaves had failed to pick up Julianne Maroney in Shannon was enough to distract Sean Murphy from farm work but not enough for him to raise the alarm. These days it didn't take much to distract him from farm work.

He'd changed into a clean jacket and hiking boots after deciding against returning to the barn to finish up the antifungal spraying he'd started that morning, one sheep hoof at a time. He hated the spraying, but it had to be done to prevent "foot rot."

He started down the lane toward the village, feeling the residual ache of injuries he'd sustained in June. Broken ribs, a punctured lung, a messed-up rotator cuff.

Sean took in a deep breath and told himself that any physical pain was in his head at this point. Fin Bracken had brought a bottle of rare, dear Bracken 15-year-old whiskey on his last visit to Declan's Cross earlier that year. Sean hadn't opened it until September. During the worst days of his recovery, he hadn't touched so much as a pint. He stayed away from alcohol when it was all he wanted.

He'd taken time to heal before he'd opened the Bracken 15, and even then, he hadn't drunk alone. He'd invited his uncle in for a *taoscán*. A few days later, he'd been able to walk into the village for a pint at his favorite pub.

Now it was early November, and what had changed? The Bracken 15 was still on the top shelf in the farmhouse kitchen. He was still walking into the village for the occasional pint.

Still working on the farm.

Sean didn't known what Fin had told Julianne Maroney about him, but it had obviously been very little. She struck Sean as feisty and yet uncertain, perhaps not fully trusting her motives for coming to Ireland. He wondered if her FBI agent friends had picked up on that ambivalence and that's why they were in Declan's Cross checking on her.

Interesting that the main offices of Sharpe Fine Art Recovery were in Heron's Cove, just down the coast from Rock Point where

Fin was. Fin had mentioned Emma Sharpe. She was the granddaughter of Wendell Sharpe, who, last Sean had heard, was on the verge of retiring in Dublin.

Had Julianne's choice of Declan's Cross for her Irish sojourn piqued Emma's interest, given the theft at the O'Byrne place ten years ago and her grandfather's interest in the unsolved case?

It had Sean's.

He hadn't been a farmer ten years ago.

Then again, he wasn't much of one now. He noticed his uncle puttering toward him on the tractor, an ancient John Deere with mud permanently encrusted on its green exterior. Paddy kept it in working order. Sean had given up. In his seventies now, his uncle liked to take the tractor out to the fields and was happy to leave the more tedious farm work to his nephew.

The wind had subsided. Sean recognized his own restlessness. He wanted to know what had happened to Lindsey Hargreaves, but he didn't trust the foreboding that was starting to gnaw at him. He attributed it to the last of what his doctors had described as a normal process of post-trauma stress recovery — or, more likely at this point, boredom.

He had no business thinking of himself as

96

bored. There was always work to do on the farm, and it was most often work he enjoyed, or at least appreciated. But that was different from loving it, wasn't it?

And it was different from being part of an elite garda investigative unit in Dublin.

An Garda Síochána. Guardians of the Peace.

The guards.

The Irish police.

Sean had joined the gardai at twenty-two. He'd never wanted to be anything else. He'd help out at the farm — it was home as no place else ever would be — but he'd never imagined being a farmer.

Technically he was still a member of his unit. He was on leave, recovering from the thrashing he'd taken during the messy arrest of smugglers back in June. He'd won the day and broken open the smuggling ring, but he'd paid the price with a long recovery.

Being back in proximity to the proprietor of the O'Byrne House Hotel probably wasn't helping.

"Ah, Kitty."

Was she suspicious of her FBI guests' motives for checking into her hotel?

She'd at least be curious.

Sean waved to Paddy and then started

97

down the lane to the village. Walking meant he could stop for a pint or two without having to worry about his blood-alcohol level. He wasn't one to over-imbibe, but better to fall over a stone wall than drive over it. Fin Bracken liked to say that walking was soul work. Sean didn't know about that, but walking had helped him these past few months. At first he could only manage to the barn and back to the couch, but gradually his stamina had improved and, with it, his distances. He'd told Fin that farm work kept him busy, but walking kept him sane.

At the bottom of the hill, instead of going past the bookshop into the village, he turned down a narrow street to the waterfront and the present and future site of Lindsey Hargreaves' marine science research field station. At the moment it was an abandoned garage she'd rented with an American friend, a professional diver. It was located just up from the small Declan's Cross pier and so far looked more like a convenient place to store diving equipment and camp out between dives. It would take vision, enthusiasm, determination and a substantial financial commitment to create a proper research facility. Even with Lindsey's family connections, Sean was skeptical, but that was his nature.

A van was parked out front, its back open, revealing state-of-the-art diving gear. Brent Corwin, the American diver, emerged from a side door of the garage. He was in his late thirties, his close-cropped hair almost fully gray. He gave an exaggerated shiver as he stuffed an oily rag into a sweatshirt pocket. "Hey, Sean. Where did the mild air go? It feels more like November in New York. I'm from Florida. Warm-blooded. What can I do for you?"

"I'm looking for Lindsey Hargreaves."

"Two Americans were just here looking for her, too. Friends of the woman she was supposed to pick up in Shannon this morning. I guess that didn't happen. That's flaky even for Lindsey."

"Has she been in touch with you?"

"Uh-uh. I haven't seen her since she left for the U.S. last week to visit her father. She arrived back in Dublin on Friday but ended up staying for a couple days. Her father had to be in London on business and decided to make a stop in Dublin and see the sights."

Sean glanced in the van at the wet suits, masks, tanks and other diving paraphernalia, none of it looking as if it had been used in the past few hours. He turned back to Brent. "Do you think she's still in Dublin, then?"

"Could be. If my dad turned up out of the blue, I'd probably forget half the things I had to do, too, but you've met Lindsey. She's not the most organized person, you know? I can see her forgetting it was Shannon and ending up at the Dublin airport, wondering what kind of flake Julianne is." Brent lifted a tank out of the van and set it on the ground. He didn't look at all worried about Lindsey or anything else. "I'll make a few calls and see if I can find out where Lindsey's off to. I'll let you know if I hear from her, or if she turns up. Would you mind doing the same?"

"Not at all."

"And Julianne — if she hears from Lindsey, she'll let us know?"

Sean nodded. "I'm sure she will."

"I'll check with Eamon, too," Brent said. "He's up in Ardmore diving with some of his buddies today."

Eamon Carrick was the younger brother of one of Sean's garda colleagues, both solid divers who looked for any opportunity to get under the water. Not Sean. He hated even the idea of diving. "How many of you were here last night?" he asked.

"Just me." Brent gestured back toward the garage. "The place has heat and decent facilities. It's roughing it by Lindsey's standards. She's looking forward to moving into the cottage. She's well-meaning but she's not reliable. She'd be the first to say so."

"She visited a friend of mine in Maine last week —"

"The priest. Bracken, right? Yeah. That's when she met this marine biologist, Julianne."

"Why did she visit Father Bracken, do you know?"

Brent shook his head. "No idea. She said he's Irish — he and his brother own a whiskey distillery near Killarney. I didn't know you were friends with him."

"We go back a ways," Sean said, deliberately vague. He'd met Fin Bracken after the deaths of Fin's wife and daughters. Not an easy subject. "When did you talk to Lindsey last?"

"Friday, after she got back to Dublin and found out her father was on his way. We only talked for a minute. We emailed a couple times after that." Brent shut the van doors and lifted the tank. "She gave me her father's cell number. If he's still in Dublin, he'll be at a five-star hotel. His name's David — David Hargreaves. We've never met, but I've done some diving for the Hargreaves Oceanographic Institute. I hear he's a good guy."

Sean could see that Brent was impatient to get on with his work and left him to it. Whether it was cynicism or experience, Sean doubted Lindsey Hargreaves was going to the trouble of launching a research facility simply out of devotion to marine science. Brent Corwin was a dedicated adventurer, good-looking, energetic. Eamon Carrick and his diving friends were the same. Temptations, perhaps, for a young woman with no clear direction in her life.

There was also her father, perhaps not an easy man to impress. Sean didn't know Lindsey well enough to have a good feel for what motivated her, but David Hargreaves' impromptu stop in Dublin could have thrown her off just enough that she'd forgotten to pick up her new friend in Shannon.

"A bored man you are, Sean Murphy," he muttered, his teeth clenched as he walked into the village, knowing his next stop would be the O'Byrne House Hotel.

Fool that he was.

Rave reviews and word-of-mouth of delighted guests had helped keep a steady flow of guests at the O'Byrne House Hotel since it opened its doors a year ago, but November was quiet. Sean went through the back gate and didn't run into another soul in the gardens. Pretty Kitty O'Byrne Doyle had seen to every detail in transforming her uncle's crumbling mansion, shrouded in cobwebs and overrun with mice, into a modern, elegant hotel that was at once tranquil and cheerful. He'd heard it was doing well. No doubt. Everything Kitty touched was a success — except, at least in her mind, her teenage son, Philip, who gave her fits.

Sean found the lad alone in the bar lounge, unloading a tray of fresh glasses onto a head-high shelf. Philip Doyle had his mother's blue eyes, dark hair and spirited temperament and his father's stubborn jaw and ambition. One minute he was eighteen going on thirteen — angry, sullen, easily bored — and the next, eighteen going on thirty — strong, mature, solid. He'd moved to Declan's Cross with his mother two years ago. He hadn't wanted to. He could have stayed in Dublin with his father, a banker, but he hadn't. And he hadn't gone back to Dublin since he'd finished school.

He glanced up and said, "Garda Murphy," with just enough sarcasm to be annoying but not enough for Sean to haul him out from behind the bar by his shirt collar.

"Not diving today?" Sean asked.

"I went out early with Eamon Carrick and a couple of his friends."

As if it's any of your business, his tone said.

Sean sat on a high cushioned stool at the polished wood bar, saved from the original fittings in the house and refurbished to Kitty's specifications. She had a background in business but loved this place. She and Aoife had been coming here since they were babies. Sean couldn't recall when he'd first noticed them. By the time Kitty was seventeen, for certain. By eighteen, she'd been in love with her banker, William Doyle.

"Where did you go?" Sean asked her son.

Philip took the last glass from the tray and set it on the shelf with the others, all sparkling in a sudden ray of sun that was there and then gone again. "We went out to the *Samson* wreck off Ram Head in Ardmore."

"I know the spot." In 1987, a trawler had run aground, its hulking, rusting wreck an eyesore to many but a popular spot for divers. "How well do you know these lads?"

"Well enough. I'm learning a lot from them. They're more experienced divers than I am."

"Diving is an expensive hobby."

"It's not just a hobby," Philip said. "I'm

thinking of becoming an oceanographic research diver."

Sean wasn't one to puncture a young man's dreams, but he said, "A college degree would help, I would think."

"It would if I decide I want one." He tucked the empty tray under one arm. "What if I wanted to join the garda water unit like Eamon's brother?"

"Think you could pull a body out of the water?"

Philip didn't flinch. "I could."

"It'd be in addition to your regular garda duties."

"Good."

Practical considerations didn't necessarily interest Philip, but that could be youth and the attitude of some of his diving friends rubbing off on him. From what Sean had gleaned in the three or four weeks since Lindsey and Brent had arrived in Declan's Cross, they'd been bouncing from place to place in order to indulge their passion for diving. Brent in particular was a respected diver, willing to cobble together a living if it gave him the freedom to dive. Their arrival in Declan's Cross had attracted local divers. Everyone had assumed they'd move on. Then came the idea for a research field station, the rented garage . . . and now Julianne

Maroney.

Sean decided to get Philip's opinion, gauge his reaction. "What's the status of this marine science research field station?"

"Lindsey's securing funding from her family. She wants it to be a proper field station." Philip opened a lower cabinet and shoved the tray inside, then stood straight, his cheeks flushed with enthusiasm. "I've volunteered to do what I can to help."

Meaning he wasn't getting paid. Same with Lindsey's new friend from Maine. "Lindsey seems to have a knack for getting people to help her."

"And what's wrong with that?"

Sean shrugged, unruffled. "Nothing on the face of it. What about Brent and Eamon? Are they volunteers?"

"I don't know, but Eamon's not involved with the field station that I can see. Brent could be on a Hargreaves Institute grant. He hasn't said, and I haven't asked." Philip was less combative, his interest in the field station plainly genuine. "Can I get you anything?"

Sean shook his head. "Just passing through. You haven't seen Lindsey, have you?"

"Not since yesterday."

"Yesterday?"

"Yeah." Philip lifted a bottle of wine from a rack and checked the cork, obviously looking for something to do. "She stopped by the garage — the field station. I was in back with the tanks. By the time I realized she was there, she was on her way again."

"Did you speak to her?" Sean asked.

"Not a word. I don't think she saw me."

"You were alone?"

"Yes. Sean — geez, man —"

"What time was this?"

"Two o'clock or so. After lunch." He gave a half nervous, half sarcastic laugh. "I wouldn't want to get into real trouble with you. I'm sweating."

Sean eased off the stool, attempting to look less as if Philip were a terror suspect. His months of inaction — healing, thinking, tending sheep — had taken a toll, and now he was overreacting to absolutely nothing. "Where were Eamon and Brent yesterday?" he asked casually.

"I don't really know. Off diving, I expect. You don't think anything's happened to Lindsey, do you?"

"I've no reason to think so."

It was a careful answer, and Philip seemed to recognize it as such. He returned the wine bottle to the rack and grabbed a wet rag out of the small, stainless-steel sink but didn't seem to know what to do with it. He finally slopped it onto the edge of the sink and scrubbed at some possibly imaginary stain. The color in his face was all the confirmation Sean needed that the lad was taken with Lindsey. She was at least a decade older, but that wouldn't stop an eighteen-year-old's fantasies.

Not much did, Sean thought. At the moment he had no desire for alcohol. He stood by the fire, burning hot with no one to enjoy it. Above the marble mantel was a mirror that had hung there for as long as he could remember. Interesting to see what Kitty had kept of John O'Byrne's and what she'd dumped.

She bustled into the room, saw him, stopped abruptly. She wore a long sweater that came almost to her knees. It was a soft wool, as blue as her eyes. "Hello, Sean." Tight, brisk. "I didn't realize you were here."

"I'm admiring your fire."

She moved deeper into the room. "You've never been even half as funny as you think you are. What do you want?"

He realized he wasn't exactly sure and said, "I'm looking for Lindsey Hargreaves."

"I see. Well, did you find her?"

"No. I talked to Philip. He hasn't seen her today."

"Good," Kitty said under her breath.

Sean watched her as she tidied books that didn't need tidying. She worried about her son. Philip didn't seem to grasp that the clock was ticking and he needed to get on with his life. His diving friends and their live-for-the-moment ways weren't necessarily the best influence, but they didn't seem bad sorts.

Then again, Sean thought, what did he know about the divers, or about Kitty and her teenage son? Since he'd arrived in Declan's Cross in June, having barely survived his smugglers' attempt to kill him, he'd kept to himself.

"David Hargreaves is arriving tonight," Kitty said. "Lindsey's father."

"Here at the hotel?"

She nodded. "He's staying in the cottage."

The O'Byrne cottage was through the gardens, a separate accommodation with its own kitchen and two bedrooms. Sean grabbed the poker and gave the fire a quick stir. "Lindsey's not staying with him?"

"Apparently not. She's supposed to be staying at your cottage. The views are gorgeous up there."

Sean returned the poker to the rack. He noticed Kitty's cheeks flame. She would be familiar with his cottage's views just from living in Declan's Cross, but he knew she wasn't thinking about looking out at the cliffs and sea from the lane. She was thinking about waking up in his bed six years ago. His father had died. His mother had moved into the village. He and Kitty had had the place to themselves.

It had been his second chance with her. He wouldn't get a third.

"It was a long time ago, Kitty," he said.

She frowned as if she were mystified. "I must have missed something because I have no idea what you mean." She moved off to adjust drapes, her back to him as she continued. "You've met my new guests. Finian Bracken's friends."

"They're FBI agents, you know."

She glanced back at him. "Are they now?"

Clearly she did know.

"They're here just for the night," she added. "They've been staying at Fin Bracken's cottage near Kenmare. The one he and Sally fixed up."

Sean nodded but made no comment. Half the women in Ireland had fallen in love with Finian Bracken after the tragic deaths of his family. They'd wanted to take away his pain and give him a new life. Then he'd gone and become a priest, and now he was in New England, thanks to Sean and, in part, to Kitty herself. On a visit to Declan's Cross in late March, Fin had talked Sean into stopping at the hotel for a drink. They'd found Kitty deep in conversation with an American priest, Joseph Callaghan, a quiet, thoughtful man in his early sixties. Father Callaghan had chosen Declan's Cross not just because of the raves about its newly opened hotel but because he served a parish in Rock Point, Maine, not far from the Heron's Cove offices of Sharpe Fine Art Recovery. He'd heard about the decade-old unsolved theft. That had tipped the scales in favor of a two-night stay in Declan's Cross.

Over too much of Bracken Distillers' finest, Father Callaghan had explained how he'd fallen in love with his ancestral homeland and dreamed of taking a sabbatical in Ireland. Sean hadn't realized what a chord the old priest's words had struck with Fin Bracken, but next thing, Fin had done whatever ecclesiastic string-pulling he'd needed to do and in June was off to Maine to replace Father Callaghan for the year.

Sean supposed the good Father Callaghan was somewhere in Ireland. He was due to return to Rock Point next June.

Not always easy to go back, was it?

Shaking off his ruminating, Sean noticed

Kitty was frowning at him again. Ordinarily he wasn't the type to ruminate. He said, "I went out to Fin's cottage once, a year after Sally and the girls died." He recalled that Fin had been dead drunk. Pasty, shaking. Not at peace with God then, for certain. Sean was of no mind to mention the incident. "It's a small place, but it's done up just right. Sally's influence, I imagine."

Kitty sighed heavily. "I expect so."

It wasn't a time he liked to revisit. He changed the subject. "Where are your FBI agents now?"

"Upstairs, I think. They had lunch here. When I saw the Sharpe name, I assumed they might be here about the theft — some new development, perhaps — but they're seeing about this marine biologist friend of theirs who's renting your cottage. Fin's doing, I've gathered."

"He was worried about Julianne, I think."

"We emailed this morning, but you know how circumspect he can be," Kitty said. "Father Callaghan never mentioned the Sharpes and FBI agents when he was here."

Sean shrugged. "Why would he?"

"Always so practical," she said with a bit of a sniff. "I suppose you're right, though. The theft's not as well-known as it was ten years ago, but it's still a curiosity for some.

It'll never be solved." Her eyes darkened on Sean. "I expect you know that better than most."

"Because I'm a detective, or because I'm Paddy Murphy's nephew?"

He thought he'd kept any harshness or sarcasm out of his tone, but Kitty nonetheless looked taken aback, as if she didn't know if she should slap him or run from him. "Neither. Both. I don't know. It makes no difference. Excuse me," she said, crisp. "I've work to do."

"I won't keep you, then."

She took a breath, but her eyes were fixed on the bar where Sean had chatted with her son. Her expression softened. "This lot Philip's diving with — they're all right, Sean?"

"I'm just a farmer these days, Kitty."

"Even your sheep don't believe that," she said with a scoff, then moved on behind the bar. She was still clearly worried about her son, but Sean knew she would never admit as much to him, or ask him to intervene.

He lingered just long enough to notice the light shining on her black hair. He could see her on a long, lazy morning six years ago, sleeping as the sun rose. Her black hair had gleamed then, too. She'd looked comfortable again in her own skin, excited about what was next for her. She'd told him she'd remembered all the reasons why she had fallen for him the first time and had forgotten all the reasons why they had gone their separate ways.

Sean exited through the bar lounge, welcoming the cool air and wind.

Kitty was a smart woman. She wouldn't forget again.

Sean stopped just past the bookshop, far enough from the O'Byrne House Hotel and its maddening owner that he could think straight again. He paid little attention to the familiar surroundings as he debated whether to call Fin Bracken about his FBI friends. He finally decided against it. It had never been easy to get information out of Fin and less so now that he was a priest. Instead he phoned Eamon Carrick's brother, Ronan, a garda in Dublin and a member of the underwater diving unit that served the entire Republic of Ireland.

Ronan picked up almost immediately. "Sean Murphy. What a surprise. How are the sheep, my friend?"

"Bleating even as we speak."

"Bleeding? Dear God. What have you done to them?"

"*Bleating.* Baaing. You know." Sean had no idea if Ronan were serious or joking.

"Never mind. It was just something to say."

"Small talk from Sean Murphy. There's something. Are you in Declan's Cross?"

"As ever. Have you any idea why Wendell Sharpe's granddaughter is here?"

"In Ireland?"

"In Declan's Cross. You already knew she was in Ireland?"

"Word reached me."

"Eamon?"

"Not Eamon. If it doesn't come in water, he's not interested. Someone I know in the art squad mentioned it. Wendell Sharpe's semi-retired now, did you know? And Emma Sharpe is with the FBI. Any reason for the FBI to be interested in Declan's Cross?"

Sean didn't respond at once. He looked in the bookshop window and saw a small boy sitting on the floor in front of a shelf of books. He'd done the same as a boy, always interested in biographies and comics. Super-heroes. Finally he told Ronan, "No reason. There's nothing new on the art theft at the O'Byrne house, is there?"

"You'd know before I would," Ronan said.

Probably true, if more because he lived in Declan's Cross than because of his garda position. "You haven't by chance run across an accident report on Lindsey Hargreaves?"

"The woman who wants to start this field

station down there? I haven't seen anything, no. I'll have a look if you'd like."

"I'd owe you one, thanks."

"What's going on, Sean?"

He told his friend what he knew.

Ronan listened without interruption, then said, "I'll let you know if I find anything. When can we expect you back in Dublin?"

"For a pint? Soon, my friend. Thanks for your help."

If Lindsey Hargreaves had driven off a road, Ronan Carrick would know it within the hour. He was famously dogged, as well as quick-witted and good-humored. Sean had relied on him many times during tricky investigations. They'd joined the gardai at the same time, fifteen years ago. Ronan was a few years older, redheaded, in good shape and the happily married father of three.

Sean turned from the bookshop and started up the hill toward his farm. He wasn't always good at dodging disaster, but he'd managed to the one time he'd set his mind to propose to a woman. That had been four years ago. She'd said yes but then decided she wanted to try her hand in New York. Last he heard she was a makeup artist in the theater district.

He couldn't see his lovely ex-fiancée spraying a sheep's hoof to prevent a highly contagious fungal disease. Strangely enough, he could see Kitty doing it, if only because it had to be done.

Thinking about Kitty O'Byrne was the road to ruin.

Sean picked up his pace, glad he felt no pain — at least none caused by his smugglers.

7

Emma stood in front of the marble fireplace in the reading room at the top of the curving stairs. She could hear the wind and a passing shower, the light fading with November's early dusk. By all accounts, it had been an even wetter, chillier night a decade ago when a thief had slipped into this very room. Later in the evening — no one could pinpoint the exact time but it had been after midnight, at least.

"A fire would be nice," Colin said from the doorway.

She turned. She didn't know how long he'd been standing there, or how long she'd been staring at the fireplace, lost in her thoughts. "It would be. I'm sure Kitty would arrange for one if we wanted to stay up here for a bit. There aren't many guests."

"Quiet time of year in Ireland. I like it."

He crossed to the fireplace, making no sound on the thick Persian carpet. The shadows accentuated the hard lines of his face, but Emma knew it wasn't always possible to read him. He was adept at burying his real emotions. In his undercover work, his life often depended on his ability to convince people he wasn't feeling what he was feeling.

He stood next to her and glanced around the room. "No alarm system in this place ten years ago?"

Emma smiled. Colin — his pragmatism — helped keep her from disappearing into her thoughts. "No, no alarm system. John O'Byrne was lucky to keep the lights on."

"Where was he that night?"

"He was on vacation in Portugal, staying with friends. A local farmer was looking after the place. He was asleep in the kitchen. The thief was in and out before anyone knew it."

"Local farmer as in —"

"Padraig Murphy. Paddy Murphy. Sean Murphy's uncle."

"Ah."

"He says he slept through the whole thing."

"You talked to him?"

"No. I saw him out in the fields but never talked to him. My grandfather did."

Emma glanced around the room, focusing

on it as it was today. Modern, gracious, with Kitty's distinctive touch. Her taste in bright, contemporary art and furnishings was very different from her uncle's shabby, traditional decor.

"Does Wendell know you're here?" Colin asked.

She nodded. "I called him this afternoon and left a voice mail. I told him I want to talk to him about our thief."

"Your thief."

She spun from the fireplace. "On my first night in Dublin four years ago, Granddad took me to a pub, and over a pint of Guinness, he told me that his best advice in art crimes work — in life, too — is to distinguish between what I know and what I believe."

Colin studied her, his eyes taking on the stormy-gray of the darkening Irish sky. "I want both, Emma. What you know about this thief and what you believe."

She sat on a chair angled in front of the fireplace. "I don't know if Julianne's presence in Declan's Cross has anything to do with the theft here."

"But you believe it does."

"I'm at least concerned."

Colin sat on a soft-cushioned love seat directly in front of the fireplace. "I'd feel better if she at least had a phone up at that damn cottage."

"It kills you that she's there by herself," Emma said with a smile, despite her own misgivings about Julianne's presence in Declan's Cross. "Ireland's pretty safe."

"This farmer's uncle is a suspect, isn't he?"

"Not for being the thief," Emma said.

"For helping him."

She didn't respond.

Colin stretched out his long legs and tapped the arm of the love seat with his fingers. Restless energy, Emma thought. Not nervous energy.

"Julianne doesn't think before she acts," he said, as if that explained everything.

"Her quick thinking saved Andy's life a few weeks ago."

"Yes, it did."

Emma didn't push him further. She couldn't get him to discuss the attack on his younger brother beyond the basic facts. Digging into the emotional impact of what had happened that day — and the prior weeks — wasn't for him.

He shifted in his seat. "Julianne would string me up if she could hear me right now. The Maroney pride. She has it in spades."

"You don't think she'd appreciate your

concern?"

He didn't hesitate. "No. I don't blame her for not wanting me around. Andy's done some stupid things in his life, like the rest of us, but getting involved with Julianne . . ." He broke off and sat up straight, as if he were about to jump up from the love seat. "He knew how it would end."

"Maybe it was inevitable," Emma said. "They've known each other forever. Did you and Andy talk about it?"

Colin looked at her with a grin. "You're kidding, right?"

She sighed. "What about Mike and Kevin?"

"Andy didn't ask any of us for our advice or opinion. Not his style. He and Julianne thought they could separate themselves from Rock Point, pretend they were a couple of strangers who met over fried clams."

"That could be fun at first."

"Then reality catches up with you. It always does. You have to look it square in the eye. Be who you are. Accept it."

Emma wondered if they were still talking about Julianne and Andy. "Colin . . ."

His gaze settled on her, but he pulled away and sprang to his feet. "Julianne's smart and ambitious. Driven. Speaks her mind. Andy's smart, but he's not as ambitious as she is, or at least in the way she is."

"He's also not ready to settle down." Emma looked up at Colin. "Are any of you Donovans ready to settle down?"

His smile caught her by surprise. "It'd help if we fell for easy women."

"Considering how easy Donovan men are."

"Are you saying my brothers and I are difficult?"

"Challenging. I'd say you're all challenging." She stood next to him in front of the fireplace. "Did you ever think Andy and Julianne's relationship would last?"

"I wasn't around much when things got hot and heavy between them."

"That doesn't answer the question, Special Agent Donovan."

He glanced at her. "You'd do fine as a field agent, you know."

"Maybe we're on edge because we've been on vacation too long."

"I think it's more than that, Emma."

She nodded. "So do I."

He studied an atmospheric watercolor painting above the fireplace. It was of an Irish sunset, all splashes of rich color against a backdrop of a churning sea and rugged hills.

Emma eased next to him, aware of how tense and preoccupied he was. "This wasn't here ten years ago," she said. "It's Aoife O'Byrne's work."

"It's quite a painting," Colin said.

"She was inspired by her uncle's art collection. The most valuable paintings he owned were here, in this room."

"The thief knew?"

"That's our assessment, yes. We think he was after specific works and he knew exactly where to find them."

Colin turned to her. "Tell me what happened."

Emma moved to a tall window overlooking the hotel gardens, its pebbled walkways illuminated against the early night. What a place to relax, she thought. Read a book. Think. Nap. Enjoy the surroundings. She knew Colin was watching her, perhaps again trying to figure out what she'd been like before she'd headed to Quantico. The Sisters of the Joyful Heart . . . Sharpe Fine Art Recovery. So different from the world he knew. She could picture him in Rock Point, lobstering, working in the marine patrol. It was his life with the FBI that was tougher for her to envision. His deep-cover work with international arms traffickers. Killers.

"Emma," he said quietly, joining her at the window.

She continued to stare out at the darkening gardens. "Two of the paintings stolen that night were by Jack Butler Yeats. The third was unsigned."

"Worth a lot?"

"The Yeats paintings, yes. Not hundreds of millions but in the millions. It's often easier and ultimately more profitable for thieves to get rid of pieces that aren't as well-known. Yeats' work has become extremely popular. He's considered one of the greatest Irish painters of all time."

"Related to William Butler Yeats?"

"His younger brother. Their father, John, was also a painter. John O'Byrne bought the Jack Yeats paintings at an auction in Dublin, before Yeats' popularity went into the stratosphere. They're earlier works — pre-1940. Landscapes of scenes in the west of Ireland."

"What about the third painting — the one that was unsigned?"

"It's an oil landscape of a local scene."

"Where?"

"The painting depicts three remarkable stone Celtic crosses at the tip of Shepherd Head."

Colin was silent a moment. "Have any of

the missing paintings turned up?"

Emma shook her head. "Not a one."

She noticed the shower had passed and some of the clouds were breaking up. There'd be more rain later on, but she'd seen weather reports. Tomorrow was supposed to be beautiful. If they heard from Lindsey Hargreaves tonight, they all could relax and enjoy the day.

"What about the cross that was stolen?" Colin asked.

"It was on the mantel downstairs. It's a small silver wall cross inscribed with a beautiful Celtic motif. It's a mini version of the largest of the crosses on Shepherd Head but much older."

"How old is old around here?"

"Granddad guesses the wall cross that was stolen might be as early as fifteenth century. He can't know for certain since he hasn't seen it and it was never appraised. John O'Byrne said he found it when he put in the gardens here about fifty years ago. He told Granddad he was devastated by its loss."

Colin turned from the window. "Where were his nieces that night — Kitty and Aoife?"

"Kitty was staying with a friend here in Declan's Cross, as I recall from the file.

Aoife had been living in Ardmore but she'd moved to Dublin by then and was home, but alone. They've both done well financially. Their uncle was a widower with no children. He struggled with money at the end."

"The cross and the stolen paintings were uninsured?"

"Right. John O'Byrne didn't arrange the theft to collect insurance money."

"That doesn't let him off the hook. He could have worked out a deal with the thief to split the profits of a private sale to a rich collector."

"There's no evidence of any financial gain," Emma said.

"What we know, what we believe and the resulting unanswered questions." Colin moved back from the window to the round table in the middle of the room. He fingered a thick book on romantic Irish country homes, then met her gaze again. "Do you think the thief is from Declan's Cross?"

"We don't know enough. That's what I think."

"Did someone from here help him? Our sheep farmers? Paddy and the nephew? Someone else?" He stood straight. "The nieces?"

"None of the evidence —"

"I'm not talking about evidence. I'm talking about instincts." His gray eyes steadied on her. "Your gut, Emma. What does it say?"

It was how Colin thought, Emma realized. He was pragmatic, unsentimental. He had investigated a wide range of crimes as a Maine marine patrol officer and then as an FBI agent, even before turning to undercover work. Her focus was the complex but particular world of art theft. "My gut says we're missing something."

"Then or now?"

"Both," she said without hesitation. "But I don't trust my gut as much as you trust yours."

"You think there's some rock you haven't turned over. It's out there, waiting for you."

"That's one way of putting it, yes."

"I know that feeling." He gestured to another painting, an oil depicting a row of bright-colored cottages. "How much of the artwork here now came with the house?"

"We'd have to ask Kitty. Her taste is different from her uncle's. Most of the art on display is likely her doing — contemporary Irish painters and sculptors, including her sister. Aoife is an internationally recognized artist herself now."

"Did her uncle support her artistic efforts in her early days?"

"I don't know."

Emma glanced again at Aoife O'Byrne's moody painting, with its striking colors and intriguing use of light. Aoife had an ability — a vision — that blended drama, open, deep emotion, reality and fantasy into a unique style that was all her own. Emma felt her throat tighten, her reaction to the painting catching her off guard.

"Who called the police?" Colin asked.

She cleared her throat and looked away from the painting. "Paddy Murphy called the gardai in the morning when he saw that the French doors were wide open. He knew it wasn't the wind, but no one realized the paintings and cross were missing until John O'Byrne returned from Portugal a few days later."

"Ouch."

"Yes. Ouch."

"He cooperated with the police?"

"As far as I know. Granddad didn't get involved until six months later, after two Dutch paintings were stolen from a small museum in Amsterdam. They're landscapes but otherwise very different from the works stolen here."

"But you're sure it was the same thief."

"That's right."

"And the subsequent thefts — you're sure?"

Emma nodded. "Yes."

"How do you know?"

She touched the cover of the book on romantic Irish houses, debating what to tell him. She looked up, saw that Colin was watching her, his eyes narrowed. He already knew the answer, she realized.

She stood back from the table. "We know because he tells us."

" 'Us' being — who? You, your grandfather, your brother, your folks? All of you?"

"Granddad," Emma said, leaving it at that.

"Not going to tell me how he lets you know, are you?"

She gave a tight shake of her head. "I can't go into detail, Colin."

"Understood." He eased next to her, his upper arm brushing hers. "Is this thief matching wits with your grandfather?"

"Possibly."

"Someone from his past?"

"Maybe. I don't know. It wouldn't narrow things down very much. Granddad's worked in art crimes for sixty years. That leaves a wide, deep pool of possibilities. The thefts are all brazen but so far not violent."

"The ones you know about," Colin said.

Emma acknowledged his statement with a

nod. "Fair point. Not everyone reports an art crime, and he might not tell us — Granddad — about every theft."

"He could escalate to violence at any time, if he hasn't already. And you're convinced it's a man."

"It's one of those things we believe but don't know."

"Irish?"

"My guess is no. Maybe of Irish descent. The art stolen from here is Irish, but the other thefts are all different. I believe he steals what he knows he can steal."

Colin walked over to a glass-front cabinet next to the fireplace and glanced at the contents, a mix of books, framed photographs of Declan's Cross and small porcelain figures of birds. "I assume law enforcement has everything you have on him."

"I am law enforcement, Colin."

"Right. Easy to forget."

She looked for humor in his expression but saw none. "Our thief is fast, clever and daring but not reckless. He doesn't strike often. The art theft squad here in Ireland is handling this case, but it's a cold trail."

"What about fingerprints, footprints, witnesses?"

"Virtually nothing here or anywhere else. He knows what he's doing."

Emma ran her fingertips over more books. She could feel Colin watching her. It was as if he could read her mind, knew what she was thinking before she could acknowledge it to herself.

"It's all right, Emma," he said. "I get it that I'm on need-to-know status with the specifics. When and if I need to know, you'll tell me."

It wasn't a question, but she said, "I will, yes. For what it's worth, I don't believe the thefts are directed at my grandfather. Taunting him is a bonus, not the motive."

"But you don't know," Colin said with the slightest of smiles.

"I also believe he works alone. He never steals more than he can handle in one trip."

"Maybe he's like Santa Claus and has elves and reindeer waiting."

Emma smiled, welcoming his lighter tone — his lighter mood. "It's dark out, but it's still too early for dinner. We could check out the spa. I had a quick look at the pool after lunch. Very inviting."

"I used to be a lobsterman, but I'm not that much on swimming." He gave her an easy grin. "I know what's in the water."

"No sharks in an indoor pool, at least."

"Or alligators," he added.

It was a reminder of his close call a few

weeks ago in Fort Lauderdale, when his arms traffickers had tried to kill him. Emma didn't always know where Donovan humor and teasing ended and Donovan seriousness began. It was the same with his brothers. They communicated with teasing and wry humor punctuated by a bluntness that could set people back on their heels. She found their approach refreshing, challenging and remarkably honest — if also sometimes disconcerting. Her family was honest but often indirect, out of respect and intuition for personal and professional boundaries, because of their natural ability to assess, analyze, reflect.

The Donovans didn't always have a keen instinct for boundaries. When they wanted to find out something, get something done, they would keep pushing until someone or something pushed back.

Then they would push some more.

No doubt that helped explain Julianne's abrupt trip to Ireland and her defensiveness with Colin.

And unlike Emma, Julianne had grown up with Donovans. She already knew what they were like.

Emma started for the hall. "I don't know about you, Colin, but I'm going to grab my swimsuit and head to the spa." She paused in the doorway and looked back at him. "Coming?"

He strode across the room to her. "Kitty O'Byrne's whiskey cabinet beckons," he said, then touched his fingertips to her cheek. "And you need some time to yourself. Emma thinking time. You can think while you're swimming. I'd either be imagining alligators or letting myself be distracted by you in a swimsuit."

"You've never seen me in a swimsuit."

"This is what I'm saying."

8

With Emma off to the spa, Colin didn't immediately head downstairs to the bar. Instead he sat by the cold fireplace and dug out his phone and found Matt Yankowski's number in Boston. Yank was the buttoned-down senior agent in charge of a small Boston-based team he'd formed in March that specialized in elusive criminals and criminal networks with virtually unlimited resources. He called it HIT. It stood for high-impact targets. Or maybe it didn't. Colin had never really asked.

Yank had personally selected every member of the team, including Emma, and now, technically, Colin, except that was more like a shotgun wedding. Yank had decided in September that after months of solitary deep-cover work, Colin needed structure, a place to light — "a damn desk," as Yank had put it.

Not that Colin had actually sat at his desk

in Boston, or ever would.

He wasn't even sure he had one.

He'd met Yank four years ago. Yank had come up from Washington to Rock Point to talk to Colin about his first undercover mission. Yank would be his contact agent. He'd griped about the rocky coast, boats and everything else about southern Maine, except Hurley's lobster rolls and doughnuts.

On that same trip — something Colin hadn't known until two months ago — Yank had also visited the isolated convent of the Sisters of the Joyful Heart and talked to a young novice, fair-haired Sister Brigid, aka Emma Sharpe. Yank had guessed that Emma, an art historian and a Sharpe, wasn't destined to spend the rest of her life as one of the good sisters. She'd grown up in Heron's Cove, just a few miles down the coast from Rock Point, but it might as well have been on a different planet, for all the Donovans and the Sharpes had in common.

Before Colin had left for Ireland, Yank had said he wouldn't mind doing a Vulcan mind meld with Wendell Sharpe. The octogenarian art crimes expert had decades of knowledge and experience, layers of secrets, tidbits filed away in his acute mind that would never be a part of any formal file. Emma had learned her ways at her grandfather's knee.

Colin put the thought aside and tapped in Yank's cell phone number.

"Donovan," Yank said on the second ring. "Still in Ireland?"

"Still here. You're missing some great rainbows."

"Tempted to chase one and find your pot of gold?"

"What would I do with a pot of gold?"

Yank grunted. "You could give it to me to pay for Lucy's trip to Paris. She's back. She went to Hermès and Chanel."

"Uh-oh."

"Yeah. Uh-oh. She bought a scarf and a pair of shoes for what my first car cost."

Lucy Yankowski probably made more money as a psychologist than her husband of fifteen years did as an FBI agent. Yank wasn't a big talker, but a few weeks ago he'd finally admitted to Colin that he didn't know what Lucy would do. He'd thought locating his special team in Boston, away from the glare of Washington, made sense, but he hadn't expected his wife to resist moving out of their northern Virginia home. Nine months later, she was still there. Yank considered the trip to Paris with her sister another of her delaying tactics.

"When you're not watching rainbows," he

said, "are you planning your new life as Cap'n Colin?"

"It'd be a good life." Colin settled back in the love seat and pictured himself down east on the Bold Coast, away from anyone he could hurt. "I'd take tourists on boat trips to see puffins, whales and seals and such. Fish between trips and in the off season. I know boats."

"Cap'n Colin does have a nice ring to it."

Colin didn't know if Yank realized that it was a serious, realistic option. "Maybe I'm not meant to do this job forever."

"You aren't. None of us is made to do it forever. There's a time to move on. You don't know if that's now. You can't when you're in Ireland chasing rainbows."

"I'm at a spa hotel with Emma."

"A spa hotel?"

"It's nice. She's in the pool now. The bar has a good whiskey selection. I think Finian Bracken had a hand in it. The hotel's on the other side of Cork from his cottage." Colin kept his tone casual as he continued. "It's in a tiny village called Declan's Cross."

Yank was silent on the other end.

Colin gripped his phone. "Yank — you know about this Declan's Cross thief?"

"Some. Not everything. Probably not as much as I should. Definitely not as much as

Wendell Sharpe does. It's tricky sometimes keeping track of what Emma knows because she's an FBI agent and what she knows because she's a Sharpe. Keeping secrets comes naturally to her. It's one of the reasons she's good at what she does."

"This isn't a secret."

"Playing her cards close to her chest, then," Yank said. "You won't be satisfied until I give you my files on her."

"Nah. I don't mind figuring her out on my own." Colin looked up at the Aoife O'Byrne painting, imagined her and Kitty in this room as little girls. What a childhood. "Do you think Emma's grandfather told her all he knows about these thefts?"

"I don't think Wendell Sharpe tells anyone all he knows about anything."

"The name Hargreaves on your radar?"

"Hargreaves Oceanographic Institute? It's up by Gloucester. That's all I know. I'm not into the ocean."

"You have a great view of Boston Harbor from your office," Colin said.

"So I do," Yank said. "That's not why you called. What's up?"

As Colin filled in the senior agent, he realized all he had was a woman who had failed to keep her word about picking up Julianne at the airport and joining her at

139

the Murphy cottage. If he was overthinking, it was because of the Sharpes and their ten years of unsolved art thefts, and it was because Lindsey Hargreaves had taken the trouble to stop in Rock Point to see Finian Bracken — and now Julianne was up at that cottage by herself. Andy had sensed something was off about her trip, and that's why he'd told Colin about it.

Colin gritted his teeth. Not only wasn't Julianne over his brother, his brother wasn't over her.

He told Yank, "I don't know if this is a Sharpe thing that sucked in Julianne or a Donovan thing that sucked her in, or if it's nothing."

"How could it be a Donovan thing?"

"Julianne's here to get over my brother."

"Andy," Yank said. "The lobsterman."

"Correct."

"She's the one who found him when your arms-trafficking friends bashed in his head and left him to drown. She told you she's in Ireland to get over him?"

"Not a chance. She'd never admit it."

"Whose side are you on in the breakup?"

"Neutral."

"Third man in rule."

"Yeah." Colin stood, even more restless. "Did Emma tell you she plans to be back at work on Monday?"

"Yes. That's good. We miss her around here. What about you?"

"I might check out Irish puffins."

"Is there such a thing?"

"They're Atlantic puffins, same as the ones you'd find off the Maine coast. The parrot of the sea —"

"You're killing me," Yank said. "Let me know when this woman turns up."

Colin wasn't ready to hang up yet. "Does the name Sean Murphy mean anything to you?"

"No. Why?"

"He's the farmer Fin Bracken knows."

"Does Emma know him?"

"Not that she's said." Colin saw that it was dark out now, no hint of dusk. "Having a Sharpe on your team is more complicated than you anticipated, isn't it?"

"Everything about this team is more complicated than I anticipated," Yank said. "Don't do anything you're not supposed to do over there. Assist as appropriate if this turns into a missing-persons case, but I don't want to make a trip to Ireland to bail you out of trouble."

"You'd love Ireland."

"That's what you said about Maine. I still don't love it. I have to go. I'm meeting with the director. I'm going to try not even to think your name."

"Why not? The director likes me."

"Tolerates you. Needs you from time to time. That's different from liking you."

Colin grinned. "Tell him I'll take him on a puffin tour."

Yank made no comment as he disconnected.

Colin slid his phone into his jacket pocket. He and Yank were opposites in most ways, but they both had good instincts, and every instinct Colin had told him that something wasn't right with this situation with Lindsey Hargreaves.

As he headed out of the reading room, he noticed how quiet the hotel was. During his months working undercover, he'd had little quiet, rarely the complete confidence that he was safe. He didn't dwell on such things. He focused on the job he had to do. His "job" in Ireland was simple. He was to relax, enjoy his surroundings, avoid anything more pressing than what whiskey to drink. Most days the past two weeks it had worked out that way.

With any luck, it would tonight, too.

Kitty was cutting lemons behind the gleaming dark-wood bar when Colin eased onto a high-backed cushioned stool. A fire burned hot in the marble fireplace. A young couple was huddled over a bottle of wine at one of the half dozen candlelit, glass-topped tables.

"You must be ready for that drink now," Kitty said. "What would you like?"

"A Guinness, thanks." He nodded to a double row of simply framed color photographs of Irish ruins and misty hills. "Local scenes?"

"Mmm. My sister's early work. Aoife had an eye even as a teenager."

"She did the seascape upstairs in the reading room, too."

"Gorgeous, isn't it? I love that painting." Kitty scooped up a handful of cut lemons and set them in a small bowl. "Aoife lives in Dublin, but she gets down here often. She's always a little embarrassed when she remembers her work's up on the walls. I've work up by other Irish artists, too."

"A lot of talent here, not that I'm an expert."

"Nor am I. I just like what I like."

"Is any of the art on display from your uncle's day?"

"Some," she said, letting his pint rest a minute, part of the process of pouring Guinness. "Aoife has some of his works, too. He only had the two Jack Yeats paintings, if

143

that's what you're asking. They were his most valuable works. You're not trying to solve the burglary, are you? It's been years, and it has nothing to do with your friend."

"I understand you were in town that night."

She set the pint in front of him. "Yes."

Head down, Kitty grabbed a lime and her paring knife and expertly hacked the lime in two. Colin drank some of his Guinness. "Seems quiet here," he said.

"It is. We've a few guests. It'll be busier this weekend."

"I saw a kid here earlier. Your son?"

She nodded. "Philip. He works here for now. He plans to go to college. He's interested in oceanography. He's learning scuba diving — he's been helping out with this marine science field station, diving with the crew there. I can't stand the thought of it myself." Kitty shuddered, slicing the lime into neat quarters. "I get claustrophobic."

"I'm not much on diving, either," Colin said. "My brothers do some. I'd rather be on the surface than under water."

"I hope this field station works out. It's more a dream for Lindsey, I suspect. A hopeless dream, maybe. I don't think it matters to the others as much. Brent Corwin, Eamon Carrick. They're serious divers.

That's what interests them."

As Kitty finished, Emma came into the bar lounge and sat next to Colin. The ends of her hair were damp, her cheeks pink from her swim and visit to the spa as she smiled at him. "You'd love the spa, Colin. Really. The pool is fantastic. I still think we should book that couple's massage."

Kitty pointed at Colin with her paring knife. "With this one?" She laughed, the spark back in her blue eyes. "I'd give you a discount."

Colin grinned at her. "I just might surprise you."

She abandoned her lemons and limes and wiped off her hands with a damp white towel. "What can I get you, Emma?"

"A glass of wine would be lovely. A red. You pick."

Kitty lifted a wineglass from a shelf and set it on her work counter. "Tell me more about how Fin Bracken is doing in Maine. Does he enjoy it, do you think?"

"Colin would know better than I," Emma said.

Colin shrugged. "He misses Ireland more than he'll admit, but the church people like him. My brothers and I think he looks like Bono."

"Bono? I suppose. Fin's a good man, but

145

I still don't see him as a priest, honestly."
Kitty chose a cabernet sauvignon from a
shelf behind her, uncorked it and poured it
into the glass. She handed the glass to
Emma and then recorked the bottle. "We
should have the peated Bracken 15 in his
honor. Later, perhaps."

"I still haven't developed a taste for peated
whiskey," Emma said, then tried her wine.
"Great choice. Thanks."

Kitty seemed distracted as she mopped
up a spill. "I hope you can relax and enjoy
your stay here, but I imagine you can no
more stop thinking like FBI agents than I
can stop thinking like a hotel owner."

"Or a worried mother," Emma said softly.

"Yes, that, too. It shows, doesn't it? But
that's part of being a mother, isn't it? Worrying. Philip could do worse than getting
caught up in diving. I swear he likes being
under water more than he does breathing
fresh air." She dropped her cloth in the sink.
"Well, then. Do you have plans for dinner?
Shall we set a table for you here?"

Colin was thinking in terms of fish and
chips at a pub instead of the hotel's more
formal menu, but Emma said, "We'd love
that," and he adjusted his thinking to roast
lamb.

He drank more of his Guinness. "How

well do you know Sean Murphy?"

Kitty gave him a shocked look, recovered quickly and acted as if she hadn't heard him. "I'll be here and there if you need anything," she mumbled, retreating quickly through the open doorway behind her.

Emma sipped some of her wine. "I wonder what that was about."

"Definitely pushed a button."

"You knew it would."

He smiled. "Believed it would." He finished the last of his pint. "I'll be more careful. I don't want to ask too many questions. She might kick us out, and I know you're itching to get me to that spa."

He saw the smile that reached all the way into Emma's green eyes and felt it tug at his insides. It wasn't just the effects of his beer. Being with her made him whole. It made him think about life in ways he hadn't allowed himself to think about it — as dangerous as that might be, given the work he did. Dangerous for her.

"Come on," he said. "Let's get some air before dinner."

"A walk in the garden?"

"Perfect."

They went out through the French doors. He could smell the ocean, and the light from the hotel and outdoor lamps shone on

147

puddles from the rain. The cool air seemed to take Emma by surprise. The aftereffects of her spa visit, Colin supposed. She buttoned her heavy wool sweater as they stepped from the terrace to a pebbled walkway. "Do you think we should check on Julianne?" she asked.

"It would just annoy her if I showed up on her doorstep again. She'd figure I don't trust her to look after herself."

"Do you?"

"That's not the point. She knows where to find us." He breathed in the clearing air, wondered if there'd be more rain tonight. "Julianne has her own demons to fight."

Emma eased in close to him, hooking her arm in his as they followed the walkway to the far edge of the gardens. "You're always warm. How do you manage that?" She didn't wait for an answer. "Julianne lost her grandfather a year ago. She's finishing up her master's and deciding what's next for her. She moved in with her grandmother — who I've gathered is still having a rough time. A lot on Julianne's plate. That could have contributed to why she got involved with your brother."

"Nothing's simple with those two."

Colin was getting used to the idea that Emma knew things about his family and friends that he hadn't told her. She'd had the run of Rock Point in October when he'd dipped back undercover to tie up loose ends with his arms traffickers. She was a natural with details and nuances. Who knew what all she'd picked up.

"I can smell the ocean," she said, tilting her head back and looking up at the dark sky. "It's not that late, but it feels like the middle of the night. Beautiful, isn't it?"

"Sure."

She sighed at him. "You're not looking at the sky."

He wasn't. He was looking at her. He pulled her closer to him. "I like how you can talk about a serial art thief one minute and admire the sky the next."

"I'm a woman of simple tastes." She smiled. "Except in men."

"I'm simple."

"Right," she said with an exaggerated note of skepticism.

"You might have simple tastes, Emma, but you're a complicated woman."

"I think I prefer complex, but I won't argue that my life has been complicated lately. Julianne's has been, too. It can't be easy being a Donovan's ex-girlfriend in Rock Point. I've also gathered that Andy has a certain reputation with women."

"Which Julianne has known since she was in pigtails." Colin noticed a rosebush climbing up a lamppost, a few pale pink blossoms on the stalky vine, even in early November. "For the most part, Mike, Kevin and I have managed to stay out of their relationship."

"Ah." Emma released his arm and jumped lightly over a puddle, turning to him. "You don't want coming here to change that."

He circled the puddle. "You got that right."

A gray-haired man came up from a narrower walkway and waved them down. "Kitty said I might want to talk to you. I'm David Hargreaves. Lindsey's father." He looked to be in his mid-fifties and wore a camel-colored sweater and corduroy slacks, a dark brown overcoat — probably cashmere — hung over one arm. "I understand you're friends with Julianne Maroney, the woman Lindsey was supposed to pick up at the airport this morning."

"That's right," Colin said. "This is Emma Sharpe. I'm Colin Donovan. Did you just get here?"

"Here to the hotel, yes. I'm staying at the separate cottage. It's quite nice. Very quiet. I arrived in Dublin on Saturday and then spent last night in Ardmore. I was there all day. It's a lovely place. . . ." He broke off, as if he didn't want to get distracted. "I haven't talked to Lindsey or heard from her since we had breakfast in Dublin yesterday morning."

"Did you expect to?" Colin asked.

"Frankly, no, I didn't. I stopped in Dublin on my way to London on business. I decided to extend my stay and come down here." The dull lamplight accentuated the lines in his face as he looked down at the ground a moment, then seemed to catch himself and smiled. "Anyway, my main purpose in coming down here is to see Lindsey and this field station she's launching."

"She knows?" Colin asked.

"Yes, of course. I have no idea where she is or why she didn't show up in Shannon." He reached up and plucked a sodden, browned rose blossom from the lamppost vine. "I'd know if something had happened to her, wouldn't I? She'd have called me, or the police — I'm sure she has me listed as an emergency contact. And if not me, Brent Corwin. I've already spoken to him. He called me as I was leaving Ardmore, and I checked in with him when I arrived. He hasn't heard anything, either."

"Have you been to the field station, then?"

Hargreaves tossed the dead rose into the

puddle. "No, not yet. I want Lindsey to show me. She's excited about it. She always has so much going on — it's not out of character for her to lose track of something she promised to do."

Emma touched a fingertip to one of the fresh rose blossoms. "Did she mention where she would be staying last night?"

"No, but I assumed she'd drive on to Shannon and stay there, since Julianne's flight arrived so early. Lindsey didn't expect to be in Dublin or she'd have suggested Julianne fly there instead of Shannon." He shifted his overcoat to his other arm, as if he just needed something to do with his nervous energy. "She could be somewhere without cell coverage."

"She has her own car?" Colin asked.

Hargreaves nodded. "That's how she got to Dublin — she didn't take the train or bus or come with a friend. I rented my own car."

He glanced around at the dark gardens, then back down the walkway to his cottage. He didn't seem to know what to do with himself. Colin didn't blame him. "Did you two have a fight?" he asked. "A disagreement — anything like that?"

"No. Not at all. I invited Lindsey to stay with me here, but she was looking forward to renting the cottage with Julianne. I'm only going to be here a couple of days. Lindsey's enthusiasm and Julianne's background in marine biology could be a good combination."

Emma stepped back from the roses. "Why did Lindsey choose Declan's Cross for this field station?"

"She says Declan's Cross chose her. She met Brent on a research dive in Scotland and they ended up here. He has solid experience, but Lindsey also consulted Irish marine scientists about whether a field station would work here. It's my first time in Declan's Cross. I was in Ardmore years ago and had been wanting to go back and have a closer look at the Celtic Christian ruins there." Hargreaves managed a smile. "Part of the classic Ireland tourist experience, don't you think? Whiskey, Guinness, spectacular scenery and ancient ruins."

"A great hotel with a beautiful spa, too," Emma said, returning his smile.

Hargreaves relaxed visibly. "I should get settled. I'll try to reach Lindsey again. I might put in a call to the Irish police."

"Makes sense," Colin said. "Let us know if there's anything we can do to help."

"Thank you. I don't want to overreact. I honestly don't believe I upset Lindsey in any way. I certainly hope I didn't." He gave another polite, awkward smile. "Thank you again."

Colin watched him head back down the walkway toward his cottage, then disappear in the shadows. "He's more frayed than he wants to admit."

Emma nodded. "Maybe we should have a word with the gardai ourselves."

"I think so, too. If a couple of Irish cops were in Rock Point wondering about a missing Irish woman, Kevin would want to know, just to be on the safe side."

"Kevin. The youngest Donovan."

"The nicest one, too."

"I feel for him."

Colin grinned and took her hand as they started back to the hotel. "Nice doesn't mean he's not one of us."

9

Andy Donovan knew he was caught the second the door to Hurley's shut behind him. He usually managed to avoid Franny Maroney, but she had broken her Tuesday routine and was at the waterfront restaurant later than usual. She was alone, without her posse of sister retirees, all of whom blamed him for breaking Julianne's heart. Not without reason, but he figured what went on between him and Julianne was none of their business.

He was just arriving. Franny was just leaving. The only positive.

It was three o'clock in Maine. Eight o'clock in Ireland. He pictured Julianne enjoying herself at an Irish pub.

Franny turned to him, her wallet in one hand as she scowled. "Julianne made it to Ireland safe and sound." Her tone said *no thanks to you.* "She emailed me from the airport. She promised me she would. I got up early to check and there it was. She said she had a nice flight."

Andy unzipped his jacket. "That's good."

"There's more. I know my granddaughter." Franny tucked the wallet back into her purse, a gaudy cloth thing covered in purple flowers, a birthday present from Julianne, who understood her grandmother. "There's something she's not saying. I can tell. Do you know what it is?"

Franny gave him an accusatory look, as if whatever she suspected was up with Julianne was his fault. Andy grinned at her. "You can't tell something's wrong from an email. If Julianne said she's fine —"

"Has she been in touch with you?"

"No, ma'am."

"I won't have you putting me off like I'm an old lady."

"You are an old lady, Franny," he said with a wink.

"Don't think your Donovan charm will work on me, Andy Donovan."

He laughed and thought she was softening some. He knew Lindsey Hargreaves hadn't turned up at the airport in Shannon or in Declan's Cross, but only because Colin had emailed him. He hadn't heard a peep out of Julianne. And he wasn't telling her grandmother about the glitch in Ireland.

It would just worry her, or she'd find a way to blame him.

He nodded toward the back of the almost-empty restaurant, where Finian Bracken sat alone at his favorite table by the windows. "Maybe you should ask Father Bracken. He's friends with the owner of the cottage Julianne is renting."

Franny scoffed. "He won't tell me anything." Her eyes — not at all like Julianne's — narrowed on Andy as if she could read his mind. "What do you know, Andy Donovan?"

"Stop worrying, will you? Colin's in Declan's Cross. Julianne's fine."

"Colin? Why's he there?"

Good question. "Passing through with Emma." He left it at that. "Nice to see you, Franny."

She pointed a finger at him. "Don't you and Colin dare keep anything that concerns my granddaughter from me."

Andy didn't argue. Arguing with her was pointless, especially in the year since her husband had died. He'd been a tough one, too. Her grief had made her short-tempered, and then Andy had gone and broken her granddaughter's heart.

Julianne's version of events, anyway. His wasn't as black-and-white.

Franny seemed more cheerful but still gave him a dark look as she headed out. She had a sixth sense or something. She always knew things, or pretended to. She hadn't predicted his breakup with Julianne or the attack that had nearly killed him, but that didn't mean Franny Maroney's gloomy view of the world didn't win out from time to time.

Andy didn't want to be too hard on her. She worshipped her granddaughter, and maybe it was understandable that she'd become more demanding and controlling in the past year as she figured out how to carry on without her husband of fifty years. Julianne adored her, but Andy was still convinced her trip to Ireland had as much to do with getting out from under her grandmother's thumb as anything else. Then again, he had a low tolerance for anyone trying to control him. Zero tolerance, in fact. One reason he was good at lobstering and restoring boats.

He crossed Hurley's dining room to Finian Bracken's table. In his email, Colin had indicated he was letting Julianne call the shots, but he didn't like that this Lindsey Hargreaves character hadn't turned up. That was Colin. He was an FBI agent. He dealt with criminals. The Hargreaves woman

...he referred to herself as a marine sci-
...enthusiast."

...hat's a marine science enthusiast?
...eone who likes whales and dolphins but
...ed organic chemistry?"

...ian sat back in the rickety wooden
... "That was my impression of her, in
...but, as I say, we only chatted for a few
...tes. I know several people in Declan's
...s. One of them mentioned me to her,
...don't know which one. It might have
...Sean. I haven't asked him. Lindsey
...t say, and I didn't think to ask."

...dy drummed his fingers on the table.
...as uneasy. Off. He couldn't pinpoint
..."You know Julianne. Her situation. Did
...mp on this trip to Ireland for the right
...ns? I was just getting used to her going
...this internship in January. Then all of
...den, she's packed and on her way to
...."

...ian glanced out the window. "Ask me
...thing else."

...aning he wasn't giving up any priestly
...dences. Andy resisted the urge to
...m at what Julianne could have told
...Bracken about him. She might not
...told him anything, if only to keep from
...ting she'd made a mistake.

...hat's cool," Andy said. "I'm not in

probably just was the type to have too many
balls in the air.

Andy sat across from Finian and realized
Julianne wasn't there to slam dishes and
give him dagger looks. She was across the
Atlantic, jet-lagged, stood up by her new
friend, alone in some cliff-side cottage
owned by an Irish sheep farmer. She had to
be feeling stupid. Not because she was
stupid but because that was Julianne. In her
world, there was nothing between perfec-
tion and failure. He, on the other hand,
lived in that broad gray area between the
two. Cs on his report card had been a cause
for celebration. Julianne had never gotten a
C, but if she had, she'd have cried for days,
argued with the teacher for a better grade,
beaten herself up.

No wonder they drove each other nuts.

Finian had a pot of tea in front of him.
"It's too early for whiskey, so I thought I'd
try Hurley's tea." He grimaced at the little
stainless-steel pot, the end of a tea bag
hanging out from under the lid. "I could
change my mind about the whiskey."

"Not many people order hot tea here,"
Andy said.

"Yes. I can see why."

"Hurley's can learn whiskey and hot tea
from you. You can learn clam chowder and

lobster rolls from them."

"And pie. I like the pie here. I should have ordered apple pie with my . . . tea." Finian shuddered, then leveled his gaze on Andy, a seriousness to him that was a reminder this was a man of conviction and depth. "I assumed you've heard from Colin. I have, too. You told him about Julianne's sudden decision to go to Ireland."

"No reason not to." Andy glanced out at the harbor, the water glasslike under the gray afternoon sky. He'd had no business telling Colin, or talking about Julianne now. It was up to her family to worry about her. But he couldn't stop himself, and said, "She's staying at this cottage by herself. Is that smart?"

"That was the original plan until Lindsey Hargreaves decided to join her. Sean will look after her."

"Sean Murphy. Your farmer friend. You know a lot of people, don't you?"

"Ireland's a small country." Finian didn't elaborate as he flipped open the lid to his teapot and sighed. "Dear heavens. There's more. I'd feel bad if I didn't drink it."

"No one will care, Fin," Andy said. "Trust me."

"You're a Donovan. You're not the parish priest."

"Fair point, but it doesn't
People won't care if you thi
is lousy. They already know.'

A waitress — one of Julia
approached the table and a
wanted anything. Cool, but
He shook his head. She ther
he wanted more hot water
smiled politely and said, "N
need to get back to the c
withdrew, he leaned over the
lie, but you will keep my op
between us, won't you?"

"Mum's the word."

Finian Bracken was more
but Andy was comfortable
found him easy to talk to. T
it was a two-way street and
talking. Andy was pretty sur
wasn't telling the whole
friend the sheep farmer.

"What did you think (
character when you met he

"She was only here for a
had coffee and left. Julian
that day and offered to s
when they discovered a m
marine science."

"But Lindsey isn't a s
Andy said.

Julianne's life anymore, anyway."

"Just a friend," Finian said as he turned from the window.

Andy let that one go. He wasn't confiding in Finian or anyone else about his relationship with one Julianne Maroney, marine biologist, hothead, dreamer and now in Ireland by herself.

Not really by herself. Colin and Emma were there.

"What's Declan's Cross like?" he asked.

Finian seemed relieved at the shift in subject. "It's a lovely village on the Celtic Sea. It's named for Saint Declan. He had a strong presence in the area in the fifth century."

"I've never heard of Saint Declan, Finian."

"He was a contemporary of Saint Patrick."

Andy grinned. "Him I've heard of. Green beer, shamrocks and snakes."

"Saint Patrick, of course, is credited with converting Ireland to Christianity, but it's not as simple as that. Some say that Declan and three other Munster saints — Ciaran, Ibar and Ailbhe — actually predated Patrick."

"There won't be a quiz later, will there?"

Finian shook his head. "No quiz," he said with a smile. "All five saints are fascinating figures of legend, history and faith. There are well-known ecclesiastic ruins associated with Saint Declan in Ardmore, not far from Declan's Cross."

"Nothing to do with marine science, then."

"I know very little about marine science, I'm afraid," Finian said.

"You know saints and whiskey."

"I do, indeed."

"I don't mean to be irreverent." Andy shrugged off his coat, but he knew he wouldn't be staying. He was too restless. "I looked up Declan's Cross on the internet last night after I got back from dropping Julianne off at the airport. She was in such a rush to get out of Rock Point that she probably didn't find this out, but I'll bet you know about the art theft there ten years ago."

"I know of it, yes," Finian said quietly.

Finian's dark blue eyes were distant, almost glazed. Andy winced, remembering that ten years ago, Finian Bracken hadn't been a priest. "Fin, I'm sorry —"

"It's all right. I'd been to Ardmore on holiday but not to Declan's Cross. Not until I got to know Sean." He added softly, "That was seven years ago. I've been there many times since."

Andy kept his expression neutral, but he

felt like a heel. Finian was saying that he and Sean Murphy had met the year Finian's wife and two daughters had died. "Forget it. I'm not in Ireland. I can wait to hear from Colin. He asked if Julianne had mentioned the theft. She didn't, not to me."

"Colin asked me the same. He also asked if Lindsey Hargreaves mentioned the theft. She didn't. I know it seems odd that she came here with Sharpe Fine Art Recovery right in Heron's Cove, but it's not the coincidence you might think. I met Father Callaghan when I was in Declan's Cross earlier this year. He had heard about the theft and was there out of curiosity, and the O'Byrne House Hotel had recently opened. It's a beautiful hotel. Kitty, the owner, has done an excellent job."

"Kitty, huh?" Andy tried to lighten the mood. "You two never —"

"Never," Finian said. "Her uncle owned the hotel when it was broken into. It was a private home then."

"Was she in Declan's Cross that night?"

"I believe she was, yes."

"This farmer, Sean Murphy, would have been there, too, right?"

The penetrating Bracken eyes leveled on Andy. "He was, yes."

Andy sat back, feeling a cold draft come

up through Hurley's floorboards. He tried to imagine Finian Bracken back then, happily married, the father of two young daughters, an ambitious, successful businessman. The priesthood must have seemed like something for other men. Maine . . . he might not have even been able to find Maine on the map. He seemed so alone now, but Andy wondered if that was his own mood creeping through.

"Did you hear about the theft at the time?" he asked.

"In the news."

"Did you know Kitty's uncle?"

"John O'Byrne and I never met, no."

"He never married?"

"He lost his wife early in their marriage. They had no children. From what I understand, he doted on his youngest brother's daughters, Kitty and Aoife. They grew up in Dublin but visited Declan's Cross regularly."

"Are they attractive?"

Again the piercing look from Father Bracken. "Most would say so, I believe."

Andy shifted in his chair. He wasn't as stiff as he had been in the first days after the attack on him, but he missed being out on the water. "Have you ever been tempted to chuck being a priest?"

"You're asking me about women," Finian said.

"Yeah. I guess. It'd be easier to ask if you weren't in that clerical collar."

"Temptation is a part of life."

"I think my law enforcement brothers and father would jump on that answer."

"John O'Byrne died five years ago. Kitty boarded up the house until she and Aoife could decide what to do." Finian pushed aside his tea. "Kitty always had a grand vision for turning her uncle's house into a hotel. It was an obvious choice when the Celtic Tiger was roaring, may he rest in peace, but she moved to Declan's Cross two years ago and took the risk."

"I looked the hotel up on the internet. Quite a place. See Colin at the spa?"

"Why not?"

"You ever do the spa?"

Finian smiled. "The bar. Kitty has an impressive whiskey collection."

"What about the sister?"

"Aoife is an acclaimed artist."

"Husbands, kids?"

"Kitty has a son by her marriage to a banker in Dublin. They're divorced. Aoife is single." Finian studied Andy across the table. "You're worried about Julianne, aren't you?"

Andy shrugged, really restless now. "I didn't like this trip of hers yesterday, and I like it even less today."

"She'd already booked her flights when she told me her plans."

"It's okay, Fin. It wasn't up to you to talk her out of this trip. I know it's at least in part because of me. Her brother says she thinks Ireland will heal her broken heart."

"I hope it can," Finian said quietly. "You're the one who broke things off between you, then?"

"It was mutual, but if that's what she told you, I'm good with that."

An easy answer, Andy thought. The truth was, he hadn't been ready for Julianne to whisper she loved him in the dark of an autumn night. He hadn't responded. He still didn't know why. He'd never been in love before. How the hell did he know what it felt like? How did she, for that matter? In the morning, she'd called him a heartless rat bastard and told him she'd had too much to drink and hadn't meant what she'd said. But she hadn't had too much to drink, and she had meant it.

"Julianne would kill us both for talking about her this way." Andy tried to keep any frustration — any worry — out of his voice. She had her own life, and, as she'd pointed out to him more than once, she didn't need a Donovan breathing down her neck. He stood abruptly, grabbing his jacket and managing a grin. "This sheep farmer. Murphy. He's good-looking?"

Finian smiled. "He's Irish, isn't he?"

Andy walked from Hurley's to his apartment on the top floor of — purportedly — an old sea captain's house on the waterfront. The owners, a pair of schoolteachers who lived on the bottom two floors, had decorated the porch with pumpkins, cornstalks and mums and hung a scarecrow in the front garden. Cheerful sorts. They were expecting a baby in the spring, their first. Sometimes their domestic bliss and stability got to him, made him look at his own life, see what he was missing — thirty years old, banging around his hometown, cobbling together a living. No responsibilities. No commitments.

Other times he looked at his landlord and figured he was in no hurry.

He dropped his jacket on a chair at his kitchen table. Julianne had said she liked his apartment. She'd never asked him when he'd buy his own place or what his plans for the future were, but he knew she'd wanted to. She was a go-getter. She liked to plan.

She *was* in a hurry.

His shoulder ached. Yesterday's long drive to Boston and back had taken more of a toll than he'd wanted to admit. Probably good for him to test its limits, give it a workout. He'd done a number on it when Colin's thugs had blindsided him and left him for dead. *"You never leave someone for dead,"* his brother Mike had said. *"You always make sure."*

Mike had added it was a definite positive the thugs hadn't been as thorough as he would have been. Andy didn't remember the attack, just waking up to Julianne tucking her sweater around him. He'd been cold, wet, semiconscious. When he'd been hit, he'd gone into the water, taking several lobster traps with him, and would have drowned or died of hypothermia if Julianne hadn't spotted him and yelled for help. Mike and Colin had dragged him to shore. He'd sustained a concussion, but it was his shoulder that was keeping him off the water.

He didn't do well being idle. He was tempted to call Kevin and review the goings-on in Ireland from the point of view of a law enforcement officer. A decade-old Irish art heist, a marine science field station in development, Finian Bracken, Lindsey Hargreaves, the Sharpes. What could he or

Kevin do on the opposite side of the Atlantic?

Not much.

Andy put a burrito in the microwave and turned on the television, imagining Julianne snuggled up next to him as they watched a movie together. He knew he was right and she'd gone to Ireland to get over him, and he'd just have to make peace with it.

He turned off the television. He'd hoped watching it would keep him from worrying about Julianne, but it didn't. He ate his burrito and got out his laptop. He figured he'd check the weather in Ireland and see what he could find on Finian Bracken and Bracken Distillers and any connection between them and the obscure Irish village of Declan's Cross.

Finian was close-mouthed, and Andy had no doubt his Irish priest friend hadn't told him everything.

10

Julianne walked into the village for dinner and decided that was a *huge* mistake when her thighs gave out on her on the hill back up to her cottage. Then it started to rain. Not a soft rain, either. Fat, cold raindrops pelted her bare head. She pulled on the hood to her raincoat. *Always* take a raincoat. Wasn't that what Father Bracken had advised her? Maybe it had been Granny. Either way, she was all set.

Just as she was about to lose cell service, her iPhone dinged, and she saw she had a text message from Andy: Heard from Colin. You okay alone in that cottage?

She debated stuffing her phone back in her raincoat pocket and not texting him back, but if she didn't, he'd hound her. He'd call her, or, even worse, he'd sic his FBI brother on her. She paused by a stone wall in the dark. She could hear the ocean washing onto the rocks at the base of the cliffs to her left. She had omitted a flashlight from her packing list. A mistake, but the light from her phone helped. She quickly typed: Yep. Thanks.

She read her message. It was enough. She hit Send.

She continued up the hill, the lights from the village below disappearing as the lane twisted farther out onto the headland. The rain didn't let up. Clouds overtook the stars and sliver of a moon. Sheep bleated intermittently in the dark fields.

Watching her feet, Julianne did her best to avoid puddles, ruts, sheep droppings and any other obstacles she might encounter on a quiet Irish lane. She didn't regret her trek into Declan's Cross. She'd sat in a booth in a pub and enjoyed a crock of steaming shepherd's pie, made with local lamb, and a glass of Smithwick's. She'd resisted dessert because she'd been too tired, and because she'd eaten every crumb of the brown bread that had come with her shepherd's pie.

She promised herself she'd indulge in every dessert on the menu before her two weeks in Ireland were up. Apple crumble. Bread-and-butter pudding. Guinness cake. Sponge cake. She'd need the long uphill walk to her cottage if she kept inhaling food.

As she'd paid for her dinner, she'd overheard two men at the bar, realized they were Lindsey's diver friends and introduced herself. In their email exchanges, Lindsey had mentioned Brent Corwin, a good-looking American and an occasional diver for Hargreaves Oceanographic Institute. The other diver was Eamon Carrick, a sandy-haired, blue-eyed Irishman. Both men had greeted her enthusiastically and apologized for Lindsey not meeting her at the airport. They'd seemed to take her behavior in stride. A great person but a flake. A lot of fun. No way for Julianne to know not to count on her.

Brent and Eamon had both agreed that with her father's unexpected arrival in Dublin, Lindsey had simply lost track of what day it was. They wouldn't have been surprised if she planned to meet Julianne at the airport *tomorrow.*

That didn't explain why no one could reach Lindsey, or why she hadn't responded to emails, voice mails and text messages, but her friends didn't seem concerned.

Julianne came to a long driveway that wound through a field to a plain farmhouse, a single front window lit against the dark night. It appeared to be the only other house on Shepherd Head. Did Sean Murphy live there alone? Did he have a woman in his life? She hadn't asked Father Bracken many questions about his farmer friend.

When she reached her cottage, she realized she hadn't left a light on, an oversight she blamed on jet lag and lack of sleep. She could have found Colin and Emma and asked them to give her a ride up from the village, but she already felt a little foolish having them — two FBI agents — interrupt their vacation to check on her. Let them enjoy their fancy hotel. She'd see enough of them at home in Maine.

The wind blew cold rain in her face as she unlocked the front door and went in, trying not to think about Granny's dark fairies. Julianne felt on the wall for the overhead switch, found it, flipped it and breathed out in relief when the light came on.

She shivered in the cold air. She could build a fire, or she could turn on the heat.

"Heat's faster," she said aloud, peeling off her dripping raincoat.

She found the thermostat and turned the knob to a respectable but not overly generous twenty degrees Celsius — sixty-eight Fahrenheit. Being a scientist, she could do the conversion in her head, automatically, even exhausted.

She stood in the middle of the living room and glanced around at the attractive furnishings, the warm-looking throw over the back of the couch, the stack of tourist maps and brochures.

Didn't help. She was totally creeped out alone in her Irish cottage.

She would never admit as much to Granny, her parents, her brother or especially a single Donovan — and probably not to Emma or even to Father Bracken.

She kicked off her trail shoes. Her wool socks were still dry, toasty warm. She told herself that Colin and Emma would never have left her to her own devices if they didn't believe she was safe.

Well. Emma wouldn't have. Julianne wasn't sure about Colin. It wasn't that he wouldn't want her to be safe but that he'd figure she'd made her bed, she could lie in it. She hadn't exactly made him feel welcome.

Nevertheless, he and Emma were FBI agents and would feel a certain duty to her. They might think she was out of her mind for coming to Declan's Cross, insisting on staying out here by herself after her housemate hadn't shown up, but that was different from thinking she wasn't safe.

She regretted biting Colin's head off, but he'd get over it — assuming he'd even noticed. She couldn't remember how many times she'd apologized to Andy and he'd given her one of his clueless looks, as if he had no idea in the world what she was talking about. She'd say, "I'm sorry for biting your head off," and he'd say, "You didn't bite my head off."

Sometimes she'd been glad that he hadn't been offended, because things didn't always come out of her mouth the way she meant them to. Other times she'd been annoyed that he hadn't gotten it that she'd been mad at him. Andy had told her that honesty to the point of rudeness was fine with him. Colin was the same. All the Donovans were. Everyone in Rock Point knew if you wanted an honest opinion, ask a Donovan.

Didn't mean they didn't keep things to themselves. Especially anything deep. Andy never wanted to have a deep conversation about anything.

Never.

Julianne pulled the shades on every window in every room in the cottage. Living room, kitchen, both bedrooms, both bathrooms. She didn't pause until she was back in the kitchen, eyeing the as-yet untouched bottle of wine. Surely she'd burned off her Smithwick's by now. She had no regrets about venturing into the village. She'd wanted to experience Ireland her first evening there instead of sitting up here alone, fretting about her missing housemate.

Drinking alone didn't seem right, and she left the wine where it was.

She heard a whoosh of wind and a spray of raindrops on the windows behind the pulled shades.

It'd be a long, dark night.

And lonely, she thought. Lonelier than she'd expected when she'd headed into the village a couple of hours ago. Now it was just after nine. Still early. Even earlier at home. If she were there instead of Ireland, she'd be gearing up for the dinner crowd at Hurley's. Right after they'd broken up, Andy hadn't stopped in as much, at least when she'd been working.

Julianne groaned. "Stop thinking about him."

When she'd walked into the village, she'd emailed Granny and her parents that she'd arrived in Declan's Cross safely and told them she was already in love with it. It was true, too. Maybe her cottage was dark and lonely, but she loved being there.

She hadn't mentioned Lindsey. No point worrying them. If Colin wanted to tell them, that was up to him. If he told Andy — well, that would be it. Even if he didn't say a word to anyone, Granny would sense it and drag it out of him.

Julianne went into the bedroom she'd chosen for herself. It was smaller than the other bedroom but looked out on the water, not that it mattered in the dark, with the shades pulled. She turned on the bedside lamp. Before leaving for the village, she'd unpacked her suitcase and shoved it in the small closet. She'd laid out her flannel pajamas on the bed. She put them on and rummaged in the bureau for a fresh pair of wool socks to keep her feet warm until the room — and the bed — warmed up.

It wasn't as if she needed to impress some man with her sexy lingerie.

She hadn't needed to even when she and Andy had been together. She'd tried once, and he'd made clear that he didn't care if she wore flannel pj's, a slinky nightgown or a ratty T-shirt, so long as whatever it was ended up on the floor.

The man was about as romantic as a crustacean.

"Sexy, though," she said as she slipped under the warm duvet.

Her eyes felt as if they'd been rolled in sand, but she was too tired to get up for the drops Granny had insisted she pack. She shut off the lamp and turned on her relaxation playlist on her iPhone but only listened to ocean waves for a few seconds before switching them off.

The rain was steady now, rhythmic, soothing.

It was perfect.

A terrifying, unearthly shriek woke Julianne in the dark. She bolted upright in her bed, her heart pounding as she clutched her chest. *A banshee.* She held her breath but heard nothing, not even the hiss of the heat. The rain must have stopped. Now it was quiet, still, so dark she couldn't see her hand in front of her.

Waking up to a banshee shriek couldn't be good, whether or not she'd imagined it.

She took a moment to breathe deeply and remind herself that she wasn't one who always believed the worst. She was an optimist. An abundance thinker.

She'd had a nightmare. That was all.

Feeling more grounded, less caught in the haze between sleep and wakefulness, she reached for the lamp on the nightstand. She knocked something off — her phone, she realized. It clattered on the tile floor. If it broke, there'd be no replacing it now that she was spending all her money on trips to Ireland.

She found the lamp and switched it on,

the light an immediate relief. She sank back against her pillows, her heart rate easing again as she shook off the eerie screech. In Granny's world, Irish saints and Irish fairies sat comfortably together. Julianne had never been as gripped by the history and folklore of her ancestral homeland as she had been by anything and everything to do with oceans. As far back as she could remember, she'd wanted to be a marine biologist. What kind of job that meant she'd have — where she'd live — hadn't been a consideration until recently, now that she was finishing up her master's degree. She'd assumed her future wasn't in Rock Point but hadn't given it much thought.

She rolled onto her side and felt around on the floor for her phone. If she fell off the bed and knocked herself out, she'd have to lie there until she came to on her own or Emma and Colin started wondering what she was up to.

Maybe that was why she'd heard the banshee. Maybe it had cried for *her.*

She snatched up her phone, turned it on and saw that it was seven-thirty. *Morning? Already?* Why was it so dark?

Because you're in Ireland.

And because she had pulled all the shades and curtains.

She threw off the duvet and stood on the tile floor, still in her wool socks. She raised the shade on the window next to her bed. The sun was just coming up in a clearing sky, the stunning landscape taking shape in the morning mist. The window looked out on the back of the cottage, a lush green lawn giving way to rock-strewn fields where woolly sheep grazed idly among spikes of gorse and the occasional wind-bent, bare-limbed tree.

"So pretty," Julianne whispered, her banshee shriek quickly fading from her mind.

She went into the living area and raised shades and pulled back curtains. She felt as if it were the middle of the night, a combination of not fully being on Irish time and the calendar. Sunrise was later in November. As she stood at the kitchen sink, she realized she liked being on her own here in her Irish cottage. It wouldn't bother her that much, if any, if Lindsey had decided she didn't want to stay here after all and was just avoiding Declan's Cross so she wouldn't have to admit it. Julianne rarely ran into people who'd rather leave others guessing than just say what was on their minds — not that she couldn't do with keeping her mouth shut once in a while.

She filled an electric kettle with tap water

and plugged it in, then added fresh grounds to a glass coffee press. The water boiled in no time, and she poured it over the grounds and replaced the filter. While the coffee steeped, she helped herself to orange juice. She'd have to get to a grocery store. She needed to stock up. In the meantime, she was starving and looking forward to scrambled eggs, toast, butter, jam and every drop of coffee in the pot.

As she dug out a frying pan from a lower cabinet and set it on the electric stove, she wondered if she'd done something to offend Lindsey. Had she found out about Emma and Colin and decided she didn't want to hang around with someone who knew FBI agents? But that made no sense. Julianne's training as a scientist and the many conversations she'd overheard among the law-enforcement Donovans while waiting tables at Hurley's had warned her about the dangers of speculating.

She cracked a window to get a bit of air, a whiff of the sea, and fixed her breakfast, then ate it at the table with its view across the lane to the sea. Would her grandfather be proud of her for the way she was spending the mad money he'd left her? Was this what he'd had in mind?

"Miss you, Grandpa," she whispered.

She left the dishes soaking in the sink and headed for her bathroom to take a shower. She welcomed the hot water on her tight muscles as she shook off her rude awakening. *A banshee.* Granny wouldn't have needed convincing. If she'd ever heard a shriek like the one that had just awakened her granddaughter, no wonder she believed in banshees.

Once she was showered and dressed, Julianne felt more like herself. She washed her breakfast dishes and left them to air-dry in the drainer. A good walk would help her adjust to Irish time before she steeled herself for the drive to the village for groceries. She'd check out the field station at the same time. Maybe Lindsey had surfaced last night.

She pulled on her raincoat and headed outside. The sky had lightened, brightened, streaks of sunlight penetrating the mist and shining on the water. The tide was coming in, crashing onto the cobbles, boulders and steep rock faces that formed the coastline. The air was cool and rain-washed, invigorating, as Julianne smiled to herself and set off up the lane, away from the village. She knew from the map she'd consulted before leaving for Ireland that the lane didn't loop all the way around Shepherd Head, but she had no idea how far it went before it dead-ended.

It didn't matter, did it? She had nowhere else she had to be.

Transfixed by the view of sea, fields and sheep, Julianne let go of any of the lingering effects of her nightmare and resisted questions, speculation and worry. She wanted to be in this moment, aware of the sounds, smells, sights, even the taste, the feel, of the breeze on her face.

The lane curved away from the water, with fields and post-and-wire fences on both sides. After another fifteen minutes of walking, she came to a metal farm gate and thought this was the dead end. Then she saw that the lane narrowed — how that was possible was beyond her — and wound past the gate, back toward the water.

Irresistible, Julianne thought, abandoning any thought of turning around just yet.

The field on the edge of the cliffs to her left gave way to a strip of windblown grass, the water a good fifty feet below. The lane deteriorated to a deeply rutted, stone-encrusted track. Despite the recent rains, she could make out partial tire marks in the mud and assumed they were from a tractor, not a car. She couldn't imagine driving out here but could picture Sean Murphy on a tractor, tending his fields and sheep. Would he notice how beautiful the scenery was or did he take such a sight for granted?

A low stone wall appeared on the lane as it dipped between two small hills. Protected from the worst of the Atlantic winds, there was more greenery here. The stone wall was overgrown with small trees, moss, vines, ferns, rushes and wildflowers, most died back for the season. Above the lane, atop one of the hills, three worn-looking Celtic stone crosses were caught in the eerie shadow of a passing cloud.

Grave markers, Julianne thought with a mix of awe and a sudden sense of loneliness that she couldn't quite explain. She knew next to nothing about Celtic crosses and such. Emma, as an art expert and a former nun, would know more. Julianne liked her, but Emma's involvement with a Donovan complicated any potential for friendship. That was part of the problem, wasn't it? Everyone in Rock Point was involved with a Donovan in one way or another.

She wished her thoughts hadn't taken this direction. "Ireland," she said aloud. "I'm walking on a pretty Irish lane on a pretty Irish morning."

She pulled her gaze from the crosses and smiled, relishing everything about where she was. Walking and sunlight would help her adjust to the time change. Even if she were working the early shift at Hurley's — which was *really* early, to accommodate the lobstermen — she wouldn't be out of bed yet. Andy didn't mind getting up before dawn.

She sucked in a breath at the unwanted image of him throwing off the blankets. Andy Donovan's naked silhouette was *not* what she needed to be picturing on her Irish walk. She'd always assumed he knew how sexy he was, but during their brief, intense, utterly insane romance, she'd discovered he didn't think about such things. He was unselfconscious about his looks, maybe the most practical, down-to-earth man she'd ever known. Since she was living with her grandmother, she hadn't stayed with him overnight that often. Not that Granny didn't get it. She got it all too well, and Julianne had avoided talking about her relationship with him. On some level, she must have known it wouldn't last.

"Ireland," she said again. "You are in Ireland."

The narrowed lane came to an abrupt end at a crude turnaround nestled in the small hollow. A pale gray Mini was parked crookedly, its front bumper almost up against the stone wall. Julianne frowned. Someone had actually driven out here?

A sudden breeze whipped her hair into her face. She brushed it back, wishing now she'd left a note at her cottage describing where she was off to. She touched a holly leaf, glistening with last night's rain. Her internship went into May. She'd be here for spring wildflowers and lambs, but she loved the feel of early November, the short days, the sense that winter was near. Father Bracken had said November was the best time for Irish rainbows.

"All of it's good," she whispered. "All good."

She stepped closer to the car. It was well concealed from anyone up in the fields or below on the sea, or even out on the lane. She'd have missed it if she hadn't walked right up to it. She peered through the passenger window. An iPhone was hooked up, and there was an unopened Diet Coke and water bottle in the drinks holder, as if the driver were geared up for a long drive. An overflowing, bright red tote bag was on the floor. Julianne was positive Lindsey had had a red tote bag in Maine.

Was this *her* car? Why come out here?

Surely the pits, ruts, sharp stones and dead end would deter even the most oblivious Irish driver. Maybe Lindsey had, in fact, gotten her dates wrong and had shown up at the airport this morning, then driven down to Declan's Cross. She could have decided to kill some time to give her house-mate a chance to get up and at it. Made sense, Julianne thought, but wouldn't Lindsey have stopped at the farm gate, especially with the car? The lane obviously worsened there, and it was a good spot to turn around or admire the view.

Julianne stood straight, hands on hips, as she tried to figure out what to do next. Bits of vegetation clung to the Mini's windshield and hood. They weren't recent — not since daylight. The state of the tire tracks also suggested the car had been out here awhile, at least overnight. She went around to the driver's side. She noticed footprints — or what was left of them — on the lane and a trail that led through the trees up to the top of the second hill. She didn't see any prints returning back down to the lane and the car.

Was Lindsey up there? Had she camped out here overnight?

Balancing herself with one hand on a holly tree, Julianne tested the wet conditions on the trail. Not too slippery. She squeezed between the holly and another small tree. Another time, this would be a grand adventure. Right now, she felt uneasy, uncertain — but she continued up the steep, narrow trail.

She came to a barren rock ledge above an angled, rocky slope down to the water. She stood on the flat expanse of gray rock and looked out at the breathtaking view of sky, sea, cliffs and fields marked off with stone walls and barbed-wire fences.

Such an incredible spot. So beautiful.

To her right, the headland sloped down to a small, protected cove with a pebbled strand. Lindsey could have hiked down there, maybe, to explore a tide pool, check out a shore bird, wave to friends on a boat — anything.

Julianne felt her heartbeat quicken as she fought against a sudden, overwhelming sense of dread. "Lindsey," she called, her voice hoarse. She cleared her throat and tried again. "Lindsey, are you out here?"

She heard only the wind and a few distant seagulls. She walked to the edge of the ledge. There was a ten-foot drop to the tumble of boulders that continued into the tide. Ordinarily the sound of waves crashing onto rocks would have soothed her, but now she only saw how dangerous this stretch of coastline could be for even an experienced hiker.

A flash of color caught her attention in the boulders below her.

Bright red, turquoise, yellow.

A cast-off scarf?

Lindsey . . .

Julianne squinted down at the black-and-gray rocks but saw nothing else out of the ordinary. The wind was steady, colder, with the tide coming in. Being from Maine, a marine biologist, she was no stranger to rocky coast, but she was always careful, always let someone know where she was, seldom went out alone — but she couldn't leave now. She had to know if Lindsey was here and needed help. If she'd continued down the trail . . . lost her scarf in the rain and wind . . .

Julianne returned to the trail, which angled under the ledge and then zigzagged into the mass of rocks. Crouched low, focused on her footing, she followed the trail until it ended among several large boulders. She placed her hand on a waist-high boulder and looked for the brightly colored scarf.

She saw something poking out from the rocks below her and leaned forward for a closer look.

A black ankle boot . . . a dark gray pant leg . . .

No sign of movement.

Julianne's breath caught in her throat, her mind resisting what she was seeing, if only for a moment, but she knew it had to be Lindsey down on the rocks.

Steadying herself, Julianne glanced up at the ledge but no one was there. She could scream for help, but who would hear her? No one was on the rocks, out on the water, down on the strand. Taking another breath, she steeled herself for what was next. She had to make sure Lindsey — or whoever was down there — was beyond help.

Julianne stayed low and crept down toward the water — toward the unmoving foot. She concentrated on the smell of salt in the air, the cold spray of the tide, until she finally stopped in a narrow crevice between two craggy, wet boulders. She bit down on her lower lip, controlling her emotions.

A woman was sprawled facedown between two large boulders. She had on the same black jacket she'd worn in Rock Point. Her hand lay palm up, discolored and still.

There was no doubt now she was dead.

"Oh, Lindsey."

Julianne suppressed a surge of revulsion, panic and grief. She had to stay focused and do what she could to alert the proper authorities. Her hands shaking, she got out her phone. She had a single bar of service. It wasn't much better than no service at all. She couldn't think of the Irish version of 911 and wasn't sure she could get a call out, anyway.

Maybe a text.

Andy's number popped up since he'd texted her last but what good would it do to text him in Maine? She had Colin's cell number somewhere. Her hands were splotchy with the cold as she found him in her contacts and typed: Call police. Lindsey is dead. We're on rocks at end of lane past cottage.

She hit Send. She had no idea if the message would go through. She didn't want to leave Lindsey — it felt somehow as if she were abandoning her — but she had to make sure help was on the way.

As she started up toward the trail, she lost her footing and banged her knee on a sharp rock. She caught herself, scraping her wrist on another rock, but at least she hadn't hit her head. Fighting tears, she forced herself to slow her pace. She'd take her time and yell for help, in case anyone could hear her.

There was, after all, nothing anyone could do for Lindsey Hargreaves.

11

"I like sheep well enough," Sean said as he arrived at the gate out the lane, almost at the tip of Shepherd Head. He'd walked from the farmhouse. His uncle had taken the tractor. They had fences to repair. Sean grinned at him. "What's not to like?"

Paddy grunted. He wore his wool jacket and cap, his standard attire for a cool, relatively dry day no matter the time of year. Although he was slowing down, he was still fit and agile into his seventies, and as clearheaded as ever. "I can think of a few things," he muttered.

"Ah, Paddy, what don't you like about sheep after all these years at them?"

Paddy paused by the tractor, white hair poking out from under his cap, the sunlight showing the lines in his face. "You're right. I've no complaints. Farming is good work. Imagine me in a factory."

"I can't. Myself, either."

It was an ongoing discussion — a friendly argument, even — about the positive and negative attributes of sheep farming, and Sean's aptitude for it. They'd been at it since Sean was a boy and Paddy had told him he wasn't cut out for a life of farming. *"I can see it in your eyes, lad,"* he'd say. Sean would argue that he loved the farm, but Paddy would say it wasn't a question of love. He couldn't see his nephew staying in Declan's Cross, doing much the same work day after day, year after year.

His uncle had been right, at least for a time.

The rhythms of the farm hadn't changed since Paddy was a boy — since *his* father was a boy. One year was much like the next. Sometimes there was too much rain, or too little, and sometimes it was warmer or cooler, but the rams were still separated from the ewes in early fall and reunited again in November, with lambs born in the spring.

Paddy was eyeing him. "We're fixing a fence. Why the garda look?"

"Habit."

"Having FBI agents in town doesn't help, does it?"

"They're friends of Finian Bracken."

"Right," Paddy said, heaving a deep sigh.

"That one."

Sean knew his uncle considered Fin Bracken a tragic soul, a man destined to live out his days in grief and misery. The priesthood, Maine — In Paddy Murphy's view, Fin was running away.

Sean pulled work gloves out of his jacket pockets. "The woman agent is Emma Sharpe," he said.

Paddy's eyebrows went up. "Sharpe, eh?"

"She's Wendell Sharpe's granddaughter."

The old man shuddered as if Wendell Sharpe had returned to Declan's Cross with new questions about the O'Byrne art theft — an investigation that stubbornly refused to be pieced together. Sean knew there was more to it than the one theft ten years ago. He doubted anyone else in Declan's Cross did.

"I see now why you have that sour look," Paddy said. "Don't worry about me, lad. I can handle myself with a Sharpe."

"I've no doubt. It's just an odd set of co-incidences that she's here."

"What about this other FBI agent?"

"Colin Donovan's his name. He and Emma are together. They're also friends with Julianne Maroney."

"The biologist. She seems all right. Pretty girl. She likes the cottage?"

"Seems to," Sean said.

"Philip helped get it ready yesterday. He's a good lad. He's got a backbone." Paddy kicked a chunk of dried mud off his boot. "You know he's the son you and Kitty could have had —"

"Let's get these fences fixed, Paddy."

"It's hard for Kitty, having you here," he said.

Sean grinned at him. "Hard for Kitty? What about me? I'm the one who was nearly killed."

Paddy shrugged. "Broken bones can be easier to mend than a broken heart."

Sean decided to wait to put on his gloves and shoved them back in his pockets, wishing now he'd left Paddy in the barn and gone out to fix the fences on his own. "I didn't break Kitty's heart."

"She broke yours?"

"It's not that simple." He wasn't discussing his love life — or lack of a love life — with his uncle. "Let's get on with it." He gestured down the lane. "We'll start at the fence break out by the church and work our way back here."

Sean had noticed the breaks when he'd been out this way on Saturday. There were no sheep in that particular field and wouldn't be until spring, but best to take advantage of the co-operating weather and get the job done while it wasn't urgent. It was a fine, clear, breezy morning, perfect for any sort of farm work.

Paddy got back on the tractor. That it was still running was a testament to his care over the years for his farm and its equipment. Padraig Murphy was also well known in Declan's Cross and among local farmers for his frugality. A thing that could still be repaired wasn't replaced, no matter how rusted, creaky and old. Paddy liked to say he felt that way about himself, too.

As Sean started past the gate, he noticed fresh footprints as the lane narrowed. Tourists sometimes walked up this way from the village, although not as often this time of year. They were attracted by the cliffs and views of the sea and surrounding countryside, some also by the atmospheric ruins of a small church and its graveyard, with their promise of ghosts and wee people. Julianne Maroney, being a scientist, might be of a more pragmatic nature, but Irish ruins, ghosts and wee people were tough to resist.

A breeze floated up from the water, carrying with it the cold of the season. Sean walked ahead of Paddy on the tractor. The footprints — recent from the look of them — continued down the lane with none returning. He assumed Julianne Maroney was out for a morning stroll.

Stone walls appeared on both sides of the lane as it wound toward the old church ruin and graveyard. Sean paused when he heard what sounded like a scream but might have only been the whistle of the wind. He motioned for Paddy to hold up on the tractor.

There it was again. Definitely a scream.

A woman yelling for help.

Paddy was already off the tractor. "Did you hear that, Sean?"

"I did. I'll have a look, but I need you to stay with me."

"All right, lad."

Sean picked up his pace, his uncle keeping up with him. They came to a gray Mini. Sean felt the cold and dampness in the shadows of the small hollow.

He couldn't hear any screaming now.

He peered into the car's front window. It looked to be Lindsey Hargreaves' Mini. It had been here awhile. Was she the woman he'd heard yelling for help? Then whose footprints had he seen?

"What's going on, Sean?" Paddy asked behind him.

"I don't know. I need to find out."

"Help!"

They both turned, looking up through the trees to the ledge above them. The cry sounded as if it had come from the other side of the ledge, down by the water.

"Can anyone hear me?" The words were distinct, unmistakable. "I need help. A woman's dead."

Sean gritted his teeth. He didn't have his phone with him. No point since there was no service out here. He grabbed his uncle's arm. "Do not move from my side. Clear?"

The old man shook his head. "Best I take the tractor back to the house and call the gardai. I can defend myself if it comes to it." He glanced up the hill, as grim as Sean had ever seen him. "Which one do you think is gone? Lindsey or Julianne?"

"Lindsey," Sean said.

Paddy nodded. "More than likely the poor woman tripped on the rocks. Either way, Sean, we need to get the gardai up here."

Sean didn't disagree. "All right. Go. Do as they say."

Paddy fastened his watery blue eyes on him. "Be careful, lad."

Sean wasn't worried about himself but said nothing more. He charged across the lane and up the trail. He knew it well. He glanced down at the lane. Paddy was already back on the tractor. It would take him a while to get to the house. Sean continued up the trail, taking long strides, feeling no pain from his June injuries. When he hit the open ledge, a cold, hard wind was blowing off the water. He ignored it and squinted down at the rocky coastline.

Julianne Maroney waved up at him. She was crouched, as if trying to maintain her balance on the wet rocks, against the wind.

He called down to her. "Are you hurt?"

"Not really. It's Lindsey." Julianne gulped in air, obviously trying to control her emotions. "She must have fallen and hit her head."

"Where is she?"

Julianne pointed to boulders below her. "Down there."

"Don't move. I'll come to you."

Sean sprinted back to the trail and jumped down to the rocks. The sun was higher in the sky, promising a glorious day. He moved fast but not recklessly. This was familiar ground. He'd explored out here countless times, as far back as he could remember. He'd never thought twice about breaking his neck.

What the devil had happened? What had Lindsey been doing out here?

He dropped down to Julianne. She was sitting on a knee-high boulder now, a bloody tear in her hiking pants, a red, raw scrape on her wrist. "Are you all right?" he asked her.

She was ashen, shivering with cold and shock. "I fell but it's nothing," she said, visibly trying to steady herself. "Lindsey . . . I know first aid, but it's too late. She's been dead at least a day —"

"Easy now."

"I texted Colin to call the police. I don't know if the text went through. I'm sure he and Emma are still at the hotel." Her voice was subdued, her eyes huge as she looked up at him. "You heard me yelling for help?"

"I was out to fix a fence. My uncle was with me. He's gone for help." Sean touched her shoulder. "Can you sit tight here? I want to have a look —"

She didn't let him finish. "No problem."

She was warm enough, Sean realized. Her shivering was primarily from the shock of discovering a body — a woman she knew. He trusted her assessment of the situation but needed to check for himself. He scanned the mass of rocks and spotted a bright bit of fabric, then a foot — a woman's unmoving foot.

He hopped from boulder to boulder, and when he reached Lindsey, he understood Julianne's certainty. The position of her neck, the color of her exposed skin — no question she was gone. He would do his best to limit any further contamination of the scene. There would be a proper investigation to ascertain the cause, manner and circumstances of Lindsey Hargreaves' death.

All the gardai could do now was get her back to her family and provide them answers as to what had happened to her. From the condition of her body, Sean estimated she'd been out here, dead, for a time — more than twenty-four hours. The medical examiner would be more precise. He saw no visible sign she'd been shot, stabbed or bludgeoned, but he didn't want to disturb the body.

Best to leave her for the gardai.

Sean stood, glancing around the area for signs of how Lindsey had ended up here. She hadn't washed ashore. That much he knew. He saw the bright fabric again and realized it was a scarf, wedged among the rocks above her. Blown up there before, during or after her death? He looked for impact marks on the rocks, drag marks, mud, other clothing — hers, someone else's — and anything else that might suggest what had happened, but nothing caught his eye.

At a guess, Lindsey had broken her neck

in some kind of fall. A wrong step hopping from boulder to boulder? She'd have had to have been going at a fast clip and gone flying. More likely, she'd gone off the ledge.

How'd that happened? What'd she been doing up there?

Once airborne, she could have struck the flat-topped boulder three meters below the ledge and her momentum then propelled her down here. As boys, he and his friends had jumped off the ledge a time or two. Stupid and dangerous, maybe, but they'd had no problem at all. If Lindsey had lost her footing in the wet conditions on the ledge, if she'd had too much to drink, if she'd hit just right, he supposed it was possible to have ended up here, dead, as the result of an unfortunate, freak accident.

Had someone pushed her off the ledge? Had she jumped with the intention of killing herself?

Sean shook his head. "Not a suicide," he said aloud. If she'd wanted to commit suicide, there were more certain methods to do the job than a free fall off this particular ledge. Why not off a sheer cliff straight into the ocean? If she'd been impaired by alcohol or drugs, she might have meant to make a straight, clean, drop into the water, but that seemed unlikely to him.

Not that it was his call to make.

Below him, high tide crashed onto boulders and cobbles, its rhythms untouched by the tragedy. A tragedy, he noted, that had occurred on the boundary of the Murphy farm. Garda though he was, he was nonetheless in the thick of a woman's untimely death.

He climbed back up to Julianne, sitting on her boulder, squinting out at the glistening sea, teeth chattering. He got down to eye level with her. "I'm sorry you had to see this," he said.

She gave a dull nod. "I'm sorry it happened."

"Are you all right staying here until the gardai arrive? I'll stay with you."

"They're the police, right? The gardai."

"That's right," Sean said.

"I'm fine staying right here." She seemed to make a physical effort to pull herself out of her thoughts. "Just trying to get my teeth to stop chattering. It's nerves. I'm not cold." She sniffled, licked her lips. "The view — it's really an incredible spot. Is this where you saw your whale?"

"It is." Sean stood straight and pointed at her injured wrist. "Is there a chance you broke a bone?"

She gave a tight shake of her head. "I just

scraped it on a rock when I tried to catch my balance. If Colin got my message — would he and Emma have a role here, since Lindsey was American?"

"No, a death investigation is handled locally."

Julianne raised her eyes to him, fear in them. "If it was murder?" She inhaled deeply. "Never mind. Sorry. You must be as out of your element as I am."

Sean didn't think this was the moment to explain his professional situation. "One thing at a time, okay?"

She shifted and again stared out at the sea. "Did she suffer, do you think?"

"I don't think so," he said truthfully. "I understand you didn't know her well, but are you aware if she had any health problems?"

"Something that could have caused her to fall off a ledge, you mean? I'm not aware of anything wrong with her — emotionally, either, in case you're thinking she might have committed suicide."

Sean sat on a taller boulder across from Julianne, his back to the water, so that he could see anyone approaching. "I'm sorry about all this, Julianne," he said with genuine sympathy. "You're not having the best introduction to Ireland, are you?"

"This isn't Ireland's fault."

No argument from him. He saw a movement up on the ledge and got to his feet. He recognized Emma Sharpe and Colin Donovan.

Julianne's two FBI agents.

Just what he needed.

12

Emma handed a pair of black wool gloves to Julianne, who'd moved up from the rocks near Lindsey Hargreaves' body and collapsed onto the stone wall by the lane. "Warm hands always help," Emma said, sitting next to her.

"Thanks." Julianne's hands trembled visibly as she slipped them into the gloves. "I didn't expect to be out here this long. I just meant to take a quick morning walk. You know. Wake up, get used to the time change. Look at sheep. Maybe see a dolphin or porpoise."

"It's spectacular scenery up here."

"Yes. Yes, it is." Julianne stared down at the muddy lane. "I couldn't remember the Irish version of 911. That's why I texted Colin. I didn't know what else to do."

"You did exactly the right thing." Emma kept her tone neutral, not wanting to say anything that would put Julianne on the defensive and shut her down. "It's 999, by the way. Ireland's emergency number. 112 also works — it's good anywhere in the EU."

"I'll remember that."

"I hope you never need it again."

"Yeah. Me, too." She ran her toe over a small, sharp stone embedded in the mud. "I wasn't sure if I'd get in trouble if I left Lindsey, but I knew I had to get help. After I tripped . . . a million things went through my head. Probably not even half of them made any sense. I started yelling for help. I figured I'd give it a few minutes before I figured out a Plan B."

Emma felt the cold of the stone wall through her jeans. She'd hoped to spend the morning at the spa. "Luckily, Sean Murphy and his uncle were within earshot," she said.

Julianne nodded. "I haven't met his uncle yet. Sean seemed to know just what to do. He's solid. I'm glad he was here."

He had stayed down on the rocks with Colin, who wanted to take a closer look at Lindsey, without intruding on the immediate scene. As a former Maine state marine patrol officer, he had dealt with more accidents, homicides and suicides than Emma had in her three years with the FBI, but this death investigation would be in the hands

209

of the gardai.

Julianne raised her chin, focused on Emma. "I'm sorry this interrupted your romantic getaway. I know you and Colin are in Declan's Cross because of me, but I'd hoped . . ." She glanced away. "It doesn't matter now."

"I'm sorry Lindsey's dead, Julianne."

She blinked back tears. "It's not what I expected. From what everyone said about her, I really thought we just had our wires crossed and that's why she didn't pick me up and I couldn't reach her. It never occurred to me she was dead." Julianne looked at the ground again and started toeing her stone free. "I never imagined she was lying out here on the rocks."

"No one did," Emma said softly.

"What happens next?"

"Once the gardai get here, they'll have a look at the scene and decide what to do."

Julianne's nose and cheeks were red from emotion and the cool wind. She seemed oblivious to the scrapes on her wrist and knee. "I've seen dead stranded whales and dolphins, which is hard, but never a dead person," she said half to herself. "Except in a casket."

"It's not easy, I know."

"Yeah. I'm glad you're here, Emma. Thank you."

Emma looked up when she heard Sean Murphy and Colin on the trail. Any evidence there had already been contaminated. They dropped onto the lane, Colin saying something about checking a nearby cove and beach for potential witnesses.

"Is the beach accessible only by boat?" he asked.

Sean shook his head. "There's a road from the village. It doesn't connect with the lane up here. The gardai will see to it." He stopped in front of Julianne. "Your color's better. That's good."

"Some of the shock is easing," she said.

"Paddy and I didn't see anything amiss from where we've been working in the fields. I wish we had. Then we'd have been the ones to find Lindsey instead of you."

Julianne made no response, but Emma thought she appreciated the Irishman's comment.

Colin glanced at the Mini, then up at the Celtic crosses on the grassy hill above them. "Declan's Cross named for those crosses up there?"

Sean leveled his blue eyes on him. "No. They were erected long after Declan's Cross was named."

Colin pointed at the remains of a stone structure overgrown with mosses, trees and vines. Mostly a foundation, but a partial wall was visible. "Looks like an old church or something."

"It is."

"Saint Declan's?"

"That's right." Sean's tone was cool. "A church was first built on this site in the ninth century, they say. It was sacked by Nordic raiders. Another was built in its place."

"And I thought my folks' inn was old. It was built in the 1890s. Just yesterday around here. Do the ruins and crosses attract tourists?"

Colin's irreverent tone, Emma knew, was deliberate, but it seemed to have no effect on Sean Murphy. He said, "Some, but not as many as the ruins in Ardmore. We do get walkers up here. The ground is wetter and rougher than they sometimes expect, but we've never had more than a twisted ankle and a few bruises and scrapes."

"Did Lindsey express an interest in coming out here?" Emma asked. "The crosses are especially beautiful. The stone is decorated in a distinctive, intricate Celtic Christian motif. They're works of art, really."

"A Celtic motif," Colin said, as if he were

translating a foreign language.

"Knots, circles, spirals, sometimes animals and human figures. The center cross — the tallest one — has a figure of Saint Declan chiseled in the middle of its shaft."

"Then you've been up here before," Sean said.

"I have, yes." She didn't elaborate.

Colin's gaze settled on her for an instant before he shifted back to the Irishman. "Do you let passersby onto your farm?"

"I don't escort them if that's what you mean. I don't always see them. People walk up here from the cove as well as the village. I wouldn't see them unless I was down here myself."

Colin gave the smallest of grins. "Don't sic the dogs on tourists, do you?"

"No. And it's one dog. My uncle sees to him." Sean's voice was even, without anger or humor. "He does the work of ten men."

"Your uncle or the dog?"

Sean cracked a smile. That was Colin, Emma thought. He could get to anyone.

He touched Julianne's shoulder. "How you doing, kid?"

She jumped as if he'd startled her. "I'm fine. Don't call me kid."

He winked at her. "That's the Julianne Maroney I know. Straight-A student and a

213

sharp tongue."

She sprang to her feet. "I didn't mean to snap at you —"

"Easy. It's okay. It's been a rough morning. The police will need to talk to you."

"I understand." Her voice was a notch above a whisper. She glanced around her, as if reminding herself that she was in Ireland. "I hope Lindsey wasn't lying out on the rocks, injured, unable to call for help."

"I don't think that's the case," Colin said quietly.

"You'd know, wouldn't you? Because of your work." She looked out the lane, in the direction of her cottage. "I heard a banshee this morning. . . ."

"Lindsey was dead long before then, kid."

She nodded, obviously appreciating his blunt response.

"The wind can shriek up here," Sean added.

"Yeah. That's probably what it was." Julianne wobbled slightly but shrugged off any help from Colin as she steadied herself. "I ran into two divers last night. Brent Corwin and Eamon Carrick. They said Lindsey spent the weekend in Dublin with her father. He was there for a last-minute visit. She needn't have worried about picking me up in Shannon, but that's neither here nor there. I've been trying to figure out why she would have come out here. I wonder if she wanted to have a look at the cottage. Then she drove out the lane not realizing it dead-ended. That doesn't explain why she got out of the car. Maybe something caught her eye. A rainbow, or she just wanted to look at the scenery."

Emma wanted to go through Lindsey's car and suspected Colin did, too — but that wasn't their job.

She heard a vehicle out on the lane.

"The gardai," Sean said. "Special Agent Donovan, Special Agent Sharpe, why don't we let them to do their work? This isn't an FBI investigation. I don't have to tell you that, do I?"

"No problem," Colin said, tilting his head back, eyeing the Irishman.

He had Emma's attention, too. His manner had changed. He wasn't as casual and convivial. There was no hint of defensiveness or irritation in his voice or manner, but still . . . something.

Then she knew. "Garda?"

He shrugged. "On leave."

In another moment, a white garda car pulled in behind her and Colin's rental and two uniformed gardai got out. The deceased might be American, but the gardai were in charge and would determine what happened next. Emma had confidence in them.

The two young gardai clearly knew Sean, even deferred to him. He briefly introduced Emma and Colin, then Julianne, who looked as if she wanted to be anywhere but on the south Irish coast. Emma touched her hand. "I'll wait for you. I'll be right here. I'm not going anywhere."

Julianne nodded. "Thanks." She looked at Colin. "I was just trying to clear my head by coming to Ireland —"

"Don't do that to yourself, kid."

She fixed her hazel eyes on him. "You don't think Lindsey's death was an accident."

"Just talk to the gardai, okay?"

"I know. I will. I don't need you to —" She stopped herself. "Never mind. Just go back to your hotel and have a massage or something. I can take care of myself."

Colin didn't respond as the gardai led her away. Sean accompanied them. Emma knew the drill. They would take control of the scene, establish an entry point for arriving support personnel, limit further contamination and do all they could to figure out Lindsey's movements from the moment she parked her car at the stone wall until her death — and, if warranted, prior to her arrival on Shepherd Head.

Her friends at the field station would have to be told of her death and likely interviewed, too. A cause of death would help decide the direction of the investigation but wouldn't necessarily provide a clear-cut determination of whether Lindsey's death was suspicious or non-suspicious. If she'd died of injuries sustained in a fall and there were no witnesses — the truth was they might never know exactly what happened.

Colin would understand that, too, Emma thought as she stood next to him in the dappled shade of what should have been a perfect morning. He said, "There's nothing I could have said to Julianne that wouldn't have gotten her back up, you know."

"I know. Right now it's easier for her to be defensive and irritable with you — someone she's known forever — than to admit how afraid and uncertain she is."

"It's not a problem. I have broad shoulders." He watched a garda van pull up behind the patrol car. "Tight quarters. It's going to get crowded fast."

"It could be a while before we can get the car out of here," Emma said. "It's not easy to be on the sidelines."

"No, it isn't. Would you mind going with

Julianne back to her cottage? I'll meet you at the hotel later. I want to talk to our Garda Murphy."

"I expected as much." Emma felt a cool breeze, no hint of dampness in it. "Julianne can't stay at the cottage by herself until we know what happened here. She must know that."

"This isn't the spa break you were hoping for," Colin said, touching a finger to Emma's cheek, settling his stormy gray eyes on her. "Is this the place depicted in the unsigned painting stolen from the O'Byrne house?"

She nodded. "The center cross is also virtually a direct copy of the silver cross that was stolen."

"There's more."

It wasn't a question, and Emma said nothing as more garda vehicles arrived.

The Murphy cottage was surprisingly warm, the kitchen sunlit and cheerful as Emma waited for water to come to a boil in the electric kettle. The gardai had been quick with Julianne. They knew where to find her if they had any follow-up questions. The walk back to the cottage had seemed to help her get her bearings. She was in a small mudroom off the kitchen, peeling off her raincoat, which she hadn't ended up needing.

Emma had appreciated the walk, too, although the beautiful weather was deteriorating. She looked out the window above the sink. A pearl-gray mist had settled on the horizon, and high clouds had moved in, the sun angling through them onto the gray-blue sea. The cottage lawn was green and trimmed, bordered by a stone wall topped with barbwire and overgrown with coppery ferns, woody vines and shrubs. A hydrangea, drooping with a few late-season blossoms, reminded her of home in Heron's Cove. Her grandmother had loved hydrangeas. Emma didn't know yet if she would have to postpone her flight back to Boston. She wouldn't be returning until she had a better idea of how Lindsey Hargreaves had died, and whether her death had any connection to a decade of unsolved art thefts.

"I can't tell Granny about this morning," Julianne said as she left her raincoat in a pile by the back door. "I just can't. For her, Ireland is all fairies, shamrocks and brown bread."

Emma opened a tin of loose-leaf tea and scooped several heaping spoonfuls into a pottery teapot. "She doesn't have to know just yet, does she?"

"I don't want her to find out from Father Bracken or a Donovan. That would just upset her more." Julianne came into the kitchen, her hair hanging in her face but her overall color improved. "Granny just wants me to have a good time and tell her how much I love Ireland."

"I have a feeling Franny Maroney's been around the block a time or two."

"Doesn't mean she needs to know I found a dead body my first morning here." Julianne winced. "Sorry. That was blunt. Do you think Colin will tell Andy?"

"Andy's his brother, Julianne."

"They're so alike but different, too. Andy's more easygoing, which isn't saying a whole lot, I know." She crossed her arms in front of her, as if she wanted to hug herself. "Colin treats me like I'm ten. Then I act like I'm ten. It's a vicious cycle, and being jet-lagged and totally freaked out doesn't help."

Emma lifted the kettle and poured the hot water into the teapot. "When Lindsey was in Rock Point, did she mention Heron's Cove or my family?"

Julianne shook her head. "She just said a mutual friend in Declan's Cross had mentioned Father Bracken. She didn't give a name. We stopped in Heron's Cove when I played tour guide, but Lindsey didn't say anything about your family. I'm sure I'd have remembered if she had." Julianne got two mugs out of a glass-front cabinet. "Hot tea right now sounds good. Later on I'll be looking for a Father Bracken–approved whiskey."

"Or Father Bracken–unapproved." Emma set the kettle back on the counter and put the lid on the teapot. "Colin will want to join us for the whiskey. He won't mind missing the tea."

"The Donovans are a hardheaded bunch. The Maroneys are bad, but Mike, Colin, Kevin, Andy — they're off the charts. They know how to get things done, though. I guess that's why I texted Colin. I knew he'd figure out what to do." Julianne yawned, covering her mouth with her hand. "My poor body doesn't know what time it is."

"The adrenaline dump this morning won't help. Toast and cheese with your tea?"

"That sounds great."

"I'll make it. Have a seat and enjoy the view. If you remember anything else about Lindsey, let me know and I'll call the gardai."

"I have the card of the one who interviewed me."

And her neighbor was one, too, Emma

thought as she poured tea for the two of them.

Julianne took hers and sat at the table, slumping, her energy understandably coming in bursts. She stared out the window. "The gardai will notify Lindsey's father?"

"Yes. He's in Declan's Cross, at the O'Byrne. They'll also want to talk to him. He and Lindsey spent the weekend together in Dublin. He could have insights into her emotional state, whether she was on medication. That sort of thing."

"I wonder if he'll know what she was doing out there. I understand it rained here most of Monday. It would have been wet. People forget how slippery rock can get when it's wet." Julianne drank some of her tea. "Do you think she was murdered, Emma?"

Emma put two pieces of white bread into the toaster. "I don't know what happened to her, Julianne. If her injuries are consistent with a fall, that still won't explain why she was out there. We might never know."

"Will this be a problem for you and Colin?"

"For us?"

"With your superiors. You're supposed to be on vacation."

"It won't be a problem for us," Emma said.

Julianne said nothing. Emma laid slices of local Irish cheese on a plate. The toast popped, and she got it onto the plate and buttered it. She wasn't hungry herself. She and Colin had indulged in a massive breakfast at the hotel before he'd received Julianne's text. He'd instantly gone into action. That was Colin Donovan. It was what people counted on him to do. His family, his friends, the FBI. Her.

She brought the toast and cheese to Julianne. "Thanks, Emma," she said, her eyes misting even as she attempted a smile.

Emma grabbed her tea and sat at the table. "Today was a lot for you. Try not to be too hard on yourself if your emotions are all over the place. It's normal."

"Lindsey didn't meet me in Shannon because she was already dead." Julianne lifted her toast, stared at it as if she couldn't imagine eating, then took a nibble. "She was so enthusiastic about the field station. No one seemed that concerned when she didn't show up yesterday. If I'd had any clue . . ."

"You didn't, Julianne. None of us did, and if we had, all we could have done was find her sooner. Lindsey was dead before you,

223

Colin or I arrived in Declan's Cross."

Julianne nodded and set her toast back on the plate. "I have to admit I'd hate to be here alone right now. If nothing else, having Colin out there gave me someone to snap at instead of the Irish police. It'd be awful if I had to call Granny for bail money."

She was only half kidding, Emma realized.

"Sean Murphy really is with the Irish police?"

Emma nodded. "I don't have any details about his role with the gardai."

"I had no idea. I thought he was a farmer. No wonder Father Bracken trusts him."

"Julianne . . ." Emma hesitated. She'd been debating whether to bring up the O'Byrne theft. She'd started to on the walk back to the cottage, but had decided to wait. She drank more tea, aware of Julianne's frown, then finally continued. "Did Lindsey or Father Bracken — or anyone else — mention an art theft here in Declan's Cross ten years ago?"

Julianne frowned. "No. What art theft?"

"The hotel where Colin and I are staying was broken into. It was a private home then. A thief stole three Irish landscape paintings and a very old Celtic cross."

"Did your family investigate?"

"After the fact. It's a little complicated."

Julianne placed a slice of cheese on her toast. "And the theft — it hasn't been solved, right?"

"That's right." Emma set her mug on the table. Outside, mist hung low over the sea, even as sunlight shone on the lush lawn. She added, "The theft isn't a secret."

"This trip is so last-minute — I didn't do much research on Declan's Cross. Just looked up a few pictures and a map on the internet. I was focused on the field station. Marine science. Maybe I wouldn't be here if Lindsey hadn't been a Hargreaves, but I liked her. Anyway, she didn't mention the theft, and neither did Father Bracken." Julianne raised her toast and cheese to her mouth but didn't take a bite. "That's why you and Colin are here, isn't it?"

"Julianne —"

"All these alarm bells went off when you found out I was staying in Declan's Cross."

"I wouldn't say alarm bells. I would say . . ." What would she say? Emma sighed. "I wanted to be sure it was an innocent co-incidence that you ended up in Declan's Cross."

"And that Lindsey chose it for her field station," Julianne added.

"Yes."

"So if I'd picked a different Irish village,

you'd have left me to my own devices?"

"Colin and I still would have wanted to welcome you to Ireland," Emma said quietly. "At the same time, we understand your reasons for being here. We didn't, and don't, want to intrude. Colin had no idea Declan's Cross meant anything until he saw my reaction when he told me it's where you were headed."

Julianne sank back in her chair. "You two must have the most interesting conversations. I'll bet you only scratched the surface these past couple weeks of what all you don't know about each other. Are there things that have to stay secret? FBI things, I mean."

"Some."

"That must kill Colin. He and his brothers like to know everything. I think that was part of my problem with Andy. He knew everything about me before I weakened and went on that first date with him. No mystery, you know?" She cleared her throat, obviously fighting fatigue and a rush of emotions. "I'm glad you're here, Emma."

"I'll do anything I can to help you get through this."

"Thanks. I really appreciate that." She ate some of her toast and cheese, then added, "And it's not a problem having Colin here.

I'm used to Donovans. I was just dumb to get involved with Andy. I thought Rock Point would be enough for us to have in common."

"It's a lot," Emma said.

"Maybe." Julianne fingered her second piece of toast but didn't pick it up. "You and Colin don't have much in common except the FBI. Rock Point and Heron's Cove are next to each other on the map but that's about it. I'm not sure exactly what he does with the FBI, but it's not art crimes."

Emma looked out at a bird swooping low toward the sea cliffs. A gull, maybe. It was too far away for her to know for certain. Finally she said, "What Colin and I have in common and what's different about us work well together. At least I think so."

"He must, too, or he wouldn't be staying at a boutique spa hotel with you. I can't imagine Andy —" She broke off and stood abruptly, almost tipping over her chair. "The two of us in a spa hotel is definitely not what I need to be thinking right now."

"When you're ready, I can help you gather your things," Emma said. "We can take your car to the hotel. Colin and I are extending our stay, and I made a reservation for you while you were talking to the gardai. We should have a better idea of what's going on

227

after you get settled. I assumed you wouldn't want to stay out here alone, at least tonight."

"Not that it would matter if I did because Colin wouldn't stand for it."

Emma smiled. "Probably not."

"I don't need him camping out on my doorstep — it's not as if I'm in any danger up here. I can't believe anyone would deliberately hurt Lindsey." Julianne went still, as if a thought — an image — had overcome her. She shut her eyes and breathed deeply, then looked out at the choppy sea and mist. "I keep seeing her foot. I knew she was dead. I'd hoped I'd find her stuck out there with a broken ankle and no cell phone. It just didn't work out that way."

"I'm really sorry, Julianne," Emma said, rising. "All we can do now is trust that the gardai will get answers. They'll do a thorough job. I've no doubt of that."

Julianne stepped back from the window and glanced around the comfortable living room and kitchen. "I know this trip was impulsive, but I thought it would be fun. A start at reinventing myself. No one here would know me. I could talk marine mammals with people as interested in them as I am, and get the lay of the land, so to speak, ahead of my internship. But it's selfish to think about myself when Lindsey is lying out there on the rocks."

"I know it's difficult." Emma gathered up the plates and mugs. "I'll do the dishes while you get your things together. Just pack enough for tonight. We can come back tomorrow."

Julianne shuddered. "I'll never doubt Granny about her dark fairies again."

Emma stayed with Julianne until she was checked into her room at the O'Byrne House Hotel. Clearly exhausted, she said she wanted to rest a bit and would meet Emma at the bar. "If I'm not there by four, come pound on my door."

In her own way, Emma thought, Julianne Maroney was as tough as any Donovan.

She debated slipping into her room to rest, too, but instead went downstairs and out to the terrace. The sun was still doing its dance with the clouds, but she sat at one of the tables out in the open and called Matt Yankowski in Boston.

"How's Ireland?" Yank asked.

"I'm looking at the Celtic Sea and pink roses. Can you believe there are still a few roses in bloom here in November?"

"You didn't call to tell me about roses.

What's wrong?"

Emma noticed a pot of cyclamen and ivy close to her. "Colin and I are in the middle of a death investigation in Declan's Cross."

"Talk to me."

She filled him in. Yank didn't interrupt. When she finished, she leaned over and touched a scarlet cyclamen petal and said, "Julianne's here at the hotel, in the room next to mine." She didn't say Colin's and hers. She didn't know why. "She's a wreck but she'll rally. She's strong, smart, stubborn."

"All those good Rock Point qualities," Yank said.

"Spirited, too."

Yank sucked in a breath. "The dead woman. Lindsey Hargreaves. Did she fall, Emma?"

She took in the quiet November landscape with its mix of colors — green, gold, copper, pinks and purples. Down the sloping garden lawn, more pale pink cyclamen were massed, naturalized, under an oak. She thought of Lindsey Hargreaves sprawled on the rocks, practically in the shadow of the trio of Celtic crosses, and shook her head as if Yank were sitting across the table from her. "No, Yank. Lindsey Hargreaves didn't fall."

"What can I do?"

"Find out more about the Hargreaves family."

"Done."

She clicked off her phone and slid it into the pocket of her leather jacket. She wondered if the gardai had located David Hargreaves yet and notified him about his daughter. If Kitty O'Byrne and her son knew of the tragedy up on Shepherd Head. Kitty hadn't been at the reception desk when Julianne had checked in.

And Brent Corwin and Eamon Carrick. What about them?

Emma's grandfather had returned her call last night. Nothing new on their Declan's Cross thief. Not in months. Wendell Sharpe was inclined to attribute Julianne Maroney's trip to the pretty village to a tangled set of coincidences.

What would he say now that Lindsey was dead?

Emma decided to tell her brother first. Lucas was back in Heron's Cove, where he ran Sharpe Fine Art Recovery, after an intense brain-dump with their grandfather in Dublin in October. Now that he was turning over the reins to Lucas, he'd felt compelled to tell him secrets and insights that weren't in the files. Emma agreed with her brother that their grandfather had undoubtedly left out a few secrets. Probably more than a few.

After their consultation, he had set out to the southwest Irish coast for his "walk-about." Emma had been terrified he was sick, but he'd looked as healthy and lively as ever when she'd seen him right after she'd arrived in Ireland, before making her way to Finian Bracken's cottage and Colin.

Lucas was appropriately shocked when Emma told him about Lindsey Hargreaves. "I haven't told Granddad yet," she added. "He's still in Killarney, but he plans to return to Dublin soon."

"For how long?"

"I don't know. He says he wants to be in Heron's Cove for Thanksgiving."

"He can only go so long without your apple pie," Lucas said, but she could hear the strain in his voice. "It's just . . ."

Emma finished for him. "It's just that we're worried about him. He's been telling us he wants to spend more time in Heron's Cove now that he's cut back on work, but I don't know."

"I think it's a tougher transition than he expected." Lucas bit off a sigh. "I'm sorry to hear about this woman, Emma. What can I do to help?"

"Find out if she was in Rock Point because of us."

" 'Us' meaning —"

"The Sharpes," Emma said.

"All right. Understood."

"Anything unusual, Lucas — any hint that our thief followed Lindsey to Rock Point, or that he's in Maine, that he's been watching you — that he's been watching Granddad —"

"I hear you."

They talked for another minute, and when Emma disconnected, she settled back in her chair. She felt the cool breeze on her face and listened to the sound of distant birds as she let her mind drift back not quite ten years. She'd come to Dublin to visit her grandfather. It had been springtime — her school vacation. She'd wanted to talk to him about college choices and majoring in art history. She'd planned to work at Sharpe Fine Art Recovery. Only later did that change.

Her grandfather — tall, rangy like Lucas — had been preoccupied. *"I have a thief I can't catch, Emma,"* he'd finally told her over tea in his back garden. *"He's going to strike again. There's no question in my mind."*

"Is he violent, Granddad?"

His incisive blue eyes had raised to her.

"Not yet."

A rabbit hopped across the lawn below the O'Byrne terrace, and Emma got up, wondering if the thief had stood in this very spot. If only the stones and bushes could talk. The rabbit paused and stared at her. "And the rabbits, too," Emma said with a smile.

She decided to call her grandfather from in front of the fire, and as she headed to the French doors, she noticed that her rabbit had disappeared under a hydrangea.

13

Colin had been involved in more death investigations in his marine patrol days than he cared to remember, and he suspected Sean Murphy had been involved in his share, too. The gardai were still on scene, doing the painstaking work of documenting Lindsey Hargreaves' last minutes. Sean had accepted Colin's offer to drop him off. The Murphy farmhouse was warm, cozy and old — not as old as Fin Bracken's Kerry cottage but old enough.

"It's my uncle's house," Sean said as they entered the kitchen. "He and my aunt never had children. She's gone to God now. I was raised in the bungalow where Julianne is staying. Paddy and I turned it into a holiday home a few years ago."

"Your uncle's the old guy on the decrepit tractor?"

Sean smiled. "That's him. He's gone home now."

"He doesn't live here?"

"He has an apartment in the village." Sean lifted a bottle of Kilbeggan 18 off the top shelf of an old-fashioned hutch, its pine wood painted dark green. "Whiskey?"

"I'll wait, thanks."

He placed the Kilbeggan on the table in the center of the kitchen and got down a glass from an open shelf. "Let me know if you change your mind." He set the glass on the table and uncorked the bottle. "They say FBI agents are on the job all the time. Rather like farmers, wouldn't you say? Something we have in common, then."

Colin couldn't read the Irishman's mood. "I suspect we have more in common than that. How long have you been on leave?"

"June. Injured on the job. I'm more farmer these days than garda." He splashed whiskey into his glass and raised it to Colin. *"Sláinte."*

Colin glanced around at the mishmash of shelves and cupboards, the scarred pine table, unmatched painted chairs, pots and pans on hooks, dog dishes by a back door. Practical, functional. An old range that looked as if it was a heat source as well as a place to cook occupied the arch of the original fireplace.

He debated pulling out a chair and having a seat, but he was restless, didn't plan on sticking around for long. He said, "Fin Bracken's been instructing my brothers and me in whiskey."

"No ice."

"Fin's first rule of whiskey. How do you two know each other?"

Sean swallowed some of his drink. "It's a long story. We're good friends. That's what matters."

And all he needed to know from the Irishman's point of view. Colin watched him set his glass back on the table, recork the Kilbeggan and put it back on its shelf.

Colin recognized Garda Murphy's faraway look. "You investigated the deaths of Fin's wife and daughters."

Sean gave a curt nod and picked up his whiskey glass again. He didn't take a drink. "It's been seven years. Hard to believe. You wouldn't have taken Fin for a priest then." He polished off the rest of his drink. "It was an awful time."

Colin said nothing.

Sean took his glass to a deep, white porcelain sink. "Fin's settling into Maine?"

"It hasn't been dull."

"He told me he was looking for dull, but I never believed him. He emailed me over the weekend about Julianne — that one of his parishioners was on her way to Declan's

Cross and needed a place to stay."

"She jumped at the chance to work on this marine science field station."

"As you saw, it's an old garage and now likely to stay that way," Sean said. "Fin was surprised at how fast Julianne acted. She met Lindsey last week, decided to fly to Ireland, booked her flights. It was done."

"Sounds like Julianne. Was Fin worried about her?"

"Not that I could tell. Fin's aware of the theft here ten years ago. That's not unusual. Many people in Ireland are aware of it."

"Did Lindsey show any interest in the theft?"

"Not to me, no."

"Did you suggest she look up Fin while she was back home?"

Sean peeled off his jacket and hung it on a peg by the door. "I didn't, no, and I don't know who did."

"Kitty O'Byrne?" Colin asked.

"I gave my answer."

"Lindsey drove down here from Dublin on Monday and was obviously up this way at some point. You didn't see her, hear anything unusual? Dog barking, a car —"

"No."

"That was a fast answer."

"I'd remember."

Colin knew he was pushing his luck, but that didn't stop him. "What about your uncle?"

"He'd remember, too," Sean said, no irritation in his voice despite his curt responses.

"Your garda pals talked to him."

"Yes, they did."

Colin hadn't talked to the uncle himself. "Paddy, right? Padraig. My mother says she wanted to name me Padraig, but my father wouldn't go for it. Patrick would have worked."

Sean scoffed, a spark of amusement in his eyes. "You're making that up."

"No, I'm serious. Well, maybe it was Seamus. Something Irish. They settled on Colin, but I don't think my father ever really liked it. He told me he wanted to name me Tom. So, your uncle grew up in this house?"

"Yes. He and my father."

"And now you're the farmer," Colin said with more than a trace of skepticism. "Hell of a day, Garda Murphy — or should I say Farmer Murphy?"

"Sean will do."

"That little hollow with the Celtic crosses and the ruins and the wild greenery and wild winds — quite a spot. Makes me wonder if Julianne did hear a banshee this

239

morning. Her grandmother's comfortable with the idea of the wee folk."

"And you, Agent Donovan?"

Colin grinned back at the Irishman. "Not so much."

Sean rinsed out his glass in the sink. No doubt he had farm work to do, but he didn't suggest Colin be on his way. "Julianne strikes me as a sensible, modern woman."

"Modern, anyway."

"You know her well?"

"We're both from Rock Point." Colin wasn't interested in being questioned. "Did you notice anything at the scene that suggests Lindsey was murdered?"

"If I did, I don't know that I'd tell you, Special Agent Donovan." Sean grabbed a threadbare, stained towel and dried his hands. "I understand it's tempting to get involved, but there's no role for the FBI in this investigation. Lindsey's father can contact the U.S. State Department if he wishes. They'll coordinate with Irish authorities."

"What you're saying is that I should book that couple's massage after all?"

Sean gave the slightest smile. "I expect you've done worse."

"I'll spare you the trouble of finding out about me the hard way. Call Matt Yankowski in Boston. He can tell you about Emma, too." Using a Bic pen almost out of ink, Colin jotted down Yank's number on the back of an envelope on the table. "You'll like him. He'll want us to mind our own business, too."

"It's not my investigation, either."

"That doesn't mean you won't be calling Yank, does it?"

The Irishman didn't answer. "I have some work I have to do."

"Farm work or garda work?"

"Do you have a farm, Special Agent Donovan?"

"I used to be a lobsterman. One of my brothers is a lobsterman. That's about as close as we get to farming. And you can call me Colin now that we've scaled a seaside Irish cliff together."

"Do you have an affinity for the ocean as I do for the land?"

"Probably not."

That brought a real smile. "An honest man."

"Blunt, anyway. I gather your uncle still works the farm."

"He's up here most days. He's a good man, Colin."

"Would I have heard otherwise?"

"It's a small village. You can hear anything,

I suppose." The smile was gone now. "Any more questions?"

"Do you have any other help?"

"When the work's more than Paddy and I can do on our own we hire out. That's not often."

"Any other family nearby?"

"A younger sister. My mother. My father is gone now."

"You're not married?"

"Not yet."

His look suggested a past, but Colin knew he'd worn out his welcome. If he'd had whiskey, he might have been able to fit in a few more questions. He zipped up his jacket and glanced out the window. It was raining. He'd learned to take Irish rain as it came. A few minutes, a few hours, a few days.

"What kind of farm work are you off to now?" he asked.

Sean shrugged. "I've time to finish up spraying the rams in the pens for foot rot."

"Foot rot. Good luck with that. I don't think I'd make much of a farmer. I've sidestepped a lot of sheep dung since I arrived in Ireland." He walked over to the door that led to a narrow front entrance, then turned back to the Irishman. "Why don't you tell me what you know about the theft at the O'Byrne place?"

"And what would I know?"

"Were you garda then?"

Sean nodded as he kicked off his trail shoes and slipped into muddy Wellies.

"Were you in Declan's Cross that night?" Colin asked.

"Kitty has an excellent selection of whiskey. Fin helped her with it. It's been a long day already. Give my best to Julianne. Please let her know she's welcome at the cottage as my guest if and when she wants to return."

He shut down further conversation by pulling open the back door.

Colin didn't blame him. "How do you decide which sheep get to live to a ripe old age and which ones end up as lamb chops?"

"Economic necessity for the most part."

"I wouldn't want to come back as a sheep, but if I did, I'd want to be one that produces wool for Irish sweaters, not one that ends up served with mint sauce."

The Irishman pulled a cap off a peg and almost smiled as he turned to Colin. "I prefer a simple roast lamb myself."

Raindrops blew against the windows. Colin watched them slide down the old glass. "What do you think happened out here on Monday?"

Sean had clearly expected the question. "I

think Lindsey Hargreaves died a quick death."

"It took more than slipping on a wet rock."

"Maybe so."

"I'll leave you to your foot-rot spraying. Why just the rams? Do I want to know?"

"It's not just the rams. We separate the rams from the ewes for a few weeks this time of year. We'll be letting the rams back into the fields soon. They'll do their work, and we'll have lambs by Saint Patrick's Day."

Colin grinned. "Maybe I will come back as a sheep after all."

The rain had ended by the time Colin pulled into the parking lot at the O'Byrne House Hotel, but he didn't get out of the car right away. He'd decided against calling Fin Bracken. Too complicated, given Fin's friendship with Garda Murphy.

No point getting further under the skin of the Irish cop.

Instead he called Andy. His brother had no idea what was going on in Declan's Cross. Colin gave him the news.

"Colin. Hell." Andy took in an audible breath. "Where's Julianne now?"

"At the hotel where Emma and I are staying. Knowing Julianne, she hasn't told her family. Is Ryan still in town?"

"He left last night. I'm not telling her grandmother, Colin. I've already done enough wrong in her eyes. She won't like me knowing something before she does."

"She won't like you not telling her, either. Can't win."

"Thanks, brother," Andy said dryly.

"I'll suggest Julianne call her, but it might not go over well. Do you know anything about Lindsey Hargreaves and her visit to Rock Point?"

"Not much. I can find out."

"No. No investigating. Just tell me what you know."

"She showed up here last week. As far as I know she was alone. She stopped at Hurley's to say hi to Fin Bracken."

"She knew to look for him there?"

"I don't know. She might have just stopped to ask directions to the church and saw him. Easy to tell he's a priest."

"Good point," Colin said.

"Jules was working. They discovered a common interest in marine science. One of those 'small world' things. I guess that's harder to believe now that this woman's dead."

"You got that right. What else?"

"Lindsey said to come see her in Declan's

Cross and check out this new field station when Jules was in Ireland for her internship. Jules decided to go now."

"Then Fin put her in touch with Sean Murphy about a cottage?"

"Yeah, I guess. I don't know much. What I do know I've pieced together from what Ryan told me and what I dragged out of Jules on the way to the airport. She's not exactly talking to me right now."

Colin heard a note of regret under his brother's matter-of-fact tone but wasn't getting into his relationship with Julianne. One of those times to stick to the facts. "How did Lindsey end up deciding to stay with Julianne at the Murphy cottage?"

"Emails back and forth and Julianne invited her."

"All right. Thanks." His brother's story squared with what Colin had heard so far from Julianne, Sean Murphy and David Hargreaves. "Anything else you can think of, let me know."

"You'll keep me posted?"

"Yeah. Sure. Do you want to talk to Julianne?"

Andy didn't respond for a moment. "I don't want to make things worse for her. If that means talking to her, I'll talk to her. If it means not talking to her, I won't talk to her. You be the judge."

"Not a chance, brother. You be the judge. You're the one who crossed the great divide with Julianne Maroney."

"Thanks a lot," Andy muttered. "How's crossing the great divide with Emma working out?"

"She wants me to do the spa with her."

That idea improved his younger brother's mood. Colin disconnected and got out of the car. Rainwater dripped off holly leaves and glistened in small puddles as the sun shone through the clouds. He bypassed the hotel's front door and took a paved walkway around to the back.

When he reached the terrace, a double rainbow had arced across the sky, its colors brilliant against the shifting gray clouds. It stopped him in his tracks, pulled him out of an Irish investigation into the tragic death of an American woman. Who wouldn't want to come here? Julianne had no reason to think she'd have anything but a great two weeks in Declan's Cross. If she'd come here to heal her broken heart, make an emotional fresh start and prepare for her Irish internship in January — what could make more sense? Who was he to question her?

The rainbow brightened even more. He'd seen a lot of rainbows, but this one got to him. The Emma Sharpe effect, he thought, entering the hotel through the French doors, just as Wendell Sharpe's serial thief — Emma's thief — had ten years ago.

Had the thief pounced on Lindsey Hargreaves' presence in Declan's Cross as an opportunity to plot another theft? She was a member of a wealthy family. It was a good bet they owned some expensive art. Maybe not a bet for the thief. Maybe he knew what art the Hargreaves family owned.

Was the thief *in* Declan's Cross? Had he learned of Lindsey's trip to Maine and decided Rock Point was too close to the Sharpes in Heron's Cove? Then how did killing her in Declan's Cross, in Ireland, make sense? Had the thief followed her to Rock Point?

Was he planning to steal art from the Hargreaves family?

What you know versus what you believe.

Anything was possible. Colin was in Sharpe territory. Art crimes weren't his area of expertise. Still, a thief was a thief, and murder was murder.

The thief hadn't been violent in the decade since his first heist in little Declan's Cross. If he'd escalated to violence and the Sharpes and FBI didn't know yet, it still didn't mean he was involved with Lindsey

Hargreaves' death.

It didn't mean he wasn't, either.

Colin entered the bar lounge. No one was there. A fire crackled in the fireplace. He could find a cozy chair and drink whiskey the rest of the day. Garda Murphy would approve. Yank probably would, too.

Colin realized he was tempted.

Who wouldn't be?

Hell.

He headed out to the stairs and up to find Emma and check on Julianne.

14

Emma wasn't normally a restless person, but she'd bounced from the terrace to the fire to her room and now was back on the terrace, at a different table from earlier. She'd spotted Kitty outside, pulling a browned, dead leaf from a vine that crawled up a trellis. Colin was upstairs in the shower. Julianne was resting in her room. A long day. An awful day.

"The gardai are talking to my son." Kitty crushed the leaf in her hand and tossed it aside. "They're at the garage Lindsey wanted to turn into her marine science research facility. I'm so sorry about her death. It's a terrible thing."

"How is Philip doing?"

"He's sad. He's in shock. He only knew her for a few weeks, but it will take time . . ." She snatched another dried leaf. "He loves diving. That will help. He knows I'm afraid of the water and tries to spare me worrying, but there's no way, is there?"

"He seems like a good kid," Emma said, sitting at a small round table, welcoming the cool air. She'd bundled up in a wool sweater.

"He might have been the last to see Lindsey alive," Kitty added, half to herself. "It was Monday afternoon, at the garage. I didn't see her myself. I was busy here all day. Well, Philip will tell the gardai what he knows, and that'll be the end of it. What can I get you?"

"Nothing, thanks. Colin says I missed a double rainbow."

"It was gorgeous, yes."

Emma wanted to ask her about David Hargreaves. Where he was, had the gardai finished talking with him, his plans now given his daughter's tragic death. But Kitty was obviously distracted and slipped back into the bar lounge, and it wasn't, technically, Emma's place to ask her anything about the investigation into the death, even of an American, on Shepherd Head.

The gardai would take their investigation step by step and only come to her about the unsolved O'Byrne art theft if warranted — if it could lead to answers about how and why Lindsey Hargreaves had died. Right now, Emma reminded herself, they had

251

nothing more than coincidences easily, if not comfortably, explained.

It was dark, overcast. The moment had passed for rainbows. Emma checked her messages, but there was still nothing from her grandfather. She'd left him another voice mail when she'd tried him earlier. He couldn't interfere with an Irish investigation any more than she could, but he didn't have Matt Yankowski to deal with if he did. Emma had known she was giving up a certain level of freedom by heading to the academy.

She wanted to talk to her grandfather because he knew Ireland better than she did, and he knew this thief.

Emma got to her feet, restless again. Maybe she'd try to just sit in front of the fire. She wondered if Colin felt like this all the time. She started for the bar lounge, but noticed the silhouette of a man down in the gardens.

David Hargreaves.

He came up the walkway and stepped onto the terrace. In the soft lamplight, he looked exhausted and grief-stricken. He'd arrived in Declan's Cross expecting to share in the excitement of his daughter's new project. Now he'd be arranging for her burial.

Emma could feel his agony. "I'm sorry for your loss, Mr. Hargreaves."

"Thank you. The police came here and gave me the news. I never did call them last night. I just thought . . ." He made a sound of pure self-disgust. "I wasn't worried enough. But it wouldn't have changed anything if I'd called. Lindsey probably fell on Monday. It was decent of them to come find me. Did you tell them I was here?"

"I didn't. Colin might have."

He nodded. "It's not a secret, of course."

Emma gestured toward the bar lounge. "Can I buy you a drink, Mr. Hargreaves?"

"David. Please." His expression softened slightly. "I'd love a drink."

They went inside. A middle-aged couple was on the love seat in front of the fire, sharing a bottle of wine. No one was at the bar. David chose a stool on the end, against the wall, but he waited for Emma to sit first. He struck her as socially awkward, which on top of his grief had to have him spinning internally, not knowing what to do, where to turn.

Instead of Kitty, an older man Emma had noticed last night took their order. David went for an expensive Scotch. Emma chose a clear, triple-distilled Bracken blend, hoping it would remind her of Finian Bracken and their whiskey sessions in Maine and help keep her grounded.

"I feel so damn helpless," David said as he stared into his whiskey. "I had planned to meet Lindsey this morning and have a look at her field station. Do you have any idea why she would have been out on Shepherd Head?"

Emma shook her head. She tried her whiskey. It'd last the evening. She wasn't much of a drinker, certainly not much of a whiskey drinker. "Tell me about your daughter," she said with a smile. "Everyone seems to agree she was a fireball of energy and loved marine mammals."

"I'm not sure I'm the right one to tell you about her." He picked up his whiskey glass. "Lindsey and I . . ." He exhaled heavily. "It doesn't matter now, does it?"

"Had you two been estranged?"

He drank some of his whiskey, shutting his eyes as he held his glass midair. Emma couldn't tell if he was debating how to answer her question — whether to answer it — or just savoring his Scotch. Finally he opened his eyes and set his glass back on the bar. He leveled his gaze on her, more awkward, she thought, than direct.

"Yes," he said finally, abruptly. "You could say we were estranged. She was already five when I came into her life. I adopted her. Her mother didn't ask me to, but I was thrilled to be a father. Lindsey's father. She was a sweet, bubbly child. After her mother and I divorced — well, it was a difficult time. Lindsey was thirteen. Her mother struggled in life."

"Did they live close to you?"

"On and off. Cynthia, Lindsey's mother, liked to move around. We lost touch. Then in July, Lindsey knocked on my door, so to speak."

"Where do you live?"

"Near Gloucester. The North Shore of Boston. I wanted to do what I could to help Lindsey get on her feet. She took a job at the Oceanographic Institute and lived in the guesthouse — her choice." He touched the rim of his glass. "She was a hard worker, Special Agent Sharpe."

Emma wasn't surprised he knew she was a federal agent. Despite his reserved manner, she suspected David Hargreaves made a point of knowing what was going on around him.

"Cynthia died when Lindsey was eighteen," he said quietly. "It's hard to believe it's been ten years. That's part of why Lindsey reconnected with me. She said she'd suddenly realized how much time had passed. She said she wanted to impress me. Prove herself. I told her that wasn't necessary."

"Unconditional love," Emma said.

"Exactly. She said she wanted to measure up as a Hargreaves. I don't even know what that means. Maybe it's something her mother told her."

"If she had a job, how did she end up diving in Scotland, then coming here?"

"Scotland was part of her job, or at least her job as she saw it. She worked in the events office and, as a diver herself, wanted to create a series of diving events. One of them was in Scotland."

"When was this?" Emma asked.

He glanced sideways at her. "Now you do sound like a federal agent," he said with a smile. "Lindsey left for Scotland in mid-September. That's where she met Brent Corwin. By the first of October, she'd quit her job at the Institute to devote herself to diving. She and Brent moved on to Declan's Cross. He's far more experienced, but her enthusiasm —" David broke off, his shoulders slumping as he drank more of his whiskey.

"From what I gather, this is a good area for diving," Emma said.

He recovered his composure. "She loved

it here. She hated to leave, but she wanted to get things started to secure funding for the field station. That's why she came home last week."

Emma waited for him to go on, but he didn't. "Were you surprised she took a day to go up to southern Maine?"

"Not under the circumstances. I'm not the best communicator. I wasn't happy about her quitting her job, of course, but I wanted this field station to work out. I'm afraid I wasn't as outwardly enthusiastic about Lindsey's project as she wanted me to be. I asked questions. I expressed concerns. It was out of a desire to help. She took off to Maine for the day." Blinking rapidly, he looked across the bar lounge toward the dark gardens and sea. "Did you notice the double rainbow earlier?"

"I missed it," Emma said.

"When I saw it, it was as if Lindsey were telling me she was okay. At peace." He cleared his throat and turned back to his whiskey. "She reminds — she reminded me so much of her mother and the good days we had together. Cynthia was everything I'm not. Vivacious, outgoing. Artistic. She was a painter. Strictly amateur but she loved it. And she loved people. Well, I do, too, of course, but I'm more selective, more reclusive. Finally that drove us apart. The divorce wasn't her fault. It was my fault. All my fault."

Emma had a dozen follow-up questions she could have asked, but she said only, "I'm truly sorry, David."

He inhaled sharply. "How's Julianne managing?"

"She's sorry about Lindsey, too."

"She's not staying at the cottage by herself, is she?"

"She's staying here tonight."

"That makes sense. Will it bother her that I'm here? I can only imagine what she's going through. I don't want to make it worse for her."

"It's decent of you to consider Julianne's feelings, but please take care of yourself. If there's anything Colin or I can do for you, please don't hesitate to ask."

His eyes misted but he kept any tears at bay. "Thank you, Special Agent Sharpe."

He drifted into silence, and she suspected he wanted to be alone and was perhaps a little embarrassed at how much he'd told her. She left him and headed upstairs.

She knocked on Julianne's door. "It's Emma. How are you doing?"

Julianne opened the door. She had on a fresh sweater and jeans, her hair pulled back in a damp ponytail. She looked less ashen, less in shock. She managed a quick smile. "I've had a bath, cried, looked at the view, cried some more. Then Andy called." She sighed. "It's annoying how good it was to hear his voice."

"Understandable, don't you think?"

"That doesn't make it less annoying. I'll put some color on my cheeks and meet you downstairs. I need that whiskey."

Emma could see it wouldn't take much to push Julianne from rallying, annoyed with Andy Donovan, to the edge of despair. "I'll meet you downstairs."

Julianne nodded, then shut the door. Emma continued down to her room. Colin was there with a thick white hotel towel wrapped around his waist.

He was so damn sexy. Solid, earthy, utterly reliable.

"Long day," she said.

He swept her into his arms. His skin was warm from the shower. She sank into his chest, wrapped her arms around him and breathed in the smell of his aftershave, the soap, the sea air coming in through the cracked window.

He kissed the top of her head. "How are you, Emma?"

"I'm glad we're here given what's happened, but I wish it hadn't happened."

"And Julianne? How is she?"

"Better. Calmer."

"If she gets sweet and sugary with me, we know she's going into shock and it's time to call the paramedics." He tightened his hold on her. "She should be enjoying Ireland, and we should be at the spa."

"At least we're here and she's not alone."

"I hate that this has happened."

Emma raised her head and kissed him softly. "I love you, Colin. You're a good man."

He grinned. "Would you be saying that if you'd caught me dressed instead of in a towel?"

"Imagine if I'd caught you in no towel."

Emma smoothed her hands down his hips, feeling his hard muscles through the towel. It would be so easy to whisk it off and fall to the bed together.

He drew her against him. "Why do I get the feeling you're about to tell me Julianne is waiting for us at the bar?"

She kissed him, then smiled. "Julianne is waiting for us at the bar."

He was dressed in two minutes, also sexy in his dark sweater and pants. He tossed his cast-off towel into the bathroom. "We have iron willpower, don't we, Special Agent

Sharpe?"

She laughed, and realized how keyed up she'd been. On their way downstairs, she told him about her chat with David Hargreaves. "He's torn up about Lindsey's death, clearly, but they didn't have an easy relationship. Her mother was a painter. I'd like to know more about that. At the same time, I don't want to muddy waters that don't need muddying."

"It's also not our investigation."

"Maybe not," she said.

Colin slowed his pace. "Emma."

She knew she didn't have to explain to him that if an international serial art thief was involved in whatever was going on in Declan's Cross, then it was very much her investigation. But that was a leap she couldn't make yet, and wouldn't without discussion with the gardai.

They found Julianne curled up in front of the fire, staring at the flames. David Hargreaves was no longer at the bar. The couple had disappeared. It was so quiet. Just the crackle of the fire.

Julianne managed a faltering smile. "What a couple of lovebirds you two are. Whiskey by the fire, you think?"

"Sounds like a plan," Colin said.

Kitty breezed in from the front hall. "You

can stay right where you are all evening if that suits you. We'll serve you dinner here, or anything else you'd like. We have a beautiful tomato bisque tonight with bits of blue cheese."

Colin sat in a soft-cushioned chair and grinned up at Kitty. "I've never had blue cheese in my tomato soup, but I'm game."

His irreverence obviously didn't faze her. "You'll love it. We'll keep the fire hot while you relax. Don't hesitate to ask for anything you need. Anything at all."

Emma found herself liking the owner of the O'Byrne House Hotel. "I had whiskey earlier, but Julianne and Colin might want to dip into your Bracken 15."

"No 'might' about it," he said.

Julianne nodded in agreement, and Kitty said, "Perfect," and bustled off, clearly less preoccupied than when Emma had talked to her on the terrace. Philip must have finished talking to the gardai.

There was definitely more color in Julianne's cheeks, some no doubt due to the heat of the fire, some to her makeup, some to time. "So, what happened ten years ago?" she asked. "Did the thief break in through the French doors, or weren't they here back then?"

"They were here," Emma said, "but this

place was quite different."

"Can you tell me about it?"

Colin leaned back. "Julianne . . ."

"Over our whiskey. I'd rather talk about an art thief than a lot of other things we could talk about. Andy, for one. We can talk about him over the tomato bisque with bits of blue cheese." Julianne swallowed. "And Lindsey." Her eyes brimmed with tears. "I don't know how we'd have done as house-mates, but I'm sorry I didn't get the chance to find out."

"So am I," Emma said.

"Me, too." Colin sat forward and winked at Julianne, obviously catching her by surprise. "Just one thing. Andy would love the tomato bisque with the blue cheese."

Julianne shook her head. "He would not."

Colin grinned. "You still have a few things to learn about him, Ms. Know-it-all Maroney."

"I don't want to know anything else about him."

"Ha."

Emma smiled, even as she recognized she hadn't known the Donovan brothers as cocky teenagers, or Julianne as a bright six-year-old with a fascination for tide pools. She was an outsider in Rock Point, and as much as she loved Colin — and he loved her — she didn't know what that meant for their future together.

A question for another time.

Kitty returned with a tray with three glasses of Bracken 15 year old, a rare, peated single-malt Irish whiskey. Emma preferred the non-peated Bracken 15, but said nothing as Kitty handed her a glass. "You didn't drink much earlier. You'll be fine."

Emma thanked her. She handed Julianne and Colin their glasses and withdrew.

Julianne held her glass and smiled through fresh tears. *"Sláinte."*

15

The rain had let up when Sean walked into the village after supper. He knew everyone in Declan's Cross and could easily distinguish local from stranger. He cut down to the would-be field station and found Eamon Carrick packing his gear into a rusted hatchback.

Eamon stood straight, a lock of fair hair falling into his face. Between his good looks, easy manner and diving skills, he had no trouble attracting women. Keeping one was another matter. "Hello, Sean. I thought I might be gone before you worked your way down here. This is terrible. I never expected it." He shut the back of the car with more force than was necessary. "Brent's taking Lindsey's death hard. Philip, too. You just missed them both."

"Where are you off to now?"

"Dublin." Eamon gave a ragged smile. "Before Ronan drives down and drags me back. My garda brother is apoplectic I'm mixed up in a death investigation."

"I can't say I blame him."

"I can't, either, to be honest. I didn't have much to tell the gardai, but I said what I knew. Any word from the medical examiner on the cause of death?"

"Not yet."

"I only knew Lindsey a few weeks, but I never saw her drink to excess, or use drugs. I doubt they'll find anything like that contributed to her death. She wasn't on medication that I know of. Just an ordinary, healthy young woman."

Sean peeked in the back of the car. Eamon had heaped his diving gear in with his personal things — clothes, boots, waterproofs. "Did Hargreaves Oceanographic Institute hire you to do any diving for them?"

Eamon shook his head, matter-of-fact. "I've done some research dives for them in the past, but this has been all for fun, at least as far as I was concerned. I've come down when I could. Weekends, mostly. Brent Corwin knows his stuff. Lindsey did, too, although she wasn't as experienced." He nodded at the abandoned garage. "I'd hoped this place would work out."

Diving was a passion for Eamon, not a

career. He taught diving, but it was his Dublin pub that paid the bills. He'd never been interested in law enforcement, joining the garda underwater unit like his brother. Eamon liked to choose when and where he went under water, and he preferred to search for sunken treasure or photograph fish than go after a missing person.

Ronan had helped recover the remains of Sally Bracken and her two young daughters. Eamon wouldn't have survived such an ordeal. Ronan barely had. Sean hadn't done any diving, but he'd led the death investigation. He and Ronan had agreed that however invaluable training was, it could only do so much to prepare anyone for the reality of what they sometimes had to do — see — in their work. Ronan had said he coped by knowing he'd helped find answers. Knowing the good he'd done always got him back into the water after a grisly scene.

"The gardai know where to reach you?" Sean asked.

Eamon nodded. "They do. Ronan would tell them if I didn't, so no worries." He looked up at the black sky, then turned to Sean, the emotional pain in his face impossible to miss even in the shadows. "I don't like to think she died alone up there, or that she was murdered. I'd rather find out she was drunk and went to God without knowing what happened."

"It'll be what it'll be, Eamon."

"Yes," he said heavily. "So it will."

Eamon was a gentle soul, if also as fit and tough as any diver Sean had ever seen. Ronan did what he had to do to be able to do his underwater work, but he wasn't as dedicated to fitness as his younger brother — nor as affable. Given Eamon's experience as a diver and having Ronan as a brother, he would know to follow evidence and try to avoid rabbit trails to nowhere.

Sean said good-night and turned back toward the village. The young couple who owned the bookshop were locking up and waved to him. They had three children under the age of four. Their children's section was second to none, and the shop had become a popular stop for children's authors. Another life, Sean thought as he waved back and continued on to the heart of the village. Paddy would be at his favorite pub. He'd seen his share of tragedy in his day, but this morning had been hard on him. Sean wanted to check on him.

As he crossed at an intersection just past the O'Byrne House Hotel, he could hear a commotion around the corner. Shouting, cursing. He tensed, immediately on alert.

Moving fast, he turned up the street and was at the pub just as two men burst out the front door, one tripping, catching himself before he could fall flat on his face. He spun around and grabbed the other man, flailing wildly.

Sean gritted his teeth.

Philip.

The lad was the one flailing wildly, pummeling — or at least trying to pummel — Brent Corwin, the second man, who had him by the shoulders. It didn't look as if many of Philip's blows were connecting with his intended targets. Mostly he was hitting thin air.

Sean jumped into the fray and hauled Philip off the American. "Settle down," he said sharply. "Do it now, Philip. Right now."

Philip was red-faced, angry, his emotions high. "Go to hell."

Sean tightened his grip on Philip's lower arm, ready to jerk it around to the small of his back and really get his attention. "Settle down. I'm not saying it again."

Brent, breathing hard, put up a hand. "Sorry, Garda Murphy. He's upset. It was nothing. No harm done."

"I lost my temper," Philip said, more sullen than apologetic.

"Not a problem. We've all had a rough

day." Brent nodded toward the pub entrance, the door still open. "I'll be inside."

Sean waited for him to go in before he released Philip, who scowled and stalked off. "Not so fast," Sean said.

Philip didn't so much as glance back at him. "I have to work."

"At the hotel?"

No answer.

"Philip."

He huffed and turned around, walking backward. "Yes. The hotel. Anything else, Garda Murphy?"

Sean shook his head. "Go on."

Philip's mother would be there. Kitty would do the lad more good than Sean would right now.

He noted that he felt no pain at all after pulling Philip off his diver friend. One good thing about this day, Sean supposed. His last fight had been with his armed smugglers. The bastards.

He went into the pub. It was a light crowd for a Wednesday evening. A few couples were at tables, and two-thirds of the stools at the curved bar were filled.

One of Paddy's longtime friends was pouring drinks and didn't look ruffled by the altercation. "A pint?" he asked.

Sean nodded. At the far end of the bar,

his uncle was seated next to Colin Donovan. Brent Corwin was on the FBI agent's other elbow, a fresh pint in front of him. Obviously not his first of the evening.

Sean took his pint down the bar and joined them, standing between his uncle and Colin.

Brent was addressing the FBI agent. "You look like the sort who knows a thing or two about dead bodies. What should I call you? Agent Donovan?"

"That works."

Brent yawned, then shook his head as if trying to counter the effects of the alcohol he'd consumed. "I should probably stick to water or Coke." He shoved his pint aside. "Damn. I'm going to miss Lindsey. I feel sorry for Julianne, too. How does an FBI agent end up knowing a marine biologist?"

"Same hometown," Colin said.

Paddy glanced up from his Guinness but said nothing. He didn't need to. His expression said it all. An inebriated diver, a suspicious FBI agent and now a suspicious garda — not a good combination.

"Have you run into Lindsey's father at the hotel?" Brent asked. "He's in Declan's Cross, you know."

Colin nodded. "We met last night."

Sean took a proper gulp of his pint. He'd

eaten a few bites of leftover stew before heading into the village, his first food since breakfast. "You mentioned you don't know why Lindsey visited Father Bracken. Did she tell you she planned to go to Maine while she was home in New England?"

Brent shrugged. "Not really. She wasn't a planner, you know?"

"Father Bracken serves a small church in Rock Point, Maine. It's a struggling fishing village." Sean was aware of Colin Donovan's scrutiny, but the FBI agent didn't interrupt. "Do you see Lindsey making a special trip to Rock Point just to see an Irish priest?"

"I don't know Maine that well," Brent said. "I've done some diving there, but it's been a few years. I don't know what Lindsey had in mind. Maybe she needed to blow off some steam and visiting this priest friend of yours was just something to do."

Sean supposed it could be the case, but it didn't feel right. "Rock Point is close to Heron's Cove and the Sharpes."

"The Sharpes?" Brent scrunched up his face as if he were having difficulty keeping track of the conversation. "Am I supposed to know them?"

It was the FBI agent who responded. "Sharpe Fine Art Recovery is based in Heron's Cove."

"Never heard of it. Did Lindsey — Wait." Brent pointed a finger at Colin. "Your sidekick. Isn't her name Sharpe?"

"Special Agent Emma Sharpe," Sean said. "Her grandfather is a renowned art detective in Dublin."

Brent frowned. "I know less about art than I do about marine science. I dive. That's it." He left a few euros on the bar, then started out, but stopped and turned to Sean. "Look, sorry about earlier. Don't hold it against Philip, okay?"

Sean made no comment, and Brent left, unsteady on his feet, perhaps more so than he would recognize or admit. Diners looked up from their drinks and plates, watched him leave. The fight with Philip would have been enough to get their attention, but word of the death of a woman on Shepherd Head would have spread throughout Declan's Cross by now.

Paddy raised his head from his pint and sighed. "You two lads can make a man sweat."

Sean grinned. "That's the idea, Paddy."

"FBI. Garda." The old man grunted. "You're a suspicious lot."

Colin obviously took no offense. "A woman just turned up dead on the Irish coast. It's got my attention."

"Are you two thinking it's got something to do with the theft at the O'Byrne place? That was a long time ago. I met the grandfather then. Wendell Sharpe." Paddy tapped his neck above his frayed shirt collar. "He wore a bow tie."

Sean stood up from his stool. His uncle had been ruminating over his pint. The effects of the Guinness had nothing to do with it. It was simply how Padraig Murphy was. All those years farming, working alone in the fields and barn with only sheep and wee folk to keep him company. That was what Sean had always figured, anyway.

"I didn't know the Sharpes ten years ago," Colin said.

Paddy looked up from his empty glass. "I'll spare you asking. I've never lied to anyone about what happened that night. Not to John O'Byrne, not to the gardai — not to Wendell Sharpe."

"Let's go, Paddy," Sean interrupted, clapping a hand on his uncle's shoulder. "I'll walk you home."

No question Paddy was reluctant to leave the warm pub and the company of an American FBI agent — even one as hardnosed as Colin Donovan — but Sean managed to get him out into the sea-tinged night air.

Paddy pulled a wool cap out of his jacket pocket and put it on. "Philip was taken with the dead woman. Poor lad. No wonder he got into a fight."

"What precipitated it?" Sean asked.

"Nothing to speak of. The American diver said they'd be shutting down the field station now, no choice given what's happened. He said Eamon Carrick's already gone home to Dublin. Philip took exception, and next thing, fists were flying."

"Just Philip's fists or Brent's, too?"

"Just Philip's. Brent doesn't strike me as much of a fighter. The FBI agent almost intervened. I could see him wanting to get up and stop them, but he kept still. Disciplined. Philip was spoiling for a fight when he walked into the pub. He said Lindsey's father had a drink in the hotel bar and now he's shut himself up in his room — he's staying in the cottage on the grounds. Doesn't want to come out. Philip brought him dinner."

"Had you heard the Hargreaves name before Lindsey arrived in Declan's Cross?"

The old man shook his head. "Why would I have?"

"It was just a question."

"No, it wasn't. Nothing's 'just a question' with you. What are you thinking?"

Sean gave him an easy smile. "I'm thinking a lot of things that probably won't amount to anything."

"It's been a sad day, Sean. A sad day."

"I know, Paddy."

"No one's done anything wrong. What happened — it was an accident."

Sean said nothing.

"I don't know why you and your friends didn't break your necks out there when you were boys," Paddy said, half to himself. "I don't know why I didn't. I wish we'd found the body instead of that poor girl. Do you think we would have if we'd gone out to fix that fence a few minutes earlier?"

"It's possible. If we'd spotted Lindsey's car, we would have."

"To think she was lying out there . . ." Paddy shuddered, then eyed Sean. "You look as if you have the weight of the world on your shoulders."

"Do I?"

"Means you're ready to go back to work."

"We need to get the rams back out to the fields."

"Not that work. Garda work."

Sean didn't respond. It wasn't a subject for tonight. He left Paddy at his apartment and debated what to do next. Back up to the farm, back to the pub or take his life in his hands and head to the O'Byrne House Hotel?

The hotel won. He'd known it would.

Kitty was alone in the bar lounge, not even a guest warming up by the fire. She was polishing glasses, looking preoccupied, but not so much so that she didn't notice Sean take a seat at the bar. She flung around at him, a glass in one hand and a damp cloth in the other. "What do you know about Philip and this woman who's died?" Her blue eyes flashed with the intensity of a worried mother. "He's heartbroken, angry. He came in all red in the face. He says he ran into you at the pub."

"He needs to settle down, Kitty. A good night's sleep will help."

She slammed down the glass. A wonder it didn't break. "What about you and this woman? She was going to stay up at your cottage. Did she fancy you, Sean? Did you break her heart?"

He settled back against the cushioned stool. "Think I'm a killer now, do you, Kitty O'Byrne? Or did I just drive this woman to suicide with my heartless ways?"

"I'm sorry." She blanched, picked up another glass. "I don't know why I said that. What would you like to drink?"

"Just water."

"We're all upset. This field station . . . this woman, Lindsey . . ." Kitty shook her head as she set down her cloth and filled the glass with water. "Philip should spend time with friends his own age."

"He needs to tell the gardai everything, Kitty."

She bristled, stood back. "The gardai? You're one yourself. And he has nothing to hide. He's told them what he knows. Which is nothing." She set the water glass down hard in front of Sean. "Lemon, lime?"

"This is fine, thanks."

"Do you have to be so blasted calm? I wish Philip didn't have to be a part of this tragedy."

Her son emerged from the back room, looking shaken as he stood next to his mother. "I'll still dive," he said. "No matter what."

Kitty moaned and spun into the back room herself, muttering about having work to do.

Sean wished now he hadn't come, but he drank some of his water and eyed Philip. "Diving's an expensive hobby. You'll be wanting to think about what's next for you."

"I'm not worried," he said, stubborn. "You shouldn't be, either."

"It's easy for trouble to find someone looking for it."

Philip snatched up Kitty's abandoned polishing cloth. "Maybe you're the one looking for trouble."

"You're bored in Declan's Cross," Sean said.

"So are you."

Getting far with this, he was, Sean thought as he set his glass on the bar. "Are you going to your father's wedding?"

Philip slapped the cloth into the sink, clearly caught off guard by the question. "I don't know when it is."

"How do you like the woman he's marrying?"

"She's all right. I'm glad he's happy. I wish my mother —" He stopped. "Never mind. I've work to do, too."

"Philip, you were up at my cottage on Monday. You helped Paddy clean up, get it ready for Lindsey and her friend from Maine. Did you see her?"

"I answered all the questions the gardai asked —"

"I'm gardai. I'm asking you a question."

He reddened. "I told you I saw her at the field station."

"Now I'm asking about the cottage."

"Why?"

"Because Julianne Maroney found Lindsey down the lane from there and because you just got into a fight for no reason —"

"A woman dying's no reason?"

"It's a reason for grief and prayer, perhaps an extra pint. Not for a fight."

Philip fingered the cloth in the sink, staring at it as if it were the most important thing in the world. "I wasn't at the cottage when I saw her. I was walking down from your place — from the barn. Lindsey was getting into her car. She left. I didn't talk to her."

"Which direction did she go, Philip?"

He looked as if he wanted to vomit. "Out the lane. Toward the old cemetery. I didn't think a thing of it. Her car was pointed in that direction. I assumed she'd turn around. Even if she didn't know the lane dead-ends, I figured she'd find out. Sean —"

"What time was this?" he asked, deliberately interrupting.

"After I saw her at the garage — three o'clock, maybe. I got to work cleaning the cottage. I don't remember her driving back down the lane, but I didn't think about it."

"Did she seem to be in a hurry, preoccupied?"

Philip shook his head. "I couldn't say."

Sean suddenly had no interest in his water

but resisted ordering a pint or a whiskey. "You need to tell the gardai who interviewed you. You know how to reach them?"

He nodded, turning on the water in the sink and soaking the cloth. "I didn't lie to them. I just didn't think of seeing Lindsey up at the cottage."

"If you remember anything else, you let the gardai know immediately. Do you understand?"

"Yeah. Yeah, I understand."

"And stay away from alcohol. It'll do you no good at a time like this."

Philip turned off the tap. The color and adrenaline from his altercation at the pub had leaked out of him. He looked young, ready to cry. He mumbled a good-night and retreated to the back room.

Kitty came out and scowled at Sean. "You're taking liberties, Sean Murphy. If you're on the job —"

"I'm always on the job, Kitty."

She picked up a fresh white cloth. "I need to hire a bar manager before we get busy in the spring," she said, more to herself than to him. She looked up, her eyes wide, catching just enough of the dim light to bring out the flecks of pure white. "I didn't want anything to happen to Lindsey, but I hoped she'd get bored with Declan's Cross and move on."

"That's understandable," Sean said.

Kitty started cleaning the small sink with her new cloth, scrubbing as if whatever dirt or bit of grime she was after would never come out. "Philip isn't happy here," she blurted.

Sean didn't disagree. "Does he want to go back to Dublin?"

"I don't know that he'd be happy there, either. His dad would have him live with him. He and his fiancée have been together for years. It's good they're getting married." Kitty took in a deep breath, let go of her cloth and stood straight, her cheeks flushed. "Life is full of change. Philip will get used to it. We all do."

"He'll want to live on his own soon."

"When he's ready. He's not yet. He's so restless. We have family in the States who'd have him. He could work there awhile, then come home. But he needs more education — and he can't leave his skin behind, can he? That's the problem. He's not happy in his own skin." She rubbed her hands together, her fingers slender, red from her scrubbing. She raised her eyes. "You know what that's like, don't you, Sean?"

He wasn't going there. Not tonight, and not with Kitty O'Byrne Doyle. He stood and grinned at her. " 'I have spread my dreams under your feet,' " he said, quoting William Butler Yeats. " 'Tread softly because you tread on my dreams.' "

Kitty gave him another scowl. "Poetry. Just what I need."

But there was color high in her cheeks and fire in her eyes as Sean left, going out to the terrace. He took the walkway to the back gate, as glad for cool weather as he'd ever been. Emotions were running high, including his own. A young woman's life cut short. He didn't like that Lindsey had planned to stay at his cottage — that she'd been to Maine to see Fin Bracken and had brought Julianne Maroney and ultimately two FBI agents, one of them a Sharpe, to Declan's Cross.

Quoting Yeats to his ex-lover. Flippant or not, what the devil had he been thinking?

He glanced back at the hotel, lit up against the dark sky. It was Kitty O'Byrne's fondest dream come true.

He was happy for her.

He walked down to the pub but didn't go in. Through the front window he could see that Brent Corwin had returned and was at the bar with an older man. Lindsey's father, at a guess. The two men seemed quiet, emotions banked as they nursed glasses of whiskey.

At least David Hargreaves wasn't mourning his daughter alone.

When he reached the darkened bookshop, Sean called Ronan Carrick, who was none too thrilled to hear from him. "Blast it, Sean, what's going on there?"

"You know as much as I do."

"I doubt that. Eamon's on his way back to Dublin —"

"I saw him earlier," Sean said.

"Was he a fool, Sean, getting involved with this marine science nonsense?" Ronan didn't seem to expect an answer and continued. "I've made some calls. In layman's terms, Lindsey Hargreaves died of a broken neck."

Sean wasn't surprised. "Any other injuries?"

"Scrapes and bruises consistent with a high-impact fall onto rocks. With death so quick, they're poorly formed and will require further examination." Ronan paused, then added, "That's all preliminary and not given up to me willingly, I might add."

Sean considered his friend's words. "If she'd been knocked unconscious, she'd have died of exposure given the conditions overnight. Blood alcohol?"

"Normal."

"Then she wasn't drunk when she broke her neck."

Ronan sighed heavily. "Was she alone out there, Sean?"

"It's hard to say. With the rain and then the number of people tramping about . . ." He grimaced, picturing the scene that morning. "I don't know that we'll get a definitive answer."

"I wasn't asking for facts."

"I know you weren't, Ronan." Sean could hear a baby crying in the small house behind the bookshop. One of the shop owners' little ones, no doubt. He debated, then asked the question on his mind. "Are you satisfied Eamon isn't involved?"

"Because it's you, Sean, I won't hang up. But I won't answer you, either. How're the sheep?"

"Busy. We're letting the rams back up with the ewes. Have a good night, Ronan. Stay in touch."

Sean didn't wait for his friend to respond before disconnecting. He started up the hill toward the farm. He could hear the wind-whipped waves rolling onto the cliffs and twice started to call Finian Bracken in Maine before finally doing it.

Fin answered on the second ring. "Hello, Sean," he said, his somber tone confirmation that he'd heard about Lindsey's death.

Sean told him what he knew, chatted with him comfortably. He heard the concern in Fin's voice for Julianne Maroney, even the FBI agents, a reminder that his friend was living a different life now. Fin was no longer the grieving, raging husband and father, or the uncertain seminarian. Seven years after the unimaginable loss of his wife and daughters, he was forging a new life for himself. Sean reminded himself that they didn't know each other because Fin was a priest. They knew each other because Sean had investigated the deaths of Sally and little Mary and Kathleen Bracken.

"Are you all right, Sean?" Fin asked.

"Kitty is worried about her son."

"Does she have good reason?"

"Yes."

"Then let her worry and figure out what to do. You'll be the last person she turns to for advice. You know that, don't you, Sean?"

"Is this how you cheer up your parishioners, Fin? Blasted blinding honesty?"

"It's not my task to cheer them up," Fin said, then added with a touch of humor, "Just don't tell them that."

"After meeting your FBI friends, I don't

know that I want to visit you in Rock Point." Sean paused on the dark, quiet lane, but he knew it wouldn't help and he was still about to lose the call. "Don't go asking or looking, but if you learn anything else about Lindsey Hargreaves and her visit to Maine, you'll phone me?"

"At once."

"Good. Right now it's time for a *taoscán* of Bracken 15."

When he reached the farmhouse, Sean poured the whiskey and sat with it in front of the cold fireplace, wondering if he could live out here for decades, alone. Four months was one thing, but forty years?

He'd get himself his own sheepdog, that was one thing for sure.

And no reading Yeats on dark November nights without a woman with him.

Without Kitty.

"Blast."

He set aside his whiskey and decided to light a fire after all, just so he could stare at the flames and contemplate how Lindsey Hargreaves had broken her neck not a thirty-minute walk from where he sat.

16

Colin found Kitty in the bar lounge, drinking whiskey at a small table in the far corner by a window. Above her was a painting of a bright Irish cottage on a lonely hill. On the opposite wall, the fire had died down, its few glowing embers the only light on that side of the room. Dim track lighting was on behind the bar, but he had the feeling Kitty wanted to sit in the dark, alone with her whiskey.

Without waiting to be invited, he pulled out a chair and sat across from her. As good as he was at reading people, he didn't have a good fix on Kitty O'Byrne Doyle and her ties to her mansion-turned-hotel, or to Declan's Cross itself.

"Well, Special Agent Donovan, it's been a day, hasn't it?"

"It has."

She touched the distinctive gold Bracken Distillers label on her bottle of whiskey. She had two glasses, as if anticipating company — wanted or unwanted — and pushed one toward Colin. "Join me?"

It was more a request than an offer. He was keeping track of his alcohol consumption. He'd made his beer last at the pub. He nodded. "I will, thanks."

She reached across the table with the bottle and poured whiskey into the glass. "Fin's happy as a parish priest, do you think?"

"Seems to be. I didn't know him before he came to Rock Point. Saint Patrick's isn't the easiest parish."

"Are there any easy parishes? It's away from Ireland. That's good. It's what he needs." She added more whiskey to her glass, then set the bottle back on the table and picked up a small water pitcher. "You won't tell him I've added water to his best whiskey. He'd be shuddering for sure if he could see me. You must know how he is about water in whiskey."

"Water or ice," Colin said.

"You being an FBI agent and all that, I'm sure you're wondering how I know him — an Irish priest from Kerry who ended up in your little town in Maine." Kitty dribbled a little water into her glass. "I was at a pub here in Declan's Cross about two years ago.

We were working on this place. Fin was having a pint with Sean Murphy. They'd known each other for several years."

Colin tried some of the whiskey. "Since the deaths of Fin's wife and daughters."

She raised her gaze to him. "You're a direct man, aren't you — is it Agent Donovan, or Special Agent Donovan?"

"Colin will do. Yes, I tend to be direct."

"You've been here a little more than a day, but you think you already know more about us than we do about ourselves, don't you?"

"Not by a long shot." Colin knew she was just trying to get under his skin, if only as a way to keep her own emotions at bay. He set his glass on the polished table. The hotel, he'd noticed, was immaculate. Kitty didn't strike him as a woman who did anything by half measures. He said, "I gather your son made it home from the village all right."

Her eyes narrowed almost imperceptibly. "I'm not discussing my son with you, Colin." She leaned back in her chair. "So, let's change the subject, shall we? When are you going to make an honest woman of Emma?"

Colin matched her bluntness. "You mean marry her?"

"Propose to her. You look the type who could use a little shove. You need to get on with it. Buy her a ring, get down on one knee and ask her to marry you." Kitty drank more of her whiskey. "Do you need permission from her grandfather?"

"I doubt it."

"Her parents, then?"

"I haven't met them yet. They're in London for the year."

"Ah. So this is a whirlwind romance. What kicked it off?"

Colin traced the rim of his glass with the tip of his index finger. "We met during an investigation," he said.

"That's the short answer, isn't it?"

He smiled. "The very short answer."

"I hear her grandfather is semiretired these days. He's still in Dublin?"

"He still has an apartment in Dublin. He's in Killarney right now. He's been on a sort of walkabout."

"What is he — eighty, at least?"

"At least."

"He came to talk to me about the theft here. It was six or seven months later. I was in Dublin. At home." She recorked the Bracken 15. "He'd already talked to my uncle and decided he wanted to talk to me, too. It's hard to believe it's been ten years. He wouldn't tell me what sparked his interest in the theft. I assumed there'd been another."

"What was life like for you ten years ago?" Colin asked.

"Complicated." Her smile had a touch of mischief in it. "Quite complicated, in fact."

"Our garda sheep farmer one of the factors complicating your life then?"

"You'll ask anything, won't you? Did you learn that in the FBI, or did you come that way?"

She hadn't answered the question, and Colin could see she wasn't going to. He drank more of his whiskey. Emma had gone up to their room. She wouldn't be asleep. He knew her, knew she'd wait for him. He hoped Julianne was getting some sleep, but he wasn't about to check on her. If she wanted his help, she'd let him know — as she had that morning when she'd texted him from Shepherd Head.

He focused again on his hostess. "Did your uncle hope Wendell Sharpe would recover the missing art?"

"Of course."

"What about you and your sister?"

"We still hope the stolen works are recovered. Why, do you think we wouldn't?"

Colin shrugged. "Just asking. Your uncle never hired anyone to look into the theft?"

She sat back in her chair. "Why would he?

292

The gardai were investigating. He wasn't a suspect, if that's what you're wondering. I wasn't, either. I'm not. Aoife isn't. I've heard that people steal, or hire others to steal art for insurance purposes, but that wasn't the case here."

"But you and your sister and your uncle all got along," Colin said.

Kitty shot him a suspicious look. "Yes, of course. What are you insinuating? His wife — our aunt — died far too young. Peggy, her name was. They never had children. They bought this place thinking they would turn it into their country home. He'd done well in business in Dublin. Money wasn't a problem, at least not then. Illness was. Peggy had cancer."

"I'm sorry to hear that."

"She died when Aoife and I were small girls. Aoife barely remembers her." Kitty looked away, her eyes shining with tears. "Dear Aunt Peggy. They had such plans for the renovations, but after her death, Uncle John didn't have the heart to change a thing."

"Did he live here full-time?"

"Eventually, yes. And he loved it. He had many friends." Kitty sat up straight. "I've had more whiskey than I should, and I've said more than I should."

"It wasn't the first time and won't be the last," Colin said with a smile.

She flushed, but she returned his smile. "No doubt at all." She eyed him again. "Your friend Julianne — she's not here just because she's a marine biologist, is she? She strikes me as a woman who's fleeing a man."

"My younger brother."

Kitty looked at him as if this explained a lot. "He's not an FBI agent, too, is he?"

"Lobsterman." Colin helped himself to some of the water. "Your sister is quite an artist. Was she in Declan's Cross the night of the theft?"

"Back to that, are we? No, she was not."

"She wasn't as well-known then. Did she and your uncle argue about the paintings and the old cross that were stolen?"

Kitty's look cooled. "Not once. Why would they?" She leaned across the table. "Just because I'm drinking whiskey doesn't mean I'm off my guard. Aoife and I didn't argue with our uncle about anything except the ugliness of the wallpaper in this place. I took her side. He didn't notice such things. You'll notice the wallpaper's all gone now. Anything else, Colin?"

"What were you doing in Declan's Cross ten years ago?"

"Mourning the death of my marriage."

"But you didn't stay here at the house," Colin said. "Your uncle was in Portugal. Paddy Murphy was here. As big as this place is, he wouldn't have been in your way. The gardai must have asked you where you spent the night."

She eased to her feet, not a woman, he thought, to underestimate. "I told the gardai I stayed with a friend in the village. They never asked who. They won't ask."

"Wendell Sharpe asked," Colin said, not making it a question.

She snatched up her whiskey glass. "Night comes so early this time of year. It's not as late as I'd like to think. I've a few things I need to do before I go home."

"What happened to Sean Murphy? Why is he a farmer these days?"

"He's not a farmer. He's garda through his bones. Always has been."

"So, what happened?"

"You could find out, couldn't you? You're the FBI agent."

"I could make some calls, but no one's obligated to tell me anything."

"Or you could look on Google for 'Garda Sean Murphy,' and there it would be. He's with a special detective unit. He was ambushed in June by smugglers he was investigating."

"Hurt badly?"

"He was in bits."

An Irish expression, Colin gathered. "Did he get the smugglers?"

"Oh, yes. Always. That's Sean."

"And you two —"

"There is no 'you two.' There never was." She nodded to the bottle of Bracken 15. "It's on the house."

She went behind the bar and disappeared into the back room. Colin was tempted to move to the fire with his Bracken 15, but he noticed a movement out on the terrace.

Emma.

He left his whiskey on the table and headed outside.

Emma was sitting on a grayed-wood bench, looking out at the stars, when Colin reached her. "I slipped out the front door," she said. "I didn't want to disturb you and Kitty."

"I found her drinking whiskey alone. She has a lot on her mind. Lindsey's death has stirred up the past."

"Maybe it helped for her to talk."

"Maybe. She could also have been looking for information."

"In a suspicious mood, are you?"

He sat next to her, the dark, quiet night capturing his mood. "It's been that kind of day, Emma."

"Unfortunately, yes, it has." She placed a hand on the crook of his arm, then leaned back. She had on her thick Irish wool sweater and didn't seem cold. "David Hargreaves walked into the village a little while ago. Did you see him?"

"No."

"I can only imagine what he's going through. Julianne's worn out. We won't see her until morning."

"Good. She needs to rest."

"I'm sorry she was the one to find Lindsey. It'll help that she didn't know her that well, but if we'd just kept walking yesterday —"

"I know," Colin said. "I've been thinking the same thing. It would have been us who found Lindsey instead."

Emma fell silent as a soft, sea-tinged breeze blew back strands of her fair hair that had found their way into her face. "Did you learn anything in the village?"

"Sean Murphy and his uncle Paddy are tight. Kitty's son picked a fight with Brent Corwin. I think the kid knows something he wishes he didn't know. The Irish diver, Eamon Carrick, is on his way back to Dublin if not there already."

"His brother's a garda diver who helped

recover the bodies of Finian Bracken's family."

Colin glanced sideways at her. "You've been busy."

She shrugged. "I got to chatting with the waiter after Julianne went up to her room. Maybe Eamon's the one who mentioned Finian to Lindsey. I'm not sure it even matters now." She paused, a few raindrops sprinkling the terrace in front of them. "Sean's something of a legend in Declan's Cross."

"He was nearly killed in June."

Emma nodded. "Smugglers."

Colin slipped an arm around her. "Easy to forget out here on the Irish coast that you're a dogged FBI agent."

"Ha. Funny."

He could feel her tension and pulled her closer. "Whatever is going on here isn't about Sean Murphy's smugglers, or his friendship with Fin Bracken."

Emma leaned her head against his arm, as if they were talking about the rain and the sea breeze. Then she turned to him, her eyes luminous, intense. "After the Amsterdam theft — six months after the theft here — Granddad received a Celtic cross inscribed in black stone. It's about three inches by an inch-and-a-half."

"No note?"

"Just the cross and a leaflet about the Amsterdam museum. They were delivered in a package postmarked from Amsterdam. Impossible to trace. Granddad checked with the garda art squad."

"That led him to Declan's Cross."

She nodded. "He realized the cross he received is a copy — at least a rough copy — of the one John O'Byrne found when he installed the gardens here fifty years ago."

Colin looked out at the silhouettes and shadows of the gardens now. "Your grandfather gets a similar stone after every theft?"

"Yes."

"The thief is taunting him?"

Emma stood abruptly, the breeze steadier, colder. "It feels like taunting. Whether or not that's the thief's intention, we can't say. We just don't know enough, even after all this time."

"Sounds like you're stuck."

She almost smiled. "That sums it up. The Sharpes, the gardai, the FBI, Interpol — we're all royally stuck." Her smile faded as she looked back at the draped windows of the bar lounge. "One positive has been that the thief hasn't turned violent."

"Now we have a woman dead out by crosses just like the one he sends your grandfather," Colin said, more to anchor the facts in his own mind than to remind Emma. Every detail about this serial thief was already burned in her mind, and had been for some time. Emma secrets, Sharpe secrets and FBI secrets all rolled into one knotted ball. He put aside the thought and asked, "Does Sean Murphy have access to all the information on this thief? The different heists, the crosses. Theories, suspects."

"Only Granddad, Lucas, Yank and I know about the crosses. And the thief, of course. And now you, too." Fatigue had crept into her voice. "Now that I've met Sean, I wouldn't be surprised if he knows as much as any of us about the case. He strikes me as the type who'd find out, just as you would in a similar position."

"What about the uncle? Kitty? Her artist sister?"

"I don't think we know everything that happened in Declan's Cross that night."

Colin sensed that she was sinking into her thoughts, sorting through all the details of what she knew about her serial thief. He moved closer to her. More hair had blown into her face. He tucked a few strands behind her ear. "We'll figure this out," he said. "You're not responsible for this woman's death. Neither is your grandfather. We don't even know she was murdered —"

"Don't we, Colin?"

He didn't respond. He could track questions back but not with the patience and logic that she could. She was as relentless in her own way as he was. Her thoroughness combined with her ability to get things done made her an asset that Matt Yankowski counted on — he'd noticed her potential four years ago when she'd still been Sister Brigid. She could explore labyrinths and dead ends forever. Her schooling in art history and her time with the sisters — her months working with her grandfather in Dublin — had only honed her gift for detail.

"We have a lot of questions that need answering," he said. "Have you talked to your brother?"

She nodded. "If Lindsey checked out the offices while she was in Maine, Lucas didn't see her and she didn't leave her name. As he points out, though, by itself a stop in Heron's Cove doesn't necessarily mean anything. People sometimes just are curious about Sharpe Fine Art Recovery."

"Has anyone with ties to Declan's Cross ever stopped by out of curiosity about the O'Byrne theft?"

"Not that I'm aware of."

"You'd be aware," Colin said.

She didn't argue. "Yank reminded me this isn't our investigation."

Colin smiled. "I'm sure he did."

She raised her eyes to him. "He told me to remind you."

"Which you just did."

He slipped an arm around her waist and brushed his lips over her hair, smelled the Irish air in it. She was as comfortable here in an upscale boutique Irish hotel as she was up on a ridge in the Macgillicuddy Reeks. The Sharpes could do sophisticated or simple. He was better at dangerous and simple. Even undercover, he had seldom played a rich guy.

"We'll figure this out," he said.

"Did you learn anything more about the sparks between Sean Murphy and Kitty? There's a history there, I think."

"There's history everywhere in this village."

"It's romantic."

"That, it is."

Emma took his hand. "Let's go upstairs. We just have to remember Julianne is right next door."

He grinned. "Worried about thin walls?"

"Not that much," she said with a laugh

that was, he thought, damn good to hear.

"Emma and Colin will kill you," Julianne said as she sat cross-legged on her hotel bed, on the phone with Andy. It was nine o'clock in Ireland. Four o'clock in Maine.

"Relax. Mike's with me."

"That doesn't ease my mind, Andy."

"What could go wrong?"

"You could get into trouble for interfering in an FBI investigation. Seriously."

"There's no FBI investigation, Jules," he said, calm. "And we're not interfering, anyway."

Julianne gripped the phone. She didn't know why she'd called him. Well, she did know. She'd wanted to hear his voice. It was just a stupid reason to weaken, and she regretted it, especially since now she knew he and Mike, the eldest Donovan, were driving to Massachusetts to check out David Hargreaves' home on Boston's North Shore.

Why did she care? Let *them* explain everything to their FBI brother.

"We'll probably get there and the house will be locked up tight," Andy said.

"Then what will you do?"

"I don't know. Mike could always break in —"

"That's not funny."

She could almost see Andy's lazy grin. "Who's trying to be funny, Jules?"

She stretched her legs out straight, under the covers. She'd changed into her flannel pj's. "I'm not going to rat you out to Colin, but I should. He and Emma are right next door."

"You okay in this hotel?"

"It's beautiful. The breakfasts have won awards. I plan on totally indulging in the morning." She could feel the tightness in her throat and wondered if Andy could tell. She felt even more alone in her gorgeous hotel room than she had last night in her Irish cottage. Was that why she'd dug out her phone? "I'm sorry about Lindsey, and I never want to go through anything like it again — but she fell. She was up there in wet conditions and slipped or took a wrong step, fell and landed badly. That's it. There's a big difference between a tragedy and what you're thinking."

"And what am I thinking?"

She sucked in a breath and didn't answer. It was a bone of contention between them — her habit of telling him she knew what he was thinking without sufficient evidence, in his mind, at least, to make such a statement.

"Never mind," he said. "Get some sleep."

"You two should still turn back."

"Got it, Jules." She could feel Andy's grin. "Mike says hi."

She disconnected and might have flung her phone across the room if she hadn't been afraid of hitting something expensive. Turndown service had been by when she'd come up to her room after her soup. The drapes were drawn, the covers were pulled back on the bed, soft music was playing. She'd felt pampered . . . and incredibly alone.

She threw off the covers and jumped out onto the warm rug. Her internal clock was so messed up, she didn't know whether to try to sleep or try to stay awake. She did three yoga sun salutations in a row, never mind that it was pitch-dark outside, then gave up and went into the spotless bathroom. Ultra-white fixtures and towels, upscale amenities, prints of romantic Irish scenes.

She filled the tub, choosing from among three different scented bath salts. Lavender, grapefruit, almond.

She felt like crying.

"Damn it, Andy," she whispered aloud. "I wish you were with me."

He'd told her he was there anytime she

wanted to talk. She didn't want to talk, she realized. She wanted to slide into bed with him and forget, at least for a little while.

But that wasn't going to happen.

She chose the lavender bath salts.

17

Andy had no misgivings when he pulled into the Hargreaves place out on its own small point on Cape Ann. Mike didn't look as if he was worried, either. He was down from Maine's remote Bold Coast, helping their folks with a project at the inn they'd opened on Rock Point harbor. He'd flagged Andy down as he'd started out of Hurley's parking lot and jumped into the truck. Donovan solidarity. If Andy was going to stick his nose in Julianne's business — potentially in FBI business — it would be with Big Brother Mike at his side.

Andy also had no misgivings about alerting Colin to Julianne's sudden trip to Ireland and this mysterious little village of Declan's Cross. It meant she wasn't alone now, in the wake of finding her new friend dead on the Irish coast barely twenty-four hours after she'd landed in Shannon. Colin and Emma were with her.

Mike didn't see that as such a great thing. On the drive down to Massachusetts, he'd said, "If I'd just found a dead woman, I don't know that I'd want those two breathing down my neck."

It wasn't an unreasonable point of view.

Andy shut off the engine and climbed out of the truck. He had on a wool shirt, jeans and trail boots and was warm enough despite the chilly November evening air. Mike had on a scarred black leather jacket over a T-shirt and jeans, and he wore L.L.Bean boots that he'd had forever.

The Hargreaves place was light on security. No gate, no guard, no sign warning of an alarm system. Andy figured he and Mike wouldn't have made it this far if there were professional security types on the premises. Then again, Mike was ex-military and had his ways.

He joined Andy on the stone walk. The house was an understated Colonial, probably no more than sixty years old, with blue-gray clapboards, black shutters and a two-car garage. Trimmed shrubs. Established landscaping with mature shade trees, leafless against the starlit sky.

"Nice place," Andy said.

Mike nodded. "Hargreaves is an educated PBS-type?"

"I guess. I know he likes oceans."

"Good thing since his back windows look out on one."

Either the lights in the front windows were on a timer or someone was at home. Andy noticed that Mike eased behind him as they mounted the steps to the front door, painted a glossy dark red.

An auburn-haired woman who looked to be in her early sixties cracked open the door. "May I help you two gentlemen?"

"My name's Andy Donovan, ma'am." He nodded behind him. "This is my brother Mike. Our brother Colin is in Declan's Cross with David Hargreaves."

"The FBI agent," she said.

"That's right."

"Did he send you here?"

Mike shrugged, slouching against a post. "Depends on your point of view, I guess. David Hargreaves your boss?"

"I'm his housekeeper. Irene Barton. I'm staying here while he's away." She didn't open the door wider. "What can I do for you?"

"Colin is doing all he can to make sure the investigation into Lindsey's death is handled properly," Mike said. "He says your boss is, too. He sounds like a good guy."

Colin hadn't said any such thing, but

Irene Barton seemed calmer, less suspicious. She said, "David is a wonderful man. He and Special Agent Donovan are staying at the same hotel." She tilted her head back, expectant.

Andy realized it was a test and said, "The O'Byrne House Hotel in Declan's Cross. I looked it up on the internet. Quite the place."

"David was looking forward to staying there for a few days," Barton said, shaking her head in sorrow. "It's so sad. He called me this morning to make sure I heard about Lindsey from him."

"That's decent of him," Mike said. "I'm sure he told you that Colin's friends with the woman who found her this morning —"

"The marine biologist."

"Right. Julianne Maroney. She and Lindsey hit it off when they met last week in Maine. They bonded over their mutual interest in marine science."

Irene Barton straightened, starchy. "I hope Lindsey didn't try to pass herself off as a scientist. She loved marine science, bless her, but love doesn't make one an expert at anything, does it? She flunked out of college twice." Irene added quickly, "It's terrible, what's happened."

Andy looked at her with genuine sympathy. "It is terrible."

"Have the police been by to talk to you?" Mike asked.

She flashed him a suspicious look. "No, why should they? Lindsey's death was an accident, wasn't it? And even if it wasn't, it happened in Ireland."

Andy didn't want to scare the woman or put her on her guard again by bringing up cops, federal agents, potential murder. "You know the cops," he said. "Thorough."

Mike stood straight, as if he had all the time in the world. "Andy and I thought we'd have a look at this guesthouse where Lindsey was staying. It'd save some time. Make your life easier. We can report back to Colin. Would you mind? We'll only be a minute."

It was hard to say no to Mike when he was turning up the charm. Irene Barton opened the door wider. She didn't look nearly as suspicious as she had at first. "If you think it would help . . ."

Mike nodded. "It would. Colin wants to get a sense of Lindsey's life here."

The housekeeper sniffed. "She had it good. David treated her well. See for yourself." She stood back, motioning Mike and Andy inside. "It's easier to come through the house. I believe you are who you say you are and that your brother is with the FBI, but I want to warn you that I'm keeping an eye on you. I have a Glock in my jacket."

Mike grinned. "I'd expect nothing less."

She clearly liked Mike. She showed them down a hall to a traditional kitchen with white cabinets and a huge island, a cutting board set up with a carving knife and a head of lettuce. They must have interrupted her fixing herself a bite to eat.

They went into a mudroom with pegs hung with coats, vests, fishing and kayaking gear. A brass tray held men's boots, Top-Siders, canvas shoes. Everything was tidy and clean.

Their hostess threw on some lights and pointed out at the expansive yard. "The guesthouse is at the end of the walk. You'll see it. There should be enough light, but let me know if you want a flashlight."

She shut the door behind them as they headed down the steps to the stone walk. "Think she really has a Glock on her?" Andy asked when they were out of earshot.

"Yeah, probably. I would."

Andy didn't own a gun. He figured if he needed firepower, he'd count on his brothers. "She could be locking the doors and calling the police."

"Nah. She wants to prove her boss isn't a bad father."

"How do you know that?"

"I can read people."

They came to the guesthouse, nestled among rhododendrons and birch trees on a bluff above the water. Andy still had no misgivings about being here, but Julianne was right. Colin would kill them both for interfering.

Mike peered into a dark window. "I could get in and nobody would ever know."

No doubt true, Andy thought, looking in another window. A light was on in a back hall or bathroom, allowing him to make out the outlines of cheerful cottage furnishings. Overstuffed chairs and love seats, big flowered pillows, painted tables and chairs. The housekeeper's or Lindsey's doing, he figured, given how different the look here was from the one in the main house.

He stepped back from the window. "Looks like a cottage rental more than a place someone actually lives."

"Yeah. I don't know that it'd do any good to have a look inside." Mike stepped onto a stone landing in front of the cottage and looked out at the dark ocean. "Wonder why the daughter bunked out here instead of in the main house with her father."

"Privacy, maybe. Still feeling each other out. Sounds as if they didn't have much to do with each other for a long time." Andy could hear the tide coming in on the rocks below them. The coast here wasn't that different from southern Maine. More populated, but the Hargreaves place managed to feel isolated, unto itself. "I'm guessing David Hargreaves is something of an odd duck."

"He's used to having this place to himself. He might not like having people around, and Lindsey was — what, twenty-seven, twenty-eight? Old enough to be on her own. Good use of a guesthouse, if you ask me." Mike hopped off the landing, back onto the walk. "Let's go see what else we can get out of Miss Barton. She's warmed up to us. She won't shoot."

"It's not her I'm worried about," Andy muttered.

"Colin?" Mike grinned. "He won't shoot us, either. He'll just want to."

By the time they returned to the house, Irene Barton had her salad made, heaped onto a plate with slices of ham and cheese. Andy could smell bread heating up and saw the toaster oven was on. She hadn't locked the doors and, in fact, seemed even more comfortable around them.

Mike swiped a carrot stick and winked at her. "You don't mind, do you?"

She blushed slightly. "Not at all."

"It's really nice here," Andy said. "It must have been hard for Lindsey to give it up."

"I'm sure it was, but she was determined to give this research field station a go. David was very good to her this past year." She wiped her hands on a cloth napkin and pointed toward the hall. "I can show you out."

She seemed intent on doing so. As she bustled into the hall, Mike glanced around the kitchen, as if imprinting it in his memory, then helped himself to a cucumber slice and followed the housekeeper.

Andy eased in behind them. "How well did you know Lindsey?" he asked.

"She was just a little girl when I first met her. She and her mother lived nearby — Cynthia fancied herself a painter. Seascapes."

From Irene Barton's tone, Andy guessed she didn't think much of Cynthia Hargreaves' artistic talents.

They came to the front entry. The housekeeper paused in the doorway of a small library, a single floor lamp lit. "I didn't see much of Lindsey after her mother and David divorced. She was always welcome here, but Cynthia kept telling her that David wasn't her quote-unquote *real* father. Isn't that a terrible thing to tell a child? David adopted her. She was very much a real daughter to him."

"Not a big fan of either the mother or the daughter, are you?" Mike asked, blunt as ever.

Irene Barton didn't seem to take offense. "Maybe so. Lindsey was a sweet little girl, but she didn't appreciate all David did for her — and for her mother."

Mike glanced into the library. "Your boss much of an art collector?"

"He'll tell you he buys what he likes."

"Ever hear of Sharpe Fine Art Recovery?" Andy asked.

The housekeeper frowned. "I don't believe so, no. Why? What do they do?"

"Recover lost and stolen art and antiquities," Mike said. "Prevent their theft. They're based in Maine. Heron's Cove."

Irene didn't react to mention of the Sharpes or Heron's Cove, but she rubbed the back of her neck, as if lost in thought. Finally she looked at her two visitors and said, "I have something to show you."

She went past them into the library. Andy glanced at Mike, then they both followed her.

She pointed at an empty space on the wood-paneled wall. "An Irish seascape was here until last week."

Not what Andy expected. "Where is it now?"

"David told me he was having it appraised."

"But you don't believe him," Mike said.

"To be perfectly frank, I don't know that I do, no. David bought it for Lindsey's mother when they were in Ireland on a sort of second honeymoon."

Mike walked over to a glass-front cabinet. "When was this second honeymoon?"

"It's been at least fifteen years. They divorced not long after that. They were gone just ten days. Lindsey stayed here with me."

"Odd coincidence," Andy said, "having an Irish seascape out for appraisal the same time his daughter's launching a marine science field station in Ireland."

"Who's the artist?" Mike asked.

"Aoife O'Byrne. I know nothing about her, but I remember the name because it's unusual, at least to me. I had to look up the pronunciation. *EE-fa.* Of course, when I saw that David is staying at the O'Byrne House Hotel . . ." She waved a hand. "I'm sure there are loads of O'Byrnes in Ireland."

"Anything else not here?" Mike asked.

Irene nodded. "Another Aoife O'Byrne piece, a beautiful Celtic silver cross. It was stored in that cabinet. Lindsey told me that her mother adored the cross and the painting but felt they belonged here."

Andy noted Irene's skeptical tone. "Do you believe that?"

"I'm not sure what to believe," Irene said.

Mike turned from the cabinet. "The mother's dead?"

"For at least ten years. She had problems. Lindsey blamed David for a long time." Irene's cheeks flushed. "I'm talking too much, and I'm sure I'm being far too critical. Having Lindsey here and then her trip to Ireland must have prompted David to finally have the appraisals done — he can be quite the procrastinator. Aoife O'Byrne was an unknown fifteen years ago."

"Now she's a rising international star in the art world," Andy said. Mike raised his eyebrows at him, and Andy shrugged. "Like I said, I spent some time on the internet."

The housekeeper's cheeks flamed an even deeper red, and she bustled out of the library. Andy didn't want to upset her further and saw that Mike didn't, either. There was no point; she'd told them all she was going to tell them. They followed her back into the hall, and she showed them

"That's pretty much what Matt Yankowski said, too. How's Jules?"

"She cried herself to sleep."

Andy's throat tightened. He didn't know if Colin was just twisting in the knife or if he really had heard Julianne crying herself to sleep in the next room. "What can I do?"

"Go back to Rock Point and stay there."

"Colin, there isn't one thing about Jules's trip to Declan's Cross that I liked before today. Now —"

"I know, Andy. That's why you need to stay out of it. Mike, too."

"How's Emma? Are the Sharpes involved

Colin was gone. Andy shoved his phone back into his jacket pocket and glared over at Mike. "We've got the feds at us."

"I'll live through it. You okay?"

"Yeah. Yeah, I'm good."

He wasn't — he was worried about Jule — and Mike obviously knew it but said nothing further.

When they reached Rock Point, Andy saw the *Julianne* at its mooring out by Hurley's. A classic wooden lobster boat that he went on restoring. Colin considered it a boat that was ready for firewood, but saw its potential. Julianne's father had

out quickly, formally, mumbling that David had nothing to hide as she shut the door behind them.

A man in a dark suit was getting out of a black sedan parked next to Andy's truck. Andy swore under his breath, recognizing Matt Yankowski, a humorless, buttoned-down federal agent if ever there was one. They'd met a few times in Rock Point, never over anything good happening.

"Easy, brother," Mike said. "Yankowski actually will shoot us."

The senior FBI agent approached them on the walk. "Andy Donovan. Mike Donovan. What are you two boys doing down here?"

"Chatting with the Hargreaves' housekeeper," Mike said. "Irene. Nice woman. Early sixties. At first she didn't want to let us inside."

"Imagine that." Yankowski didn't let up on the stony gaze. "Didn't your brother tell you two not to meddle in an official investigation?"

"Which brother?" Andy asked. "We have two in law enforcement. Kevin and Colin."

"I'm not amused," Yankowski said.

Andy shrugged. "I didn't think you would be. Why's the FBI involved? If this woman's death was in Ireland, and it was an accident —"

Again the stony gaze from the senior FBI agent. "Who told you it was an accident?"

Mike nodded to the house. "You going in? We charmed Miss Barton, but I wouldn't be surprised if she's calling the police now, with the three of us out here. She says she's armed, by the way. Glock in her jacket."

The FBI agent grimaced. "I'll talk to her. I can show her my credentials. You two, on the other hand, can get back in your truck and go home."

Andy wasn't a hundred percent sure Matt Yankowski would want to know what they'd discovered in the Hargreaves house. "Should we tell you what we learned?" he asked.

Yankowski took an audible breath. "What did you learn, Donovan?"

Andy kept his tone even. "David Hargreaves is more of an art collector than he's let on. A seascape and a small Celtic cross by an Irish artist named Aoife O'Byrne were in his library last week and aren't there now. Irene Barton says he told her they were being appraised."

Mike ran the toe of his boot over the clipped grass on the edge of the walk. "Aoife is spelled *A-o-i-f-e*. Nice Irish name."

"You two don't know anything about art,"

Yankowski said.

Mike raised his gaze to the feder[al] [...] "I think I'm insulted."

Yankowski was clearly unmov[ed ...] you're not."

"Lindsey Hargreaves and her [...] estranged for years," Andy [...] showed up a few months ago —

"Good night, gentlemen," Yan[...] then brushed past them.

Mike looked at Andy. "Gue[ss ...] go."

Andy asked Mike to do the [...] Maine. That way he cou[...] although he had no idea if [...] would be awake in Ireland [...]

He was. He called thr[...] Andy hit Send.

"Where are you now?"

Andy had planned to l[...] but Mike raised his vo[...] I-95. "Just talked to [...] housekeeper. You've [...] brother."

"Talk to me," Col[...] without interruption [...] had transpired on t[...] he finished, Colin [...] again."

named it for her, but it had been her grandfather's boat. She was convinced Andy had swindled her father out of it, taking advantage of him when he'd been grieving over his father's — her grandfather's — death, but they'd had the deal in place for months.

The truth was, Julianne wanted a different life from the one Andy had. He didn't have a chip on his shoulder. He wasn't unambitious. He was a lobsterman, but the boat restoration work he did on the side was going well. If he couldn't handle both jobs, so be it, but he'd cross that bridge when he got to it.

It was all so simple to him, but Julianne was good at complicating everything.

Mike pulled into Hurley's parking lot. The place was dead on the cold November night. He turned off the engine. "You should text Julianne."

"Why?"

"Tell her you got back from the Hargreaves' place okay."

"It's the middle of the night in Ireland."

Mike was unmoved. "If she's awake, she'll see the text and won't worry. She won't feel abandoned. If she's asleep, she'll see it in the morning and realize you were thinking about her."

Andy stared at his eldest brother. "Mike,

are you giving me advice about women?"

"No, I'm telling you to text Julianne. You were a son of a bitch to her, and she's still getting over you. Be nice now and text her. She's like the little sister I never had. Colin, too."

Great. Just what he wanted to hear. Andy complied and texted her: Are you crying?

She texted him back almost instantly: I'm asleep. Leave me alone.

Andy showed the text to Mike. His brother shrugged. "Okay, she's fine. Come on. I'll buy you a whiskey."

Fin Bracken was at his table by the windows at Hurley's. Kevin was with him, his cop face on, meaning he'd heard about Lindsey Hargreaves and possibly about Mike and Andy's trip to the North Shore. Mike looked unconcerned as he sat down. "So, Fin, do you know this spot in Declan's Cross where Lindsey Hargreaves died?"

"I do, indeed," the priest said.

"How do you get there?" Andy asked, sitting between Mike and Finian, with Kevin across from him at the round table. The long drive down to the North Shore and back hadn't done great things for his shoulder, but he ignored the dull ache.

"By car?" Finian asked, but didn't wait for an answer. "There's a road up from the village, through the Murphy farm, out to the tip of Shepherd Head where this terrible tragedy occurred. On foot, you can walk out the road, of course, but there's also a trail up from a small beach."

"How do you get to the beach?" Kevin asked.

"Another road winds onto the headland from the south. It doesn't connect with the other road, except by the trail."

Mike helped himself to the Bracken 15. "So there are two dead-end roads onto the headland," he said.

"That's right," Finian said.

Kevin frowned. "Is it difficult terrain?"

"Fairly difficult, yes." Finian eyed the three brothers. "Have any of you talked to Julianne tonight, or to Colin and Emma? I was busy with visitations all day. Now it's very late . . ."

"I haven't talked to them," Mike said. "Andy's talked to Colin and Julianne. Special Agent Sharpe remains enigmatic."

Kevin grinned at him. "Enigmatic, Mike?"

"Hard to figure." He turned to Finian. "Have you talked to your friend in Declan's Cross?"

"Briefly."

It was, Andy saw, all Finian intended to say on the matter. Across the table, Kevin pushed aside his glass. "You look tired, Andy. Shoulder hurt?"

"Some."

"Where were you and Mike?"

"Hargreaves place," Andy said.

Mike gulped his whiskey. "Colin already yelled at us."

"Good," Kevin said.

"Yankowski, too," Mike added.

Kevin said nothing. Andy sometimes wondered if he'd missed his calling and should have been a cop, but not tonight. Tonight, hearing Julianne's voice, then Colin's voice, seeing Kevin now — remembering the housekeeper's bridled emotions — he knew he wasn't cut out for law enforcement work. He liked being out on the water. Restoring boats. Exploring tide pools with Julianne.

Hell.

He really was tired.

"Franny Maroney was here earlier," Kevin said. "She was looking for you, Andy, but she settled for badgering me. Julianne had been in touch and told her about Lindsey. Apparently she didn't want Franny to worry, but at the same time she didn't want her to hear about what happened from one of us."

"Telling Franny herself was the lesser of

two evils," Andy said. "Did Franny tell you she knew something was wrong?"

"Yeah." Kevin kept his gaze on Andy. "She wants you to go to Ireland. I told her Colin's there and that was already one too many Donovans as far as Julianne's concerned."

"It didn't help," Andy said, predicting Franny's response.

Kevin sighed. "It did not."

Finian Bracken poured more whiskey into Andy's, Mike's and his own glass. Kevin put his hand over his, signaling he was done for the night. The priest said, "I didn't see this coming. I feel responsible somehow . . ."

Andy sensed that a dark mood was descending on his brothers, Father Bracken, himself. He took a swallow of whiskey. "What do you all think will happen with Colin and Emma?"

Mike grunted. "When? The next two weeks, two months, two years —"

"You know what I mean."

"I keep hearing wedding bells," Kevin said. "That would please the folks."

Finian Bracken sighed. "That's not a reason to have a wedding."

"As good as any," Mike said with a grin.

"You're not an easy lot," the Irish priest said.

"Some women like that," Mike said. "Emma might be one of them. I always thought Julianne was." He glanced at Andy. "We all figured you two would have the first Donovan wedding."

"What about you, Mike?" Fin asked. "You're the eldest brother. Any desire to settle down?"

"I live alone in the woods. Works for me."

Andy wasn't sure if Mike was kidding. He'd always been blunt but private, and never an easy man. Andy was more open about what was going on with him. Julianne was even more forthcoming. No secrets. He didn't know how things had gotten so hot with them. Inevitable, maybe, but he still should have resisted. Anything between them was always destined to be temporary, and since she was a Maroney and he was a Donovan, he should have never had a bite of that apple.

Mike polished off his Bracken 15. Finian muttered about just using Hurley's cheap stuff if it was going to be belted down. Mike grinned at him. "This is what happens when you start talking weddings with us." He nodded to Kevin. "Need a ride home, or are you sober?"

"I'm sober, but I walked. I could use a ride."

They left together. Andy stayed behind, watching as Finian Bracken lifted the whiskey bottle. "I don't drink every night but tonight . . ." He sighed heavily. "Another *taoscán,* my good friend Andy?"

"Sure. Have you heard from your friend Sean Murphy?"

Finian looked pained. "I fear I sent trouble his way."

"I have a feeling it's not the first time."

Finian stared out at the dark harbor.

"Were you trying to fix him up with Julianne? I don't know if I can see her with an Irish sheep farmer."

"Sean's heart belongs to another and has for a long time. And farming is what his family does."

"He's a cop," Andy said. "I want to know the rest, Fin. What you haven't told me. I want to hear all of it."

18

Julianne only mildly regretted her tart response to Andy's middle-of-the-night text. What she *really* regretted was responding to him in the first place. Now he knew she'd been up, unable to sleep. He'd think it was in part because he wasn't there.

If she could do it all over again, she'd dump him first, before he could dump her.

She put him out of her mind. Despite her tossing and turning, she was up early. It was only two o'clock in the morning at home and barely daylight in Ireland, but she was wide-awake as she grabbed her coat and headed into the village. The pretty streets were quiet, only a few people about as she found her way to the waterfront.

The garage that Lindsey had adopted as her "field station" was about what Julianne had expected. The location near the pier was good, but it took real vision to see a modern marine science facility here. It would take funding to make it a reality, and that was unlikely to happen now, with Lindsey's death.

Brent Corwin came out a side door. He looked as if he'd done his own share of tossing and turning and still couldn't decide if he should give up on trying to sleep.

He gave Julianne a ragged smile. "Thought you might make your way down here eventually."

"It's weird being here. I feel like I'm stepping into someone else's unfinished dream."

"I know what you mean." Brent cleared his throat. "Lindsey had big plans. She was excited about having you here and getting your input as a marine biologist."

Julianne averted her eyes, glanced at the van parked crookedly in front of the garage. "Have you talked to her father?"

"We had a drink last night. I think he was going to step in and see if he could make this thing happen. Least of his worries now. Mine, too. Without Lindsey, this place will stay an old garage." He shoved a palm over his short-cropped hair, as if the meaning of his own words had just hit him. "Where are your FBI friends this morning?"

"We're meeting for breakfast." Julianne saw the dark circles under his eyes and felt guilty at her own bad night. He'd known

Lindsey far better, even if he hadn't been the one to find her body. She said softly, "I'm really sorry about what happened."

He nodded grimly. "Same here. Wasn't your fault. Wasn't anyone's fault." He blew out a breath at the sky, then looked again at Julianne. "Have you seen Philip this morning? Do you know him — Kitty's son?"

"I saw him at the hotel yesterday, but he was working. I haven't seen him yet this morning."

"He lost it last night at the pub. I hope he's okay. I should have handled the situation better. I forget he's just a kid. The police had been here, asking questions — they want to piece together Lindsey's last day, figure out what she was doing out on the rocks. Philip was probably the last one to see her alive. It's eating him up." Brent shivered in a gust of wind. "Damn. It's colder out here than I expected."

Julianne turned so that the wind was at her back. "Did Lindsey plan on tearing down this place and building a new facility?"

"Lindsey had a million plans." He sniffled, whether from the wind, the cold or raw emotion, Julianne couldn't tell. "I feel like we're all under the microscope."

"Maybe that's because we are."

He grinned at her. "Not one to beat around the bush, are you?"

She smiled back at him. "I guess not."

But she saw his seriousness return and felt her own smile fade as he walked over to the van and pulled open the door on the driver's side. It still disconcerted her that it was on the right. He shut the door again. "I don't even know what I'm doing. I've been spinning in circles since yesterday."

"That's understandable."

"I know the police have a job to do, and it must look weird to them that Lindsey stopped in Declan's Cross on Monday without telling any of us. None of us saw her. Well, except Philip, but that was just on the fly — he didn't talk to her."

Julianne put her hood up against another chilly gust of wind. The tide would be up, she thought. She glanced at the diving gear piled by the side door of the garage. She wasn't much of a diver herself and wondered what Lindsey had had in mind for her to do here. Maybe just get ideas from her, as a marine biologist? Bounce ideas of her own off her?

She turned back to Brent. "The police will keep asking questions until they're satisfied Lindsey's death was an accident. Even if it was, they'll want to know if anyone was with her."

"And left her out there, you mean?"

"Panicked, maybe."

He nodded thoughtfully, less shocked than Julianne expected him to be. "I can see that. The police wanting to know, I mean. Not someone panicking and leaving her out there and the rest of us to wonder. I feel like a royal jerk for assuming she'd stood you up because she was a flake." He pivoted, gravel crunching under him, and went to the back of the van. "All the diving we did together and never a mistake, never a close call. Then one wrong step up on an Irish ledge and she's gone."

Julianne shoved her hands in her pockets. It felt like November this morning. Cold, wet, no promise of Indian summer. "You and Lindsey . . ."

"There was nothing serious between us," Brent said. "She knew that. It's what she wanted. Sharing the cottage with you was a way to get some space. She was thinking she might rent it herself and stay here through the winter. Get this place set up."

"You?"

"She knew I would move on eventually."

"The bad-boy diver," Julianne said with a smile.

He laughed, despite his obvious sadness. "Yeah, I guess. Her dad thinks all divers are bad boys." He tugged open the back of the van. "What about you? Any bad boys in your life?"

"Don't I wish." She wasn't sure her tone came across as joking as she'd meant.

"Special Agent Donovan's a bad-boy type, isn't he?"

"He comes across that way sometimes."

"He and the lady FBI agent are an item. Isn't that a little awkward? Three's a crowd and all that?"

Julianne noticed the back of the van was crammed full of gear. She suspected Brent would want to get out in the water again as soon as possible. "Are the police finished with you? Can you leave if you want to?"

"Yeah. No problem." He bit down on his lower lip as if he were trying to control a wave of emotion. "I've gone through some tough stuff, but losing Lindsey — it's awful. I liked her a lot. I'll miss her."

"Where will you go after here?"

"Caribbean. I'm not exactly sure which island. I can pick up some work there. Clear my head. Lindsey rented this place. I wasn't involved. I'll help her dad close up shop if he wants me to, but it's up to him to figure out what's next. It's not easy to be here. I

335

found that out last night. I don't know if I ever saw what it could be the way she did." He paused, visibly holding back tears, then cleared his throat and nodded to the van. "I have a few more things to toss in here."

"I'm really sorry, Brent," Julianne said, the words sounding empty to her despite the genuine sentiment behind them.

"Me, too." He pushed a cardboard box, making a few more inches of room in the back of the van. "What about you? It's not the Ireland trip you imagined. What are your plans? Will you stay at the cottage on your own?"

"I don't know yet. I'm at the O'Byrne House right now."

He stood straight. "Your FBI friends insisted?"

"It didn't take much insisting."

"I have a couple friends in law enforcement. They're great, but they tend to think the worst. Trust me, no one around here is worried about a killer on the loose."

"I hope not," Julianne said.

He walked over to diving gear heaped by the side door. "This is all lightweight stuff. I've got most of the heavier equipment loaded into the van." He grabbed two pairs of high-end goggles and brought them to the van. "What's your specialty in marine science? I don't think Lindsey ever said."

"Cetaceans."

"Can't go wrong. Everyone loves cetaceans. Toothed whales and baleen whales. Dolphins, porpoises, humpback whales, right whales, beaked whales. Every kind of whale. *Cetus* meaning whale, or 'large sea mammal.' " He grinned, looking more animated, less exhausted. "See? I picked up a few things diving besides a bad-boy reputation."

Julianne smiled, more at ease herself. "Very good, Mr. Corwin."

As he placed the goggles in the van, she noticed Philip edging onto the parking area. He looked haggard, his hair sticking out, his jacket hanging half off his shoulders.

"Morning," he mumbled.

The wind was dying down, but Julianne still felt the chill in the air as she nodded at him. "Good morning."

Brent stood back from the van. "Philip. Hell, man. Sorry about last night. How are you this morning? Hanging in there?"

"Never better," Philip said, his appearance belying his words. "I'm not staying. I need to get up to the hotel to help with breakfast. Just wanted to see if anything was going on here. You're leaving?"

"Not yet," Brent said. "Soon, though."

"Nothing to keep you here, I guess."

"I thought I'd go out for a dive later on. Clear my head. Join me?"

"If I'm able with work, yeah. Sure thing." Philip sniffled, clearly awkward. "Well, I'll be on my way."

"Breakfast sounds good," Julianne said. "Mind if I walk with you?"

He shrugged in what she took to be the affirmative.

"See you both later." Brent resumed his packing. "Thanks for stopping by, Julianne. Join us on the dive if you'd like. We can suit you up."

She thanked him as Philip spun around and started back up toward the village without a word. She quickly caught up with him.

"Sorry," he said.

"Not a problem. You had a bit of a crush on Lindsey, didn't you?"

"I suppose I did. Doesn't matter now, does it?" He didn't wait for an answer and pushed on up the quiet street. "She wanted people to like her. Nothing wrong with that unless you manipulate them, lie to them so that they'll like you."

Julianne had to hurry to keep up with his long strides. "You seem to have good instincts about people. I don't. I guess that's why I'm a marine biologist and not a psychologist."

He glanced at her, slowing his pace. "Do you have a fellow back in Maine?"

"Not anymore. I did for a while. We live in the same small town. You must be able to imagine what that's like."

"I can, for sure. Does he know you're here?"

"Oh, yes."

Philip smiled at her. "There's a lot in that *oh, yes,* isn't there?"

"I've known Andy — that's his name — my whole life. Actually, he's Colin Donovan's brother."

"Is that right? He looks as if he's a good one to have around in a pinch."

"All the Donovans are. There are four brothers." Julianne grinned at the Irish teenager. "You pity me now, don't you?"

"I suppose I have to," he said easily, then drifted into silence as they came to the hotel and went through the gate.

"Philip, is something on your mind? You can tell me. I'm not an FBI agent or a garda detective. If you want to talk —"

"Sometimes it's best to keep your mouth shut. My mother taught me that. My father didn't. He's always saying the wrong thing."

"I can identify with that."

He laughed a little but said nothing. He had to get to work, but Julianne was in no hurry. She wanted to savor her time in the hotel's pretty gardens. Coffee and scones, however, did sound inviting.

She pulled off her hood and unzipped her jacket, warmer given the fast clip up from the waterfront. She decided not to pressure him to talk. Instead she asked casually, "Were you here when this place was broken into ten years ago?"

He seemed almost relieved at her question. "I was in Dublin with my dad. He and my mother had just split up. I was only eight. I thought the theft was exciting."

"Cary Grant, Robert Wagner."

"Lindsey said it made her think of Pierce Brosnan in *The Thomas Crown Affair*."

"A good Irish actor. You and Lindsey talked about the theft?"

"Only for a minute." Philip's voice was barely audible. "It was nothing. We were just chatting and it came up."

"Did she bring it up or did you —"

"Why does it matter?"

"It's okay. Sorry." Julianne smiled. "I don't mean to interrogate you. Will you go diving with Brent today?"

"I don't know."

He was sullen again, preoccupied, but he

didn't break off from her. She said, "Where would you dive? Any idea?"

"He said last night he wants to go out to Shepherd Head. He thought it'd be good for us to do. We've done some diving up there. Brent, Eamon, Lindsey and me." He kicked a small stone. "I guess that's done. Back to washing dishes and sweeping floors for me."

"I imagine you're a big help at the hotel, but I understand you want to go into marine science."

"It's just a dream."

"If you don't take any action, yes."

"Now you sound like my mother," he said, but he managed a strained laugh.

"Yikes," Julianne said, wincing slightly. "Seriously, Philip, if I can answer any questions, point you in the right direction — just let me know, okay?"

He thanked her and excused himself, ducking quickly into a staff entrance at the back of the hotel. Julianne paused by a stone statue of a woman with a water pitcher. Sunlight sparkled on the sea and glistened on the lush grass and flowerbeds, a beautiful, calming sight.

If only she didn't have Lindsey's death on her mind.

And Andy, she thought.

He was always on her mind.

Colin and Emma were in the dining room, at a table set for three. They already had coffee and a basket of scones, toast and brown bread. "Sorry to keep you waiting," Julianne said as she sat down, ignoring Colin's scowl.

"I was just about to send out a search party for you," he said.

"Meaning you were about to come look for me yourself. I didn't realize I had instructions to stay put."

"I didn't think I needed to give them."

"I appreciate your concern, and I'm sorry to worry you."

He grunted at her. "You're not sorry."

She gave him a cheerful smile. "Good morning, Colin."

He picked up his coffee cup. "Good morning, Julianne."

She smiled at Emma. "Sorry. We're done now. Good morning. It's such a romantic hotel, isn't it? Are you sure you want me to join you two for breakfast —"

"We're sure," Colin said. "We need to talk."

"Does this have anything to do with Andy's escapade last night? I told him you'd kill him."

"Julianne," Emma said, "did Lindsey tell you how she ended up in Declan's Cross?"

"Not that I recall, no."

"Did she talk about her mother at all?"

"Her mother? No. Marine mammals, diving, how pretty it is here. We talked some about my internship, and she told me a bit about her father — not a lot. I got the feeling she'd landed here by accident and fell in love with the area." Julianne frowned, noticing how serious Emma was. Colin, too. "What's going on?"

Colin put his cup down. "Did Andy tell you what he and Mike learned last night?"

"No. What?"

Emma answered as she broke open a scone. "Fifteen years ago, David Hargreaves and his wife at the time visited Ardmore and bought two works by Aoife O'Byrne."

Julianne reached for a scone. "O'Byrne as in —"

"John O'Byrne's niece and Kitty's sister," Emma said. "The two works — a seascape and a silver Celtic cross — were in David Hargreaves' library until last week. He told his housekeeper he sent them out to be appraised."

"Well, that's quite the coincidence. Do you think that's why Lindsey ended up in Declan's Cross?"

"Her mother was a painter herself," Colin said, his eyes — so like Andy's — on Julianne.

Using the silver butter knife, she put a pat of Irish butter on her bread plate. Hurley's didn't have separate butter knives. Suddenly Maine seemed so far away, even with Colin and Emma at the table with her. She looked up from her scone at them. "Have you talked to Lindsey's father about this?"

Emma shook her head. "Not yet. Colin and I are meeting my grandfather this morning in Ardmore. I want to talk to him first. We'd like for you to join us. He might want to ask you a few questions."

"No problem. I'd love to meet your grandfather, and I want to see Ardmore. You guys can read all the emails between Lindsey and me if you want. I don't mind." Julianne spread the butter on her scone and tried to keep her mind from racing. "When did you talk to Andy?"

"Last night," Colin said. "Late. He and Mike ran into Matt Yankowski on their way out of the Hargreaves' place."

Julianne knew Yankowski from the attack on Andy in late October. "And they're not under arrest?"

"They're lucky it was Yank and not me."

She looked at Emma. "He's not kidding,

you know."

Emma smiled. "All's well that ends well. Can you meet us at reception in forty-five minutes?"

"I'll be there."

"Please don't discuss the Aoife O'Byrne works with anyone else," Emma added as she and Colin got to their feet.

They headed out of the dining room, and Julianne slathered thick rhubarb jam onto her scone. She'd seldom seen Colin in full-blown FBI mode. Never Emma. "Scary, those two," she muttered under her breath. Then again, they had reason to be in FBI mode.

She ordered yogurt and fruit to go with her scones. The trip to Ardmore would be interesting. Wendell Sharpe was a legend in southern Maine. She did want to meet him. She replayed in her head everything Lindsey had said to her from the moment they'd met at Hurley's to the moment they'd parted that evening, promising to stay in touch. Julianne was positive not a word had come up about art, the O'Byrnes or the Sharpes. There had been so much to see and talk about, given their mutual interest in marine science. It hadn't occurred to Julianne to mention Sharpe Fine Art Recovery, even with Emma in Ireland.

She finished her breakfast and headed up to her room. Housekeeping had already slipped in and done their thing. The bed was made, the bathroom was clean, fresh towels were hung. The drapes were open, sunlight streaming in. She looked out at the glistening ocean and suddenly felt lonely. Her thoughts automatically went to Andy. He wasn't easy, but he was good in a fight. Was she in a fight?

She checked her messages. He'd called and left a voice mail, probably while she was consuming her third scone. *"Woke up thinking about you, Jules. I don't know if that's welcome news or not, but I'm here if you need me."*

She didn't know if it was welcome news or not, either.

19

Emma walked among old graves on the uneven ground at the base of the Ardmore round tower, a twelfth-century landmark rising a hundred feet above the picturesque village. The view of the bay from the hillside location was enough reason for a visit, but the early Celtic Christian ruins, the scattered graves and the inescapable sense of history made it a must-see for tourists, at least as far as she was concerned. Today, though, with the cool, crisp air, they had the cemetery and its ancient structures to themselves.

Colin had hung back, reading worn headstones splotched with orange and white lichen as he watched for her grandfather. Julianne had joined Emma for a closer look at the tower. She squinted up at the impressive block-and-mortar structure. "What's the purpose of a round tower?"

"We don't know for certain," Emma said.

"Dozens of round towers were built throughout Ireland, most between the eighth and tenth centuries. This one offers a bird's-eye view of the coastline, so some think it might have served as a watchtower against invaders."

"Kind of elaborate for a watchtower."

"I think so, too. Notice the door and how high it is above-ground — at least twelve feet. One theory has it as a deliberate defensive measure. During raids, monks would hide inside with their valuables."

"Pull up the ladder, so to speak, and play possum until the bad guys sail off again," Julianne said. "You'd want enough food and water to last awhile."

Emma hunched her shoulders against a gust of wind that went right through her leather jacket. "More likely using the tower as a hideout was opportunistic and the high doors were necessary for structural stability."

Julianne smiled. "Pretty amazing, though."

Colin joined them, his jacket unzipped despite the wind. "Leave it to your grandfather to have us meet him in a cemetery."

"It's historic," Julianne told him. "Saint Declan established his monastery here over a thousand years ago. Can you imagine?"

"Some other day, maybe," he said.

Julianne rolled her eyes, but Emma just smiled. She appreciated their company — their easy familiarity with each other — and was glad she wasn't meeting her grandfather alone.

"Granny would love this," Julianne said. "I don't remember learning anything about Saint Declan. I like the name Declan, though. A cute guy in my college organic chemistry class was named Declan."

Colin muttered under his breath, but Emma suspected he was relieved to see Julianne more animated, more herself, today. "Saint Declan believed God guided him to Ardmore," Emma said. "According to accounts of his life, when he and his companions set sail from Wales, they inadvertently left behind a small bell that Declan believed God had sent to him as a gift early in his priesthood. They prayed, and the bell appeared on a large stone that then guided them to Ardmore."

"Saint Declan's Stone," Colin said. "It's in the harbor. It's actually a large boulder. We could walk to it from here. The bell's gone, though."

"You read that on the internet," Julianne said.

He grinned at her. "Always so smart."

Emma led the way among the headstones

and grave slabs — some new, most very old — and the plantings of junipers, yews and euonymus to what was left of Ardmore cathedral. It was without a roof but was still recognizable as a church, part of it dating back to the ninth century. More graves were located inside its intact walls. Stone panels depicted biblical scenes, perhaps the most well-known of the Archangel Michael weighing souls, but Emma didn't point it out — she'd spotted her grandfather by the end gable.

So, clearly, had Colin. He picked up his pace, but she and Julianne kept up with him as they made their way to the gable. Wendell Sharpe, Emma thought, was still a good-looking man in his early eighties. He was tall and lean, with thinning white hair and a penchant for bow ties, although today he wore a Burberry coat that he'd had for as long as Emma could remember. "Hi, Granddad," she said, giving him a quick kiss on the cheek. "Thanks for meeting Colin and me. This is our friend Julianne Maroney."

He took Julianne's hand. "I'm sorry to meet you under such strained circumstances," he said, then stood back and eyed her. "Are you related to Jack Maroney? I used to buy lobsters from him years ago."

in Declan's Cross —"

ust tell us what you know."

mma intervened. "Granddad, we need now if the thief is back — if he's in some responsible for Lindsey Hargreaves' th."

m doing my best to help," he said. he touched his shoulder. "Colin knows ut the crosses. I told him."

er grandfather made a face. "I suppose had no choice."

olin swore under his breath. "Emma, might want to remind your grandfather I'm a federal agent —"

don't care if you're the prime minister Ireland," Wendell said. "The details of investigation are closely held for good son."

olin didn't back down. "What do these ss-inscribed stones tell you about our ef? What's the point — what's he trying say?"

f I knew that, maybe I could catch him."

Granddad," Emma said, "do you know if ty and Aoife O'Byrne have a suspect in nd?"

e stepped back from the gable, into the d, and turned up his jacket collar. "It sn't matter who either one of them sus-cts."

"My grandfather. He died last fall."

"Sorry to hear that. Good man. Did he ever get to Ireland? He talked about it frequently."

Julianne shook her head. "He never did."

"That's life, isn't it? I'll never do half the things I talk about doing." He glanced at Colin. "You don't look happy, Special Agent Donovan."

"I'm in a cemetery, Wendell."

"Ha. Yes, indeed." He sighed out at the view, the tide washing onto the sand of a horseshoe-shaped beach far below the hilltop cemetery. "I love this place. I haven't been down here in far too long. Did you know there are two ogham stones here? They were moved some time ago to within the walls of the cathedral."

"So that's how you pronounce it," Julianne said. "*OH-am*. Early Celtic alphabet inscribed on stone monuments. I read about it. Lots of arguments and theories."

"These particular ogham stones probably date from the fifth century, around the time we think Saint Declan established a Christian settlement here." He beamed at Julianne, obviously already charmed by her. "Have you had a chance to look around?"

"Some. It's fascinating."

"Your Declan's Cross thief doesn't just

steal Irish art," Colin said.

"And he's the reason for our visit," Wendell said with a sigh. "He's an interesting character, our thief. We don't really know if he has a particular interest in Saint Declan. It could be the O'Byrne house was simply his first heist. He's like rain through our fingers."

Julianne gestured vaguely. "I'll go wander about and let you guys talk art thieves and such."

"The oratory is worth a look," Wendell said, nodding to a small building above them on the hill. "It's the reputed burial site of Saint Declan, although his remains have long since vanished. Quite an unusual market over the years for the relics of saints."

"I'll check it out," Julianne said, the wind whipping her hair as she headed to a narrow dirt path that wound through the graves, shrubs and grass.

Emma drew her grandfather into a sheltered spot between two slanted stone supports on the outside of the gable, out of the wind off the bay. She noticed that he looked happier, healthier, since venturing into the Kerry hills a few weeks ago — unless he was just energized by talk of a thief that had eluded him for a decade.

Colin touched a bit of white old stone. Emma understood necessarily appreciate the ro Fine Art Recovery in a decad art thefts. He turned from th studied her grandfather. "Ha from your thief since Lindse arrived in Declan's Cross?"

"No," Wendell said.

"Would you tell me if you ha "If Emma said to."

If he'd meant to get Colin didn't work. "What do you Kitty and Aoife O'Byrne?"

"Pretty. Smart. Headstron Kitty is good with business a artistic flair to work in the h more of a mystery." Wendel Emma. "Ten years ago, they five and twenty-seven. Kitty son. Her marriage had just end just moved back to Dublin. S few years living and working more."

"Who do they think brok uncle's house?" Colin asked.

Wendell eyed him. "Is this a rogation?"

"Like it would matter."

"I'm not the thief, and I di

Colin eyed him. "Was Kitty with Sean Murphy that night, Wendell?"

He sighed. "Not all night."

Emma noted her grandfather's matter-of-fact tone. "Granddad, that's not in the files —"

"No reason for it to be. Sean arrived in Declan's Cross that evening and stopped by the O'Byrne house to tell his uncle he was there. He was the last person Paddy saw before retiring to the kitchen. Kitty had already left. She had dinner at a restaurant in the village and walked up to Shepherd Head."

"How do you know she and Sean weren't together all night?" Colin asked.

"She told me she left her friend's house for a short time to take a walk by herself."

"You didn't ask if the friend was Sean?"

"I didn't need to." Wendell smiled. "Not being an officer of the law, I can just know what I know."

"Granddad . . ." Emma reined in her frustration. "Why didn't you tell me?"

"I didn't think to."

"Didn't think to," she repeated, but forced herself to take a deep, calming breath. "There's a difference between 'didn't think to' and 'just didn't.' "

He shrugged. "Not enough to matter.

Whatever was between Kitty O'Byrne and Sean Murphy obviously didn't end well, and exactly where they were that night won't tell us who the thief is. Even if they could provide each other with an alibi, it wouldn't be reliable." He toed a tuft of grass with his walking shoe. "I've been through this in my head a few times over the past ten years, you know."

Emma gritted her teeth, but she saw Colin bite back a smile, as if she'd just had a taste of her own medicine. "What about Aoife?" he asked. "Do you believe she was home alone in Dublin that night?"

"I don't know where she was," Wendell said. "From all accounts, John O'Byrne and his nieces got along well. He was a convivial fellow. He loved Declan's Cross."

Emma stepped out from the protected enclosure, but the wind had died down. The sky was clear, the small village bathed in the bright morning sun. "Granddad, have you told Irish authorities all you know about the thief?"

He bent down to peer at a grave marker, then stood straight, rubbing his lower back. "I'm not as spry as I used to be."

"Granddad . . ."

"Never could stall with you. I've told the gardai all I'm required to tell them. The

356

same goes for the FBI."

Wendell Sharpe, Emma remembered, could be exasperating. "If you're withholding evidence, I wouldn't blame the gardai if they lock you up and throw away the key."

He didn't look concerned. "Will the FBI meet me at customs when I go back to Heron's Cove?"

"It could be arranged," Colin muttered.

Wendell grinned at him. "Good answer. I wish I could be of more help. The Declan's Cross thief has never resorted to violence. That doesn't mean he won't. I've always felt he's responding to loss, regret, heartbreak — maybe all of them rolled into one — and it got mixed in with entitlement, control and a desire to best someone who wants to put an end to his party."

"You," Emma said.

"Us now, I think," he said, matter-of-fact. "He's trying to fill a black hole that can't be filled no matter what he steals, or how much he steals. That's my judgment, anyway. I worry the rage is building inside him and one day it will explode. If it already has and he did kill Lindsey Hargreaves . . ." He shook his head. "I just don't think that's what's happened."

"Let's go find Julianne," Colin said.

He dropped on the dirt path. Emma

suspected his timing was deliberate, that he wanted her grandfather a little off guard for what came next.

As they walked the short distance to the oratory, Colin said casually, "We suspect David Hargreaves might have had art stolen last week."

"What kind of art?" Wendell asked.

"Early works by Aoife O'Byrne. An Irish seascape and a Celtic cross. David and his wife at the time — Cynthia, Lindsey's mother — bought them here in Ardmore fifteen years ago."

"Ah."

Emma recognized her grandfather's tone. "You knew?"

"About the purchase. Not that they might have been stolen." He winked at her. "Don't be mad. I'm always careful about what I say when I'm dealing with the FBI."

Colin looked as if he could throttle him. "Dodgy answer, Wendell."

He waved a hand, dismissive. "I've had ten years to figure out who's bought Aoife's work, especially anything to do with Saint Declan and Declan's Cross. The Hargreaves name didn't jump out at me at first. Not until I asked Lucas to check the files."

"Lindsey met her father in Dublin over the weekend," Emma said. "He drove here to Ardmore on Monday and stayed on his own. It seems he was recreating his last good time with his wife before their divorce and her death a few years later."

"Do we know where David Hargreaves was when the O'Byrne house was broken into?" Colin asked.

"I don't." Wendell gave him a half smile. "I like how you say 'we.' I'm not in law enforcement for a reason, you know."

Colin continued along the path without comment. Emma walked beside her grandfather. "Aoife was living in Ardmore fifteen years ago," she said. "She couldn't have been more than twenty when she did the pieces the Hargreaves bought."

Wendell nodded, less combative. "She was experimenting with seascapes then, and she did several copies — variations on a theme — of the cross on her uncle's mantel. She stopped after the original was stolen. Now one of those copies and one of her seascapes are — what did you say? Missing?"

Emma had no doubt he remembered, but Colin glanced back at him and answered, "We said we suspected Hargreaves had art stolen. We don't know it for a fact. He told his housekeeper he sent the two O'Byrne pieces out to be appraised, but she doesn't believe him."

Wendell's eyebrows went up. "Do I need to know how you found this out?"

"You do not," Colin said. "Aoife's work is worth a lot more now than it was fifteen years ago. Have you ever met her?"

"After I talked to her uncle in Declan's Cross, so it's been almost ten years. I visited her at her studio in Dublin. She's something of a recluse. She's also one of the most beautiful women I've ever met." He glanced at Emma. "No, that's not in the files."

"What did you two talk about?" she asked him.

"We didn't talk. She shut the door in my face."

They came to the oratory, a small, square, stone building with a slate roof covered in white lichen. Julianne was standing on a stone used as a step, peering into a barred window. Colin stood next to her. "Having fun?"

"This place is creepy but fascinating." She pointed through the bars. "See the coffin-shaped hole? That's where Saint Declan was laid to rest."

Colin had a look, then stepped back. "I wonder if Saint Declan's body was ever in here."

"Always the skeptic." Julianne jumped off the stone. "That the grave is empty is

360

creepier somehow."

"Yes, it is," Colin said with a grin. "Do you want to have a look, Emma?"

She shook her head. "I've seen it."

Julianne adjusted her jacket, her cheeks rosy from the wind, the cool air and, perhaps, the excitement of finally getting to play tourist. "Saint Declan was a healer. Could that be why your thief stole the cross from the O'Byrne house? To capture Saint Declan's healing powers somehow?"

"It's possible," Emma said.

Her grandfather nodded in agreement. "Then again, so much is."

"If Lindsey stole the Aoife O'Byrne cross from her father, it didn't do her much good, did it?" Julianne glanced back at the oratory. "If the police found a cross on Lindsey's body or in her possessions, would they tell us? Would they tell you and Colin, as FBI agents?"

"Not necessarily," Emma said.

"Even if she stole the painting and cross, that doesn't mean she was murdered. Maybe she regretted what she did after spending time with her father in Dublin, and she went out to Shepherd Head to think — because of its connection to the stolen art."

"We can speculate all day," Colin said,

not harshly, and turned to Wendell. "I take it you're going straight on to Dublin?"

"I've some work to do," he said vaguely.

"I'm sure you do," Colin said with a trace of sarcasm. "Let's get you off so you can take your time getting back. I hate the thought of you on the Irish roads as it is."

"I've been driving the Irish roads since before your father was born."

"That's my point."

Wendell glanced at Emma. "This is what he's like?"

She smiled. "He's great, isn't he?"

Her grandfather sighed. "I say nothing. Let's at least have a bite to eat before you send me off. Follow me. I'll drive past where Aoife had her studio when she lived in Ardmore."

"Are you sure, Granddad? I don't want you falling asleep at the wheel —"

He kissed her on the cheek. "You and Lucas are worried about me. Don't be. I'm not on death's door, but at my age, whether it's a good day or a bad day, I still have more years behind me than ahead of me." He headed down the path, moving with his usual energy and agility.

"He's cute," Julianne said. "Larger than life but very cute."

"I think you're the only one on the planet

who thinks Wendell Sharpe is now or ever has been cute," Colin said, then glanced at Emma. "He cooperates with authorities when it suits him, doesn't he?"

"He'd tell you that he follows the law."

"Not quite the same thing, is it?"

Julianne laughed. "And I thought dating a Rock Point lobsterman was complicated." She paused by a rock wall covered in moss and heather and looked out at the view. "Granny would so love this. Andy would, too, but he'll be like Grandpa and never go anywhere —" She broke off and smiled cheerfully. "But it's thanks to Grandpa I'm here right now."

Emma understood Julianne's volatile emotions. "Lunch sounds good," she said, starting back up toward the round tower and their car.

Colin slung an arm over her shoulders. "Nothing like traipsing around in ancient ruins and old graves to work up an appetite."

20

Colin warned himself to be patient with Julianne as she flung off her seat belt and ran ahead of him into the cottage. He'd dropped off Emma at the hotel and then had driven Julianne up here to pack her things. Another night at the O'Byrne made sense to him. Less so to her. She wanted to stay at the cottage on her own. She'd made her case all the way up from the village. He'd finally realized that staying at the cottage wasn't the point — normalcy was the point. She'd fallen silent on the drive back from Ardmore, and he should have guessed the events of recent days — weeks, even — were taking their toll and eroding her cheerful mood at lunch.

He got out of the car and followed her to the front door. The small bungalow did look inviting. The afternoon had turned warm and pleasant, with little wind and no sign of rain. The sea was quiet under a clear blue sky. Emma's ewes were back at the fence, *baaing,* nudging each other as if he was the most exciting thing to come along all day.

No gardai in sight. They could still have a team out at the tip of Shepherd Head where Lindsey Hargreaves had died.

Julianne had left the door open. He went inside. "Go ahead," she said, staring out the window by the dining table. "Have a look around. Satisfy yourself that everything's fine."

Colin remained by the open door. "At least stay at the hotel one more night. Then we can see what's what in the morning."

She threw up her hands. "Fine."

"I'll wait here while you pack up."

"You don't need to wait. I can carry my suitcase down the hill. No problem."

He didn't answer. Answering, he saw now, would only give her more fodder for fighting with him. Didn't matter what he said.

She sniffled as she looked out the window at the impressive view. "I don't blame you for Andy. I don't even blame him." She glanced at Colin, her cheeks flushed with obvious emotion. "I was stupid. It never was going to work between us."

"You knew that going in, did you?"

"Yeah. I did. Andy did me a favor by dumping me. That's what he said, too. 'I'm doing you a favor, Jules.' Sounds like him, doesn't it?"

Colin shook his head. "Not answering that one, Julianne."

"I know talking about this stuff makes you squirm. I planned to go to the grocery yesterday after my walk." She went into the kitchen. She sounded calmer. Not as prickly. "I don't think anything in my welcome basket is in danger of rotting."

"No one will mind if it does."

"Good point." She stood still, one hand on the refrigerator. "Whoa. Colin."

He heard the fear in her voice and bolted into the kitchen. She pointed at the mud-room. The back door to the cottage was partially open.

"Goldilocks moment," Julianne said.

"Have you gone out this way?"

"I haven't touched that door since I got here."

Colin glanced at her. "Stay close to me."

"Happily, but you're not armed, are you?"

He winked. "Shh."

He stepped into the mudroom. He saw no obvious sign the door had been forced open. There was a washer and dryer, white wire shelves with cleaning supplies, a vacuum, broom, mop. Nothing seemed amiss.

He opened the door the rest of the way

and went outside. A strip of gravel along the back of the house gave way to green lawn and, in another ten yards, a post-and-wire fence. More sheep grazed in a rolling field.

To the left of the back door was a small shed that looked shut up tight. A gravel walk led around to the front of the bungalow.

"It was probably just the wind," Julianne said from the threshold.

"Maybe," Colin said. "Your landlord could have stopped by to check on the place and didn't shut the door tightly. The wind was pretty stiff this morning. It could have blown the door open."

"Yeah. I guess. Can we have a look at the rest of the cottage?"

He'd been thinking the same thing and returned to the kitchen with her. "Stay with me. Tell me if you see anything different from when you and Emma were here yesterday."

"Sure. Don't you want a broom or a kitchen knife or something to arm yourself?"

He grinned at her. "A broom, Julianne?"

Her eyes sparked. "Don't make fun of me."

"Never. Come on. I'm not going to let anything happen to you."

"I'm not worried about me. Honestly. I'm

just freaked out in general."

"I know, kid."

She sighed at him. "Would it do any good if I told you I'm going to punch you next time you call me kid?"

He laughed. "Probably not."

She stayed with him and didn't say a word as they checked the two bedrooms and bathrooms. No one was hiding in a closet or under a bed, and the only indication he saw that anyone had been inside the cottage was the back door.

"Wait," Julianne said, her face pale as they went back into the living room. "I shut the bedroom doors yesterday when Emma and I were here. I know I did."

"Could Emma have opened them after that?"

"No."

"What do you think happened, then?"

She took another quick breath. "It must have been the wind. Maybe I didn't shut the doors as tightly as I thought. Then the wind blew them open. Happens all the time at Granny's house. I never think twice about it."

Colin glanced around the quiet cottage. "No windows are open."

"The back door was open. Maybe that was enough. Maybe I left a window open, and

Sean or his uncle saw it, came in and shut it, then left through the back."

"We can ask them," Colin said.

"It could be my imagination. Jet lag. Shock." If possible, her face drained of more color, but she sighed and made an effort to smile. "Maybe it was one of Granny's dark fairies."

"I wouldn't doubt it. Grab your stuff. Let's get you back to the hotel."

"Are you going to report this to the police?"

"Report what, Julianne?"

She sighed again, looking tired now, even a little weepy. "I should have asked Lindsey more questions before I barreled into her life. I fell in love with the idea of coming to Ireland. Coastal Ireland is a whale and dolphin sanctuary and that's my field of expertise." Her eyes shone with tears. "It's beautiful here. It's exactly as I imagined. I know I can't erase yesterday from my mind, but I hope at least what happened wasn't the result of anything nefarious . . ." She shook her head. "I'm so sorry about all this, Colin. You and Emma —"

"Emma and I are fine. We're glad we can be here for you." He gave her a second, then grinned. "You just said 'nefarious,' didn't you?"

She told him to go to hell and disappeared into her bedroom.

When they went back out to the car, he offered to carry her suitcase, but she said, "No, thanks, got it," but at least didn't argue about walking into the village with it. As she set it on the ground and opened the passenger door, Colin noticed Sean Murphy and his uncle ambling down the lane together.

"We just found the back door open," Colin said when the two Irishmen reached him. "One of you?"

Paddy shook his head, and his garda nephew said, "It wasn't one of us. We'll have a look around. You'll be at the hotel?"

"On our way there now," Colin said.

"Good."

"Anything on the autopsy?"

The Irish detective's blue eyes were steady. "Broken neck. Her father knows."

"Must have been a hell of a fall."

Colin could see it was all he was getting. Sean Murphy said nothing as he started up the walk to the cottage.

Julianne didn't object when Paddy Murphy offered to help get her purple suitcase into the back of the car. She thanked him, and he wished her a good day and caught up with his nephew.

Colin called her on it when he got behind the wheel, but she had no apology. "It's not just the Irish accent," she said. "Sean and his uncle are totally charming."

"And I'm not?"

She gaped at him as if he'd turned shamrock-green. "Donovans are a lot of things, Colin, but charming? No. You are not charming."

"Ask Emma. She thinks I'm charming."

"Bet she doesn't."

He liked seeing the color in Julianne's cheeks as he started the car, but he wanted to know why the back door to her cottage had been open. He couldn't think what someone could have hoped to find there. Ten to one the door hadn't been securely latched and a wind gust had popped it open — but like so much of the past few days, a hard-and-fast answer wouldn't necessarily be easy to come by, or even possible.

Colin left Julianne in front of the fire in the bar lounge and went upstairs to find Emma. She'd left a note on the bed, in her neat handwriting, saying she was at the spa. *"I'm having a massage. I need to think."*

He didn't need to think. He needed to do something. He just didn't know what — and that, typically, was when he tended to get into trouble and make mistakes.

He checked his messages. Nothing from Yank, or even his brothers. Just as well, but he still had no desire to go back downstairs and have tea and cookies with Julianne.

Then again, it beat pacing in his hotel room.

Julianne was having tea and scones. She was settled in front of the fire with a book on Irish country cooking open on her lap. She looked so damn young. Colin decided not to tell her so.

She looked up at him. "I'm glad you were at the cottage with me just now. I mean that. When I walked into the kitchen and saw that door — I didn't think. I knew you were there and I yelled for you."

"That's what you should have done."

"I don't like seeing an open door and thinking something bad has happened. Here I am having tea and scones in Ireland as I've dreamed of doing since I was a little girl, and I keep thinking about Maine. It seems so far away." She shifted her gaze to the low fire. "It *is* far away."

Colin stood closer to the fire, welcoming its heat. "That was the point, wasn't it?"

"Yeah, I guess. Seeing you and Emma huddled with Wendell Sharpe reminded me that you do this sort of thing all the time. I don't. I'm writing a thesis on cetaceans."

"It sounds like an interesting paper."

"Thank you. It was nice of Emma's grandfather to ask about it at lunch, even if it was only to give us something else to talk about besides Lindsey's death and a ten-year-old art theft."

"I think he was genuinely interested," Colin said. "I know I was. Emma was, too."

"I appreciate that. My self-esteem's been kind of in the dumps lately." She ran her fingertips over a photograph of a tempting array of Irish cheeses, but Colin could tell her mind wasn't on cooking. She looked up at him again. "Do you think Emma made the right decision leaving her family business and joining the FBI?"

"It's not for me to say, but she's a top-notch agent."

"Granny wants me to stay in Rock Point and teach biology at the high school. It's a good option, but it's not for me."

"Ireland and far-off places call," Colin said.

"I have other options — lots of them are a comfortable middle between staying in Rock Point and wandering to far-off places."

"I imagine you have all kinds of options."

"Andy does, too."

"I'm not discussing my brother with you,

Julianne."

She gave him a half smile. "That's the hard-ass Colin Donovan I know." She closed her book on her lap. "I love having tea by the fire. I love being here. I never should have asked Lindsey to stay with me. What if she died because she went to check on the cottage? What if she'd still be alive if she'd stayed in Cork, or in Dublin with her father, or even at the field station with the divers?"

"Don't do this to yourself. Lindsey's death isn't your fault."

"I've never heard you so — I don't know. Concerned about me."

"I didn't need to be concerned when you were ladling out chowder at Hurley's."

"You needed to be concerned when I started dating your brother," she said.

Colin shook his head. "Still not going there, kid."

She set aside her book and picked up her tea. "Sean Murphy told you how Lindsey died, didn't he?"

"Julianne —"

"She broke her neck, right? I'm guessing death was quick, maybe instantaneous."

He watched the fire a moment, noticed it had died to hot coals. He said, "That's right."

"Do you think she could have sustained that kind of catastrophic injury in a freak fall off the ledge? It's a good drop, but I don't know. I guess it'd be hard to tell from the autopsy if she was pushed."

"I'm not a medical examiner," Colin said.

"Neither am I, but we both grew up in Maine. People fall on the rocks all the time. How many end up breaking their necks? Some, I know, but . . ." She didn't finish. "Can the medical examiner tell if she was killed first and then someone flung her body off the ledge?"

"Julianne . . ."

"I know. Gruesome talk over tea and scones. I wouldn't have brought it up if there were other guests in here. I wonder where Lindsey's father is." She drank some of her tea and returned the cup to its saucer. "All right. I can see you're not going to tell a non-FBI agent what you think. Will you miss being an FBI agent if you quit?"

"You've been talking to Emma."

"Andy, actually. He thinks the past six months in particular have been tough on you. I told him you like it tough, but now I don't know." Julianne lifted her book back onto her lap. "Maybe it's Emma. Her influence on you."

Even worse than talking about his brother

and high-impact falls with Julianne Ma-roney was talking about Emma. Colin moved back from the fire. "Try to rest. Have dinner tonight with Emma and me in the restaurant here." He winked at her. "We'll do fancy."

"You have a tie?"

He grinned. "In my closet at home."

"I can see the Donovans when you all dressed up in suits for my grandfather's funeral. Colin, I swear I'm here just for the marine science and scones and walks on quaint lanes."

"You don't have to convince me. Do you have anything to wear to dinner that doesn't involve mucking about in a tide pool?"

Some of her fight sparked in her hazel eyes. "You sound like Andy. You're all rat bastards, you know. Handy in a fight but not that great at a candlelight dinner."

"Hey, don't sell us short."

"Maybe the Sharpes are rubbing off on you."

He ignored that last comment. "I'll see you at dinner."

She didn't argue with him. He didn't know if that was a good sign or a bad sign, but she seemed stronger, more sure of herself, as he headed outside to the gardens.

He was walking past beds of pansies when

Emma joined him. "I'm telling you," she said, tucking her hand into his, "you would love the spa."

"Think a deep-tissue massage would help me?" He squeezed her hand gently. "Am I too hard on people, Emma? The work I do on top of being a Donovan . . ."

"Where are you going with this, Colin?"

"Beats the hell out of me."

"I don't think so." She knotted her fingers into his. "I'm getting to know you, don't forget."

"Sometimes I wonder if I'm the right man for a woman like you."

"A woman like me. Are you referring to my being a Sharpe, an art crimes specialist, an FBI agent or an ex-nun?"

"All of the above."

"I see."

He had a feeling she did see. "I've pushed you hard, Emma. I know I can be rough on people. I know I look for all the sharp angles and dark corners. It's not just my under-cover work."

"It's who you are." She eased her hand from his and slipped her arm around him. "Don't soften your hard edges on my ac-count. I like who you are. I like your hon-esty, your toughness, your instincts." She put her head against his arm as they paused by a low rock wall, covered in moss, heather and died-back ferns. "And I love you."

He held her close. "I love you, too, Emma. Always."

"But you don't think it's enough, do you?"

"Emma . . ."

She smiled. "It's okay. It's a beautiful afternoon. We don't have to get deep. Let's just walk." She lowered her arm and took his hand again. "You've got a big heart, Colin. All you Donovans do. I see that."

"Even Mike?"

She laughed. "Especially Mike."

They wandered through the O'Byrne gardens and down to the sea, tossing rocks into the tide, and when they returned to the terrace and saw David Hargreaves at a small table in the shadows, Colin felt Emma stiffen next to him. The intrusion of reality. The end of their short pretense that they were on a romantic getaway.

Hargreaves had a glass of white wine in front of him. His face was ashen, but he motioned with one hand and said, "Please join me."

Emma pulled out a chair and sat down, but Colin remained standing, ready to excuse himself if she proved more able to deal with the grieving father and his relationship with his daughter. "We were in Ardmore this morning," she said. "My grandfather met us there. We had lunch at the Cliff House Hotel. Is that where you stayed on Monday?"

He nodded. "It's a wonderful place. It's built into the side of a cliff. Every room has a view of Ardmore Bay. Lindsey's mother would have loved it." He picked up his glass. "Would you care for wine?"

Emma shook her head. "We're having dinner here at the hotel soon. Do you have plans?"

"An early bedtime. I'm exhausted. I walked out to where Lindsey died. I could have asked one of the officers to take me, but I wanted to go alone." He inhaled deeply. "It was difficult. Very difficult."

"Had you ever been out there before?" Emma asked him.

"No, never. This is my first time in Declan's Cross. My last, too, I'm certain, as lovely as it is. I'm returning to Dublin tomorrow. The gardai tell me they'll release Lindsey's remains as soon as possible." He set his glass down without having drunk any of the wine. "I'm sure having two FBI agents in town got their attention, but nothing suggests foul play was involved in her death."

Colin debated taking a seat but instead peeked in a window. Julianne had vacated her spot by the fire. Someone had added another log. He watched it burn, while behind him, Emma let David Hargreaves talk. She had a way of drawing people out, and Colin only wanted to insert himself into the mix at the right moment.

"Of course," David continued, "you and Special Agent Donovan are in Ireland on vacation. I understand that. I feel terrible that Lindsey's death interrupted what must be well-deserved time off, and that it's marred this place. At least it's not the high season. By spring people will have forgotten a young American woman fell out here on a wet November day."

Colin turned from the window to a large stone urn and feigned interest in its array of flowers and vines.

Emma sat back in her chair. "Did your wife visit Declan's Cross when you were in Ardmore fifteen years ago?"

David obviously didn't expect the question. "Special Agent Sharpe —"

"We're trying to understand why Lindsey chose Declan's Cross," Emma said evenly.

"I thought you had no role in the investigation." When she didn't explain, his shoulders slumped, as if the energy to stay offended, on alert, had gone out of him.

"Cynthia drove to Declan's Cross by herself one day. She told me she wanted to test her Irish driving skills. She had lunch at a pub and then drove back to Ardmore."

"Was that —"

"It was after I'd bought the Aoife O'Byrne works." His gaze steadied on Emma. "That was your next question, wasn't it? I'm aware that a senior FBI agent spoke to my housekeeper last night."

So Yank was accounted for but there was no mention of Mike and Andy, Colin noted.

"I thought you might be," Emma said.

"The Aoife O'Byrne works are a personal matter with no relevance to Lindsey's death."

"Did you or your wife know about Aoife's connection to Declan's Cross?"

"I didn't," he said, reaching for his wineglass again. "I don't know if Cynthia did. She never said."

"If she drove down here —"

"She was a painter herself. She was always looking for scenes, especially seascape, to paint."

Emma waited as he sipped some of his wine. She touched a finger to a bit of a red flower petal that had landed on the table. When she didn't continue, Colin realized she wasn't going to bring up the connection between the cross Aoife O'Byrne had made fifteen years ago and the cross on the hill near where Lindsey had died. Not only would Emma not want to tread on an Irish investigation, she would take great care with her own.

Colin abandoned the urn. "Where are your Aoife O'Byrne works now?" he asked, sitting next to Emma.

David set his glass down with exaggerated patience. "If it turns out Lindsey's death wasn't an accident, it's far more likely to be because she stumbled into the middle of a Sharpe or an FBI vendetta than because I bought two works by an emerging Irish artist fifteen years ago." He pushed back his chair and rose, formal, awkward. "I've answered every question the Irish authorities have asked me truthfully and to the best of my ability. Now I just want to take my daughter home."

"Let us know if there's anything we can do to help," Emma said, her tone neutral.

"Thank you. Please excuse me. I'm very tired, and I've suffered a terrible loss. I hope you understand."

He left quickly, without waiting for any response. Colin watched him march through the gardens back toward his cottage. "He knew we'd ask about last night," he said.

"He just hoped we wouldn't."

"He's lying about the appraisal."

Emma's expression tightened as she shot to her feet. "Yes, he is."

Colin stood next to her. Time to lighten the mood. "So, I noticed you packed that cute little skirt you bought in Killarney. Going to wear it to dinner?"

It worked. She smiled. "Anything for you, Colin."

"I'll remember that." He noticed that now her smile reached her green eyes, and he leaned in close to her and whispered, "Best part of that skirt is getting it off of you."

"And I," she said, "will remember that."

21

Sean resisted kicking in the door to the
O'Byrne House kitchen but only because it
was unlocked. Even then, it was a near
thing. He hadn't been this agitated in a long
time. Not since he'd come to blows with his
smugglers.

He heard a muffled sob coming from a
side office and ducked in there instead of
continuing on to the main cooking area.

Philip was seated at a tidy desk, a first-aid
kit torn open in front of him as he dabbed
antibiotic ointment on a bloody cut on his
hand. He looked up, the left side of his jaw
and his left cheek also bloodied and bruised.

Sean ground his teeth. "Philip."

"It's nothing." He squirted more cream
out of the tube. "Go away."

"Did someone catch you sneaking around
on the farm and knock your head in?"

"I don't know what happened. I didn't
see."

Sean stepped deeper into the small, airless room and adjusted a desk lamp to get a better look at the lad's face. He had to be in pain, but the cuts were superficial — they wouldn't need stitches — and Sean doubted there were any broken bones.

He stood back. "You were at the cottage. I saw blood splattered out by the shed. Were you hit there, or somewhere else?"

"I didn't say I was hit at all."

"You left the back door open. Our FBI agent Donovan took a look but didn't go as far as the shed — only because he had to see to Julianne Maroney. If he'd found the blood, believe me, it wouldn't have mattered that Lindsey's death isn't his investigation."

Philip touched his swollen jaw. "This has nothing to do with Lindsey."

"Doesn't it?"

Kitty swooped in, one hand on the door latch as she gasped at her son. "Philip — dear God in heaven, what's happened? Should I call the gardai?"

"No need to now," Sean said.

Kitty didn't seem to hear him. She edged in closer to her son. "Do you need a doctor?"

"It's not as bad as it looks," Philip said, his words slurred, no doubt from the swelling. He pointed to a plastic bag filled with partially melted ice. "I know what to do."

Sean jumped in while Kitty absorbed what she was seeing. "Why didn't you come to me for help?" he asked.

Philip stood and shut the first-aid kit, then shoved it back onto an open shelf above the desk. "Why would I have?"

A fair point, but Sean didn't let up. "Why didn't you call the gardai when you got here? If you were assaulted —" He softened his tone, although it took some effort. "Talk to me, lad."

"I went out to the rocks where Lindsey —"

"Where this woman *died*?" Kitty shrieked. "What were you thinking?"

Sean shot her a look. "Wait in the kitchen."

She stood straight and glared at him. "I'll do no such thing."

"You will, Kitty. Don't coddle him. He's a man. He can answer for himself."

Her mouth dropped open, but she told her son she'd be in the kitchen and then stepped out of the tiny office.

Philip sank onto the edge of the desk and picked up his bag of ice. "I didn't get hit out on the rocks. I was hit at the cottage."

"What were you doing there? Why did you sneak inside?"

"Aren't gardai trained to ask one question at a time?"

Sean knew the sarcastic remark was intended to get a rise out of him — to divert him. "You're lucky it's my cottage and I'm the one who saw the blood. An American woman just died, Philip. There are a lot of unanswered questions. You don't want to be sneaking around FBI agents."

"I wasn't. Lindsey was staying at the cottage." He sounded less confrontational. He placed the ice on his hand and winced, clearly in pain. "That was her plan, anyway. How did you know it was me? It could have been anyone's blood."

Paddy had spotted him, but Sean said, "It doesn't matter. What I need from you is the truth. What are you hiding?"

"I'm not hiding anything."

Sean reined in his impatience. "You are. The FBI agents know it and so do I. So does your mother. I'm not worried about them. I'm worried about you."

Philip put the ice to his jaw. "I don't believe you."

Sean ignored him and checked Philip's bloodied hand. "This looks like a cut."

"I fell after I got hit in the face. I don't know what I landed on. By the time I got to my feet, whoever ambushed me was gone."

"*Ambush* is a strong word. Did you see who hit you?"

Philip made a fist, as if testing his first-aid job and the extent of the swelling. "People are on edge."

"Who did it, Philip?"

"Sean . . ." He looked away, putting the ice back onto his injured hand.

Sean could feel the heat of the small room, so close to the kitchen. "Who?"

"You'll tell the guards —"

"I am one, Philip. I'm just on leave recovering from a thrashing of my own."

He raised his eyes, reminding Sean of his mother. "I thought you fell."

"I did. I also got thrashed." Sean leaned in close to him. "Who hit you?"

"It was your uncle, Sean. At least I think it was. That's why I didn't want to say anything. We're all on edge with what's happened. Paddy —"

"How do you know it was Paddy?"

"I got a glimpse of his jacket and cap," Philip said, clearly reluctant. "I can't say for certain it was him."

"Did you see his face?"

"No."

Eyewitnesses weren't always reliable for a reason. Sean sighed. "You need fresh ice. Get some and think about telling me the rest. I'll see to Paddy."

Philip touched the tip of his little finger to the worst of the swelling on his cheek. "Will you tell the guards? I mean the ones investigating Lindsey's death."

"You will. Your mother will take you. You'll tell them everything that happened. Don't leave out anything." Sean paused. "D'you understand, Philip?"

He tried to nod but moaned in pain.

Kitty was back in the doorway, fighting tears. "I'll get the ice, and I'll see to it he talks to the gardai." Her voice was low, calm, a reminder that she ran an upscale hotel and could handle herself in a crisis. She raised her eyes to Sean. "Where will you be?"

"I don't know. Call me if you need me."

He left them and went outside through the kitchen door. He'd never be a patient man, but he'd always and forever be a loyal one, and that, he feared, would one day be his undoing.

He welcomed the cold evening air as he walked out through the garden and into the village. He found Paddy on a wooden stool in his favorite pub. Sean almost went back out again. He could be up at the farm mucking out stalls or carrying in turf for a fire. There was always work. Then again, he'd never been bored as a garda, either. Wasn't in his nature.

He sat next to his old uncle. "Did you throttle Philip Doyle this afternoon?"

"Kitty's son? What happened? Is he all right?"

"Paddy —"

"I didn't throttle him. That doesn't mean I haven't wanted to from time to time." Paddy narrowed his eyes. "You wouldn't be sitting here if Philip was hurt badly."

"Ice and a good night's sleep will take care of him. He says he was blindsided up at the cottage by someone wearing your jacket and cap."

"My jacket and —" Paddy frowned as if his nephew had lost his mind. "What are you talking about?"

"You're wearing a sweater tonight."

"It's all I need, and I don't wear my barn jacket and cap to the pub."

"Where are they now, Paddy?"

"Hanging off the kitchen up at the farm, same as always."

Sean waved off the barman, although he wanted a pint. He focused on his uncle. "You'd tell me if you'd hit the lad, wouldn't you, Paddy? A lot's been going on. It'd be easy to hear someone and get nervous —"

"The only time I was at the cottage today

was with you, when we saw the marine biologist and that FBI agent." Paddy spoke calmly, not sounding particularly offended at his nephew's questions. "After I told you I saw Philip."

"Where were you again when you saw him?"

"On my way back to the house from the upper field. I'd let loose some of the rams. Philip was on foot — he was almost to the cottage."

"Coming up from the village?"

"Other direction. I figured he'd gone to see where Lindsey was found. The gardai have finished their work out there. Philip was alone."

"What did you do after you saw him?"

Paddy shrugged. "I went on to the house, cleaned up and did some paperwork."

"Could someone have slipped in through the back and borrowed your jacket and cap?"

"I don't hear as well as I used to, so I suppose it's possible. Why take that chance? Me right there. You right in the barn."

Sean nodded. "More likely Philip caught a glimpse of a jacket and cap similar to yours." Or he'd lied, Sean thought. "You didn't wear them when we walked down to the cottage —"

"I wouldn't have. I was through with the farm work for the day."

Sean would have liked to have asked Philip more questions — when he'd gone up to Shepherd Head, what he'd done, why he'd stopped at the cottage. But the gardai investigating Lindsey's death would ask all those questions. By rights, Sean had no business talking to Paddy now.

"Did you see anyone else?"

"An older man — the dead girl's father, I think. That was earlier, before I saw Philip. I let him be. He had the look of a man who needed to be alone with his grief."

Sean supposed that Paddy, a widower himself, would recognize that in another man. "Did you talk to anyone?"

"The sheep." His eyes twinkled ever so slightly. "I've always talked to the sheep, you know."

"I suspected as much." Sean relaxed a little at his uncle's half-hearted stab at humor. "What did you do after you saw Philip?"

"I ran into you, and we walked to the cottage together. Ah, Sean. I'm sorry I've disappointed you."

"You've never disappointed me."

The old man stared into his Guinness. "I wasn't drunk that night."

Sean knew what night he meant.

"I was in the room down by the kitchen, just as I told the gardai and the Sharpe fellow. I wasn't asleep, though." He took in a long breath. "Old John O'Byrne and I didn't have much in common, but we'd both lost women we loved with all our hearts far too soon. Your aunt Ruth had a soft spot for him, and she adored the house. Her mother used to clean it, before John's day. Ruth would help from time to time. I got to thinking of her as a little girl, and I couldn't stand it, Sean. I sobbed my blasted eyes out. I missed her so much that for a time I thought I wouldn't go on and . . ." He didn't finish. "I miss her still. I think of her every day."

"I'm sorry, Paddy."

"She's gone to God, lad. She's gone to God." He shook his head in despair. "I was too embarrassed to tell anyone, but I might as well have been asleep. I didn't see the thief. I didn't hear a blasted thing."

"Kitty should have been there. You shouldn't have been alone in that house and then had to bear the suspicions —"

"Do you think I cared about that? That people wonder if I was drunk that night, or that I let in the thief myself? I care that because of what I did, you threw away a chance at happiness, lad. I know where Kitty was that night." Paddy stood up from his stool. "You two were good together."

"It was an illusion."

"It was a fine illusion, then."

"It was," Sean said, standing next to his uncle. "I have the devil to pay for my mistakes, Paddy. You had nothing to do with them. Come on. I'll walk you home."

"Do you think Philip lied to you, Sean?"

"I don't think so. I think he just didn't tell me everything."

Paddy nodded thoughtfully. "He's still a fish out of water in Declan's Cross, but he's been here long enough that he is in Dublin, too. He doesn't know where he wants to be. Understandable at that age. You were the same."

"The same?" Sean grinned at his uncle. "It's a good thing you're a farmer, because you're better at analyzing sheep than you are people."

Paddy didn't argue. "Anyway," he said, buttoning his heavy sweater, "I can walk home on my own. You needn't worry about me. I can still take care of myself in a fight."

"I know you can," Sean said. "It's your company I want."

Paddy's barn jacket and wool cap were

hanging on their pegs off the kitchen as always. Sean didn't see blood stains or anything else that suggested they'd been involved in thrashing Philip Doyle.

He walked down to the cottage, imagining himself as a boy, loving this place — loving the farm — and yet knowing he wanted something else for himself, and it wasn't in Declan's Cross.

The gardai had just arrived with Philip. Sean opened up the little bungalow and turned on the outside lights for them. Philip was pale, subdued, his bruises blossoming into ugly splotches of purple and blue on his face. His hand was bandaged. His mother's doing, no doubt, but Philip was alone now with the gardai. Kitty hadn't forced her way up there. That was a good thing, Sean told himself, even as he felt an urge to protect Philip himself.

He left the gardai to their work. They'd lock the cottage after they'd finished, and they'd decide without his help if they wanted to check Paddy's jacket and cap for themselves.

When he got back to the farmhouse, Sean wasn't surprised to find Colin Donovan on the front step. "Busy up here lately," the American said. "It's usually quiet, isn't it? Just you and your uncle and a lot of sheep?"

Sean went past him and opened the door. "What can I do for you, Special Agent Donovan?"

"I'm walking off my dinner. Thought I'd have that whiskey."

"Come in, then."

Sean knew he didn't sound particularly hospitable, but Colin didn't seem to mind. They went into the kitchen, and Sean got down the Bracken 15 and two glasses. "I've worked with FBI agents before," he said. "You and Emma are unusual."

Colin took a seat at the table. "That's why our boss likes us."

Sean grinned. "I can just imagine."

"He wants to do a Vulcan mind meld with her grandfather — know what he knows."

"He's not the only one, I can tell you. Emma can be a Sharpe one day and an FBI agent the next?"

"She's both every day. That's what I've finally figured out."

"It's not always easy, is it?"

"I don't know that it's ever easy, but it works."

Sean poured the whiskey and handed Colin a glass, then sat across from him with his own. "How do we know her grandfather isn't our Declan's Cross thief? He was living in Dublin ten years ago."

Colin settled back in his chair. "Is that what you think?"

Sean shrugged. "I keep an open mind and follow the evidence. Isn't that what you do, Special Agent Donovan?"

"Sometimes I operate on pure gut instinct. It's great when it works. When it doesn't —"

"It can get messy," Sean finished for him.

Colin grinned. "Almost caused me to be eaten by alligators a few weeks ago." He raised his glass. "Which is only the slightest exaggeration. So, is there any evidence that points to Wendell Sharpe?"

"It's not my investigation."

"Right. That's what I say when I don't want to answer another law enforcement officer's question. You don't trust many people, do you?"

Sean swallowed some of his whiskey. "I don't distrust you. If I did, I wouldn't have offered you the Bracken 15. Does Emma ever think about quitting the FBI and returning to her family business?"

"Sometimes."

"When her background as a Sharpe complicates her work instead of enhances it?"

"More like when she feels like baking pies in Maine."

Sean almost smiled. He found himself liking Colin Donovan, but he realized the FBI agent had come to ask questions, not to answer them. Sean nodded toward the window, rattling in the wind. "You should be off soon. I can give you a lift if you'd like."

"Who attacked Philip, Sean?"

"I don't know that anyone did."

"Think he tripped on his shoe laces and made up an attack?"

"I think these are difficult days and we should see what the gardai come back with."

The FBI agent assessed him with a frankness that Sean recognized as calculated, deliberate. "Fair enough," Colin said finally, rising. "Thanks for the drink."

"Care to borrow a hat, Special Agent Donovan?"

He just grinned and left. Sean stood in the front door and watched the American walk out to the lane. He didn't look as if the thought of the cold and wind troubled him at all.

Sean noticed headlights.

The gardai and Philip leaving the cottage.

He shut the door and went back into the kitchen. He built a fire and poured himself another *taoscán* of Bracken 15, fighting an image of walking in the cold and wind with pretty Kitty O'Byrne.

22

Emma was explaining what she had learned about whiskey from Father Bracken to Philip as he slumped next to her at the bar. He had a Coke and a fresh ice pack for his cuts and bruises. His mother looked on from behind the bar. Kitty was clearly controlling her emotions, putting on a good face to her guests even as her son turned black-and-blue.

"The Bracken brothers do know their whiskey," Emma said. "Twins who set about opening an independent distillery in their early twenties. Quite a dream."

"Most dreams don't come true," Philip said.

Emma understood his mood. Attacked at the Murphy cottage, in the wrong place at the wrong time — she believed his story but was also convinced he was holding on to things, perhaps things that were of more consequence to him than to the investigation into Lindsey's death.

She guessed what one of them was. "You told Lindsey about Father Bracken," she said.

He nodded, an effort that caused him obvious pain. "It's why you're here. Because I told her we had a friend in Maine, and she went to see him. And now she's dead."

Kitty stiffened visibly behind the bar. "How does one thing lead to the next? You can't think Lindsey died because she visited a priest in Maine who knows two FBI agents."

Emma could see there was more to it. She kept her gaze on Philip. "When did you tell Lindsey about Father Bracken?"

"Right before she left to visit her father in Massachusetts. She was here for a drink and we got to talking about the theft. I took her upstairs to show her where the paintings had been stolen. I didn't think a thing of it. I was showing off."

Kitty sucked in an audible breath. Emma glanced up at her, but Kitty busied herself behind the bar and said nothing.

"Lindsey was happy here," Philip continued. "She told me that. She loved diving and would go on about whales and things, but she was interested in everything. She'd been out to the ruins on Shepherd Head and said she was fascinated by the old graves and crosses."

"Did she mention your aunt?" Emma asked.

His eyes widened in surprise, but it was Kitty who responded. "Aoife? Why in heaven's name would Lindsey Hargreaves be interested in my sister?"

Emma decided to answer. "Her parents bought two of Aoife's works fifteen years ago on a visit to Ardmore."

"Fifteen . . ." Kitty paled. "I had no idea."

"It's one piece of what's become a rather complex puzzle," Emma said, keeping her tone even, neutral, as she turned to Philip. "Did you tell Lindsey that my grandfather had looked into the theft?"

Tears pooled in his eyes, and he sniffled, placing an ice pack again on his jaw. "I did." His voice was barely a hoarse whisper. He cleared his throat before he went on. "I was a small boy back then. To me it was all an adventure. No one was hurt."

And telling Lindsey was a way to impress an older, attractive, well-connected woman. Emma eased off the comfortable stool. She'd had two sips of whiskey, but they were enough. "Philip, you don't have to protect Lindsey or anyone else. Just tell the investigators everything you know. Let them sort out what's relevant."

"That's what I told him, too," Kitty said, defensive. "And now he has. Haven't you, Philip?"

"Not about Father Bracken and the Sharpes. I'll tell them now."

Philip seemed stronger, more certain of himself and what he had to do. Kitty, on the other hand, looked shaken, but she nodded at her son. "I'll let you handle it, then."

Emma left them. She had a rush of questions of her own to process. She went upstairs and noticed Julianne was alone in the reading room, sitting on the floor in front of the fireplace, a fire burning behind a screen.

"Mind if I join you?" Emma asked.

Julianne smiled. "Please do." She nodded up at Aoife O'Byrne's seascape. "I don't know much about art, but that's an amazing painting."

Emma sat next to her on the thick carpet. Julianne was in leggings and an oversize sweater, no shoes, as if she'd tried to settle in for the evening and found she couldn't stand being alone. She hadn't joined Emma and Colin for dinner, instead ordering a sandwich in her room. Emma still had on her skirt from dinner, but she kicked off her flats and wiggled her toes, welcoming the heat of the fire.

"It's weird how life can throw people together at intense times." Julianne leaned back against the love seat. "You've been all over the world, Emma. Monday was my first time on a transatlantic flight. I had this whole trip rationalized in my head, but the truth is, I was running away from Rock Point. From myself."

"Maybe that's what you had to do."

"You're very centered, aren't you? At peace with yourself."

"I don't know about that," Emma said.

"It's hard to stay at peace with yourself when you're in love with a Donovan."

"Are you, Julianne? In love with a Donovan?"

Julianne gave a small moan. "Andy. Just who I want to think about while sitting in front of an Irish fire."

"It doesn't answer the question, does it?"

"No, it doesn't, Special Agent Sharpe." Julianne sat up straight. "I don't have a Donovan in love with me. You do. Where is Colin, by the way?"

"He went up to see Sean Murphy."

"Sean. Now, he's an interesting guy. Good-looking, too. Who knows, if the field station had worked out, maybe I could have become a staff biologist and . . ." She paused and looked at Emma. "He's, what, thirty-six or thirty-seven? That's not too old for me, is it?" She looked again at the fire. "I don't know what to do, Emma. I keep thinking about Andy. It's not healthy."

"You've been taking the steps to move on with your life," Emma said.

"Running away to Ireland on a whim?"

"Julianne —"

"I ruined Rock Point for myself by getting involved with Andy. Maybe deep down that's why I did it. A bad, inevitable breakup with Andy Donovan would force me to leave."

Emma listened to the wind gusting against the windows, the crackle of the fire, and felt Julianne's exhaustion — felt how much she wanted Andy with her right now.

"I'll be fine," Julianne said. "Really. I'm not lying dead at the base of an Irish ledge."

"You're strong, Julianne, and you're resilient. Maybe you don't have to be so hard on yourself for falling for Andy." Emma touched Julianne's hand. "Or for still being in love with him."

Julianne stood quickly, wiping tears off her cheeks. "Thanks, Emma. I'll rally. I'll figure all this out."

"You don't have to do it alone."

"I appreciate that, but you and Colin have

enough going on. I'll pull myself together. I'll figure out what to do in the morning. Going back to the cottage now that Kitty's son got bloodied up there . . ." She sighed. "That wouldn't go over well with Colin, would it? Not that I need him to stop me this time. The past week to the contrary, I do have some common sense. I'm glad Philip's okay. That's what matters."

Emma got to her feet. "We could get you out of here tomorrow. Maybe drive over to Killarney and hike up to Torc Waterfall, or do a boat tour of the lakes. Now that the field station hasn't worked out, you don't have to stay in Declan's Cross. You could spend the rest of your two weeks over there. It's incredibly beautiful."

"That's tempting. When do you go home? You haven't told me already, have you?"

"I was booked on a flight tomorrow."

"What about Colin?"

"He'll be staying a bit longer," Emma said.

Julianne studied her, but said only, "You two are something," then smiled and headed into the hall.

When Emma returned to her room, Colin still wasn't back yet. She filled the tub with water as hot as she could stand and added scented salts — rose geranium, she saw —

and slid in. She closed her eyes and let the pieces of the puzzle of this little village and its ties to Rock Point, Heron's Cove, a theft a decade ago — a death a few days ago — drift past her.

She heard Colin come into the room.

"It's me," he said.

"I'm in the tub."

"Are there bubbles?"

"There are no bubbles."

"Good."

He opened the bathroom door. He'd pulled off his jacket and had on the sweater he'd worn to dinner — Irish cashmere that she'd bought for him on a shopping-and-lunch day in Kenmare. It seemed like a hundred years ago but had been just last week.

He sat on the edge of the tub. She let a facecloth float strategically over her. "Are we any closer to knowing what happened to Philip?" she asked him.

"I'm not. I doubt Sean Murphy is, either."

"Philip doesn't know. He's racked with guilt because he talked to Lindsey about the theft. He told her about my family. I doubt she went to Maine just to clear her head and say hello to Finian."

"It doesn't mean she stole the Aoife O'Byrne pieces from her father, either.

That's what you're thinking, isn't it?"

She smiled. "I'm trying not to think."

He returned her smile. "I was hoping you were going to say that."

He stole her facecloth and cast it aside, then lowered his mouth to hers in the sexiest kiss ever. Him dressed . . . her naked in the tub . . . the hot water swirling over her breasts, between her legs . . . his tongue parting her lips, plunging deep, insistent, erotic. Sensations bubbled through her. Desire, love, dreams that she'd once thought impossible.

Then his fingertips slid ever so lightly over her wet skin . . .

"Colin." She couldn't breathe. "I'm going to drown. I swear."

He dipped his hand into the water, skimmed his fingertips over her hips. He had to know he was torturing her. He plunged his hand deeper into the water, until his fingers found their mark. He stifled her cry of pleasure with his mouth, his tongue matching the rhythm of his fingers.

Ragged, aching, she raised up out of the water, throwing her arms around him, ready to pull him in with her.

He lifted her out of the tub. Water went everywhere, but she didn't care — and obviously he didn't, either. He laid her on the soft, thick bathroom rug. She pulled him down on top of her, and he feasted on her — tongue, teeth, fingers exploring, taking her to the edge and back again, not letting her go over.

She tore at his shirt, pulled at his pants, making little progress . . . until he helped. Then his clothes were off in seconds, cast onto the edge of the tub, in the scented water.

"Emma, if the floor —"

"The floor's good. It's perfect."

And it was. The moment he touched her again, she was lost — there was him, and only him. She arched to meet him, and, when he plunged into her, felt his heart racing with hers. This time when he took her to the edge, he let her go over . . . and went with her.

Later, when their bodies had cooled, he pulled a towel off the heated rack, wrapped it around her and carried her to bed. In the darkness, she held him close, skimmed her hands over the familiar shape of his muscles, the sexy roughness of his callused hands, and she splayed her fingers on his chest, felt his heartbeat and knew she loved this man, and would forever.

23

Andy Donovan had never thought much about Heron's Cove. It was a good spot to take a date for dinner or to check out cute shops, fancy yachts and big summer houses. Sharpe Fine Art Recovery was located in a gray-shingled Victorian tucked between an upscale marina and a picturesque inn at the mouth of the tidal Heron River. Wendell Sharpe used to work in a front room. Now, except for a small apartment in back, the entire house was being transformed into offices.

Andy went around back and found Lucas Sharpe on the porch overlooking the water. The tide was out, the marina quiet on an early November afternoon. Lucas was tall and sandy-haired, with a strong enough resemblance to Emma that people would recognize them as brother and sister. He had on ratty khakis and a canvas shirt spattered with white paint, as if he'd been helping prime walls — but he said no, not here. He'd been painting at his house in the village. "The carpenters don't like me helping here."

A couple of them were from Rock Point and had told Andy the same thing. He'd met Lucas since his sister had taken up with Colin in September, but didn't know him well.

"I'm short on time," Andy said. "Sorry to cut to the chase. Why wouldn't someone report an art theft?"

Lucas eyed him for a beat, then answered. "Ransom. The thief threatens to destroy the art if the owner doesn't pay up. Insurance fraud. Inheritance disagreements. Ownership disputes. Those are some of the most obvious reasons. Does this have something to do with Declan's Cross?"

"You've talked to Emma?"

"And my grandfather."

Andy noticed an empty easel in the corner of the porch. Emma was an amateur painter. Any artistic talents he had went into his boat restoration work. He didn't know about Lucas. Looked more the type to relish the cerebral aspects of his work. "Any theories why David Hargreaves wouldn't report the theft of the two Aoife O'Byrne pieces he owns?"

"He could have thought he was protecting his daughter, his reputation — his family's reputation."

"Avoiding publicity, then."

"A prison sentence for Lindsey, too, perhaps, unless she could claim ownership." Lucas picked up a paintbrush drying on the porch rail and tested the bristles. "Hargreaves isn't giving a straight story."

"Doesn't sound like it," Andy said. "There's more to this unsolved theft in this little Irish village than you and Emma and Colin are saying, isn't there?"

Lucas returned the paintbrush to the rail. "I don't know that it has anything to do with what's happening there now. Lindsey's mother was a painter, but she never got a toehold and spiraled downhill after the divorce." He nodded toward the back door. "I spoke to the carpenters just now. A woman fitting the description of Lindsey Hargreaves stopped in last week asking about the Sharpes."

Andy frowned. "Asking what?"

"Vague questions. They gave her the address of our temporary offices, but she never showed up there. This was in the morning."

"Before she arrived in Rock Point, then. How much are these Aoife O'Byrne works worth?"

"A lot."

"More than the pieces stolen ten years ago?"

"Not more than the Jack Yeats paintings. Not yet, anyway. Why? What's on your mind, Andy?"

He could see that Lucas was quick-minded, no-nonsense, probably relentless as hell. Andy decided not to mince words. "Do you think David Hargreaves could have pushed his own daughter off that ledge?"

Lucas's blue eyes narrowed. "I think someone did."

Andy thanked him and went back out front. Mike was waiting in his truck. Andy climbed in. His brother looked over at him. "You still want to do this?"

"Yeah." Andy put on his seat belt. "I hate flying, though. I'm not afraid. I just hate it."

"Flying's better than listening to Franny Maroney go on about her dark fairies. She raised the hairs on the back of my neck."

She'd hunted Andy down at Hurley's. Mike had been there, too. She'd told them she'd heard a banshee keening last night. She had dark circles under her eyes and her sweater buttoned up crooked, as if she hadn't slept. She'd thumped the table with her bony finger and told Andy that he had to do something.

Finian Bracken had arrived, and Andy and Mike got out of there, leaving their Irish priest friend to deal with Franny. Andy was sorry she was so worried, but he also hadn't told her that he'd already booked a flight to Ireland and was leaving tonight.

"Do you think it's a bad sign Franny heard her banshee after I bought my ticket?" he asked Mike.

"Andy, it's Franny Maroney. Even if there are such things as banshees, she likes scaring the hell out of us, and she's a pessimist. She can find the negative in fixing oatmeal for breakfast."

"She's still getting over Jack's death."

Mike pulled out onto the quiet street. "So is Julianne."

"I know. That's part of why she weakened and fell for me."

"What's the other part?"

"My natural charm."

Mike rolled his eyes. "Why'd you weaken and fall for her?"

Andy looked out his window. "Some things just can't be explained, Mike."

"Like Franny's dark fairies," his brother said with a grin as he headed toward the interstate.

Andy would arrive at Logan just in time for his flight. He'd be in Ireland for breakfast. In Declan's Cross by lunch. "I haven't told Colin I'm coming."

"Good. Don't until you land."

That was Mike. Mr. Communicator.

"You're not second-guessing yourself, are you?" Mike asked. "That would be Julianne rubbing off on you."

"She should trust her instincts more," Andy said. "She knew this trip to Declan's Cross was nuts, and she was right."

Mike grimaced. "Might not want to tell her that."

24

Sean had poured himself another glass of Bracken 15 and had a good fire going in the kitchen when there was a knock at the door. He knew who it was even before he stood and opened it with his glass in hand.

Kitty had her hands in her jacket pockets, her dark hair flying in the wind. The night air was raw and cold. "Drinking whiskey alone. Never a good thing, is it, Sean?"

"Sometimes it's the best thing. Do you want to come in?"

"For a minute. To get warm."

She walked past him into the kitchen and stood by the fire. He joined her and set his whiskey on the table. "You walked up here?"

She nodded. "I tried to sleep. I couldn't keep still. Philip's at the hotel. He's safe."

"Kitty . . ."

"I'm not afraid of walking in Declan's Cross alone, Sean. Someone pushed Lindsey Hargreaves off that ledge. There's no doubt in my mind. But whoever it is has no reason to kill me, and if I'm wrong — well, better to be pushed off a cliff up here than murdered in my own kitchen."

Sean smiled. "Practical Kitty."

"The gardai gave Philip a good talking to. I'm glad they did. The FBI agents are in for the night. Julianne's tired but more settled in her skin, I think. David Hargreaves can't wait to wipe the dust of Declan's Cross off his feet. Poor man."

"You still shouldn't be up here alone."

"I'm not," she said. "I'm here with you."

He could hardly get a breath.

"Sean . . . our timing has never been good, has it? Ten years ago, we were in bed together the night that blasted thief helped himself to Uncle John's paintings and that old cross he loved so much. I was still a mess from my divorce, more so than I realized — more than I'd ever have admitted. You were this dashing, ambitious garda. I didn't trust how much I loved you."

"Some days that night feels like yesterday. Other days . . ."

"Other days it might as well have been a dream. Then six years ago —" Kitty touched her hand to his cheek. "Oh, Sean. I didn't realize until a few months ago what the investigation into the deaths of Sally

Bracken and her daughters must have been like for you."

"I did my job, Kitty. That's all."

"Fin was a wreck that first year. For you to have to consider — even for a minute — that he could have been responsible for what happened must have been horrible."

"It's in the past now."

"I don't know about that. I think it's right here, still eating at you. It makes it harder for you to commit." She turned, the flames glowing in her blue eyes. "Sit by the fire with me, and talk to me — I know you, Sean. I know you've never talked to anyone about it."

"You don't want to hear about smugglers breaking my ribs?"

"Oh, that you had coming, I've no doubt," she said with a spark, but her blue eyes were warm, filled with emotion. "Ten years ago, you were so ambitious, I could have killed you myself. Six years ago, though. That one night we had together before you threw me out. You were a tortured soul, and I don't know why I never put two and two together."

"How much talking do you want me to do, Kitty?"

"As much as you want."

"I had a job to do when Fin's wife and

daughters died. It was as hard a job as I've ever had to do, and I did it. It took all I had. Fin and I became friends, and you and I . . ."

"You and I made a mess of things. Then you fell for sexy and glamorous with your makeup artist."

"I did. She was also very shallow."

"I'm not shallow. I can be sexy and glamorous in a pinch, when I'm not thinking about work."

"Even when you are." He touched her hair. "Ah, Kitty, you and I are as star-crossed as a pair can be."

"So we are," she said, her mouth finding his.

25

Colin awoke to a text from Andy saying he'd arrived in Shannon and was driving to Declan's Cross. Emma leaned next to him in bed, read the text and kissed him on the cheek. "Two Donovans here at the same time. Ireland may never be the same. Do you think Julianne knows?"

"I doubt it, but Andy's on his own. I'm staying out of it."

"That's why we're in Declan's Cross. Because you stayed out of it."

"We're in Declan's Cross, sweetheart, because of your thief. Otherwise I'd have left Julianne to her own devices."

"Uh-uh." Emma sat up straight and shoved a pillow at him. "You wouldn't have known Julianne was here in the first place if Andy hadn't told you."

"No secrets in Rock Point."

"There are a million secrets in Rock Point. You just don't care about most of them and dig out the ones you do care about. Anyway," she added, throwing off the covers, "I'm starving. I'm going down to breakfast."

"Feel free to warn Julianne that Andy is on his way."

Emma grinned at him. "Not a chance." Colin watched her slide into a white hotel robe and pull clothes out of a drawer. She'd unpacked her overnight bag after they'd arrived at the hotel, explaining she always did when she was on the road. One of the countless little things he'd learned about her during their time together in Ireland.

She was dressed and on her way before he got out of bed. He was in no hurry. Let Emma and Julianne start breakfast together. If Julianne was like her grandmother, she'd sense that something was up and get it out of Emma.

Of course, Emma was a disciplined FBI agent and unlikely to weaken and tell Julianne about Andy's arrival in Ireland.

Colin knew there was no way Emma was letting him off the hook. If he stalled long enough, Andy would roll into the O'Byrne driveway and could explain his presence to Julianne himself.

Not that Colin really gave a damn. It was just a fun distraction from everything else he had on his mind — in particular, who had killed Lindsey Hargreaves. He and Emma were setting up a chat with the investigating gardai.

He showered and got dressed. Lucas Sharpe had texted Emma late last night to tell her Lindsey had turned up at Sharpe Fine Art Recovery on her way to Rock Point, a tidbit she'd kept to herself when Julianne had driven her through Heron's Cove.

Lucas had also reported that Andy had been by.

Probably on his way to Logan, Colin thought as he headed downstairs. His brother insisted he didn't regret splitting up with Julianne.

"Yeah, right."

When he arrived in the dining room, Colin saw that Julianne was alone at a table by a window. She looked content, but he had no idea if she realized Andy would be there soon. Hunger and the need for coffee won out, and Colin went over to her.

"It was a gorgeous sunrise this morning," Julianne said. "Did you see it?"

"Nope. Didn't see the sunrise."

"Emma just grabbed toast and coffee. She's gone to talk to David Hargreaves. She said to tell you."

"Thanks." Colin sat down. "I'm not stay-

421

ing, either. What are your plans for the morning?"

"I thought I'd take a walk and have a look at the spa. Then . . ." She popped a chunk of apple in her mouth. "Then I'll figure out what to do when your brother gets here."

"Emma told you?"

"No. He did. He texted me when his plane landed." She sank back against her chair. "You weren't going to tell me, were you?"

"It's none of my business."

"As you can see, I have taken the news well. Better than you expected, huh?"

Colin reached for the silver coffeepot. "So far, so good."

"Andy isn't in Ireland because of me, Colin. He's here because he told you about my trip, and he feels guilty that you and Emma are stuck with me."

"We're not stuck with you, Julianne."

"I know that. You're FBI agents. Whether you knew I was here, or even if I wasn't here, Lindsey's death would have caught your attention. Emma's, anyway."

"Andy won't stay here if you don't want him to."

"He told you that?"

"No, but I know my brother."

She put her white cloth napkin on the table. "I know it's awkward for you because

Andy and I . . ." She rose, her hair falling in her face as she looked down at Colin. "It'll get better. Time heals all wounds, right? I just don't want either of you to worry about me out of some sense of guilt or responsibility. I can take care of myself."

"No doubt about it," Colin said. "But you'll let Emma or me know where you are this morning?"

"Garden, spa or room. I'm checking out today, though. Emma suggested Killarney, but you guys have done enough for me. I have my own car. I'll figure out what to do next. Thank you, Colin. Really."

She spun off before he could respond. Just as well, he thought, because he had no idea what to say. He downed coffee and brown bread and headed out to the O'Byrne gardens. He hopped off the terrace and started down a walkway. He could hear birds twittering in the shrubs and could smell the ocean, glistening in the morning sun. According to Emma, the next few days were supposed to be sunny and relatively warm. She'd planned to leave today — to go home without him. He thought of his brother landing alone in Shannon, and his own solitary arrival there in late October. But Andy hadn't come to Ireland expecting to be alone.

Of course, if Julianne sent him packing, that could be how things turned out — in which case Colin would let him sleep on the sofa at Fin Bracken's cottage and drag him off to hike in the Irish hills.

Andy could help him plan his alternative life as Cap'n Colin.

Not the same as having Emma there.

"Not even close."

Colin came to the walkway that led to the O'Byrne cottage. With the unanswered questions in Declan's Cross, Emma was unlikely to be boarding a plane for a while, anyway.

The O'Byrne cottage was newer construction than the hotel, situated behind a gate, with its own garden and a large, private deck. Colin stepped in through an open glass door. The living area was sleek and contemporary, its colors more muted than at the hotel. Emma was standing in front of floor-to-ceiling windows and glass doors that opened onto the deck and looked out onto an endless view of the ocean.

David Hargreaves had his bags packed and ready to go by the door, but he was pacing.

"Your daughter was murdered, David," Emma said. "You know that. Colin and I know it. I'm sure the gardai do, too, even if they haven't stated so publicly. Help us find her killer."

"I know you mean well, but please —" David took in a breath, pale, emotional "— just let me bury my daughter."

Colin stayed by the door. "Maybe you killed her yourself," he said, blunt.

David spun around. "*Me?* I did everything I could to help her. I was thrilled when she discovered a passion for diving and marine science."

"Were you thrilled when she quit her job?" Emma asked him. "Were you thrilled when she said she wanted to turn an old Irish garage into a research facility?"

"I was impressed by her enthusiasm and vision."

"Not enough to help her secure funding," Colin said. "You told her she was on her own, didn't you?"

The older man's gaze hardened. "You've never been a father, have you? If Lindsey was murdered, it's your thief who's responsible."

Emma jumped on that one. "How so?"

"He followed her."

"He's contacted you?"

"I didn't say that —"

"Then why do you think he followed your

daughter?"

David turned even paler, some of the fight going out of his eyes. "We're not friends, are we? You're FBI agents. It doesn't matter that I've lost my daughter . . ."

"Just be straight with us," Colin said.

Emma nodded in agreement. "You believed, if only for a moment, that the Declan's Cross thief was responsible for stealing the Aoife O'Byrne works from your home. It's what Lindsey wanted you to believe. She tried to strike a balance between being too obvious and too subtle, but it was her contingency plan. She hoped you'd pay the ransom and never trouble her with the details. Never confront her."

David looked out at the view without meeting Emma's eye. "You have it all figured out, don't you, Special Agent Sharpe?"

"Why did you lie about the appraisal?"

He looked at her then. "I didn't know what else to do. I'm not impulsive. I don't make decisions quickly. I needed time."

"Did she steal the painting and cross the night she got back from Maine?" Emma asked, moving back into his line of vision. "Just tell us what happened, David."

He averted his eyes, staring at an arrangement of dried hydrangeas on a glass-topped dining table. "Lindsey got home late. She was so excited about having met Julianne. She was still angry with me for refusing to help her get funding for her field station here, but I was confident we could move past it. The next morning after breakfast, she told me she'd accidentally left the back door to the house unlocked that night. I wasn't concerned. She had a habit of leaving the back door unlocked."

Emma kept her gaze on him. "When did you notice the Aoife O'Byrne pieces were missing?"

"After Lindsey left for Ireland," he said.

Colin noticed a gull swooping low over the water. "How did you learn about the unsolved theft here?"

"Lindsey told me. I never imagined she was in danger. Perhaps she was getting too close to the thief, or her presence here worried him. He could have known I owned two works by Aoife O'Byrne that had appreciated substantially in value. Perhaps he keeps an eye on the Sharpe offices in Heron's Cove and recognized her. I don't know." David sounded exhausted yet also preoccupied, as if he'd been running through all the possibilities on an endless loop. "I just know that I wanted to do what I could to make things right."

"What did that look like to you?" Emma

asked quietly. "Making things right. Tell me."

"Keeping Lindsey safe. The painting and cross, too, but I'd gladly have sacrificed them —" He broke off and burst out to the deck, Emma on his heels.

Colin followed them outside, but he wasn't getting in Emma's way. She stood next to David at the rail. "David, you're still lying to protect your daughter, and maybe yourself, too."

He leaned over the rail, clasping his hands together and staring out at the sea. "It really is beautiful here. I can see why Lindsey fell in love with it. Her mother, too."

Colin thought he could sense Emma's exasperation, but she leaned over the rail and clasped her hands, too, as if in solidarity. "David, the way I read this, Lindsey stole the painting and the cross in order to get money she felt entitled to, and maybe to exact a little revenge against you — for herself, for her mother. You knew in your gut that's what was going on. You'd tried to get her to be accountable, responsible, by not getting involved with this field station idea of hers. You knew she'd chosen Declan's Cross because of her mother. When the two works of art you'd bought with her disappeared, you knew what Lindsey had done. You went to Dublin. You spent time with her. You tried to —"

"I tried to get her to realize that she was my daughter and I loved her very much." His voice was laced with fatigue and agony. He stood up from the rail and looked at Emma. "I wished I'd simply told her that, but I was so angry — so confused. I saw she would never admit what she'd done."

"So you decided to confront her," Emma said. "When you told her you were going to Ardmore and then coming to Declan's Cross, she panicked."

"Lindsey blamed me for her mother's problems, and ultimately for her death. Cynthia wanted the Aoife O'Byrne pieces. She picked them out, recognized Aoife as a remarkable talent. I'd have never noticed. As true as that is, giving them to Cynthia would have been a mistake. She'd have sold them for a song, then hated herself for having done it. I'd planned to give them to Lindsey, but I didn't tell her. I wanted her to get on her feet first." He clearly struggled to go on. "I'm sorry. I didn't know what else to do."

"You didn't report the theft," Colin said.

"I didn't see it as a theft. I still don't. I see it as a family matter. I received an anonymous email about the same time I discovered the painting and the cross were missing. The painting isn't large. It's easy to transport. The cross is no bigger than a rabbit's foot. Lindsey had only to slip them in her suitcase, or overnight them to herself. The email said I needed to pay up or they'd be destroyed."

Colin watched the gull perch on a rock out in the water. "Did you follow the instructions?"

"To the letter," David said. "It was surprisingly simple. I fly to London often. Arranging a last-minute business trip wasn't a problem. I keep a considerable amount of cash on hand at home and arranged for the balance of what I needed — a hundred thousand dollars, total. I left it in a designated spot in St. Stephen's Green. The art was delivered to my hotel. I made no effort to find out who was responsible. I didn't want to take that chance. I suppose I also didn't want to know."

"Where is the art now?" Emma asked.

"At another hotel in Dublin. I planned to go there after Declan's Cross. My own daughter stole from me. That's how I thought of her, at least. She never really accepted me as her father. I didn't want her hurt. I didn't want myself hurt. I just wanted it all to go away. I wish I'd confronted her in Dublin and gotten her side of the story. I would have helped her if she was in over her head — in danger."

Colin leaned back against the rail. "Did she give any indication she thought she was in danger?"

"No. None." David shivered in a cool breeze. "I know you believe Lindsey was murdered. Maybe I do, too, but it's just as possible she was upset and reckless and fell."

Emma buttoned her leather jacket and stood straight. "You'll need to talk to the Irish authorities," she said. "We can ask them to meet you here, but it's their call."

David nodded, gray, miserable. "She really did want the field station to become a reality, even if originally it was just a prop in a ruse. She was pursuing additional grants and in touch with Irish scientists. I thought she was genuinely excited about having Julianne here. Ironic that it might have turned into a real project for her. I'd like to think that. I can't explain why I have no animosity. I suppose it's because I feel more responsible than I should for the rough start she had in life. For the bad choices her mother made for her."

"Guilt," Colin said.

"That sums it up, doesn't it? I never should have married. I'm a solitary sort. I enjoy the company of friends and colleagues, but I'm not one for intimacy. I tend to be in my own world. Oblivious. I wish I could be oblivious again." He started back into the cottage but stopped. "I've done nothing illegal. Unwise, perhaps, but not illegal. I wish I'd done things differently. Called the police when I discovered the theft, or the gardai when I arrived in Dublin. I thought I could handle this on my own, and I couldn't. And now my daughter is dead."

Colin walked with Emma back through the O'Byrne gardens, his mind on their conversation with David Hargreaves. "Lindsey wasn't as interested in getting police to blame the Declan's Cross thief as she was in getting her father to blame him. Hence her day trip to Maine. She'd see the sights. Stop at Sharpe Fine Art Recovery in case he checked, but not make a big deal of it — avoid being too obvious."

"She hoped it wouldn't come to that," Emma said. "She wanted her ransom scheme to work."

"It did work. It just got her killed."

"What if her father killed her after all?"

"And all that back there was a show?" Colin considered the possibility. "I think he played her game until Dublin. Then when Lindsey didn't fess up, he'd had it. The question is whether he went to Ardmore to get his head into confronting her — or whether he used it to cover for sneaking into Declan's Cross and killing her."

Emma ducked under a low branch of a rhododendron. "Maybe he arranged to meet her on Shepherd Head and confronted her there. Then things got out of hand, they argued — whatever — and she fell. He panicked. Here we are."

Colin shook his head. "There were no other tire marks on the lane. He doesn't know his way around up there. He'd have had to hike up the trail from the cove or hike out the lane."

"If Lindsey met him and drove him out there . . . then how would he have gotten back to Ardmore?"

"We'll be talking to our gardai friends soon. They'll check out his movements in Ardmore, if they haven't already."

Emma slowed her pace as they came to the hotel terrace. "If we assume David is now telling the truth — which I tend to think he is — then why did Lindsey come down here on Monday and drive out to the tip of Shepherd Head?" She paused at a large flowerpot overflowing with bright cyclamen. "And where's the money?"

"Maybe she was making a last stab at trying to blame your thief by hiding the money up by the crosses and church ruin."

"And someone else found out —"

"Or was in on it from the start," Colin said. "No one who knew Lindsey describes her as a good planner."

Emma sank onto a bench overlooking the gardens and sea. "That's what was going on at the Murphy cottage yesterday. Whoever knocked Philip was looking for the money."

"She had an accomplice." Colin got out his phone and called Yank, who picked up on the first ring. Colin didn't wait for him to speak. "We need all you can get on Lindsey Hargreaves. Who her friends were. Her work at the Hargreaves Oceanographic Institute. Her diving. Everything."

"You know it's the middle of the night here, don't you?"

"If you were a lobsterman, you'd be up."

"Your brother Andy is in Ireland. He tell you?"

"He'll be here any minute. We'll have a pint together later." Colin filled Yank in on David Hargreaves' story. "I think he's finally leveling about what happened."

"This fits with what we've learned here," Yank said, sounding less groggy. "Cynthia

Hargreaves liked to brag that she owned two of Aoife O'Byrne's early works and her ex-husband was holding on to them for her. She wasn't a big talent herself, but she prided herself on recognizing talent. That she knew early on that Aoife would be a star meant a lot to her."

"Whether or not Cynthia was lying, if her daughter believed her, then she wasn't just after the money. Stealing those particular works was personal for her. She wanted her father to suffer because of them."

"I wouldn't be surprised if she didn't want to return them," Yank said.

"An accomplice would be interested just in the value, and in not getting caught." Colin thought he heard pots and pans clanking on the other end of the phone. "Yank — where are you?"

"Rock Point. I'm at your folks' inn. It's nice. Everybody's up. Your father's making muffins."

"Hell, Yank."

"I had whiskey with Finian Bracken last night." Yank's voice turned serious again. "He vouches for the garda detective, Sean Murphy. Your brother Mike was there. I told Mike that in no way, shape or form do I need his help doing my job."

"What did he say?"

"Nothing."

"Sounds like Mike."

Colin disconnected and sat next to Emma. He'd heard the concern in Matt Yankowski's voice and appreciated that he was personally looking into the situation.

"How are things in Rock Point?" Emma asked.

"Yank's having muffins with my folks."

"Life could be worse."

"Nope. I don't think so."

Emma placed a hand on his thigh. "I want to go back up to Shepherd Head where Lindsey died."

He covered her hand with his. "I thought you might. I do, too. I want to talk to Sean Murphy and Lindsey's diver friend, Brent Corwin."

"It would be good to know what he was up to this weekend and on Monday when Lindsey died."

"Yes, it would."

As they got up, Colin saw he had a text from Julianne: I'm at the spa. It's gorgeous.

At least she was safe. He texted her back: Good. Stay there.

26

Sean was out at the barn when Ronan Carrick phoned him. "David Hargreaves was in Dublin, as he says. He checked out a day early. Also as he says. We talked to a waiter at his hotel who described tension between him and his daughter. The accommodation manager remembered being in the elevator with them. Lindsey was trying to explain something, and he just stared straight ahead and didn't respond."

"Subject?"

"Marine science."

"It's not much, Ronan."

"It's not anything. We checked with the housekeeping staff. One of the housekeepers accidentally walked in on Lindsey. She was hyperventilating. She'd been sick."

"Not a happy reunion with the father."

"She also had a package on the bed. Nothing like it was found on or near her body, in her car or at her field station."

"Any idea what was in it?"

"Not a clue."

Sean bit back a sigh of frustration. "Ronan . . ."

Ronan ignored him. "So, Eamon is back in Dublin. He's down to the pub and talks to the lads, and what do they tell him? Brent Corwin was there for a pint on Saturday. He told us he was diving all weekend."

"He could have popped into Dublin and still said he'd been diving."

"He never mentioned dropping in at the pub to Eamon. They went diving together on Sunday."

"Monday?"

"Eamon worked out on his boat most of Monday. He's got a good life, that one. He'll dive with anyone, though. Put a mask and tank on the devil, and Eamon will go underwater with him."

It took more to earn Ronan's trust.

"What do you think, Sean?"

"It's something."

"It's just not enough, is it?"

"Did forensics find anything on Lindsey Hargreaves or in her car that suggests she'd been up to the crosses or the church ruin? Any mud or grass or dung that's not from the lane, the trail, the rocks?"

"I don't think so. I'll ask. What's on your

mind, Sean?"

"Liver fluke. It's a terrible parasite that affects sheep." But Sean couldn't work up any real humor. He thanked Ronan, who promised to stay in touch.

In the quiet of the barn, Sean noticed the smell of hay, manure and wet sheep. Good smells. So many times since June, as he'd made his slow recovery, he'd told himself that becoming a detective had been the wrong turn in his life, and it was farm work he was meant to do.

He went back to the house. Paddy came into the kitchen, still in his jacket and cap. He'd gone out to the fields early, ignoring Sean's concerns about the attack on Philip yesterday.

"No gardai up here today, thank God," Paddy said, pulling off his cap. "Just the American diver. He must want to have a look at where his friend died."

"You saw him just now?"

"Not ten minutes ago. He was in his van. I assume it was him. I was too far away to see who was inside."

"I'm going out to see what he's up to," Sean said. "You stay here and watch yourself. Lock the doors."

"What's wrong, Sean?"

He wanted to make a joke, say he'd been

off the job too long, but he couldn't. "I don't know that anything's wrong. Let's just be on the safe side."

The phone rang. Paddy answered it and handed it to Sean. Kitty started talking before he could say hello. "Is Julianne Maroney up there?"

"I haven't seen her —"

"She isn't at the hotel. She hasn't checked out. Her car is here. She was at breakfast and said she'd be in the spa, the gardens or her room, and she's in none of those places. Normally I wouldn't think a thing of it."

"Where are Emma and Colin?"

"They just left. Sean, they said the guards investigating Lindsey's death will be here soon to talk to her father."

"Did you see Brent Corwin at the hotel?"

"Brent? No, why?"

"I don't have time to explain. Where's Philip?"

"He's working in the kitchen."

"Keep him there. Trust me, Kitty."

"I always have."

"You never have. You thought I was your blasted thief."

Julianne shivered in the damp shadows of the hollow where she'd discovered Lindsey's car. The cool air and her mud-soaked clothes made her ripe for hypothermia, but with a 9 mm pistol shoved in her ribs, freezing to death wasn't her most pressing concern.

"You've got your money," she said, trying to keep her teeth from chattering. "Just take it and go."

Brent Corwin shook his head. "It's not that simple."

He sounded almost sorry. He was close enough that she could smell his sweat and the mud caked on his hands and jacket. The money was inside the backpack he had slung over one shoulder. It, too, was muddy and wet. He'd dragged her out of his van and shoved her at the ancient stone wall and moss-covered ruins. He'd ordered her to start searching. A package wrapped in black plastic, a backpack, maybe even a small suitcase — it was here, he'd said. He'd finally figured it out. This was where Lindsey had hidden the money she and Brent had manipulated David Hargreaves into giving them.

It hadn't been on her body or in her car. It wasn't at the field station. It wasn't at the Murphy cottage.

"The stupid bitch. The money's here."

They'd found her hiding place, a gap in the stone wall, almost inside the church ruin. Lindsey had chosen it well, and covered her tracks well — not that she'd have left much evidence of her presence in the moss, grass and rock.

Brent had leveled his gun at Julianne and made her do most of the work — digging through the browned, sodden mass of leaves and ferns that Lindsey had used to conceal the gap. She'd pulled out the muddy backpack. He'd unzipped the main compartment, and Julianne had seen a black-wrapped package inside.

He'd seemed satisfied and marched her back down to the lane at gunpoint.

She nodded to the backpack. "Are you sure it's actually money inside the package? The wrapping is opaque. What if it's newspapers and Lindsey hid the money somewhere else? The reason you're in this mess is because she double-crossed you in the first place, right?"

He motioned his gun at her. "Up the trail, Julianne. Let's move."

She didn't want to go up the trail. It led to the ledge, and the ledge was where Lindsey had died. Where he'd killed her. Not that he'd confessed, but Julianne knew. She'd known when she'd run into him in the O'Byrne gardens. She'd never been good at a poker face, but it wouldn't have mattered. He'd needed a hostage. What had he said? *"You're a soft target, Julianne."*

She'd gone out for a quick walk ahead of her visit to the spa. She'd hoped pampering herself a little before Andy arrived would help clear her head. She'd been dressed for the spa. Yoga pants, yoga top, lightweight zip-up fleece — they weren't intended for digging in cold mud and muck in an Irish ruin. Even her shoes were useless. She'd slipped into pink flip-flops Granny had given her, insisting they'd come in handy on her trip.

If she died out here, she could hear the Donovan brothers now. *"What the hell was she doing out there in yoga pants and flip-flops?"*

No socks, even.

She'd been at the far corner of the gardens, already cold, eager to get into the sauna and a soft hotel robe. Brent had come through the trees, up from the water, saying he'd heard about the attack on Philip Doyle and wanted to know if he was all right. Julianne hadn't liked his flat tone, his sleepless eyes, and had suggested they go up to the hotel together and talk to Emma and Colin — then it was out with the gun, through the trees to a parking area by the water and into his van.

She wished she'd found a way to jump out of the van, knock him out while they'd searched for the money or just run away without getting shot. So far, all she could do was keep stalling for time until Colin realized she wasn't at the spa. He'd be pissed, and he'd come looking for her.

Brent leaned in close to her. "Julianne."

She was so damn cold. Her shivering was nearly uncontrollable now. "You don't have to push me off a cliff. I'll die of hypothermia first."

"Just do as I say and you'll be fine. It's worked out so far, right? I have my money, and you haven't done anything stupid. I just want to keep you with me until I'm free and clear of the gardai and your FBI friends."

"Then leave now — by yourself."

"I have a car down by the cove. I just need to make sure I get there without any trouble. Then we'll part company. I get out of Ireland. You go back to your Irish vacation."

"That's what you did on Monday — you hiked up from the cove." Julianne nodded at the dead-end lane. "But the trail's that way. It's not up on the ledge."

"There's a shortcut. You probably didn't notice it the other day. It's a little steeper, but we'll be fine."

She could hear in his voice he'd lost

patience. Any words to the contrary were a pretext. The car-at-the-cove line was a ruse — a way to manipulate her so he didn't have to actually shoot her. A gunshot would draw attention. He wanted to push her off the ledge, then get back in his van and drive away as the bereaved friend who had gone out to the spot where Lindsey had died and said his goodbyes on his way out of town. By the time anyone came up here, he'd be long gone.

On the other hand, he might have a car down at the cove, too — a backup plan.

There still was no shortcut from the ledge.

Julianne tried to stall him. "Where are you going from here?"

"Somewhere warm and sunny."

"New identity?"

He pushed her toward the trail. "No more talking. One stupid move, and I'll shoot you. I don't want to. I want to let you go after you've served your purpose."

He had her go first up the trail. She cut past the holly tree. She could hear him close behind her, no question he still had his 9 mm pointed at her. He'd have no trouble on the steep hill. He was in good shape.

Her feet, numb with the cold, nearly slipped out of her flip-flops, but she continued up to the ledge. Wind gusted off the water, penetrating her thin, wet clothing. She struggled not to fall to her knees into a ball. It'd help conserve body heat. She was already slurring her words. The wind would only speed up the onset of serious hypothermia.

If she collapsed, would Brent shoot her? Risk the sound of gunfire alerting Sean Murphy and his uncle — even people in the village?

He moved in front of her and watched her shiver, his gun steady in his hand. "Your lips are purple."

"I'm freezing."

"It's okay. We'll get you warm soon. I should have grabbed a jacket for you out of the van."

She drew her hands up into the sleeves or her sodden fleece. "You didn't come up here with the intention of killing Lindsey, did you?"

His look told Julianne that no, he *had* come up here with the intention of killing Lindsey.

And now me.

"I didn't kill her." His tone was distant, as if he didn't care if Julianne believed him or not. "I just wanted my share of the money. She got crazy and fell."

It wasn't what happened.

"You didn't realize she'd already hidden the money," Julianne said. "You must have freaked out when it wasn't in her car."

"It didn't occur to me she'd hidden it in the damn ruins. If it had, you and I wouldn't be here right now. She didn't do you any favors when she invited you here, did she? She liked you, you know. You're everything she wasn't. Smart, a go-getter, a self-starter. Hardworking. All she wanted was to please her father. When he put his foot down about the field station, it was the last straw."

"That's when you two cooked up the theft."

"Everything worked like it was supposed to. I knew her father would figure out she stole from him, and all Lindsey's efforts to make it look like this guy who pulled off the theft here was responsible wouldn't amount to anything. I just also knew he wouldn't do anything about it. He'd cooperate. He'd pay. He might confront her, but he'd never go to the police. He has his own reputation to consider. I had a drink with him after you found her. He really did love her in his own lame way."

Another gust of wind howled up from the rocks and sea. Julianne tightened her arms around her. *Keep talking, keep talking.* "When did you realize she wasn't going to keep up her end of the deal?"

"We were supposed to meet on Monday. When she didn't show up . . ." Brent blew out a breath. "She started to get weird over the weekend. I shouldn't have let her pick up the money. I should have been more careful when I was in Dublin helping her pull this thing off — but this was such a no-brainer. I wasn't that worried about covering my tracks."

"You weren't thinking you'd have to explain your whereabouts to the Irish police."

"You got that right."

Julianne glanced at the waves rolling onto the rocks. She could hear birds in the distance. Crows, she thought. She turned back to Brent. "Lindsey wanted the field station to work. Maybe she came to Declan's Cross because of her resentments, and maybe she was angry with her father for not helping her —"

"She knew he was onto her, but she still thought she could pull it off and get him to blame the thief. That's why she hid the money out here. She figured it's where the thief would hide it."

"But she didn't want anyone to find it, did she?"

"She wanted to keep it and put it into the

field station. She thought I'd go along with her. The field station would be a success. I could work for her."

"That's what she told you on Monday?"

"I didn't go along with her."

"You wanted all the money for yourself."

He shrugged. "I have bills to pay." He raised his gun. "Your lips really are purple."

"It's mild hypothermia . . ."

"I know. Lindsey was so excited after she met you. She didn't see the field station for what it was — an old garage, another of her ideas that wouldn't work out." Brent shook his head. "I wish she hadn't met you, Julianne. I'm sorry she did."

"You like having your way, don't you?"

"Guilty as charged." He kept his gaze steady on her. "I know you're cold. I've had hypothermia. It's no fun."

And it could be fatal — would be now, Julianne knew, if she didn't get warm soon. She looked down at the rocks below the ledge, at the spot where she'd spotted Lindsey's bright-colored scarf. Brent wasn't going to shoot her, and he wasn't going to make her death look like an accident — he was going to make it look like she'd come out here in despair, not dressed for the conditions . . . searching for answers to her new friend's death. Julianne could see it.

She'd be the young woman who came to Ireland to heal a broken heart and help with an exciting project, and instead everything went wrong.

She looked at Brent. The son of a bitch was just going to watch her freeze. When she collapsed, he'd walk away. By the time anyone found her, she'd be dead, and he'd be on his way.

Julianne heard voices down toward the lane. Brent swore, and his reaction told her the voices weren't just in her head, a result of hypothermia.

Emma and Colin.

At home, they'd be armed. In Ireland . . .

Julianne knew what she had to do — and even as Brent lurched forward to grab her, she leaped over the ledge.

She dropped onto a flat-topped boulder, landing on her feet, her knees bent, but her momentum propelled her off the edge, into the crevice between more boulders.

She hit hard. She couldn't move, couldn't breathe.

She heard a gunshot . . . shouting . . .

Emma reached her first. "Easy, Julianne."

"It's okay. I just got the wind knocked out of me." She struggled to sit up. "What happened?"

"Brent refused to put his weapon down —"

"You shot him?"

Emma shook her head. "Sean Murphy did."

Colin dropped in next to her. "The paperwork is a lot easier that way. We make a good team. Emma and I had rocks. Sean had a gun."

Julianne saw that he wasn't kidding. "You aren't hurt? And Sean — you guys are all okay?"

"Yeah, we're good." Colin got off his jacket and draped it over her shoulders. "That was a gutsy move, kid."

"I heard you and Emma —"

"A deliberate distraction," he said. "We'll talk back at the hotel. The gardai are on the way."

Now that she was warmer — and safe — Julianne felt steadier. She got to her feet, but didn't shake off Emma's help onto the trail.

Colin shook his head. "No socks, Julianne?"

"I was at the spa."

"That's where Brent grabbed you?"

She tightened Colin's jacket around her. "No, I was in the garden."

"The garden isn't the spa."

Julianne looked at Emma. "You know the Donovans have been fantasizing about throwing me off a ledge forever, don't you?"

Colin grinned. "Especially Andy."

Sean Murphy met them at the top of the trail. He had a serious, take-charge look that reminded Julianne he was a law enforcement officer — one who'd just had to use deadly force.

She could hear vehicles down on the lane. "Gardai," Sean said.

Colin clapped an arm over the Irishman's shoulder. "Getting the jump on a man with a gun and a hostage — you're going to have a tough time convincing your superiors you shouldn't be back on the job."

Sean squinted back at the ledge where Brent Corwin lay dead. "I am back on the job."

27

The sun had returned when Emma arrived back at the O'Byrne House Hotel with Colin and Julianne. The gardai had finished there, taking David Hargreaves with them to discuss the particulars of the ransom and why he hadn't told anyone. It would be a while longer, Emma knew, before Sean Murphy and his garda colleagues left Shepherd Head.

Andy Donovan was waiting, pacing in the bar lounge. Muddy and bruised, Julianne burst into tears, then sniffled and glared at him. "I don't need you here. Go back to Maine."

"Jules," he said, taking her into his arms. "Damn."

Emma stood next to Colin by the stairs. He rolled his eyes, but Julianne's close call had clearly affected him. When he and Emma had arrived at the church ruin and saw Brent Corwin's van — heard Julianne up on the ledge, fighting for her life — they had focused on the job at hand. An armed Sean Murphy had only helped.

Julianne needed a hot shower and dry clothes, but Emma saw that her assistance wasn't required. Andy was more than up to the task. He wanted to carry her up the stairs, but she insisted she could walk — and then stumbled, and that was that. He had her up and off her feet in a flash.

"I'm all wet and smell like mud," she told him.

"Nothing new with you, Jules."

Colin sighed, watching them go up the stairs. "Let's see what happens when the adrenaline and jet lag wear off."

He and Emma went out to the terrace. He checked in with Yank while she checked in with Lucas and her grandfather. Kitty sent out tea and trays of sandwiches and desserts. Julianne and Andy came out to the terrace — both freshly showered and in clean clothes — and as they sat at the table, smiling, for a moment Emma pretended they were all on an Irish vacation together.

Julianne, however, was still pale, and a bruise had blossomed on her wrist. She grabbed half a ham sandwich. "It bugs the hell out of me that Brent Corwin thought I was a soft target. That's what he told me.

Soft target."

Andy grinned at his older brother. "You see what she's like?"

"She's been like that since she was two. I remember." Colin turned to Julianne. "Don't beat yourself up because you got nabbed."

"I'm not beating myself up. I know I'm not an FBI agent. That doesn't mean I can't fight."

"No kidding," Andy said.

"You did what any one of us would have done," Emma said.

The Donovan brothers disagreed and discussed various ways they would have disarmed Brent and stopped him from dragging them off at gunpoint. Julianne didn't seem to object. She was, Emma saw, used to their talk.

Sean Murphy arrived, coming through the bar lounge. "Please join us," Emma said, and he sat across from her, next to Julianne. Kitty came out to check on them, and Emma invited her to join them, too, but she had her hands full keeping up with the gardai's comings and goings.

"How's Philip today?" Sean asked her.

She seemed to avoid his eye. "He's as well as can be expected."

"He has good instincts, Kitty," Sean said.

"He did well under pressure, and he must know now that nothing he told Lindsey put this scheme of hers into her head."

Kitty blinked back tears. "Thank you for asking about him," she mumbled, then whirled back inside. Sean watched her in silence.

Julianne abandoned her sandwich and wandered off to look at a bed of pansies just off the terrace. Andy made no move to join her.

"You're a lucky man," Sean told him. "Julianne's a lovely woman."

"She still wants to drown me in the Celtic Sea."

Sean grinned. "You probably deserve it."

No argument from either Donovan.

The Irishman got up, and Emma followed him inside to the whiskey cabinet. "We still don't have our thief," he said.

"Not yet."

"I like your attitude, Special Agent Sharpe." He peered through the glass at the array of whiskey bottles. "Fin Bracken is almost as good a judge of people as he is whiskey, and he considers Colin a friend."

"Colin needs his freedom," Emma said.

"From what?"

"A desk."

"You don't tie him down. He's an undercover agent, isn't he? A valuable asset for the FBI, no doubt. They'll have another job for him. He'll do better, not worse, knowing he has you to come home to."

"You're a wise man."

"I'm dumb as a post." He winked at her. "Luckily I know where Kitty keeps the key to the whiskey cabinet. Let's help ourselves while she's in a generous mood."

Sean left a bottle of Auchentoshan with the Americans and found Kitty in her office. She didn't look up from her desk. "I'd have turned you in if I'd had proof you were the thief."

"I'd have done the same with you."

Now she looked up. *"Me?"*

Sean smiled. "If I wasn't with you part of the night, then you weren't with me part of the night."

"I don't know if I should be insulted you'd think I'd do such a thing or complimented that you think I could pull it off."

"Either way, it's not what came between us. You've done well with this place, Kitty, and you've a good lad in Philip."

"He looks up to you."

Sean grinned. "And well he should."

"I'm glad you're not this thief. Maybe just as well we don't know who it is." She got to her feet. "Ah, Sean. What a mess we've made of things."

"Maybe we just have our own timing."

"Philip's father wanted an old-fashioned wife, and that I'm not and will never be. He's a good man but . . ." She sighed. "He has what he wants now, and he's happy. Philip will be off on his own soon enough. I'm still young, Sean."

"You want more children?"

She didn't seem that surprised by his question. "It could happen. I love babies. I always thought I'd have a brood. I've this place. I have such happy memories here. I deal with wonderful people every day, as guests, workers, contractors. I love Declan's Cross. I'm blessed."

"Come up to the farm tonight, Kitty. We'll open a bottle of champagne and watch the stars come out over the sea."

"That sounds wonderful." She tilted her head back. "Did you steal the champagne like you just stole my whiskey?"

Starchy Kitty, Sean thought, laughing as he left her to wonder.

As far as Andy was concerned, the spa at the O'Byrne House Hotel was heaven, but he was jet-lagged and still getting over the shock of arriving in Declan's Cross to all hell breaking loose. Julianne had talked him into a couple's massage, and now they were in the couple's lounge, relaxing, supposedly, on a double chaise lounge with deep, sleep-inducing cushions.

Quite a first day in Ireland.

It was almost dark now. The lounge over-looked a peaceful garden that was lush even in November. He had spa-provided head-phones so he could listen to music. The spa attendants had left a pot of special herbal tea, a pitcher of ice water with lemons and oranges, a plate of cut-up fruit. All perfect, but he was jumping out of his skin.

He noticed Julianne didn't have her head-phones on, either. She looked tired enough to melt into the cushions, and the bruise on her wrist had darkened. Andy hated think-ing about how close Colin and Emma and Sean Murphy had come to finding Julianne dead on the rocks.

"I've missed you," he said finally.

"I haven't been gone long enough for you to miss me. I left Rock Point on Monday night. It's now Friday —"

"I mean since we broke up."

She sighed. "We didn't break up, Andy. You dumped me."

"You remember everything, don't you? I

459

guess that's why you're such a good student."

"You weren't a good student because you had other things on your mind. You're good at lobstering, and you're good at restoring boats."

"A few other things, too, Jules, as I recall you saying on occasion."

"I love Rock Point. You know that, right?"

He didn't know how they'd gone from him referring to making love to her talking about Rock Point, but that was how her mind worked. "I know that," he said. "I just want you to do what's right for you."

"Let me be the judge of what's right for me, okay? Don't you try to be the judge of it. I'll have options when I finish my degree."

"We don't have to figure out everything today. This hotel's great, but I think I prefer the Murphy cottage."

While Emma and Julianne had taken a walk in the hotel gardens, Andy had gone with Colin to have a look at Shepherd Head. The gardai wouldn't let them onto the ledge where Lindsey Hargreaves and Brent Corwin had died, but Andy had gotten a glimpse of the Celtic crosses that had inspired Aoife O'Byrne. He could see why.

"The cottage is nice," Julianne said, subdued now.

"We can take walks on the cliffs and out to the ruins."

"After someone's died there?"

"There's a cemetery out there, Jules."

She smiled. "Ever the pragmatic Donovan."

"Not so pragmatic since I'm here. The massage was pragmatic, though. My doctor said I should have regular massages for my shoulder."

She rolled onto her side, and he saw the gold flecks in her hazel eyes. "We rushed things this fall. *I* rushed things." She touched her fingertips to his jaw. "Anyway, thank you for being here."

His throat caught. "It's where I want to be. I'm sorry I broke your heart, Jules. I was an idiot."

"You were scared, and that's not easy for a Donovan to admit. Maine's home for me. Rock Point. I'm not going to work at Hurley's forever, but I don't need to go out into the big wide world to be a research biologist. I can do it there."

"You'd miss us Donovans out in the big wide world."

"I'd miss you."

"Yeah."

She rolled onto her back again. "I'm still doing my internship in Cork in January."

"I'll come visit then, too."

"I hope so. I'm going to use the last of the mad money from Grandpa to bring Granny over here in the spring. I can't stand the idea that she'll die wishing she'd just done it and gone to Ireland once in her life."

"Like your grandfather did."

"Yes. Oh, Andy. I've tried so hard to stop loving you, but I won't push myself on you after today. If you want me to get lost —"

"Do you think I'd have flown to damn Ireland if I wanted you to get lost?"

He kissed her, and she snuggled against him. She was so damn warm. He thought she'd fall asleep, but she said, "I still want my boat back."

w people."

Murphy?"

didn't answer.

n didn't push for more information. can stay here. There's a loft and a sofa. your pick."

rget it, Donovan. I'm not bunking with

ou'll have the place to yourself. I'm ing to Dublin tonight." He gave Yank key. "Hike the Irish hills. It's good for soul."

What about the rain?"

Buy a raincoat."

ife O'Byrne was, indeed, a truly beautiful oman — all black hair, porcelain skin, blue yes, angles and energy. She told Emma he'd already talked to the gardai and wasn't nterested in talking to the FBI, too, but let her into her Dublin studio, a large, open room with exposed brick walls and views of the Liffey River.

"I remember David and Cynthia Hargreaves," Aoife said, pacing on the tile floor. "I was just twenty. I was thrilled to sell my first works. He was a wealthy man with poor social skills. She was an artistic woman with no patience to learn her craft. She wanted instant results and then was disappointed

28

As Colin walked up the driveway to Finian Bracken's cottage, he noticed a red Micra parked out front and thought it might be Andy and Julianne in for a visit. Instead he saw Matt Yankowski standing in the drizzle.

"A Micra, Yank? Really?"

"I know. I almost got out and carried it, but I like a small car on these damn Irish roads." He nodded toward the view over Kenmare Bay. "I just saw a rainbow."

"You didn't just see a rainbow, Yank."

"I never see rainbows. It's my lot in life." He had on a dark suit and tie, ever the proper agent of the Federal Bureau of Investigation. He grinned at Colin. "I think I might hate Ireland more than I hate Maine."

Colin smiled. Yank didn't hate Maine, or Ireland. He just liked to gripe. "You didn't pick the best day. Come back in the spring. There'll be lambs. You'll love Ireland then.

Bring Lucy."

"Lucy. She loves lambs and rainbows. I was in Dublin four years ago when Emma was working for her grandfather. I didn't see a rainbow then, either. You've been hiking all day?"

"All day."

"All day every day since you left Declan's Cross?"

"It's just been three days, Yank."

"Emma's in Dublin. She's working on this art thief case. She picked me up at the airport. We had breakfast."

"Good." Colin wasn't discussing Emma with Yank. "Want to come inside?"

"Nope. I'm still shaking off driving across Ireland in that little car. I don't need to be in a little cottage. You like it here alone?"

"It's fine." Just better with Emma. "The weather's been great the past three days."

"The Donovan luck does have its moments."

"You didn't come here to talk about the weather, Yank."

Yank opened his hand, and in the palm was a round black stone inscribed with a Celtic cross. In the center was a tiny figure — Saint Declan and his bell.

It got Colin's interest. "This is one of the cross-inscribed stones the thief sends Wen-

dell Sharpe?"

"It came for me yeste...

"At your office? Yan... knows about your office...

"The Sharpes' thief d... how. He must have foun... just happened in Declan's... from there." Yank pocketed... likes the game. I think he... scalp."

Colin stood back. "How d... didn't get that rock in an I... shop?"

"You won't if you go off an... tours."

"Emma would tell me."

"Nope. Against policy. Besides,... suming she would want to stay wi... boat operator instead of a rugge... cover federal agent."

"Tour-boat operators can be rugge...

Yank didn't seem to notice the fin... collecting on his suit coat. "The di... wants me to bring you back to Boston... me."

"How long are you staying?"

"A few days. I'll be in touch with the... fice, but I need to do some thinking. I wa... to spend a day in Declan's Cross and wa... the ground where this thief first struck. Tal...

when they didn't live up to the image in her mind. I didn't know a daughter was involved."

"Lindsey was thirteen at the time," Emma said. "She stayed at home with the housekeeper."

"And now she's dead, and so is the man who killed her." Aoife raked both slender hands through her hair. "I can't believe something I created was a part of such violence."

Emma glanced around the studio and its utilitarian shelving and cabinets, filled with books and art supplies. A large industrial-looking table occupied the center of the room. Not so much as a pencil was on the scarred wood. There was no artwork on the walls. Everything in its place, and no distractions.

"Aoife," Emma said, "did you and your uncle ever talk about the cross and the paintings that were stolen from his house?"

"Very little, before or after the theft. He just knew I loved them."

"What about Saint Declan?"

"Saint Declan? Because of the crosses? No, Special Agent Sharpe. My uncle and I never discussed Saint Declan. Truly, there's nothing you can ask me that I haven't been asked already by the gardai — that I haven't asked myself." Aoife crossed her arms on her chest and stared out at the river, gray on the quiet November afternoon. "I want this thief caught, and I want what he stole recovered. I hope that's clear, but if not, so be it."

"Do you get to Declan's Cross often?"

"Not often enough."

"Have you stayed at your sister's hotel?"

"I haven't. I hate hotels, but I love the house, and Kitty. Uncle John left the house to both of us, but I had no interest in owning it." Aoife lowered her arms and turned to Emma. "Kitty and Sean . . . it was destined, you know. Since we were girls. It was always Sean for Kitty, but Philip needed to be born first."

Aoife O'Byrne had her own way of looking at life, Emma thought. "It was good to meet all of them, but I wish it had been under better circumstances."

"Will you be going back to Declan's Cross soon?"

"I return to Boston tomorrow." Emma placed her business card on the worktable. "We'll stay in touch."

"I'd rather not," Aoife said.

A fine, cold mist was falling when Emma reached the street. She pulled up the hood to her raincoat and walked to the Dublin pub where her grandfather had first taken her. She was staying in the small guest room at his apartment near Merrion Square. She'd postponed her return to Boston, but she wasn't on vacation. She'd pored through everything that she and Sharpe Fine Art Recovery had on their elusive thief, and she'd sat with her grandfather for hours, probing, digging, trying to make sure he'd finally told her everything.

Matt Yankowski had arrived in Dublin early that morning, and she'd filled him in over breakfast. But she knew she wasn't the purpose of his trip. He was in Ireland to see Colin.

"Puffin tours, Emma. Hell. I thought he wasn't serious."

The mist had turned to a hard rain when Emma entered the busy pub. She sat in a dark booth in a quiet corner and ordered beef stew and a pint. Her annual Guinness. Or maybe she'd had her annual Guinness already, given how complicated her life had been since meeting Colin in September.

She'd been thinking of him constantly, but she'd told him she wouldn't call him or email him until she got back to Boston. He needed this time on his own. He knew it, too, and didn't argue with her. She'd be going back to Boston tomorrow, without him.

"Thinking again, Emma?"

For a split-second she thought she'd imagined his voice, but when she looked up from her Guinness, he was there, sliding onto the cushioned bench across from her. He shed his wet jacket and shoved it onto the seat next to him.

"Colin." She collected her wits. The dim light made his eyes seem even smokier, and his smile took her breath away. She managed to say, "I didn't expect you."

He winked at her. "Hi, Emma."

She saw that he had on the sweater she'd given him. She took in the shape of his broad shoulders, the rain-soaked ends of his dark hair, the small scars on his right cheek, by his left eye. "You know the effect you have on me, don't you?"

"I do." He leaned back, but there was nothing casual about him. "How's old Wendell?"

"Pacing. He came back here reenergized."

"Does he know about the cross-inscribed stone our thief sent to Yank in Boston?"

Then Yank had caught up with Colin before he'd left for Dublin. "Yank told Granddad himself this morning. Granddad received one, too. So did Lucas."

"And you?"

She picked up her glass and nodded. "A

470

package arrived at Granddad's apartment addressed to both of us. There were two cross-inscribed stones inside. One for each of us."

"So this guy's watching you," Colin said.

"For the moment, at least."

"He didn't like Brent Corwin and Lindsey Hargreaves stealing his thunder, or trying to."

"So it seems."

"You've got your work cut out for you, Emma. I'll do whatever I can to help."

"I go home tomorrow."

A waiter set a pint of Guinness in front of Colin. He kept his eyes on Emma as he drank some of his beer. "Is your grandfather flying back with you?"

"No, but he still plans to be in Heron's Cove for Thanksgiving."

"My folks invited Fin Bracken to join us for Thanksgiving. He isn't sure what he'll do. I told him the main thing is not to try choosing between pumpkin pie and apple pie. Have both."

Emma smiled. "I can only imagine what a Donovan family Thanksgiving is like."

"Join us. You, Lucas, old Wendell. Your folks will still be in London. You could bake a pie."

"I love to bake pies. Does this mean you

471

plan to be back for Thanksgiving?"

"Sooner than that." He leaned forward over the table, his eyes lost now in the dark shadows. "Emma . . ."

He got up, and for a moment, she thought he would bolt out of the pub, but he came around to her side of the table and eased in next to her. He put an arm around her and held her close. Her heartbeat quickened. She started to speak, but he touched a finger to her lips, then slipped back out of the booth.

"Kitty O'Byrne said I should get down on one knee. People tend to do what Kitty says." He winked, and did just that — got down on one knee. He took Emma's hand, kissed her fingers and looked up at her with a warmth and intensity that reached right to her soul. "Emma Sharpe, I'm madly in love with you, and I want to be with you forever."

"Colin —"

"Will you marry me, Emma?" He placed a simple, beautiful ring in her palm and closed her fingers around it. He kissed her softly on the forehead. "Don't answer yet. I saw the ring in a window in Kenmare yesterday, and I knew it was meant for you. Take your time. Think. I'll wait."

"I don't need time. I don't need to think."

She draped her arms over his shoulders and smiled. "I love you with all my heart, Colin Donovan, and yes, yes, yes — yes, I will marry you."

A shout of approval came from nearby tables, and soon the entire pub was caught up in the celebration, people clapping, singing, dancing and cheering. Emma laughed as Colin swept her into his arms and spun her across the worn floor.

He whispered that he'd arranged for a room at a romantic hotel tonight, and he'd be on her flight tomorrow.

They'd go home together.

AUTHOR'S NOTE

A huge, special thank you to my good friend John Moriarty and all the people he consulted in answering my questions and generously sharing their knowledge, expertise and opinions on everything from Irish gardens to liver fluke — and, of course, whiskey. I look forward to many more visits to Ireland. I love wandering in the Irish hills, and I'll never tire of Irish rainbows . . . and I'm developing a taste for whiskey. Without ice!

Declan's Cross is a fictional Irish village, but "nearby" Ardmore, the round tower, the monastic ruins and the Cliff House Hotel are all real and worth a visit. Whether you're an armchair traveler, planning a trip or just want to have a look, I'm always posting pictures — and, now, videos — of Ireland on my website and Facebook page.

If you're new to my Sharpe & Donovan books, I hope you'll look for the first two books in the series, *Saint's Gate* and *Heron's*

Cove. There's also a prequel! "Rock Point" is my first e-novella original, and we learn more about Irish priest Finian Bracken and his arrival in Maine . . . and Irish detective Sean Murphy and his smugglers.

I have more in store for the Sharpes, the Donovans, Matt Yankowski and his elite FBI unit!

Thank you, and happy reading,

Carla

ABOUT THE AUTHOR

Carla Neggers is the *New York Times* bestselling author of more than 60 novels, novellas, and short stories. Her work has been translated into 24 languages and sold in more than 30 countries. She is a popular speaker around the country as well as a founding member of the New England Chapter of RWA, past president of Novelists, Inc., and past president of International Thriller Writers. She lives with her family in New England.

The employees of Thorndike Press hope you have enjoyed this Large Print book. All our Thorndike, Wheeler, and Kennebec Large Print titles are designed for easy reading, and all our books are made to last. Other Thorndike Press Large Print books are available at your library, through selected bookstores, or directly from us.

For information about titles, please call:
  (800) 223-1244

or visit our Web site at:
  http://gale.cengage.com/thorndike

To share your comments, please write:
  Publisher
  Thorndike Press
  10 Water St., Suite 310
  Waterville, ME 04901

The beginnings of a book like This one
will take on a life that Gale book, For
our partners the Wheeler and Kennebec
Large Print titles are designed for easy
reading, and all our books are made to
last. Other Thorndike, Large Print books
are available at your library, through selected bookstores, or directly from us.

For information about titles, please call:
(800) 223-1244

or visit our website at:
http://gale.cengage.com/thorndike

To share your comments, please write:
Publisher
Thorndike Press
10 Water St., Suite 310
Waterville, ME 04901